Is this Love?

Is this Love?

Sue Moorcroft

Copyright © 2013 Sue Moorcroft

Published 2013 by Choc Lit Limited
Penrose House, Crawley Drive, Camberley, Surrey GU15 2AB, UK
www.choc-lit.com

A CIP catalogue record for this book is available
from the British Library

ISBN 978-1-78189-055-4

Printed and bound by CPI Group (UK) Ltd, Croydon, CR0 4YY

For my gym buddies
Gail, Jo, Sue, Sheila, Alison, Olivia and Debs
Because their laughter is good for my mental health.

Acknowledgements

Huge thanks go to everyone who gave up time to help me with this book. The yoga came from Gail Willis, instructor and columnist. Between us, we constructed a thriving business for Tamara and decided how it would be affected if she got a rich hermit for a client and had to sign a non-disclosure agreement. Sue and Adrian Hall invited me onto their farm to meet their gorgeous alpacas, talked me through owning a starter herd and answered endless questions. Alison Turnbull shared her veterinary knowledge over what would happen when Jabber the mutt had a mishap. An overview on caring for adults with learning disabilities came from Bernardine Kennedy. Dan Yeager (who has a really cool job) helped me with the life and skills of a close protection operative. Mark Lacey taught me about money laundering and tax evasion (it's all right, he's on the side of the good guys) and why homeless young men live outside the system. And Jo Askew selflessly attended a spa with me.

As always, I'm indebted to my valued beta readers, whose feedback on an early draft of the novel provided reassurance, put me right, gave me insight, pointed out when things changed colour, made me think and made me laugh – Sue Hall, Mark West, Dominic White and Gail Willis. Thank you.

To my wonderful family and friends, thanks for the love, support and friendship.

And, as ever, to all on the Choc Lit Team, who make my books possible.

Chapter One

Tamara breezed in through the front door of her childhood home, Max in tow, and on into the sitting room, fending off an exuberant doggie welcome from Jabber.

'Hel— Oh!' She stopped short at the sight of the man talking to her parents and Lyddie, her sister.

A jolt of recognition. Jed. Jed Cassius.

The last time Tamara had seen Jed, he and Lyddie had been thirteen, a huge three years older than Tamara. Her heart twisted to remember how Lyddie had been 'seeing' fun, good-looking Jed Cassius, writing his name on her books at school and being told off at home for hanging out with him, instead of getting her homework done. Now, there wasn't even recognition in Lyddie's eyes as she treated him to her usual open and guileless smile.

'Um, hello,' Tamara began. When Jed Cassius only stared in response, she glanced at her parents for clues to the mood. Her father, Sean, wore his usual genial expression. But Cheryl, her mother, looked wary.

Lyddie stumped across the room, flinging herself on Tamara with a big hot hug and a wet kiss. 'Hey, 'Mara! Way to go!' Way to go was Lyddie's latest phrase. She latched onto certain combinations of words and used them over and over. Beaming, she hauled Tamara forwards, almost into Jed Cassius. 'This is my sister, 'Mara, and her boyfriend, Max.'

Gently, Sean took Lyddie's arm, a signal that she needed to calm down. 'Yes – remember Jed, Tamara? We used to be friendly with his family.'

Jed's eyes were the green side of hazel. They hadn't changed. But the gangling, laughing teen of Tamara's memory had been overlaid with a self-possessed, assured man; taller, built from muscle, jaw like a blade, his hair darker. She swallowed. 'Yes, I remember you. You lived right down Main Road, not far from Gabe Piercy's place.'

He smiled faintly. 'I remember you being around but I wouldn't have recognised you.'

Lyddie was fixed firmly in chatter mode. 'Isn't 'Mara's dress pretty? I like the way it shows the tops of her boobs.'

Jed Cassius was surprised into letting his eyes flicker to Tamara's neckline and, though well used to Lyddie's lack of inhibition, Tamara felt the beginnings of a blush.

'Max,' Lyddie beamed. 'Do you like the way—?'

'Oh, yes, Saucepan Lid.' Max gave Lyddie's long hair a friendly tug.

Lyddie, eyes bright, roared with laughter at the familiar joke. 'My name's Lyddie, not Lid! I can't fit on a saucepan. Maxie-Max, did you buy a house?'

'I've seen one I like. But it's not in the village—'

'Let's talk about that later.' Tamara shot Max a warning frown. She turned back to Jed. 'We used to call your parents Uncle Don and Auntie Fiona. Your family moved away not long after Lyddie's accident.'

Their departure had been only a spark of sadness in a furnace of grief, as Tamara had been forced to watch Lyddie struggling to talk in her new laborious voice and to grind through physio with her new awkward body.

Jed nodded. 'That was us.'

Cheryl slid a brisk arm around Lyddie. 'Come on, darling, it's nine thirty, let's get you ready for bed.'

If Lyddie didn't get enough sleep she turned grouchy and difficult. But challenging behaviour had to be accepted from someone who was thirty-three-going-on-eleven, who had bits of her brain that seemed to have set like the tarmac her head had crashed onto when a speeding car had knocked her old life right out of her.

Lyddie's mouth turned down. 'I don't want to go to bed. Tamara's not going to bed.'

'But you need your sleep, darling.' Cheryl took her hand.

Reluctantly, Lyddie allowed herself to be guided towards the stairs. 'Can Jabber sleep with me tonight, Mum? Just tonight? Just once? Just *once*? He'll be good, he's a good dog, Jabber is.'

She was wasting her breath. Cheryl never allowed Jabber to sleep upstairs and he always seemed perfectly content with his green beanbag and leopard-print fur fabric throw in the kitchen.

Sean sent Tamara a smile. 'Jed's come to talk to us about something.'

Jed had been watching Lyddie's exit with eyes that were dull with shocked compassion. He switched his attention back to Sean. 'I'd like to wait till Cheryl's back downstairs.'

So this was no impetuous visit. Tamara's neck prickled. 'Would you like coffee?'

'Thanks.' Jed's hair was the bronze brown of a new chestnut, straight and silky, falling into his eyes. He had the look of someone who wanted to be somewhere else: stiff, watchful.

Max followed Tamara into the kitchen. 'I thought we were only popping in for a minute so that you could say goodnight to Lyddie? I want to talk about the house.'

She shrugged a half-apology. 'But I want to know why Jed's here. And it's your house, Max. I've already got one, here in Middledip.'

He reached round her for the sugar canister, trapping her against the cupboards as he spooned sugar into mugs. 'But mine will be big enough for both of us. And it's the right side of Peterborough, so you wouldn't be that far from your precious Middledip.'

From upstairs, Lyddie yodelled, 'Goodnight ev-er-y-bodeeee.'

'Goodnight, Lyddieeee,' they all yelled back. Her bedroom door clacked shut.

Tamara bumped Max out of the way with her bum, and picked up the tray. 'Mum will be down in a minute. Let's get this into the sitting room.'

Cheryl trod down the stairs to rejoin them, took her coffee with a nod of thanks, and perched on the edge of an armchair. 'Well, Jed?'

Jed accepted the cue, looking from Sean to Cheryl and then to Tamara, cradling his coffee mug. 'My dad died recently, from cancer.' He lifted his voice to override the murmurs of sympathy and dismay. 'And in his last days of coherence he told me something that he made me promise to come and tell you.'

The room went still.

Tamara felt her heart clench in anticipation.

'It was Dad,' he said. 'It was Dad who was driving the car that ran down Lyddie. He was the hit-and-run driver.'

Chapter Two

Shock and grief sucked the air from Tamara's lungs, as if she'd plunged into icy water.

Jed's frown was black across his brow. 'He asked me to … I know there's no way to make it up to Lyddie, to you. But Dad asked me to sell his house and give Lyddie the money as compensation. He was eaten up by guilt, but he could never make himself face you with the truth.' And he added, inadequately, 'I'm sorry.'

Tamara felt Max take her hand. But all she could do was stare at Jed Cassius.

After all these years of hating the driver who hadn't stopped to help when his car flung a girl through the air, it turned out to be Don Cassius. Uncle Don, sharer of picnics and even a wet camping trip in Somerset. *Uncle Don*'s car had slammed into a healthy teenager with the loudest *bang!* and left Tamara staring at a Lyddie turned rag doll.

Cheryl sank into her chair as if she were a rag doll, too. 'Get out.'

Jed put down his coffee mug and rose, face set. 'I'm so sorry. On behalf of my family, I'm so, so sorry. But I'd like to explain what Dad—'

'Just get out.' Cheryl's face began to crumple.

Sean turned to her, face anxious but voice gentle. 'It's not Jed's fault. We shouldn't shoot the messenger.'

'*Get out! Get OUT!*'

Tamara found herself on her feet. 'It's probably best if I see you out,' she said through numb lips.

Out in the hall, Jed paused, eyes haunted. 'I'm sorry,' he repeated.

'I know.' Tamara's heart seemed to be having trouble

with its usual easy beat. 'It's not your fault. It's the shock. Mum can't make herself be reasonable or listen.' Her lips twisted. 'She has fixed ideas about things.'

He took a step, dropping his hand on the front-door latch. 'Even if your parents don't want to listen, will you?'

Her stomach lurched. 'I don't know. Not right now. It's come too much out of the blue. Ripped into the old wound.'

Sombrely, Jed nodded.

Tamara opened the door, watching him walk down the garden path, climb into a sporty black car close to where Max had parked his old red Porsche, and rumble away.

Max came up behind her. 'That was pretty intense. Shall I stay with you tonight?'

She wiped a sheen of sweat from her forehead as she shut the door. 'Do you mind not?'

He sighed. 'You want to be with your family?'

She was grateful that she didn't have to explain and, although he might sigh, he wouldn't get in a huff. Max was such a best friend kind of boyfriend. 'It was a bombshell. I'll stay with Mum and Dad, but you've got a car show tomorrow and you'll need to be up early.'

'I'll manage.'

Tamara shook her head. 'You'd hardly get any sleep before the photographer calls for you to whizz off to Birmingham to spend the day on your feet.'

Working a noisy, colourful show, from stand to stand. Max the journalist would have to be smiling, personable, jokey, falling into conversation, looking for the stories, the personalities, and above all, the cars. Outrageous colours, dark windows, wide rubber, flared arches, neon lights: the cars that the readers of *Charge!* adored.

'I'll leave you to it, then.' He gave her a big, long, comforting bear hug, dropping a kiss on her hair before running out to his Porsche.

After he'd roared off, Tamara trailed back into the sitting room. She found her parents facing one another. Cheryl looked as stiff as the pink-beige brocade of the sofa. 'I don't want him near us.'

Sean clicked his tongue. 'It wasn't Jed's fault, Cheryl. It was Don's.'

'I can't help it. I don't want him near.'

'That's irrational. I know it's a shock and bizarre that the hit-and-run driver turns out to be Don, after all these years. I feel as betrayed as you. But Jed was a nice kid and he's been left with a horrible job.'

'I just don't want him near me!' Unreasoning fury burned in Cheryl's eyes.

Sean appealed to Tamara. 'What do you think?'

Slowly, Tamara let herself sink onto a chair. 'I agree it's not his fault. But … it all just feels weird. Seeing him as a man feels weird—'

'—when Lyddie didn't get a chance to grow up, properly,' stuck in Cheryl. 'I don't want to see him again.'

Tamara had arrived in Max's car, which he'd now driven off to his flat in Bettsbrough. A ten-minute walk across the dark village in the drizzle with no jacket wasn't appealing, so she opted to stay the night in her old room. Her first yoga class on a Saturday wasn't until eleven, so she'd have time in the morning to go home and change.

Lying in the single bed, remembering Cheryl shaking in the wake of Jed's visit and Sean trying to comfort her while refusing to blame Jed for Don's crime, it washed over Tamara, as it had a thousand times, what her parents had lost when Lyddie was injured – the 'when the children have grown up and left' part of their lives. Greater choices. Putting themselves first. Freedom: both personal and financial. Lyddie wouldn't leave home unless they put her into some kind of institution or supervised dwelling, which Cheryl had so far refused to countenance. Lyddie did spend one weekend a month in respite care at lovely warm, airy Mountland Hall, between Bettsbrough and Peterborough, and Cheryl wasn't even keen on that. But it was kinder on Lyddie in the long run, because one day her parents were going to be too old to look after her and if Mountland Hall was her best option, the transition would be easier if it was already part of her life.

But Tamara went curly inside at the thought of Lyddie in an institution and couldn't somehow see herself letting it happen. Lyddie leaving the village that was her world? Her job in the shop? And the people she knew, the kindly middle-aged dog walkers and Gabe Piercy, whose menagerie was a Lyddie-magnet?

It seemed as if she'd barely dropped off to sleep before the bedroom door burst open. 'Mor-ning 'Ma-ra,' sang Lyddie. 'Mum said you were here, can I get in with you?' And in a moment she was shoving her way into the small bed in her pink and white dressing gown, her arms cuddling clumsily, her kisses wet on Tamara's cheek.

Tamara didn't sigh. There was no point. Returning her sister's hug she blinked heavy eyes at the morning light filtering around the curtains.

Lyddie wriggled free to delve in her dressing gown pocket and produce a pack of *Star Wars* cards, shoving back a curtain so that she could see, making Tamara blink even more. 'Look, 'Mara, here's Queen Amidala. Isn't she pretty? I like Queen Amidala better than Queen Jamillia, don't you? Her hair's really cool. Can I have—?'

But Tamara had been in this conversation before. 'I don't think me or Mum could do your hair like Queen Amidala. They must have highly trained people to do that.'

'Movie people?' Lyddie passed several cards from one

hand to the other. 'Yucky, Darth Maul.' She slapped Darth Maul's red and black face to the bottom of the pack. 'Yoda ... Yoda's really liddle, isn't he? Dot six six metre, it says. But Luke Skywalker's one dot seven two. That's bigger.' Lyddie didn't see the necessity for distinguishing between 'point' for numerical values and 'dot' for website addresses.

She crammed the cards back into her pocket and kissed Tamara's face again. 'I'm going down to see Jabber now.'

'OK, I'll be there in a minute.' Tamara flipped the curtain back into place, as Lyddie let herself out into the slice of brightness on the landing, then crunched up her eyes, willing sleep to return. But her thoughts flitted and circled like bats. Were they going to tell Lyddie who Jed was? Apparently she now had no recollection of Jed, but at one time he'd been embedded in her thirteen-year-old heart. Tamara cringed to remember hooting with laughter on discovering Lyddie writing his name on her hand and surrounding it with careful pink hearts.

Lyddie was aware that she'd had an accident that had changed her life, but she didn't remember it and had always seemed to accept that the driver's identity was a mystery. It was just so poignant, and ironic, that it should be Jed Cassius who'd returned to identify the bastard they'd all hated so thoroughly and for so long, who'd knocked Lyddie down speeding through the village as if it were a race track. How would Lyddie react to the news that it had been Jed's father? Conveying momentous information to her was hard. Confusion was never far from emotion with Lyddie.

Tamara shivered, missing her sister's heavy-breathing warmth.

Yes, she was angry with Don. But ... Jed? She tried to conjure up a share of her mother's antipathy towards him.

Nope. She just couldn't make him guilty for his father's crime. Sighing, she gave up any ideas of sleep, threw off the duvet and climbed into yesterday's clothes.

Downstairs, Lyddie had parked herself in front of the television and Tamara paused in the sitting room doorway to watch her rapt, open-mouthed concentration, as a celebrity chef chopped stalks of celery with a noise like a machine gun. Tamara's heart swelled. Lyddie's condition made for challenges, but they all shared the responsibility – Tamara, Cheryl and Sean – with help from a social worker called Ginny, and Mountland Hall. Lyddie was why Tamara hadn't moved out of Middledip, why she hadn't said she'd move in with Max, although it was the next logical step in their relationship.

Tamara's heart melted whenever she looked at her sister, her tallness, the way she walked with her legs a bit stiff and her bottom sticking out, her delighted smile, her idiosyncratic perspective on the world.

Lyddie loved Tamara, too.

She also loved Jabber the Mutt, who was now lying across Lyddie's feet, lifting his head to glance at Tamara as he sent her a wave of his feathery tail. Jabber, Lyddie's doggie companion, was her protector in her wanderings about the village, making feasible small pockets of independence in her restricted life. It was only when she was doing three-hour stints in Gwen Crowther's shop at The Cross in the centre of the village four times a week, that Jabber would doze beneath the cages of O B One Canary and Lyddie's white mice, Jar Jar and Chewy, waiting for Lyddie to burst back into his world.

Tamara turned and followed the aroma that told her someone was making coffee in the kitchen.

'I can't understand your mother,' her father proclaimed, the moment she appeared.

Yawning, Tamara took down a mug and lined it up with his in front of the kettle. 'Oh?'

O B One Canary flicked his creamy yellow tail feathers and fluted a couple of notes.

'To be furious with Don, yes. But not with Jed. Now she's insisting that if Jed turns up again, I make sure he knows he's not welcome. But I always liked the lad and it was good to see him.' He studied his reflection in the kettle, as if it could explain his wife to him if he just glared at it hard enough. Then he sighed and slid an arm around his daughter. 'And how are you?'

'A bit shocked.' Tamara stopped spooning coffee into her mug to hug him. This was the man who'd always had a cuddle for her if she'd bumped herself; the one who was most likely to find time for her when she was a teenager and everyone's attention had been on Lyddie. 'But it's not your fault, Dad, and it's not Jed's. It's Don's ... and he's dead.' She paused. 'Are we going to tell Lyddie?'

Sean blew out his cheeks. 'That, at least, we're in agreement about. No. What's the point in upsetting her? It won't help her in any way.'

'Where is Mum?'

He nodded at the kitchen window. 'Outside, massacring the hedge.'

With a sigh, Tamara took down another mug. 'I'll take her coffee out.'

Cheryl glanced around as Tamara walked up the crazy paving that ran between two sections of close-cut lawn. She was setting about the dark green privet with savagery in every snip and snap of her garden shears. Just as well that she didn't have an electric hedge-cutter, she'd probably take off someone's legs. 'You shouldn't be out here in your bare feet.'

Tamara ignored this routine scolding. 'I've come to see

how you are.' She put the coffee down on a handy garden chair.

Her mother hmmed and shrugged, side-stepping along the hedge. But Tamara heard a small squeak, as if she was trying to suppress a sob. She gave her a minute, knowing better than to offer a hug while Cheryl was showing her vulnerability. Snip. Snip. *Snip*. Sniff.

'Do you want to talk things over with Dad? Shall I take Lyddie out somewhere so you can?'

'We talked last night, thank you. We've agreed to differ.' Snip-snip-snip. 'You really shouldn't be out here without shoes, you should wear slippers.'

Lyddie was a slippers person; Tamara was more spike-heeled, snakeskin boots. She waited, thinking her mother might ask her how she felt – about Jed, not about slippers.

Snip-snip-snip. Snip. *Snip*. She didn't.

Chapter Three

It wasn't that Jed was disrespecting Cheryl Rix's feelings – much. But yesterday Cheryl had seemed unbothered about how this mess made him feel or how difficult it had been to make his dad's confession for him. How rocked he'd been to see Lyddie as an adult with learning difficulties, when he'd last known her as a bright, giggling teenager who he'd kissed in the cornfields.

The more he thought about Cheryl throwing him out of her house, the more it rankled. Especially with Tamara watching with her wide amber eyes, her russet hair a curtain past her shoulders. Last time he'd seen her she'd been a stick-drawing in village school uniform. Now she was lean and curved and all grown up. Her image had hung before his eyes all last night and as soon as he'd woken today.

He shifted his mind off Tamara and wished he'd got Sean's phone number. But he hadn't, which was why he was now striding back up the path to the square pebble-dashed house on the corner of Church Close and Port Road, this time with his stepbrother in tow, feeling a bit as he had when he had been a paperboy in Middledip and worried that a slavering dog would fly around the corner of a house and clamp its fangs on his leg.

'House looks the same,' Manny observed, glancing around at the walled garden, the bay window and the door with the black letterbox, as Jed rang the doorbell. And then Tamara Rix was standing before them, her eyes wary, and Jed was aware of Manny's whispered, 'but she's changed.'

Tamara was dressed as if she was just off to an exercise class: black top and bottoms and a bright purple cardigan tied over the top. You'd have to search with a magnifying glass to find an ounce of spare flesh on her, everything was perfectly formed and beautifully put together.

'Have you come to see Dad?' she asked.

Swallowing, Jed rubbed his chin and found himself hoping that she liked stubble. 'I don't know. Who hates me least?'

Her smile flashed. 'Dad. But he's out.' Then she looked contrite. 'Sorry. I don't hate you, either. You can speak to me.' She didn't ask him in, though, just stood on the doorstep like a gatekeeper to the household. Her gaze flicked towards Manny.

Jed remembered his manners. 'I don't know if you remember Manny, my stepbrother?'

'I just about remember you having a cool older brother.'

Manny took Tamara's hand. 'That's me, the cool older brother. You going out for a run?'

'I'm a yoga instructor. I've just called in after a class to see everyone. Things have been a little … unsettled, here.'

Jed propped a shoulder against the house wall and interrupted before Manny got too deep into impressing Tamara. 'I'm sorry I upset your mother.' He managed to stop himself from referring to her as Auntie Cheryl. 'Auntie Cheryl' belonged to another life, the one before the shit storm from which he'd never quite recovered.

'What happened to Lyddie was a tragedy and I can only guess how your mum must feel. And to discover that it was Dad who was the driver …' He shifted uncomfortably. Tamara was watching him gravely and he was annoyed to feel his face heat up. Blushing wasn't something he did. Emotion sometimes felt alien; he'd covered his for so long.

'Look,' he said, more sharply than he'd intended. 'It wasn't a job I wanted to do, to come here and pass on my dad's deathbed confession. It was a shock for me, too. And I'm sorry if this makes your mum even more upset, but me and Manny are living back in the area, so that could be problematical if we all started falling over one another. I think it will be easier if we clear the air.'

Tamara's lips parted in surprise. 'Back in the village, you mean?'

Jed was saved from a reply when the door swung wider and there was Cheryl, her bonnet of hair framing her graceless expression. 'I suppose you'd better come in. Wipe your feet.'

Jed didn't kid himself that there was conciliation in Cheryl's eyes. Her face was like a slap as she ushered them into her sweetly neat sitting room.

'I suppose your mother's still a teacher?' she demanded without preamble, putting up a hand to halt Tamara, who had begun to offer refreshments.

'A head teacher, now.' Jed could see where this was going, but he might as well get the awkwardness over with. And, sure enough …

'Teaching's the career I gave up to look after Lyddie.' Cheryl's eyes locked onto Jed accusingly, then moved on to Manny, who, damn him, had gone into his strong silent act, standing half a step back. And Fiona was Manny's actual mother, rather than the stepmother she was to Jed.

Jed took a moment to smooth any irritation from his voice. 'Everything about Lyddie's accident is hard on you. We're the first to acknowledge—' He was interrupted by the sound of Manny's phone.

'Sorry, duty calls.' In an instant Manny was away up the passageway and had managed to ninja out of there.

Inwardly, Jed cursed, wishing it had been his phone ringing. But he'd made a promise to his father and, in his view, he hadn't yet tried hard enough to keep it. He returned doggedly to his task. 'You've no idea how sorry we were—'

Then the back door banged and Lyddie and Jabber burst

through from the kitchen in a flurry of fresh air and Jed still didn't manage to get out what he was there to say, as Lyddie started talking at the top of her voice.

'Hello, Jed! I've been to see Gabe and his puppies! 'Mara, do you think Jed would like to see them?'

'Mum and Jed are talking just now, Lyddie.' Tamara took her into the kitchen, telling her gently to calm down a bit.

Jed began again, but Cheryl, glaring pickaxes at him, made him feel like the adolescent she used to know.

Then Lyddie stumped back into the sitting room with a white mouse in each hand. 'Look, Jed. I've brought Jar Jar and Chewy.'

Jed gave up on his speech. 'They're beautiful.'

'I'll let you hold them.'

And Jed found himself with his hands full of mice, letting them run over-and-over his fingers, laughing when Jar Jar tried to woffle off up his sleeve. 'Whoa!'

Lyddie giggled. 'Jar Jar loves you because he wants to be in your clothes. Jar Jar poos on people sometimes.'

Jed pulled a horrified face. 'Rescue me, Lyddie, this is a new shirt – it's white and not poo proof. Don't let him poo up my sleeve.'

Lyddie curled over with laughter, plaits swinging. 'I can't stop him. He just *does*.'

'They're not supposed to be in here without their cage, are they Lyddie?' Cheryl reminded her quietly.

Still snorting with laughter, Lyddie gathered up Jar Jar and Chewy and ambled back to the kitchen.

From the doorway, Tamara sent Jed a look that might be approval and he was glad he wasn't the type that freaked at rodents up sleeves. In fact, Lyddie had lit up like Piccadilly at Christmas at his gentle humour. Maybe, somewhere in Lyddie's memory, a breeze of familiarity had stirred.

And then, under Cheryl's scrutiny, Jed took a breath and

began what he'd come to say, starting with the fact that he and Manny were living locally – news that Cheryl greeted with a face like stone. 'About Dad's money,' he went on.

'I thought I'd made it plain that I don't want to hear about that.'

'If you could just let me finish—'

'It's time you went.'

Tamara shot her mother a reproving look, but said, 'I'll see you out.'

Jed tried to dodge around her to maintain eye contact with Cheryl. 'If you could give me five minutes—'

Tamara hooked his arm determinedly and turned him around. 'I'm sorry but, to be honest, you're doing more harm than good. Mum said she doesn't want to hear it.'

Torn between anger at Cheryl's unreason and a dart of desire at the distracting touch of Tamara as she escorted him up the hall, Jed allowed himself to be shown the door in the Rix household for the second time. But out on the pathway, he dug in his heels and wrestled back his arm. 'I get that your mother thinks I'm a demon, but there's stuff I need to say to one of you and I'm not going to give up until it's said. So can you give me Sean's number?'

Tamara stared up at him, thoughtfully. 'Will I do for you?'

An inappropriate response rushed to the tip of his tongue, but he swallowed it. 'Definitely.'

'It can't be right now. I'm going out with Max.' She glanced at her watch.

'So when? I'm not going to go away on this.'

'Tomorrow afternoon?' Tamara took Jed's arm again to direct him down the path.

Nostalgia for a summer Sunday hangout from his teen years took him by surprise. 'How about a walk along the embankment?'

She smiled, suddenly, as if sharing the same memories. 'We can buy ice cream. Two o'clock?'

Max had a hug waiting for her at his flat. 'How are things? Still crappy?'

Tamara groaned as she closed the front door behind her with her foot, shutting out the world, family travail and all need for diplomacy. 'My mum. She's really gone off on one about Jed Cassius. He's just shown up again with his stepbrother, Manny, so that was two of them for her to be rude to.'

They collapsed onto Max's battered blue sofa. 'Mum's gone all kind of shocky, as if the accident has only just happened. And Jed let Jar Jar and Chewy go up his sleeve.'

Max did a theatrical sharp-intake-of-breath. 'So he's gone straight to the top of Lyddie's list of favourites and that's pissed Cheryl off even more?'

Companionably, Tamara laid her head on the familiar ledge of his shoulder, his T-shirt that said *Racing drivers are my rock stars* warm against her cheek. 'How cool that you understand without having to be told.'

'Crap for Jed, by the way.'

'You know that and I know that. Mum doesn't want to know. Let's talk about something else. How was the car show?'

'Fantastic!' He paused.

She lifted her head, suddenly aware of excitement thrumming through him, glowing in the depths of his dark eyes. 'What?'

'Now's probably not a good time.'

'Yes it is. Distract me from the whines and woes of Tamara Rix.'

'At the car show I was approached by an editor, Marie Mundy. She's headhunting me for deputy editor at *Rush*.

It's a grass-roots motorsport magazine, so I'd have to get into rallying and banger racing and stuff. But it would be brilliant and about four thousand a year more, too. It'll be great to move on from *Charge!* James is so preoccupied with the budget that the only attention he pays to editorial is to make cuts.'

'Wow, congratulations! Get in there, Max. I'm so proud of you.' Tamara planted a kiss on his cheek.

'You don't mind? A new challenge would be fantastic.'

'What is there to mind?'

'About moving. Lucky I didn't actually put an offer in for that house. I'll have to tell the agents not to send me any more local details.'

Tamara jerked back, frowning. 'Moving? House?'

'*Rush* is in Liverpool,' he explained, as if she ought to have known.

'You're moving to Liverpool?'

He gathered her close again. 'I'd like *us* to. I know it would mean a lot of work for you, finding new classes to teach in the area. But that's the beauty of being self-employed, isn't it? You can move around.'

A weasel of dismay slunk down Tamara's back.

'I'll help you,' Max rushed on. 'Or, at least, as much as I can. But I'll be out a lot at weekends, at least at first, immersing myself in race meetings and stuff. It comes with the territory. But you can work at weekends when the gyms are busy with all the Monday-to-Friday wage slaves queuing up for classes. I've Googled gyms and clubs in Liverpool and there are loads. We can have time off together in the week. Once I've settled into the new job.'

Tamara gazed at him. At the excitement in his eyes. And the apprehension. Because he knew, and she knew, what she was going to say next. 'I can't move to Liverpool, Max.'

'You can.'

She sighed gustily, dragging herself back out of his arms. 'You know I can't, because of Lyddie.'

Max took her hand. 'That's *won't*, Tamara. Nobody expects you to stay in Middledip your whole life. I know your mum will have a tantrum when you say you're leaving, but she'll get over it.'

'Somebody expects me to stay – me. How long do you think it would take Lyddie to get over it? To realise that she can only see me every few weeks or months? That I'm not there to get her out of Mum's hair? She mopes even when we go for a fortnight's holiday and cries when I come home.'

His eyes slid away. 'Even Lyddie will get used to it. You can talk to her every day on Skype. It's your life, Tam. You can leave.'

She stared into his face, the face she'd known since the first day of senior school in Bettsbrough, when he'd plonked himself down next to her in maths with a grimace and said, 'This bloody teacher's making us sit next to people we don't know.' And the bloody teacher had heard him and he'd been the first of the new intake to be kept in at break time.

She'd waited outside the detention room to say, 'That wasn't bloody fair, was it?' prompting instant friendship. It had eventually grown into something else when Max had finished university, and somehow she'd hardly noticed her female friends leaving the village, or settling into relationships that involved babies. Max had been enough.

Sadness pinched her guts. 'I know I *can* – but I can't. I can't do that to Lyddie. I can't. I'm not talking about whether Lyddie or Mum would get over it, but whether I would. I might have made living with you work in Bettsbrough or Peterborough, but I can't go as far away as Liverpool.'

He captured her hand and rubbed it against his cheek.

'But it's a fantastic job. My dream job. And Marie headhunted me, she's been following my columns. It's huge, Tam.'

'I know.' She cleared sadness from her vocal chords. 'I know.' She took a long deep breath to psyche herself for what she had to say next. 'I think you have to take it. We'll see each other at weekends.'

Max dropped her hand and drew away, dark eyes flat. 'The weekends we don't have? I know how you feel about Lyddie, but I always thought that if it came down to a straight choice I'd win.'

Tamara's heartbeat thumped heavily as she tried not to say, 'Where did you get that idea?' and hunted for a compromise instead. 'People have long-distance relationships, Max. It's the age of communication. We have phones and Skype and email. I don't have to choose —'

'I think you do. It's not only about whether a long-distance relationship will work – it sounds pretty crap, actually – but about whether we mean enough to each other.'

For long seconds they stared into each other's eyes. The air became hard for Tamara to breathe. 'You don't understand about Lyddie,' she said, flatly. 'And I always thought you did.'

Chapter Four

Lyddie couldn't cope with anything too complex, tiring, or emotional, so her job with Gwen Crowther at the village shop was ideal. A few days a week, a few hours a day, she served the steady stream of villagers calling in for snacks or cigarettes, got the papers ready for the delivery kids and, sometimes, took on an afternoon round, less muddly than a morning round when different households ordered different papers.

Lyddie loved being at the shop, although, as she didn't do punctuality, Cheryl had to orchestrate getting her to work on time. Changing her into a clean glittery top, denim skirt and trainers was pretty doable, but the hair brushing could take forever if Lyddie clamoured to be 'like Legolas' in *Lord of the Rings*. Unlike Tamara, Cheryl never had the patience for YouTube tutorials on how to do lace braids and a fish tail, and would just plait each side and pull them back to join another plait at the back.

Lyddie probably couldn't have held the job in the days before the electronic till, because her numeracy wasn't a strong point. Her vocabulary was OK though, and she was a magnet for sayings that were regurgitated at frequent intervals. Presently, as well as her favourite 'Way to go!' she was into 'Much obliged'.

'*Thank* you, that's four pounds sixty please, much obliged. Much obliged, here's your change, much obliged. *Thank* you.'

Gwen never lost patience with Lyddie's clumsiness or the slight thickness in her speech and seemed to have no problem with keeping her on task. 'Have you finished putting the beans out, Lyddie? The sweeping's still waiting, dear.' Gwen's eyes would smile kindly through her glasses.

Lyddie adored her employer and never minded if Gwen phoned on her days off to ask her to do an extra hour or two. 'I've got to go in,' she'd report weightily. 'Someone's ill so Gwen wants me to take over.' And she'd bustle off to do a paper round in the old village. Not in the 'new village', Bankside, where too many houses and roads looked alike.

Tamara made a point of calling into the shop as often as possible when Lyddie was working. Strolling through the village on Sunday morning to buy a magazine, she was in a dream, watching the clouds bob across the sky looking like she felt: swept around by outside forces. As she reached the shop her eyes fell on a figure jogging up from the opposite direction in a vest and tracksuit bottoms, a compact man, moving like an animal, demonstrating the control of movement that goes with extreme fitness. His trainers were dark grey and looked expensive, like reptile skin. It took a second for Tamara to realise that the smile he was smiling was for her, and that it was Manny.

Ian 'Manny' Mansfield had been in his late teens when his family left Middledip, 'a grown-up' to the Tamara of the time and she wouldn't have recognised him with a shorn beard and longish dark hair, if he hadn't been reintroduced to her by Jed. Whereas Jed she had known in a heartbeat.

Tamara smiled back, then stepped into the shop. She waited for a mum with a toddler on her hip to be served. It was Louisa, who'd been a year above her at school.

'Hiya, Tamara!' Louisa hoisted up her little boy and turned for the door.

Gwen beamed a greeting and Lyddie sang, '*Hel*lo 'Mara.' She adored standing at the important side of the counter as Tamara, a mere customer, looked on. Manny entered as Lyddie was handing Tamara her magazine and a white paper receipt. 'Much obliged, 'Mara, three pounds fifty pee, please, much obliged, thank you. See you at Mum and Dad's.'

Tamara handed over the money and said, 'Lyddie, this is Manny, Jed's brother.' She decided not to bother her with the complexity of a step relationship.

'*Hel*lo Manny,' Lyddie chimed. 'Jar Jar went up Jed's sleeve. Didn't he, 'Mara? And Jed laughed.'

'That's right.' Tamara saw Manny's puzzled expression. 'Jar Jar's a white mouse.'

'Good to know it wasn't Jar Jar Binks. So you work here, do you, Lyddie?'

Lyddie beamed. 'Yes, it's my job. Have you got a job?'

Manny nodded vaguely up Port Road. 'Along there. Jed, too.'

Tamara said her goodbyes and left, glancing up the road in the direction Manny had pointed. She wondered if he meant at a house beyond the curve in the road, where a team of men was stripping off the slate and replacing it with tile. But he didn't look like a roofer. And Jed certainly didn't; his hands were smooth and clean, not roughened or stained by the heavy work of carting tiles up ladders.

She'd noticed his hands.

As arranged, Tamara met Jed at 2.00 p.m. in the car park near the embankment, where the river snaked between Middledip and Bettsbrough.

As June had decided to award the area a day of scudding grey clouds, only a bin full of wrappers marked where the ice cream van usually stood. Tamara wrapped herself into a long burgundy cardigan that swung around her calves and waited as Jed pulled a denim jacket from the back of his black BMW Z4. The denim was grey, like lead, and had that designer-expensive cut; the car looked like a small Batmobile.

'You remembered your way here,' she observed.

'I remember a lot.'

He led the way to the gate and yanked it open to let her through to the footpath. She glanced at him in thanks, though she would have been happy to open it herself, and something in his eyes connected with the very pit of her stomach like a static shock. She looked away, telling her insides to stop fizzing. It was just that, for a second, her body had remembered the strength of her adolescent crush and reached out to the young, carefree Jed that must be buried somewhere in this self-assured man, who was watching her now with a small frown between his brows.

Down at the river a mist settled around them, making the day dank as well as cool. Dozens of swans dragged their reflections through the rippled olive water, keeping pace with Tamara and Jed, peering through black masks like stately bank robbers. Tamara wished she'd brought bread; feeding them would have given her something to do. Being enclosed by the mist with Jed seemed to emphasise his presence, especially when even the swans left them alone and sailed to the other bank to investigate the possibilities of a row of fishermen.

Towering weeping willows punctuated the riverbank, flopping over as if awaiting some giant shampoo girl. Jed, thrusting aside armfuls of the unruly greenery, wasted no time in small talk. 'I'm sorry my news stirred up bad feeling. It was obviously a hell of a shock and I see how difficult things are for you. They're not easy for me, either.'

'I suppose not.' She took a long stride to avoid a muddy brown puddle, pulling her cardigan more tightly around her.

'After we left the village, relations deteriorated between Dad and the family. He cut himself loose a couple of years after moving us all to London. Me and Manny stayed with Mum. Then Manny moved out.'

'You stayed with Fiona even though she's your stepmum and Don's your real dad?' Tamara glanced at his unsmiling profile.

Jed pulled a wry face. 'I know the facts are that my dad married Manny's mum, but my real mum died when I was a baby and Fiona is the only mum I've known. Anyway, Dad didn't give me the option of going with him. He'd changed. He'd become very morose and quick to lose his temper. Alcohol issues. I hung on with Mum, hoping she'd move us back to Middledip, but she was settled in a new school and was up for head of her department.

'Dad leaving scrambled my brain. I was so furious. Mum and Dad seemed to have cocked everything up between them and not cared how I felt. I expect I gave Mum a shitty time. Then I left home at sixteen.'

Tamara couldn't keep the surprise from her voice. 'Wow. That young?'

'Too young. I knew that what people did was to get a job and a place to live – but didn't have the first idea how to do those things. If it hadn't been for Manny, I don't know where I would have ended up. Manny was living in a squat and he got me in there. We slept on the floor in sleeping bags with dirty old pillows. There were no real rules to live by. I'd dumped school before I should, before my exams, so I got whatever work I could, cash-in-hand and being ripped off pretty regularly. I grew up quickly.'

The mist dulled the greens and browns around them and even muffled the *wheeow* of the traffic. In contrast, their footsteps and the rushing of the river seemed loud. They left the grey paving slabs as the path became dark beaten earth, striding between hedgerow and river and under the bridge, where traffic whizzed over the water and past a small mill on the other bank. Tamara knew the path; if they carried on far enough – a couple of miles through uninviting brambles and sharp-smelling nettles – they'd eventually arrive in Bettsbrough. The Boatman pub would be on this bank, probably full of families determined to eat in the beer garden, despite the weather.

Jed had fallen silent, pushing aside spiky hawthorn twigs and watching the flow of the water.

Tamara found herself feeling incredibly sorry for him. The Jed she remembered had smiled, made jokes, lived a settled life in a home with two parents. It was odd and poignant that not much more than two years later, he'd become one of those teens you read about, who fall through the cracks in the system, living like a stray dog. It was far from her own experience of life with hands-on concerned parents, especially Cheryl, who had no idea how to keep her hands off and her concern to herself.

'Did you keep in touch with your mum and dad?'

'Not really. Once they knew I was with Manny, they pretty much accepted the situation. I was too angry to be reasoned with, anyway.'

'So they didn't get the police, or anything?'

He shrugged. 'No point. I was safe, they couldn't compel me to return home. They wished things were different, they said, and I said so did I.' He laughed, without humour. 'Manny saw I was OK. Well ...' He paused. His face softened and his hair lifted on the breeze. 'He was a bit of a chancer, I suppose. We didn't trouble the taxman with what we earned, but we didn't claim benefits so it seemed reasonable. There aren't many handouts for homeless young men, anyway. Manny was into martial arts and as long as he had enough money to keep that up, he was happy. I liked hanging out with the other guys at the squat and not having any responsibility, except for myself.'

They reached a point where the path widened and sat down on a bench dedicated to a fisherman called Alf Barnes. The breeze was flipping across the Fens and whisking the mist away and now they could see further across the river to where the flat fields were brown and green. The deep drainage ditches that sliced between the fields and prevented the land reverting to seabed weren't visible from their bench, but Tamara knew that they were there. People were like that. You saw the surface without knowing what sliced them up beneath it.

Jed stared out over the land. 'I was angry at my parents for taking me away from the village, my mates and my school, but I suppose I didn't really know how to come back. There are no squats in Middledip and I'd missed a chunk of school. I was living outside of normal society. It's distressingly easy to begin feeling like an outcast.

'A couple of years after I went to live in the squat, Manny made the bizarre decision to join the military police. He was attracted by the yomping and the stomping, the physical challenges and the intellectual stimulus. He wanted me to join up, too, but I couldn't see me in that mob. He told Mum he was going, perhaps to let her know that he wouldn't be around to see I was OK. She was horrified, she said the army was all wrong for him.'

'Why?'

He shrugged. 'She was right, as it turned out. It didn't bring out the best in him, even though he got to train all day and play every sport going. He's motivated and likes to take the initiative, but I think the army likes you to do things their way and Manny likes to do things his way. So I suppose that it taught him to do things his way, but hide it.

'I felt ... empty, with him gone. He'd been the constant in my life. And around the same time, I got a regular job at an electronics factory because I did a bit of cash work for the builder who was building an extension to the factory and while I was doing that I got friendly with the factory foreman. He said he was looking for a lad to train. It wasn't bad work, making up electrical products from components on an assembly line. You started on really easy stuff, like switches, and they'd move you up if you did OK. I did OK and after a while I was able to move out of the squat and into a tiny studio flat. It wasn't a palace, but it wasn't the dump the squat was. I felt part of the normal world again. The factory was part of a group and I caught the attention of someone who doesn't just value an employee by the certificates he's earned. I moved up, and I'm still working for the owner.'

Jed seemed lost in his thoughts. At their feet stars of cow parsley burst from ridged stalks and fat-bummed bees hummed and bumbled from one to another. A moorhen peep-peep-peeped up to have a look at the two humans sitting so still. Unimpressed, evidently, it peep-peeped off again, rippling the water.

'And you still didn't see your mum and dad?'

Jed sank his hands in his pockets. 'Not if I could help it. Dad was moody and drinking. Mum had her career. I had my sense of injury. We didn't completely lose touch, but we got along without each other. Then, two years ago, Dad wrote to me. Said he had cancer and he was on his way out.'

Tamara swung to look at him, the hard slats of the bench digging into her back. 'I'm sorry.'

Bleakly, he nodded. 'It was a nightmare wake-up call. I suddenly saw that letting my teenage rebellion go on too long had hurt me more than anybody. I mended fences and spent time with my parents, getting to know them again. I spent a lot of time with Dad.'

His gaze had settled on her. Tamara found herself unable

to look away from his eyes and the way the light gleamed in them. From them. 'I've given you my life story because I want you to try and understand what it was like to realise that my dad wouldn't always be there, waiting for when I decided to forgive him. How ready I was for him to open up to me. How much I wanted to absorb and remember every moment, every word.

'And then he told me that it was him that hurt Lyddie. All the details about how he'd disposed of the car by taking it to a scrapyard a hundred miles away, one where the bloke paid cash and didn't ask questions. I don't know if you remember that he had a sideline doing up cars and selling them on? I felt sick. Horrified. Outraged. Mortified.'

The breeze flicked his hair into his eyes and he thrust it back. 'I felt compassion for him, too, though I don't expect you to. The guy was in agony from guilt; it had been a life sentence. The alcohol abuse had stemmed from trying to forget that he'd had a few lunchtime beers at the pub and then driven stupidly – the moods and temper had come from self-hate because forgetting was impossible. I wanted to help him find some kind of peace before he died. So, when he asked me to find your family and do his confessing for him, I agreed.' He drew in a ragged breath. 'It was about him, not you, not the realities of life for your family – and for Lyddie. I failed to empathise with you and your parents.'

Caught up in the story, mesmerised by the fierce light in his eyes, Tamara could hardly breathe.

'He so wanted me to come back and do what he couldn't bring himself to.' The muscles in his neck worked as if he had to swallow his emotion. 'When you promise somebody something on their deathbed, you just think about getting it done.' His eyes bored into her, as if he could compel her to see things his way if he tried hard enough. 'I agreed that he could make me executor of his will and I've spent the time since he died last year sorting out his affairs and selling his house. Mum's remarried and he left everything between me and Manny, but he asked us to give some money to Lyddie. I want to give her my half. I want to make your mum accept that.'

No matter whether she had compassion for Don, Tamara's heart did go out to his son, sitting beside her, so obviously trying to do the right thing. He hadn't tried to defend the indefensible and his honesty touched her.

'All Mum will see is that your dad's life sentence was nothing compared to Lyddie's. In her mind, the money's tainted.'

Shutters came down over his face. He blinked and looked away. 'She's probably feeling cheated because she didn't see him sent to prison for what he did,' he said, bitterly.

Awkwardly, Tamara touched his arm. 'Maybe she is. Can you blame her?'

Silently, he rose and they made their way back along the path. It wasn't until they were right back at the embankment and the swans had sailed over to inspect them again, that he spoke, staring at the big white birds as if they might hold the answers. 'Sean's OK with me.'

'Dad's a more straightforward person. He can see that it's not your fault and you're trying to do what you think is best. But Mum's blinded by grief and anger.' She paused to formulate her argument. 'Why are you trying so hard to give Lyddie this money?'

His gaze flicked to her. 'Because I made a promise to Dad.'

'And why did he want you to promise?'

'Because he wanted to make up for what he did.'

Slowly, Tamara nodded. 'That's why Mum's so angry. You think that making it up to Lyddie – and to her – is possible. And she knows it's not. Money won't give Lyddie back what she lost.'

Jed kept his gaze on hers. He didn't want her to think that he couldn't meet her eyes. 'That's a skewed argument. Nothing can return Lyddie to what she was, but money can help. It can make life easier, even if it's just so that your parents can take her to Disneyland or something.'

Interest flickered over Tamara's face. 'That's a point.'

'Can you make your mother see it?'

Ruefully, she smiled. 'I wouldn't hold your breath.'

'Because it would destroy her argument against me?'

She snorted. 'She hasn't really put forward an argument against you. Blind rage is all she needs.' Her eyes softened. They were an unusual colour, like scrumpy. 'I'm sorry that she's making you a scapegoat.'

They'd reached the cars and he realised that she was going to get into her car and drive away. 'Meeting the boyfriend, now?'

'No. You meeting the wife?'

'Not married. I got too used to seeing myself as the outsider.' He'd meant it to be a joke, but somehow it came out bitter. 'I lived with someone once, but it didn't work out. Do you live with your boyfriend?'

Tamara fished her car keys out of her pocket and checked her watch. 'No. I have stuff to do, so I'd better get going.'

And in moments she was in her car and starting up the engine. Damn. Why the hell had he brought the boyfriend into the conversation? He should have just said, 'It's cold. Let's go somewhere warm for coffee.' He hadn't liked the boyfriend, Max. Not because there was anything wrong with him, but because Tamara had held his hand and her parents and sister had treated him like one of the family.

He shook his head, impatiently. *You're going to have to stop all this 'outsider' pity shit. It's getting to be a habit.*

Arriving home in his shiny car, driving in through the gates of Lie Low, Jed tried to shake off the feelings that had crowded back with such unsettling force, as he had told Tamara about his past.

He left his car in the garage and strode round to the side entrance of the fabulous house that lay elegantly in its landscaped grounds, and ran up the stairs. He, Manny and Carrie lived in the staff apartments in the roof of Lie Low, visible from the outside as a row of dormer windows at the back of the house. His apartment was the furthest along the blue-carpeted corridor, and the largest.

He let himself into the square hall. The walls were pristine white, the carpet cream. He sniffed appreciatively as he put down his car keys and took off his shoes and socks, leaving them on the big mat inside the door, so that he could step off onto the thick carpet and feel it on his skin. The air smelled of herbs and bleach, as if the cleaners had just been in. Not like the squat. He breathed in harder as he walked down the hall, past the kitchen, past the room that housed his cross trainer and rowing machine, trying to quash the memory of the stink – like bonfires and old hay and septic wounds.

Padding into his bedroom, he looked at the bed. Twice a week the cleaning staff changed one set of white cotton for another. He threw himself down on the pillows and closed his eyes, wallowing in the lemony scent of freshly laundered bedclothes, the softness of the bed beneath him. He shoved aside memories of achingly bare boards and a squalid sleeping bag.

Today he lived in cleanliness, hot water flowed in his bathroom, lights lit when he flicked the switch, the fridge was full of fresh food. He concentrated on thinking about bright clean things. The apartment. His car, which he had valeted to retain that new-car smell. The breeze off the river. Tamara Rix, the picture of health, the kind of girl who took care of her skin and nails, her hair blazing in the sunshine and smelling of shampoo when he got close enough to catch it.

He'd left the stink of the squat behind. Way behind.

It was just that, sometimes, he was frightened that it wasn't far enough.

Chapter Five

The little house in Bankside had been home to Tamara for several years. Compared to the eclectic and aged old village, it was ordinary, part of a rank of two-bedroom houses tucked into the corner of an estate of mainly posher houses with sweeping drives and porticoes that had earned Bankside the name of 'Little Dallas'. Tamara, at the end of the row, had only one immediate neighbour. On her other side, a towering hedgerow separated the estate from surrounding farmland and hosted fluttering or scurrying wildlife. She liked the lack of passing traffic and, though she was a child of the old village, she liked her house for its newness. Clean, square and airy, she'd painted its interior in creams and yellows.

She spent Tuesday afternoon catching up with laundry and household chores, but her mind kept slipping back to Jed and his story. She hadn't said anything to her parents yet, although Jed had plainly wished to get her onside with the aim that she should mediate.

Her thoughts were overlaid with the surreal feeling that had come with her boyfriend/best friend announcing out of the blue that a) he was going to move miles away b) he wanted Tamara to move with him, regardless of what such abandonment would do to Lyddie and that it would necessitate Tamara dumping the yoga classes she'd carefully built up and starting from scratch elsewhere and c) that he didn't want a long-distance relationship. If Tamara wouldn't accommodate b) so that he could have a), then c) would suggest they'd reached the end of the road.

How did she feel about that? It was a shock … but not a huge shock, as if somehow, somewhere, at the bottom of her heart, she'd always known that Max wasn't the love of her life. Suddenly she'd been made to acknowledge that relationships that never burned red hot were always going to fizzle out.

After a shower, Tamara jumped into her exercise gear, ready for her six o'clock class at the village hall in Middledip. As she ate half a sandwich and drank two cups of coffee, her phone bleeped. Text from her mother: *Lyddie has a note for you. Ian Mansfield took it to the shop and asked her to pass it on.*

Tamara's eyebrows flew up. Why would Manny send her a note? But then she glanced at her watch and dismissed the subject. It was time for her to go and do her instructor thing.

It was a ten-minute walk to the village hall, which was off Ladies Lane beside the playing fields. Tamara had grown up with the long, low stone building that hosted every type of village activity, from the playgroup to wedding receptions or funeral teas. It might not be such a glamorous venue as a gym or leisure club, but the profit margin was greater if she got a big class.

Arriving early, she gave herself time to turn the heating up and fetch the stereo out of the cupboard in the foyer, plug her iPod into it and fill the room with the soothing tinkle of piano music. People began to arrive, laying out their mats – territorial over their favourite spots, some of them – throwing their shoes and jackets to the side of the room. The stone floor wasn't exactly perfect for yoga, but the villagers never complained and Tamara always had spare mats, if anyone needed extra padding.

'Good evening, yogis. Anyone have any injuries or issues I should know about? OK, if you'd like to roll down on your mats, let's forget the hustle and bustle outside of this room.' And taking her own advice, she put aside her thoughts about Max, her mum, Lyddie and Jed Cassius as she turned her attention to her yogis.

She hoped she'd never get tired of being a yoga instructor. When she saw the stress that other people put themselves under with deadly office jobs and backstabbing corporate climbing, the work they brought home, the hatred with which they greeted Monday mornings, she almost felt guilty as she stretched her way through her working week, watching people hurrying into class as taut as piano wire and drifting out, an hour later, with languid steps and calm smiles. She loved the sensation of her muscles working their way into poses that kept her body elastic and disciplined.

Yes there were new routines to plan, admin to do like anybody else and sometimes living in a village made travel hairy in winter. But, other than that, Tamara stretched and toned her way through each session, assessing yogis and their individual needs, adapting her planned routine where she saw it was necessary, soaking up energy from the final deep relaxation as everybody shut out his or her clamouring worries to take a mental walk along a tropical beach or through a sun-dappled wood. By the time she roused them to a few last gentle stretches and twists, the room was an oasis of serenity and she sent them off with, 'See me with any feedback or I'll see you next week or at the Friday morning class.'

After some of her other classes there would be a gathering at a coffee shop, which was another agreeable aspect of her job. But there was no coffee shop in Middledip so, after switching off the lights and chatting to Shelli, the hall custodian who was waiting to lock up, Tamara strolled over to Church Close to satisfy her curiosity over Manny writing her a note. And she supposed she'd better tell her family about the unexpected developments with Max.

She found Lyddie and Jabber had just returned home from visiting Gabe's creatures, a particular lure for Lyddie while he was rearing an abandoned litter of puppies. She stepped into the hall, Jabber bouncing and barking, Lyddie beaming as she grabbed Tamara's hand and pulled her into the sitting room, where Sean and Cheryl had settled down with newspapers and the TV.

"Mara, I've got a letter for you from Manny. He gave it to me in the shop.' Lyddie took a square white envelope importantly from the mantel.

Cheryl eyed the envelope with disfavour. 'I can't imagine what he wants with you, Tamara.' Her tone was faintly accusing, as if Tamara had deliberately invited unsavoury correspondence.

'Me neither.' Tamara ran her nail under the flap and took out a single sheet of plain white paper. '*Hi Tamara, I'd like to speak to you about a yoga course. Please can you call me?*' she read out. His name and phone number were printed at the foot of the page. 'It looks as if he wants to add yoga to his fitness regime.'

Cheryl sniffed.

Tamara decided that if Cheryl was in a sniffy mood, then she hadn't mellowed at all from last week's bad temper. This seemed to be supported by Sean not joining in the conversation. If that was the case, it definitely wasn't the time to try to talk her mother down from her moral high ground about Jed. Nor was it the right time to tell her that it looked like the end for Tamara and Max, because Cheryl would be bound to say give Max time and he'd charge round and admit he'd been an idiot. Which wasn't going to happen.

Although Tamara couldn't expect Max not to take the fantastic career opportunity that had fallen into his lap, she couldn't even imagine herself telling Lyddie that she would be living many miles away and wouldn't be around to take her on long walks or play *Star Wars* Top Trumps.

The idea of not being part of a couple with Max did spawn a curious emptiness. But a chasm cracked open inside her at the thought of deserting Lyddie, and Lyddie's woebegone lack of comprehension, tears and tantrums.

Max was sad about the situation, she knew, but not bereft. If anything, he'd been pragmatic, admitting that he'd known he would have to ask her to choose between him and Lyddie one day. That her first instinct was to put Lyddie first, and his was to put his wonderful new job first, suggested a big problem with their relationship. He'd ended sadly, 'I've loved you for such a long time, Tam. I still love you.'

'I still love you, too, but—'

He nodded. 'But. You love me "in a way". In the easy, comfortable old way, which obviously isn't enough. One day you're going to have to realise that you can't put your sister's life right for her and you don't have to give up your own life in the attempt.'

The statement had sounded to Tamara like an accusation and suddenly the conversation became a quarrel. Not their first quarrel; they both had strong opinions and, occasionally, the expressing of them became robust. But, this time, her frustration at his lack of understanding about Lyddie had ignited more than momentary anger.

After the rage had faded, she'd searched for the hurt that she felt she ought to be burning with. But, with regret, all she could come up with was a sense of inevitability.

Tamara was jolted out of her thoughts by her mother clicking her tongue. 'What on earth's the matter with you, Tamara? Lyddie's asked you twice to watch a *Star Trek Voyager* DVD with her.'

With an effort, Tamara smiled. 'Sorry, Lyd. Come on then. A quick episode before bedtime.'

No, she wouldn't say anything about Max until she'd had time to let her own thoughts settle. Lyddie had a hard time comprehending that suddenly somebody you liked could be out of your life. In a while Tamara would get Cheryl alone and explain about Max and they'd strategise about how to distract Lyddie with things to look forward to and lots of positivity to ease her into the change. You couldn't just throw bad news at Lyddie.

At least there would be no pressure to leave Middledip now.

It was the next morning before she responded to Manny's note.

'Thanks for calling,' he said. 'I had quite a chat with your sister in the shop. I hope that it was OK to leave a note, but I didn't have your number and it was that or turn up at your parents' house.'

'It's OK,' she said, appreciating why he would rather not wave himself like a red rag in front of Cheryl. 'Are you looking for a yoga class? I do two in Middledip village hall – Friday mornings and Tuesday evenings. Or, if you're taking gym membership, I do classes at Caradoc Gym and Oasis Leisure, both in Bettsbrough, and the leisure clubs in Port Manor and Bettsbrough Park hotels.'

Manny hesitated. 'It's a bit more than that. I was hoping we could meet for coffee and a chat.'

'We can't sort it out now, on the phone?'

'I prefer face-to-face. Does later this afternoon work for you? Or some time tomorrow?'

She got the impression that he was looking at his watch and felt mildly irritated that he should be making such a production of trying a new yoga class. For most people it was enough to take a taster class, where she'd chat to them. She pulled her diary towards her. 'OK, I can do this afternoon, here in Middledip.'

'Where's the coffee shop in the village?'

She laughed. 'There isn't one. Unless you want to go to the mums and tots group in the village hall? I think they serve tea and coffee. Or we could meet at The Three Fishes pub.'

'The pub,' he said, promptly. 'At four?'

'It opens at five thirty.'

'Five thirty. Jed will be there, too. He asked me to arrange this. Thanks, and see you later.'

'What—?' she began. But the call had ended. She stared at her phone. Odd enough that Manny should feel the need for a meeting before committing to a yoga class, but to do so at the request of his stepbrother?

She snapped her diary shut. Weird.

It was only hours later that Tamara answered her phone to find her mother in a near panic. 'Tamara, I've got a bit of a situation, here. Jabber's hurt his paw, so Lyddie's beside herself. The dog obviously needs the vet, but I can't put Lyddie in the car while I drive, not in the state she's in. Can you come, darling?'

Tamara jumped up and reached for her keys, as she caught Lyddie's wails in the background. Rallying round was automatic when a family member had special needs. 'Be right there, Mum.'

A few minutes later, she stepped into her parents' house and into chaos.

Jabber was yelping and whimpering, a thick piece of rusty wire sticking right through his paw. Lyddie, sobbing and howling, 'Jabber! Jabber!' was casting herself around the kitchen, wild-eyed at the horrible protrusion from the dog's front left pad and the splats of blood on the kitchen vinyl, shoving at her mother with the flat of her hands.

Lyddie could get pretty challenging when she went off on one. Cheryl was trying to soothe both Lyddie and the distressed dog but, in his pain, Jabber kept lifting his lip at her.

'Thank God you're here, Tamara.' Cheryl tried to avoid Lyddie's hands, while Jabber tried to avoid Lyddie's feet. 'Poor Jabber.'

'Poor Jabber,' keened Lyddie.

'I've rung the vet and she says to take him straight to the surgery, but I can't get Lyddie calm enough to let me lift him in to the car. It's all right, Lyddie, honestly darling, he'll be all right. You need to stop crying so we can help Jabber.'

'Jabber!' roared Lyddie, 'Jabber's hurt, Jabber's really hurt. He stepped on it and I didn't see it and he screamed, Mum! Jabber really, really screamed. And he hopped all the way home.' Lyddie began a panicky paddling of her feet.

'I'll help Jabber, Lyd.' Tamara slid her arms around her sister for a big reassuring hug, uncomfortable as that was in view of Lyddie's flailing limbs, then moved in to grab Jabber's collar.

Cheryl then turned her full attention on Lyddie, her normally neat hair ragged around her face. 'It will be all right, Lyddie, honestly. Now Tamara's here you and me are going to go and sit in the other room and calm down and Tamara's going to get Jabber to the vet. You know which one it is, don't you Tamara? The one by the dentist's. The vet's going to make Jabber all better. OK, darling? Come on then, good girl, let's go through to the sitting room.'

Her voice and Lyddie's sobs dwindled, and Tamara was left stroking the head of a very-sorry-for-himself Jabber, his paw trembling in mid-air. 'Poor Jabber,' she soothed. 'Poor old Mutt. I'm going to help you, puppy, but I don't think this is a one-person job.'

She worked her phone out of her pocket and rang Gabe, explaining briefly the fix she was in, and Lyddie's distress. Gabe Piercy was Lyddie's best friend, calm and quiet, thoughtful and kind. One of the more eccentric villagers, he clip-clopped around the village on an ancient trap pulled by Snobby, his shaggy black pony. He might look like a gypsy, but actually he was a retired bank manager who'd stopped shaving and cutting his grey hair when he stepped out of the banking hall for the final time. Now he lived like a refugee from a folk tale, in a little house with a big plot of land where he kept chickens and ducks and every lame animal that found its way to him. Lyddie loved helping with what she called 'Gabe's creatures' and one of the chickens, Princess Layer, was 'hers'.

'Hang on, I'll be there.' His voice was reassuring. Gabe was a good bloke to have in a crisis.

He arrived at the house in ten minutes, silver hair sweeping his shoulders. Tamara met him at the door before he could ring the bell, whispering so that Lyddie wouldn't hear them and come rushing out to see Gabe.

Using Jabber's blanket from his beanbag, between them they got him wrapped up and into Gabe's arms and from there onto the back seat of Tamara's car, although with a couple of yelps that made Tamara wince. Gabe got in beside him, and as Tamara drove across the village and took the road towards Bettsbrough, he stroked Jabber's broad head, crooning. Jabber panted, but didn't whimper any more. Gabe was fantastic with animals.

'How are Max's house plans coming on?' he asked, as they left the village.

A lump settled in Tamara's stomach. 'They're not.' And she found herself telling him what she hadn't yet felt able to tell her family, about Max's new job. 'He's angry, of course, because I can't leave Lyddie,' she finished. 'And he thinks it's some misplaced sense of duty or neediness to see myself as indispensible. But I just can't bear to hurt her like that. It's weakness, not strength.'

'Ah well,' said Gabe.

She flicked her gaze from the road ahead to the rear-view mirror, trying to glimpse his face. 'What does "Ah well" mean?'

Gabe laughed. 'It means that I'm being non-committal.'

She changed down and turned right at a T-junction, trying not to shake poor Jabber around too much. 'Be committal.'

After a pause for thought, Gabe said, 'Max is a great guy. But he never looks at you as if he'd like to shut himself in a bedroom with you for a fortnight.'

Tamara nearly swerved into a ditch beside the hawthorn hedge starred with the last few blossoms. 'Gabe!' Then, curiously, 'What exactly does that expression look like?'

'You'd know it if you saw it. And I think that a pretty young girl like you should be seeing it on her boyfriend.'

'Right,' said Tamara, comforted by the thought that if Gabe could detect a lack of passion between Max and her, passion definitely wasn't there. It made things easier to accept. She wondered how it would feel to be looked at by a man as if he'd like to shut himself in a bedroom with her for a fortnight. And then Jed Cassius popped into her mind, and the arrested look in his eyes when she'd arrived in her parents' sitting room to find him there. The memory shivered down her backbone.

Max had been her best friend. The sex had been fine because they knew each other so well that trust and comfort played their roles. But ... she couldn't recall the last time he'd looked at her that way. Or she'd shivered at the thought.

It was several hours later that they lifted a sore, bandaged Jabber back into the car, the vet having reversed the deep sedation she'd put him under while she cut the wire and eased it out, flushed the wound and applied a poultice.

'I don't need to keep him in overnight,' she'd said, giving Jabber's black silky ears a rub. 'He'll be well on the mend by the time he's had a night's sleep.'

Back in Middledip, Lyddie dashed out the moment the car drew up. 'Jabber? *Hel*lo Jabber.'

Gabe lifted Jabber carefully from the back seat. 'Easy, Lyddie. Let's try and keep him calm. You stand still and let him show you how he can walk on three legs.'

Lyddie froze with exaggerated care while Jabber hopped up to her, hooked tail swinging and ears back in greeting. Delight flooded her face. 'He's not bleeding now.'

'He's been a good dog and let the vet help him. But we all need to be very careful of his paw.' Tamara gave Lyddie a hug and a kiss on the cheek. She kissed her mum, too, who was hovering, looking strained. She probably hadn't had an easy time with Lyddie while the Jabber rescue party had been away.

They all watched Jabber three-leg it to the fence and, with a bit of creative paw-work, discover a way to balance while he cocked his leg, before heading indoors towards his beanbag in the kitchen, Lyddie providing an anxious escort.

'I'll be off home.' Gabe brushed off Tamara's and Cheryl's thanks, tucked his hands in the pockets of a jacket that looked as if it had once been part of a good blue suit, and set off, whistling.

Tamara glanced at her watch. She ought to be leaving for her meeting with Manny and Jed at The Three Fishes.

'Jed Cassius's money,' she said, impulsively. 'Don't you think you might as well take it?'

Cheryl turned an astounded face on her. 'Why?'

'I know that no amount of money can put the clock back, but you could use it to give Lyddie treats. Disneyland or something.'

'Not with blood money.'

Tamara sighed. 'Jed seemed to genuinely want Lyddie to have all of the money his dad left him.'

Cheryl snorted. 'To quiet his conscience, I suppose.'

Irritation flared in Tamara. 'He has no reason to have a bad conscience. He was just a teenager, like Lyddie, Mum. He wasn't driving the car. He didn't know who was, until his dad was dying. It couldn't have been easy for him to come and tell you what had happened, to lose his dad and have to face up to something so horrible on his behalf.'

Yanking her cardigan around herself, Cheryl swung away to follow Lyddie and Jabber back indoors. 'I'm not going to be beholden to any Cassius. I didn't ask him to come here, making up to Lyddie and your dad. And you! I saw the way he looked at you.'

Tamara stared after her. Why was the way men looked at her today's hot subject?

Chapter Six

The Three Fishes: the fragrance of beer, dark red velvet curtains, roughcast rendering, too much brass and copper. Though it was early, the local noisy beery blokey blokes, Ben Bell and his mates, were watching Sky Sports on the TV in the corner.

Manny sat waiting, his back propped comfortably against the bar. His chest stretched his white T-shirt, his beard looked freshly shorn.

Jed lounged beside him in a black T-shirt with a black jacket, feet on rungs of two different stools, his hair a satin curtain he flicked from his eyes. He watched as the blokey blokes looked away from the TV screen with brightening eyes when Tamara entered, instantly embarking on their favourite comedy routine. 'Tamara! It's your round. But we'll let you off if you give us a kiss.'

Tamara was only too familiar with the blokey blokes. Two of them had been in the same year as her and Max at school. She'd never shared a single one of their endless rounds, but it seemed to amuse them to pretend she did. 'Another time,' she said.

But they didn't seem to want to be brushed off.

'Aw, come sit with us, Tamara.' Spherical heads reddened through their stubble, eyes disappearing into creased flesh as their shoulders shook with silent mirth. She tried to ignore them, but Bell tipped back his chair so that she had to either squeeze past or take a detour. She heaved a sigh. It wasn't that there was anything wrong with Bell and co. They were just so hairy-arsed with their chorused male guffaws, face-and-head stubble, fierce arguments about footie and their cigarette-induced coughs.

From long experience, she knew that the best approach was to ignore them and not let them know they were irritating her, because that would increase their belief that they were comedians.

She turned away, intending to circle the next table and try not to feel self-conscious that they'd probably all be eyeing up her rear view. But a yelp and a thunderous clatter from behind made her spin on her heel.

Bell and his chair were lying on their backs. Bell's empty glass was in his hand, while the erstwhile contents soaked into his combat trousers and T-shirt. Jed stood over him with an expression of deep concern. 'Sorry, mate,' he said. 'I was helping you get out of the lady's way.'

The blokey blokes gaped.

Manny remained on his stool, watching expressionlessly.

Gingerly, Bell rolled off his chair and climbed to his feet, face red and wary, shaking away beer that dripped down his arms.

Jed's eyes were cold. 'As you're on your feet, you might as well stand aside to let Tamara through, hadn't you?'

Silently, Bell complied, not meeting Tamara's eyes as he stood the chair up out of her path.

Slowly, she walked through the space he'd made. 'Thank you.'

Jed looked meaningfully at Bell. 'You're welcome,' Bell muttered.

Jed dismissed the situation with a turn of his shoulder and transferred his inscrutable attention to Tamara. 'What would you like to drink?'

Behind the bar, Tubb, the pub's landlord, stared warily at Jed. The optics twinkled behind him in the late afternoon sunlight, filtered through a galaxy of dust motes disturbed by Bell's considerable carcass crashing to the carpet.

Tamara noticed that Manny's gaze was still on the

blokey blokes, as if watching that they behaved while his stepbrother's back was turned. 'Frothy coffee, please.'

Jed nodded at Tubb. 'Three, please. And what was the big bloke drinking?'

Tubb's turned-down mouth didn't open far when he spoke. 'A pint of Adnam's.'

'A pint of Adnam's, too, then.'

With practised movements Tubb pulled the pint, then paused while he watched Jed return to the still-silent blokey blokes and position the full glass precisely in front of Bell. Bell eyed him cautiously.

Jed returned to the bar and indicated a table across the room. 'We'll have the coffee over there, please.'

Tamara allowed herself to be ushered to the comparative peace of a corner table, its dark wood scuffed at the edges, taking the chair that Jed pulled out for her as Manny closed in smoothly behind them like a bodyguard.

What had just happened? Had Jed Cassius really kicked Bell's chair out from under him because Bell had childishly blocked Tamara's way? She glanced at Jed under her lashes. He was seating himself calmly, not betraying by a flicker that he was even ruffled. But for a few seconds he'd been like a Hollywood cowboy in a saloon, taking the law into his own hands, meting out justice and apparently unaware of – or unconcerned at – creating an atmosphere of wary tension in a local pub that usually reposed in somnolent bonhomie.

Tubb arrived with a tray and set three thick white coffee cups on the circular table, giving Jed a look that suggested he might have something to say but wasn't sure it was a great idea to say it, then sailing ponderously off towards the bar.

'That was ... interesting,' Tamara said, neutrally.

Jed made a small movement of his eyebrows. 'The guy's a dick.'

She didn't argue. Bell always had been a dick but, so far as she was aware, nobody had ever felt the need to dump him on his capacious arse in front of his assistant dicks before.

Arms folded on top of his belly, Bell ignored the pint that Jed had just delivered, ignored his wet clothes and gazed studiously at the television. The rest of the abnormally subdued blokey blokes cast uneasy glances Jed's way.

Jed just added sugar and cream to his coffee as he spoke to Tamara. 'So how did you get into being a yoga instructor?' His eyes were more green than hazel in the light from the window.

She wasn't sure if she approved or not of him putting some manners on Bell, but no way was she going to let him think that he could intimidate her with his abrupt questions. 'I wanted to do it. I did it. The actual training was well within my capabilities and I like it. The business side of keeping myself employed for a certain number of hours each week, hiring halls, getting myself taken on in gyms and leisure clubs, is less appealing, but I'm good at it.' She sipped her coffee.

'Do you work with people with physical challenges?'

'Lyddie,' she replied, succinctly. 'But, yes, people often come to yoga when they've hurt their backs or ankles, or whatever. They suddenly see the value of strengthening and lengthening muscles and improving bone density. I would think all instructors work with people with physical challenges, to some degree.'

He nodded. 'We need an instructor.'

Tamara glanced at Manny, who was listening silently. What the hell physical challenges did Jed or Manny have? Each looked the epitome of masculine health: lean, muscled and confident. 'I take fifteen classes a week in the area, so there's bound to be something to suit you. Like I said to

Manny on the phone, you could join a gym or leisure club or come to a class at the village hall or Port Community Centre.'

Jed lifted his coffee cup. 'Classes wouldn't work. Do you give private lessons?'

She hesitated. Going to wherever these two unreadable men lived to give them private yoga tuition sounded like the kind of thing women were warned against. Though ... this was *Jed Cassius*, who she'd known since childhood, who'd been Lyddie's teenaged boyfriend. Yeah, the Jed Cassius who had just kicked Bell off his chair. 'I have worked one-to-one, if that's what you're asking.'

He frowned. 'We're not approaching you for ourselves, but for Emilia.'

'Who's Emilia?'

'Emilia's our employer's wife,' he explained. 'She had an accident and she's coming to terms with life on crutches. She's had physical therapy, but when I met you again I mentioned it to her and she's interested.'

Now she felt more on solid ground. 'What kind of injury does she have?'

'She smashed her ankle, broke her tibia and fibula and suffered ligament damage in a fall. It was about a year and a half ago, but the leg won't take much weight.'

'It may always be affected. That kind of damage needs time and physio. Does she have a realistic picture of what yoga can do for her?' Tamara felt it best to be honest about her capabilities. Presumably, Emilia and her husband enjoyed 'a certain lifestyle' if they could afford employees to arrange private instructors for them, so it was possible that Emilia had taken up the idea of yoga in the spirit of *throw money at the problem and fix it*.

Jed looked at Manny and Manny answered. 'Emilia has been used to having a high level of fitness. Gym, aerobics, swimming, she did them all daily until the accident. She thinks yoga is a good option for her right now, and I agree. It'll give her a gentle stretch and tone and help her with her balance and posture.'

'It would be great for her general mobility and to augment her physiotherapy,' Tamara agreed. 'Depending on her injury, it could help with problems of weight bearing, too.'

'I've acted as her personal trainer, sometimes,' Manny said. 'She had good fitness and endurance levels before the accident.'

'Then that fitness should help her now. Of course, I'd need to meet her to make an assessment and to see if she would want to work with me, and where she'd like it to happen,' Tamara added. 'If she'd like to give it a try, we'd need to discuss fees.'

Jed took back the conversational ball. 'Our employer's able to finance what Emilia wants to do.'

'What do you two do for "your employer"?' she asked, curiously. 'And who is he? You make it all sound mysterious.'

Another of those little movements with his eyebrows. Jed was pretty economical with his expressions, as if they'd wear out if he used them too often. Which was a shame because when his smile flashed out, it was a real megawatt example.

'I manage things for him. Whatever it is he needs me to manage: his household, aspects of his business, his general comfort. Manny takes care of security and travel, that kind of thing. It's not the sort of job that requires three shifts a day of close protection officers, guys working in pairs. More low key than that.'

He studied her for a moment, as if debating what she needed to know. Eventually, he added, 'He's a successful businessman, but in the last couple of years one of his businesses has been targeted by protestors. It was OK when the protests were peaceful and legal, but the extreme faction lost their heads and made it personal and threatening. That's why the move up here from London and why our employer is cautious about who he and Emilia come into contact with.'

Though conscious of a pang of disappointment that Jed's employer wasn't a celebrity businessman like Alan Sugar or one of the Dragons, Tamara gazed at him, fascinated. 'Wow. What was the protest about? Was his company unethical or something?'

'How do you evaluate that? Ethics isn't just a matter of acting lawfully. It's all about moral judgements and appropriate behaviour. And judgements vary. Some people hold strong opinions and easily fall victim to moral outrage. They get impetuous, take matters into their own hands.'

She glanced pointedly at the blokey blokes who were watching News 24 in almost unprecedented hush. Bell still hadn't broached his pint, as if in silent protest at his treatment. 'And you don't take matters into your own hands?'

He shrugged. 'My action wasn't impetuous. It was prompt, but controlled. And I made certain that only that guy's dignity was hurt. No innocent workers found themselves fighting their way out of a building filled with fumes from a home-made gas canister flung in through a window. Nobody received rotting animal parts through the post.'

Tamara sobered. 'That's serious stuff. But I think that if you're suggesting that I commit to working in the home of an employer who attracts that kind of attention, then I need to know the company's business.'

'Knickers.'

She hesitated.

Manny smothered a laugh.

A rare smile lit Jed's face. 'The Hilton Group is made up of diverse businesses, but the particular company that attracted the protestors manufactures knickers, bras, basques, suspender belts and bustiers. You may wear the products yourself, it's all sexy, pretty stuff. Some of the work was outsourced to China, to a company who were later proved to be using unethical and abusive working practices. Our employer ended the contracts as soon as practicable, but the damage was done. The activists had targeted his concerns.'

Trying not to think about Jed thinking about her underwear or the memory of Cheryl's 'I've seen how he looks at you', Tamara said, 'OK, so long as I'm not in danger from anti-lingerie protestors, I'm up for meeting your employer's wife. If you think she's comfortable that this is the time to improve her fitness.'

'She says it's exactly what she needs. I was hoping to arrange for you to get together on Monday.' Jed had obviously come to this meeting with clear aims.

'That would be possible. Is her doctor aware of her plans? I need to be happy about that.'

'A letter from her doctor is no problem. Emilia's keen to get started. Our employer will want to meet you, too.'

Hmm. Tamara made her reply careful. 'I'll be happy to meet her husband, of course, but it's Emilia who would be my client.' She wasn't sure that allowing herself to be vetted by an anxious husband was the best way to build rapport with a new yogi.

'Emilia's well-being is high on Mr Hilton's list of priorities.'

Tamara was ruffled at Jed's obvious intention to be in control, but let it pass. 'OK. Let's talk fees.' To test how serious he was she named an hourly fee that was somewhere around what a competent city accountant would charge. 'Because I could be using the time to instruct an entire hall full of yogis, couldn't I? And that's what I'd expect to take in a hall session.' She didn't offer a discount for not having to hire a hall.

Jed didn't flinch. 'I'll pass that on.'

Wow. Emilia and Mr Hilton were evidently used to paying for what they wanted, which was fine by Tamara.

Jed pressed the conversation forward. 'My employer will want you to sign a confidentiality agreement.'

'A what? What for?'

One corner of his mouth lifted at her astonishment. 'I've explained the problems. Our employer needs to assure himself that his, and Emilia's, privacy is maintained. It's a standard non-disclosure document, just stating that you won't share information with third parties about Emilia, your work with Emilia, our employer, their home or any of their business.' And, as Tamara gazed at him, 'Is there a reason you can't?'

'No,' she answered, slowly. 'It's just a novelty in the life of your average yoga instructor. And if I sign an agreement like that the work can't then go on my CV, which is a pity because it would act like a recommendation for anyone else looking for one-to-one sessions.'

After a moment's consideration, Jed nodded. 'Perhaps our employer will agree to a premium on your fee to compensate you for that. I'll recommend five per cent. If you're happy to go ahead, I'll take your contact details and be in touch to arrange for you and Emilia to meet. As long as you're aware of the need for discretion, I think we can leave the signing of the NDA until your first visit.'

Tamara studied his face to check he was serious, but his level green gaze said he was. It all felt a bit unreal.

Chapter Seven

As the meeting broke up and Jed was courteously holding the big wooden pub door for Tamara to pass through, her phone rang.

It was Max. 'We ought to talk,' he said.

Tamara nodded goodbye to Jed and Manny as they turned towards the car park. 'Good plan.'

'Your house in about an hour?'

'That's fine.' She drove home to switch on the coffee machine and open the sitting room windows to the summer evening breeze, then curled up on one of the two small sofas with a newspaper until she saw his car draw up in the road outside. She watched him step over the low wall and cross the grass. He had a key, but she got up to open the door to save him from having to decide whether he was still allowed to use it.

He hadn't shaved and his stubble scraped her cheek as he gave her a hard, brief hug. 'I couldn't leave without seeing you.'

Her heart dipped. It wasn't because of grief that Max wasn't going to do the what-was-I-thinking-of-because-I-can't-live-without-you routine, it was more dismay at the uncomplimentary speed with which he was adjusting himself to the new situation.

'So, you're leaving this soon?' She shut the door and turned to the kitchen to take refuge in the automatic movements of coffee making.

He turned her around, milk carton in her hand, his face anxious. 'Are you OK?' And then, before she could even answer, 'That was a bit lame, wasn't it? Sorry. I suppose that we've just been together so long. Even though—'

'Even though?'

'We're not really together any more.' There was sadness in his voice, and maybe surprise. A pause. 'This is like a chick flick, isn't it? In a minute, one of us is going to say, "I love you, but I'm not *in* love with you" and rush off to find someone more exciting.'

He was more rueful than upset. Max, who had been such a huge part of her life that she'd fallen into the trap of thinking he would carry on being so, was cutting himself out of it.

Tamara took the coffee jug off the machine and filled two mugs, leaving plenty of room for milk in Max's. 'Or maybe, "It's not you, it's me"?'

'Weird, isn't it?' He took the coffee without even brushing hands. 'But I'd hate to lose you as my friend.'

'Me, too.' And she realised that the disconnection she'd been feeling was all about losing him as a best friend, not as a boyfriend. Which was sort of sad. But curiously liberating.

After Max had left, Tamara felt restless. There had been no emotional scene, just a couple of heartfelt hugs and probably relief and, yes, guilt at feeling relief. It seemed wrong that breaking up was so easy.

She grabbed a jacket and the door key Max had left and set off on a circuit of the village, letting herself get used to the idea that doing the right thing for Lyddie had turned out to be the right thing for Tamara, too.

Inevitably, her route took her past Church Close and she crossed to her parents' house, letting herself in through the front door. 'Hello?'

''Mara!' Lyddie burst from the sitting room, arms out, anxiety tugging at her mouth, her denim skirt twisted so that the embroidery that should be on the front was on the side. Jabber limped beside her, putting a little weight on his bad paw already, a smaller dressing now in place of the poultice. "Mara, can I have a puppy? Gabe's puppies. I want one. It's a really, really nice one, he's black nearly all over.'

Tamara gave her sister a big reassuring hug, aware from the agitation of Lyddie's hands that she was emotional. She made her voice gentle. 'But Lyddie, Jabber wouldn't understand you getting a puppy. He's been brought up as an only dog.' She gave Jabber's silky head a consolatory pat.

Lyddie's lip quivered. 'He would,' she muttered, unconvincingly, rubbing her trainer on the carpet.

'Poor old Jabber, he'd think you didn't love him any more. You'll have to ask Mum, but I think she'll say no.'

'She's already said it.' Lyddie heaved a big dramatic sigh, lifting her hands and letting them slap down onto Tamara's shoulders, her eyes full of sudden tears. 'Dad said it, too. I thought you might say yes.' She sniffed. 'Would you like a puppy?'

'No,' Tamara responded instantly, visualising Lyddie landing her with a whole litter of puppies, and probably a few rescue chickens, too.

Lyddie fixed her eyes grumpily on the floor. Then she heaved a huge sigh and dropped her hands with a flounce. 'I'd better give him back then.'

Tamara's jaw dropped. '*What*? You haven't brought him home, have you?'

Lyddie flushed a dull red, her eyes glittering with guilty tears. 'He's so liddle I thought—'

'Oh Lyddie! I'll bet Gabe doesn't know you've got him. Have you fed the puppy?'

She hunched her shoulders. 'I was going to. But I haven't got any of those bottles Gabe feeds them with.'

'Lyddie, a puppy has to eat every few hours.' Tamara tried not to groan. 'Where are Mum and Dad?'

'In the garden.' A tear tracked down Lyddie's cheek. 'I haven't told them about the puppy.' One hand began to grab at the air, as if seeking words and logic to feed to her mind.

'Come on, you'd better show me.' Tamara took Jabber into the kitchen, shutting the door on his eager black-and-white face, and took Lyddie's large hot hand.

Upstairs, the puppy was stowed under Lyddie's duvet. Poor little rat of a thing, he was boiling hot and breathing in side-heaving gasps, his eyes half-blind above his seeking mouth. Predictably, he hadn't suspended his bodily functions while in Lyddie's bed.

He was desperately cute, though, black with white paws, one white ear, and a tiny pink nose.

'He's called Luke,' Lyddie whispered, breathing heavily on Tamara as she scooped up the furry baby.

To spare Lyddie a talking-to, and to spare Cheryl the shame of Lyddie becoming a puppy-napper, Luke had to travel out of the house the same way he'd apparently arrived – in the big front pocket of Lyddie's hoodie.

'Lyddie's going to show me Gabe's puppies,' Tamara shouted through the back door to her parents, who were discussing something in the garden. Then she and Lyddie scurried out of the front door as if they were still children not wanting Cheryl to know they were sneaking biscuits.

Jabber tried to shoot out behind them in a limping rush, but Tamara shut the door before he achieved escape. Judging by his pricked ears and gleaming eyes, he'd got a whiff of the competition and Tamara didn't need him being obnoxiously doggy all the way through the village. Luke had enough to cope with – like starvation.

Gabe was shutting his chickens away for the night when Tamara and Lyddie turned onto the track to the back of the large plot around his little house.

'Evening,' he smiled. As the sun went down it lit Gabe's pearl-grey beard pink like one of those fibre-optic things bought from a pound shop. His silver hair was tied back in a ponytail and he wore the jacket of an old brown suit over navy deck trousers. When he'd left his bank manager's job he must have decided to renounce all personal material considerations. Of course, he'd left his wife at the same time and she probably got a good wodge of his pension, making recycling his old work suits a sensible economy.

Tamara fished the poor little puppy out of Lyddie's kangaroo pocket. 'I'm afraid he's very hungry,' she apologised, easing the furry scrap into Gabe's capable hands. 'But Lyddie just couldn't resist him. She's sorry, aren't you, Lyd?'

Lyddie nodded, eyes filling again with tears. ''M sorry,' she gulped.

'Good gracious,' Gabe said in his precise tones. 'I didn't think to count the damned things at feeding time. Perhaps I ought to frisk you, young lady, before you leave in future?' He frowned and cupped his hands over the pup to keep him warm.

Lyddie stared at her feet.

'Come on,' he said, gently. 'Let's get this youngster some milk. He's a bit dehydrated but he's only missed one feed.'

In the spartan, but clean, kitchen, Tamara nursed the mewling scrap that was Luke, while Gabe tucked his ponytail down the back of his jacket out of the way. He boiled the kettle, mixed up puppy milk and stood several bottles, like baby bottles but smaller, in a bowl of cold water. As if by magic, the other puppies woke to squeak and squirm in the cardboard box Gabe had lined with paper, blankets and a heat pad, a thermometer hooked over the side, wriggling over each other in their rootling for food.

When the milk was cool enough, Tamara passed Luke

back to him and watched as he made a cradle from his large hand, guiding the teat to the puppy's mouth, which fastened feebly to this mother-substitute. 'You'd better start on the others,' he observed as the puppy gulped more strongly. 'His brothers and sisters have got the idea that it's time for supper.'

Lyddie was sheepishly subdued, worn out by the upset, but Tamara sat her down on the floor with her back to the wall and she fed one of the more robust puppies, a little black-and-white patchy one, laying him face down on her lap and cupping the little head in her palm. Gabe had brought up more than this abandoned litter over the years and Lyddie and Tamara had both received training in puppy feeding. Tamara watched to ensure that Lyddie was squeezing the bottle and not the puppy, then picked up a white female with a black eye patch and saddle.

By the time the litter was fed it was past ten. Lyddie wanted to see her chicken, Princess Layer, but Gabe flipped his ponytail and yawned. 'Princess Layer and all the chickens went to bed hours ago. And now I'm going, too. The old girls get up early.'

Tamara counted the puppies to make sure Lyddie hadn't swiped any more, then walked her home through a beautiful dark blue evening dotted with stars. The village seemed to belong to them as they walked up Port Road, arms linked. Lyddie heaved a big sigh. 'I'm sorry I took him.'

Tamara kissed her sister's cheek. 'I know you won't do it again.' Actually, she knew no such thing, but there was nothing to be gained by being angry with Lyddie. Just nothing. Setting boundaries only worked sometimes, depending on the degree of importance Lyddie attached to her goal.

But Lyddie's mind was already moving on in one of its random strides. 'I had chops and roast potatoes for dinner.

I love pork chops more than anything. I *love* them. More than anything, except pizza. And lasagne. And chips.'

'They're all great,' agreed Tamara.

'And I really, really, really like gravy. But not with chips. Or pizza. Or lasagne. Max loves lasagne, too. I haven't seen Max for days, 'Mara. Where is he?'

Tamara felt her neck tighten. Normally, she'd forewarn her parents before she spilled any beans to Lyddie. But she suddenly had the urge to confide, as if Lyddie was really the big sister she ought to have been and would comfort her as she accustomed herself to the idea of life without Max.

She took a deep breath. 'I've got some news about Max.'

Lyddie turned expectantly, sidling crabwise so that she could keep her eyes on Tamara's face. The sweetness of her smile hit Tamara hard under the breastbone.

'It's not good news though.'

Lyddie's smile slid away. She hated 'not good'.

Tamara squeezed her sister's arm again. It went against the grain to deliberately upset Lyddie. 'Well, some of it's good news. Max has got a fantastic new job.'

A bright beaming smile blazed across Lyddie's face. 'Yay!'

'But it's not in Peterborough. It's in Liverpool.'

Lyddie nodded, still smiling.

'So we won't see as much of him as before.' Tamara sounded as matter-of-fact as she could.

Lyddie stopped dead with a ludicrous expression of dismay. Tamara waited out one of her longer pauses for thought. 'But won't he come to see you?' Lyddie said, in the end.

'Sometimes, maybe.'

'Don't he like you any more? Don't you like him?' The all-too-familiar sad and confused expression dragged at her sister's features and Tamara found it very difficult not to babble comforting fibs.

With an effort, she summoned up her calmest, most matter-of-fact tones. 'We do like each other very, very, very much. But Max wants to take this new job. It's a wonderful job. So we've decided that with him living quite a long way away, there's no point us being boyfriend and girlfriend any more. We're still best friends though.'

Lyddie shuffled uneasily. 'Did you have a horrid argument?' There was dread in her voice. All arguments were horrid to Lyddie. 'A really, really bad one? Really bad?' Her hands rolled over and over and over each other.

'No, we didn't have an argument. We still love each other – a bit.' Not enough. But there was no point telling her things she wouldn't understand. 'That's why I think Max taking his lovely new job is the best thing for him. I want what makes him happy.'

They set off again, Lyddie in glum silence. Tamara knew her less-than-perfect thought processes would be ambling unhappily around this new prospect.

She was too cowardly to point out at this stage that the fracture in her relationship might mean that Lyddie would never see Max again. She just couldn't face the rawness of Lyddie's grief.

But she didn't get long to worry about it because Lyddie halted in consternation. 'I need a wee.' Lyddie needing a wee was a sudden thing, she didn't seem to get much warning.

Tamara picked up her pace. 'Can you wait until we get home?' Home was still half a mile away.

'Nope, nope!' Lyddie did a little dance, her forehead furrowed. 'Can't wait. I'll go behind that bush where it's dark.' And she rushed off towards a shrubby area in front of someone's garden wall, clutching herself inelegantly, while Tamara glanced round to check no one was coming and hoped that the householder didn't look out and freak. It wasn't worth protesting, better for Lyddie to let it all out than wet herself. It was why she usually wore a skirt, not trousers.

In two minutes Lyddie was back, lurching through the dewy weeds that overhung the path. 'I got wet socks,' she announced, cheerfully. 'I stood up.'

Tamara couldn't help smiling as she turned her sister for home. 'Couldn't you crouch, or something? Standing up's for boys.'

'*I* just did it. I'm not a boy.'

'But you got wet socks.'

'I like wet socks.' Lyddie kissed the side of Tamara's face, moistly.

There didn't seem much point in going into techniques of female al fresco urination for the nth time, especially if the need to pee had jumped Lyddie's thoughts out of Maxlessness, so Tamara laughed. 'If you like wet socks, your way's fine.' She returned the kiss and they linked arms and strolled on towards Church Close.

As soon as Tamara opened the door to their parents' house, Lyddie yodelled, 'Mum, I got wet socks!' The sound of the television came from the sitting room.

'I'll sort her out,' Tamara called. 'Leave your trainers outside, Lyddie. And your socks. Yes, definitely, your socks, I'll see to them when you've had a shower.' She could quickly change Lyddie's bed, too.

Cheryl came out into the hall. She looked strained. 'Couldn't you wait, darling?'

'No. I went in a bush.'

'I stood guard,' Tamara supplied, automatically. These were things that the family of a learning disabled adult dealt with. No point making a fuss. No point wishing things were different.

''Mara's not Max's girlfriend any more,' Lyddie announced, proving that her thoughts hadn't entirely jumped out of Maxlessness. She started up the stairs, holding on to the handrail because her co-ordination for steps wasn't good.

Cheryl swung her surprised gaze on Tamara, and Tamara shrugged apologetically. 'Sorry. I was going to tell you as soon as I'd seen to Lyddie. Max has been offered a brilliant job in Liverpool. I don't want to go with him and he doesn't want to miss the opportunity, which has made us re-evaluate things and we've realised that we're more friends than anything.'

Sean emerged from the sitting room, newspaper in hand and concern written on his face. 'Sorry to hear that, darling.' He hugged her and Tamara had to swallow a sudden lump in her throat.

Cheryl, on the other hand, sighed. 'Oh dear, Tamara, aren't you ever going to settle down?'

Sean clicked his tongue. 'There's nothing wrong with her being single.'

And as they bristled at each other, Tamara escaped up to the bathroom, not sure if her heart felt more squashed by her father's sympathy or her mother's lack of it.

Once Lyddie was clean and dry, Tamara went with her to her room. 'Can we webcam?' demanded Lyddie.

Tamara agreed, getting out her phone, preferring conversations via cyber space to the usual demands for the computer games that Lyddie loved for their bright colours and clanging music, but which inevitably made her cross when she lost in shoals of counters or animated characters shaking sorrowful heads. Tamara had taught her to use Skype so that she could chat with cousins. It entertained her and was something Ginny, Lyddie's social worker, had put down as a new skill when Lyddie demonstrated how to open the software and click on Tamara's picture.

When the software sprang to life on Tamara's phone, she touched *answer*.

'Hellooooo 'Mara!' Lyddie's face filled the screen, concave from being too close to the webcam. 'We're doing the webcam, aren't we? I can see you. My name is Lyddie Rix and your name's Tamara Rix, isn't it 'Mara? I can see you.' And she laughed, a long, deep rolling chuckle, lighting her on-screen eyes and filling the room.

Tamara laughed back. Life was always easier when Lyddie was happy. And when Lyddie was happy, Tamara found it easier to be the same.

Chapter Eight

The more Tamara considered Emilia, her potential new client, the odder her situation seemed, a feeling that increased when Jed phoned to request that she meet Manny along Port Road and follow him to the Hilton residence. 'It's just that it's easy to miss.'

And, sure enough, at the appointed time on Monday she found Manny waiting in a big dark blue Mercedes. Tamara drove up and flashed her lights and they cruised half a mile past the last straggling houses of the village, before slowing and turning left between the hedges, up to a spinney of hawthorn and poplar that filtered the sunshine into jiggling dapples and green shadow.

Tamara had lived in Middledip all her life and had only a vague memory that this track existed. Muddy tracks off country roads were usually the preserve of farms and tractors and faded into the scenery. Threading its way among the trunks, the track emerged suddenly at a chunky pair of black iron gates in a high fence. Behind them, further along the curve, lay a more elegant set of gates set in another fence. Tamara saw Manny point a remote control and both pairs of gates swung open, allowing the cars to drive past a discreet sign, *Lie Low*, onto a cobbled drive. Behind them, the gates glided shut.

Surrounded by what seemed to be acres of manicured garden, the house was wide, low, gabled and built of dark red brick. It looked big enough to provide twenty people with en suite bedrooms and, very likely, their own sitting rooms. Pulling on the hand brake, Tamara stared around at terraced lawns, a pond with a bridge and a fountain, pagodas, gazebos, rockeries, and all the other requisite features for a garden to shout, '*Money! Serious, serious money.*'

She climbed from her car, holding back her hair against the breeze, just as Manny closed the door of the Mercedes. 'I had no idea this place was here.'

Manny grinned. 'That's one of its attractions.'

He showed her the way through black double doors into a lofty hallway, wide and cool, with a dogleg staircase and polished oak panelling. Watercolour landscapes and oil portraits followed the line of the stairs. The carpet was midnight blue, which must be hell to keep clean. But no doubt that was their cleaner's worry.

Jed appeared from a corridor on the left wearing black trousers and a crisp white shirt, open at the neck. He still looked like a cowboy, just one who'd shaved and put on his Sunday clothes.

'Tamara. Can we talk for a moment?' He led her down the corridor to a small office. As she walked into the neat room, she noticed that Manny had melted away.

Jed took the seat behind a desk made of sleek glass the colour of sea foam, with a black phone and computer monitor and a set of black drawers to one side.

'Thanks for coming. Before I take you to meet Emilia, could we go through this agreement? It's a straightforward document both in language and intent.'

Reading it didn't take Tamara long. It contained her name and the reason that she was coming into contact with the household at Lie Low, and stated that she wouldn't share with any third parties information about Thomas and Emilia Hilton, or their property, conversations, images, or household staff in respect of their duties, whether such information was made known to her in connection with her own duties or otherwise.

'So,' she said, cautiously, 'I just keep my mouth shut about everything that's said or done here and I'm fine.'

Jed nodded. 'Here or anywhere else, if it affects Mr Hilton

and Emilia. Absolute discretion. They lead a quiet life and they want to keep it that way.'

Tamara supposed it was a sign of growing trust that 'my employer' had now become 'Mr Hilton'.

'OK.' She signed and dated the bottom of both copies of the agreement. Jed filed one and gave her the other, then ushered her back out into the corridor, across the hall and deeper into the house. 'I'll make the introductions then leave you and Emilia alone. I hope you can help her.'

'So do I.'

Jed took her to a sitting room where cream upholstery contrasted with dark polished wood and delicate green silk lampshades. Acres of cream carpet stretched away to a run of French doors and the splashy Monet-like pastels of the beautiful garden beyond. The fireplace could have held a roasting ox.

In the centre of it all, her back to the view, a young woman lounged like a princess waiting to be set free. She smiled a brilliant smile and dropped a glossy magazine on the sofa as Jed led Tamara into the room. She was about Tamara's own age, which was somehow younger than Tamara had anticipated; slender and beautiful, dark and fidgety. Crutches stood beside her sofa, as if on guard. Disconcertingly, close by was a portrait of her looking hauntingly beautiful and fragile. The way she looked up from behind her hair might have hinted at shyness, but her greeting, in a soft, silvery voice, was confident. She cut across Jed's introduction. 'Thank you for coming to see me, Tamara.'

'It's lovely to meet you. What an amazing house. Have you lived here long?'

Jed half smiled at Tamara and left, the door clicking gently behind him. Emilia hardly glanced his way.

'No. We came because my husband wanted to get out of

London.' Her eyes were dark and quick and her smile took her loveliness and made it glow as she waved Tamara to a cream silk chair.

Tamara imagined that if you were a man that smile would hit you between the eyes. It was no effort to smile back. 'I understand that you're looking for a yoga instructor. Have you done yoga before?'

'A little bit. I was more into high impact stuff before I broke my leg. I was a real gym bunny.' Carefully, she straightened her right leg. Her feet were bare beneath black exercise pants and Tamara could see that the right foot was swollen and mottled, a scar like a dull red seam peeping out at her ankle.

'Are you still in pain?'

'It's not acute.' Emilia looked down at the offending limb distastefully. 'But my leg's stiff and weak and won't take my weight for long without aching. It's difficult to get comfortable at night. I can't run or dance any more and I feel like I'm turning into an old granny sitting here all day.' She laughed. 'But tell me about you.'

Tamara felt in her bag. 'I've brought copies of my instructor certificates from the British School of Yoga and my insurance details—'

Emilia waved it away. 'The paperwork can be dealt with later. Shall we wander in the garden and chat? See if we like each other?'

'Fine.' Tamara was all for establishing a rapport. In a class situation she'd always seek out any new yogis and ask about their physical condition and explain what they could expect from the class, but she was willing to adapt her approach if Emilia had other ideas. Essentially, she was being interviewed.

She waited as Emilia slotted her arms into her crutches and opened one of the French doors, limping out into the luminous summer day and tipping her face to greet the sun, before leading the way along a paved, winding path towards the pond that was almost a small lake. Tamara noted that she favoured her right leg, but didn't avoid putting it to the floor altogether. It seemed to her that one crutch might have been sufficient – but that was for Emilia's physical therapist to decide.

'So you live in the village and Jed said you knew each other as children?'

Tamara fell into step beside Emilia, explaining how her parents and Jed's had been friends until Jed's family left the area. She didn't talk about Lyddie's accident or Uncle Don being the driver. Still too raw. Still unsettling to have the focus of all that anger and pain assume a face and it being someone her family had called a friend. She began a rundown of her yoga instructor experience, but Emilia broke in as they reached the bridge over the water.

'There are enormous carp in this pond – big ugly goldfish, really. Look at them coming up to gawp at us and check us out for food.' She gazed down at the carp gazing up through the water at her. 'A *Carry On* star used to own Lie Low, did you know? He had secret house parties here, apparently. It was his hidey-hole. His wife didn't know about the place – he'd tell her he was on location, filming, then hide out here with a couple of mates, a bimbo or two and a big stash of alcohol.' She smiled dreamily. 'It must have been a bit more exciting here then. He owned the house for over twenty years and came here right up until two years ago, bringing his own staff to avoid using local people and having them talk, apart from Roland, who lives down the hill in a tiny house and looked after the place. The only time Roland talks is to give the gardeners their work, so he was the ideal caretaker for the *Carry On* star. Then the star had a stroke and died a few months later. His wife inherited almost everything, but he left Lie Low to one of the mates who used to come here with him and it was the mate who sold it to us and told Tom all about the wild times they used to have here.' She glanced around wistfully. 'Not like now.'

Tamara had listened with growing astonishment. 'I'm amazed I never heard about this place. I've lived less than two miles away all my life.'

Leaning her elbows on the bridge rail, Emilia smiled secretively. 'Oh. You know. People with money. They don't all drive around in huge black limos, wearing Versace and living in ostentatious villas in Monte Carlo. You'll notice that Tom's Mercedes is even de-badged so you can't see that it's actually top of the range – an AMG. People with money find ways not to draw attention to themselves.'

'That's probably why I don't think I've ever seen you before,' Tamara agreed, thoughtfully.

Emilia straightened. 'No. Well. I've been a bit holed up here, with my leg.' And she set off again, over the bridge and across a lawn, hopping down stone steps on her good leg onto another lawn and across to a post-and-rail fence. She seemed to have reasonable mobility and could move at a walking pace utilising crutches on flat ground.

As they reached the fence, Tamara's attention was caught by what was beyond. Halfway down the slope, five animals stood in a loose group, three black and two fawn, long necks extended like fuzzy periscopes as they stared at their visitors, ears pointing up and inward, punk-rocky top knots over enormous dark eyes. 'Wow, llamas!'

Emilia unthreaded her arms from her crutches and leaned on the fence. 'Alpacas, not llamas. Do you like them? This area was meadow when we arrived and I'd always loved alpacas, so Tom bought me five pregnant ladies as a starter herd. They are due to have their babies any time.'

'Amazing.' Tamara gazed at the beautiful animals, elegant

necks and barrel bodies supported on slender legs. 'They look as if someone knitted them. Aren't they incredibly hot in all that fur?' The sun was pleasant on her shoulders, but she wasn't wearing what looked like a fireside rug.

'Fleece. They've just been shorn, too. You should have seen them when they arrived. But aren't they gorgeous? I've seen babies at an alpaca farm and they're *so* cute. The proper name for the young is cria, and I can't wait to have some of my own.'

'Is that their stable?' Tamara indicated a wooden building down the slope.

'Their field shelter, yes. They need to be able to get out of the rain, but they're tough cookies as they come from up in the mountains.' She swept up her crutches and slotted them in place. 'Shall we go back up to the house? Over coffee, you can ask me about my wonky leg and tell me what we're going to do in yoga class.'

Tamara turned to follow Emilia who, it seemed, had decided she was OK and was ready to move things on. Excitement twisted suddenly inside her. She'd never hankered after riches or material things – Lyddie's accident had taught her early that the most precious things were what money couldn't buy – but she was aware of entering a completely different world, where non-disclosure agreements, film star's houses and pet alpaca herds were the norm.

'Let's go to my favourite spot.' Emilia hopped back indoors, through a different run of French doors on another side of the house. And suddenly they were in the midst of cream tiles and pot palms and heading for the still turquoise water of a slinky, sparkly indoor pool, the smell of chlorine heavy on the warm air.

'Wow!' exclaimed Tamara in involuntary admiration.

'Isn't it fantastic? It's a bit like a private spa.'

'Exactly like one, with the hot tub and steam room and everything.' And, behind an array of chairs and loungers, even a proper masseur's couch with a cut-out for the face – probably Emilia's physio came to the house. Jed must be kept busy with those non-disclosure agreements.

They settled themselves on the loungers and Emilia took out her phone. 'Coffee? Or there's tea, juice, wine …'

'Coffee would be fantastic.'

Emilia used her phone to call somebody named Carrie. 'Would you bring coffee to the pool?'

Five minutes later, a smiling woman in a navy dress appeared with a tray bearing a cafetière and two pale pink porcelain cups, with biscotti in their saucers.

Emilia watched her set it down. 'So, what about the yoga? I was thinking twice a week.'

'That's possible,' Tamara agreed, feeling a bit as if Emilia was a princess granting favours. She slipped her pad, pen and diary from the pocket of her bag. 'I have classes that I need to work around, but they leave some availability. What are you hoping for from your yoga? Recovery? Relaxation?'

Emilia nodded. 'If it helps my leg, that's great.'

'Do you mind me asking about the injury?'

A shadow passed across Emilia's fine features. 'It was a stupid accident, a freak thing with the guardrail on a first-floor balcony. My ankle snapped completely, so there's a plate in there, now. Lots of connected damage – tendons, ligaments, everything. I've had three operations and now the surgeons say that I just need time to heal.' She pulled a glum face.

They went on to talk about mobility and how long Emilia felt she could exercise without undue pain.

'We need somewhere warm and quiet to work in,' said Tamara. 'This pool area would be ideal, in fact. I think you'd be comfy and relaxed here.'

'Good.' Emilia pushed down the plunger on the cafetière and poured dark, fragrant coffee into each of the two pink cups.

'We'd start and end each session with relaxation and breathing techniques,' said Tamara. 'Start low with the stretches and postures, mindful of your weight-bearing issues, working towards improved mobility and flexibility.'

Emilia sipped her coffee and listened, nodding occasionally. Her eyes were as dark as the coffee she drank without milk.

'Do you have a letter from your doctor passing you fit for yoga, by the way?'

Emilia put down her cup and picked up her phone. 'Jed? Tamara has paperwork that needs sorting.' She stretched, leaning her head back against the lounger. 'Can you do Mondays and Fridays?'

Tamara opened her diary. 'Ten in the morning on Mondays I can do, and two in the afternoon on Fridays. An hour each time?'

'Allow an hour and a half. That's how long it's taken today, and we'll have coffee after. I hate it when people just rush in and out. My husband, Tom, likes me to have what I want.' She'd started fidgeting, tracing a pattern on the lounger with her fingernail. Maybe Tom Hilton had acted with good intent when he brought Emilia somewhere quiet to convalesce, but Tamara suspected that what was meant to be cocooning had become isolating.

A door at the other end of the pool area opened and Emilia glanced up. 'Jed, did you get the letter from Dr Bertram to say that I'm OK to take a yoga class? Good.' Then, to Tamara, 'Jed will take you off and you can show him your certificates and stuff. See you on Monday at ten? That will give me time to buy some new exercise kit.'

Realising that she'd been dismissed, though she'd barely

touched her coffee, Tamara tucked away her things. Emilia perhaps tired easily. She stored the detail in her mind as something to watch out for. 'Fine. Shall I bring you one of my exercise mats?'

Surprise flickered in Emilia's eyes. 'No, I'll buy my own.'

Tamara flushed. Naturally Emilia's yoga mat would have to be pristine, probably one that was sold as 'deluxe' or 'luxury'. Maybe one of those silk things she thought were a waste of money. Or even one of those self-heating jobs that cost hundreds of pounds and sounded to her like a good place for a nap.

Jed stood aside and Tamara passed by doors until she reached the hall, then crossed to the corridor that she recognised as leading to his office and soon they were again facing each other over the glass desk.

'Here's the letter from Emilia's doctor. It looks short and to the point.'

Running her eyes over it, Tamara agreed. 'Great. No problems there, then. And here's what you need from me.' This time she succeeded in passing over the photocopies of her teaching credentials and insurance cover. 'Emilia has asked me to come for an hour and a half on Monday mornings and Friday afternoons.'

Jed nodded. 'And how do you need payment? Each session? Or for a number of sessions in advance?'

'Each session, please. I've been here for an hour and a half today.'

He nodded again, receptive, efficient and controlled, as if there was nothing anybody could ask for that he couldn't provide. He opened one of the black drawers to the side of the desk and counted out the cash.

Tamara wondered whether the set of drawers was where Jed crammed all his junk. The gleaming glass desk was unnaturally free of clutter. 'Thanks.'

'I'll introduce you to Mr Hilton before you go.'

'Oh. OK.' For some reason, she'd assumed that Emilia's husband wasn't in the house. She followed the blinding white of Jed's shirt into a different, den-like sitting room done out in fir greens, where a saturnine, solemn man sat by the window tapping at a large laptop computer.

Then she looked properly at Tom Hilton, and blinked. He was at least thirty years older than Emilia. Maybe she went for the father figure?

Tom Hilton didn't smile, but he put aside his computer to rise and shake Tamara's hand. 'I hope your meeting with my wife went well?'

Tamara smiled. 'Yes, thank you. It was a pleasure.'

He nodded at Jed. 'I'm sure you're looking after Tamara.'

Tamara accepted this new dismissal with grace. When all was said and done, she was working for these people. Well, for Emilia, anyway. 'It's been interesting to meet you.' Which was true, because who wouldn't be curious about everybody in this unreal, monied-but-quiet household?

Once in the gracious hall again, Jed escorted her past a security TV monitor displaying a black and white view of the gates, then they were out on the drive.

Tamara slid into her car. Jed settled down on his heels in the space created by the open door. 'Next time you come, look for the keypad on the gatepost. There's an intercom button in it – someone will let you in.'

'Right,' she said, as if gated estates were all in a day's work for her.

'Is it OK to ring you?'

She looked at him. His eyes were a darker version of the glass of his desk in the sunlight. 'If Emilia needs to rearrange her session, you mean?' She'd need to get used to the Hiltons employing Jed and Manny to arrange their lives for them.

His mouth curved in one of his small smiles. With his elbow on the door, he seemed to be almost in the car with her. He never actually invaded her space, but somehow it felt as if he did. Or maybe just that she was sensitive to his presence, his clean smell, the way he moved. 'That as well.'

'As well—?'

But his phone rang before he could answer and he felt for it inside his trouser pocket, simultaneously pointing a small remote at the gate. He stood back and watched her putting the car in gear and moving off, his hair like autumn leaves in the sunlight.

Jed watched Tamara's red car roll down the drive, through the gates and out of his sight.

Manny's voice came down the phone. 'Sorry if I interrupted you making a move.'

Bloody Manny. He ignored the teasing laughter in his stepbrother's voice. 'What's up?'

'Mr H wants to go to the lingerie factory and he wants you with him to talk to the production manager.'

Instantly, Jed's mind snapped back to his job. The lingerie business, the centre of discord in the Hilton Group, hadn't stopped causing issues just because production had been returned to British workers as a result of protests over the unethical use of overseas labour – an overseas labour force that Jed suspected had encountered disaster following the loss of their jobs. In the hands of Midlands manufacturing, strikes were now threatening over looming redundancies created by labour-saving new machinery.

'I'll drive him while you stay here,' Jed said.

Chapter Nine

On Thursday evening, Tamara arrived home after her class at Port-le-bain community centre. Still wearing her yoga gear, she took a glass of wine outside into her garden. The grass was spangled white and yellow with daisies and dandelions because it needed cutting. Max used to cut it. Living in a flat as he did, he quite liked to take his shirt off and get his hands dirty with her high-pitched electric mower, which he called The Mosquito. She missed Max and was feeling loose-endy. She took a big mouthful of the wine and let it seep slowly down her throat. On Thursdays she usually went to Max's flat or met him in The Three Fishes for a drink, but that wasn't going to happen now.

Apart from coffee or the occasional meal with people from her classes, her social life had revolved around being Max's girlfriend for so long that there wasn't really anyone she could just ring and say, 'Fancy going out for a drink?' Lyddie would be thrilled to see her, of course, because Lyddie was thrilled to see her any time, any day. She could go and buy a round for the blokey blokes in The Three Fishes, she supposed ... From the front pocket of her top, her phone buzzed and she leaned backwards to extract it with finger and thumb, without putting down her glass. A number was on her screen, but no name, which happened a lot as her contact details were up on various posters, or given out by gyms.

'Hello? Tamara Rix.'

'It's Jed. You sound formal.'

'Sorry, I thought it would be a yoga enquiry.' Tamara found herself smiling. It wasn't that it was Jed's voice, sounding warm in the middle of her feeling out of things – it was just that she needed to get on with him, despite her mother's baleful attitude, as there was every prospect that she'd meet him at Emilia's house.

'I was wondering what the chances were of going out for lunch? Maybe Saturday?'

She answered automatically. 'I have classes late morning and early afternoon, so I'll have to pass.' Normally, what time she did have on Saturdays involved Max, but that was another thing that wasn't going to happen.

'Ah.' He hesitated. 'I was hoping for a chat.'

Tamara frowned. 'And you can't just say whatever you have to say, now, on the phone?'

A thread of caution entered his voice. 'It might be a tricky situation.'

'I'll be at Lie Low on Monday, for Emilia's session.'

'I was hoping for before that.'

She thought she heard him smother a sigh. And was that exasperation in his voice, as if she wasn't saying what he wanted to hear? Or hearing what he was trying to say? Why did it have to be before Mon— Ah. She felt a dip of disappointment. If Emilia had changed her mind about a personal yoga instructor, dumping Tamara was a task she'd give to someone else, and Jed was the one whose job it was to make the lives of Emilia and Tom Hilton as carefree as possible. She could imagine her saying, 'Give her lunch or something, Jed,' in that casual way she had of ordering things as she'd like them to be.

Damn. It had been nice to have her job take a different direction from her usually strictly regimented round of classes, certain times, certain venues, and to have the prospect of working in such a swanky environment. Emilia had seemed enthusiastic.

Jed had fallen silent. Probably wondering how he could get the bad news delivered before Tamara was due to present herself at Lie Low.

Annoyance flared. If she was going to be fobbed off, she might as well get something out of it. 'Maybe we should make it dinner?'

Jed sounded surprised, but was quick to accept. 'Yes, I can do dinner on Saturday. There's a good tapas bar just opened on the square in Bettsbrough. I could pick you up?'

'There's no need, I know the one you mean.' You didn't let a man do the door-to-door service thing if it wasn't a date; everyone knew that. Even if it would be quite nice to act as if it was a date, just to try out her rusty date muscles and see if they still worked.

'OK, I'll meet you at the bar. About eight?'

And then he was gone. Oh well. Might as well grab the free meal and put the cancellation down to experience. The non-disclosure agreement hadn't been any form of contract for her services.

And then her phone rang again and this time the screen said *Max*. She smiled as she answered. 'Hey, you.'

'You didn't come round after yoga.'

She leaned back on one elbow in the cool grass, suddenly feeling normal and grounded again. 'I wasn't sure whether to.'

He laughed. 'I haven't left yet.' And then he added, 'And we have to swap stuff, don't we? I think you've got half my CDs and at least four of my T-shirts.'

Ah. The new kind of normal, not the old kind. 'I've just had a great big glass of wine, so I can't come round now.' She took a huge swig from her glass to make it nearly true.

'I'll come to you. Be there in twenty minutes.'

Max was being efficient, she had to give him that. At exactly the time he'd predicted, she heard the rumble of the red 1975 Porsche 911 Turbo he kept on the road through willpower and having the right contacts in the right places. In contrast to many *Charge!* readers and their love of outrageous modifications to elderly, but gutsy, vehicles, Max kept the Porsche true to its original condition. Except for the sexy stereo with the circular speakers set into the door cards in highly polished circular walnut frames, the CD changer lodged in the boot ready to blast out 96 dB of Sabbath or Chili Peppers on demand, above the roar of the sports exhaust.

Leaping out of the cracked leather seat, as Tamara opened the front door to let him in, Max scooped up an armful of her CDs and DVDs, a jacket she left at his house against sudden squalls of rain and her overnight supplies of toothbrush, moisturiser, cleanser, shampoo, conditioner, make-up and hair brush. Tamara smiled weakly as she extended her arms to receive his haul. There was something particularly poignant about the half-used toiletries. 'Thanks. All I've done is empty another glass of wine and find a few bin liners.'

'No problem.' Max kissed her cheek. 'I'll just grab my stuff.' Brushing past, he began on the CD stand in the sitting room, flipping out three Frank Turner albums and dropping them into a bin liner. '*Charge!* is bringing in someone from one of the other titles in the group that's folding, so they're releasing me to go to *Rush* straight away. I'm going into a B and B for a couple of weeks while I find a flat and get sorted. I've given a month's notice on my place here. Good job I hadn't gone any further buying the house in Bettsbrough.'

'Good job,' she agreed, letting the stuff he'd bundled into her arms slither onto the sofa, watching him home in on the DVD stand and pounce on *Fight Club*, *Fast and Furious* and *Iron Man 2*.

Suddenly, Max dumped the DVDs and dropped down beside her. 'You didn't want to live in Bettsbrough anyway, did you? I know it feels really weird but it's time for us both to move on.' He gave her a bracing squeeze. 'There's probably something fantastic around the corner for us both.'

Chapter Ten

By Saturday, Tamara had decided that if she was going to be dumped by Jed on Emilia's behalf, she was going to dress like somebody who didn't give a fuck. Over-the-knee grey-green needle-heeled boots – as June was going through a chilly phase – led to her selecting the thigh-high skirt in olive satin, with black, cobweb overlayer, that she hadn't yet dared to wear because of its price tag. Reluctantly, she rejected a black bustier on the grounds that it made the overall effect more dominatrix than don't-give-a-fuck and chose a silky, clinging T-shirt instead.

When she arrived, Jed was waiting at the bar at the front of the restaurant, looking hot in a white shirt and charcoal-grey jeans. His eyebrows lifted fractionally when she swung in through the heavy plate-glass door. 'You look … great.' He rose from the black leather barstool to kiss her cheek. Behind him, a wall of segmented mirrors refracted his reflection a thousand times. To the side, past the bar, Tamara could see candles on tables and a long counter containing Stonehenges of cheese, platters of cooked meats and pyramids of olives. Cheese, spices and wine mingled pleasantly in the air.

'Thanks,' she said, carelessly, hooking a needle heel over the rung of the barstool next to his and hopping up, anchoring her hemline with a couple of fingertips so that it was a flash of leg he got, not underwear. She was quietly triumphant to see that it still made him blink. 'What are we drinking?' She glanced at the pint of lager in front of him and lifted an eyebrow. 'Beer?'

His eyes smiled. 'I like beer. I've ordered what I like and you should order what you like.'

'Champagne, then.'

He grinned suddenly, as he signalled the barista and requested the wine menu. Something about her was obviously amusing him. The barista was young and blonde, her straight white apron sweeping her ankles. Her eyes flashed 'interested' as she looked at Jed. 'We carry Laurent-Perrier or Moët. Or the house champagne.'

Jed looked at Tamara who, belatedly, realised that as she'd just driven in from the village, she'd have to drive back. 'Does the house come by the glass? I'll have that, please.'

'Perhaps you'd like to go through to your table? I'll bring your drinks.'

Jed surprised Tamara by handing her down from her stool, his skin warm and smooth as his fingers closed around hers. He stood back to let her precede him into the cave-like interior of the restaurant, where they were shown to an alcove table at the back of the room. The barista lit the fat white candle, smiling, especially at Jed, then brought them a jug of iced water and Tamara's champagne.

'Visit the tapas bar whenever you're ready,' she cooed, 'and just let me, or one of the other servers, know when you'd like more drinks.' She headed back to the bar and new customers.

Tamara seated herself, glancing around at the many tables already occupied by men draping their arms over women with their hair in Saturday-night updos. Thighs nudged thighs. Smiles became lips that kissed. One guy was all but making love to his girlfriend's hand, her fingertips to his lips as she talked and he tasted her skin. The woman suddenly slid her other hand to the back of his neck and pulled his mouth to hers, hard, demanding.

Tamara felt almost envious of their Saturday-night-datedom. She'd spent plenty of Saturday evenings out with

Max, but she couldn't remember the last time that she'd wanted to drag his head to hers for urgent public kisses. Or to lean in to him as if he were magnetic, like the girlfriend was doing now, her fingers fluttering up to touch her boyfriend's hair.

'So,' said Jed, interrupting her study of the love lives of strangers, 'am I still public enemy number one with your mother?'

She transferred her gaze to him. His hair was sliding forward over his eyes as he watched her face. His scrutiny made her feel fluttery, but she supposed that was a natural product of him being about to give her the chop by proxy. She took a sip of her champagne. 'To be honest, she hasn't mentioned you much recently.'

'Maybe that means that she feels less antipathy now that the shock's passed.' His expression became bleak. 'I can only imagine how it must be for your parents. It was hard enough for me seeing Lyddie as she is. They must look at her every day and think about the woman she ought to be, with a career and maybe a family of her own. She was so bright and funny. Life's played a horrible trick on her.'

Tamara hesitated. She wasn't sure how to take the adult Jed. Although that speech proved him to be capable of empathy and sympathy, he wasn't entirely the man she would have expected the boy to grow up to be. He had a hard edge that unsettled her, honed, probably, by throwing himself on the mercy of an inhospitable world less than three years after he'd left the cocoon of Middledip village. He had a strange job working for an odd couple; wealthy hermits in a particularly luxurious cave. There was no degree on his CV – well, there wasn't on hers, either. They'd both been too busy dealing with the hand life dealt them to skip off down the route that they would probably otherwise have taken.

What he wasn't, she decided, was a bullshitter. His hazel gaze was frank as he waited for her to contribute to what was probably an uncomfortable conversation for him to have begun. She thought about his expression when he'd looked at Lyddie. 'It must have been weird for you.'

He grimaced. 'Horrifying, to be honest. The Lyddie who was still in my memory was the one I had a bit of a teenage thing with, because I never saw her after the accident. And for you, the grief must be much deeper. No matter how loveable the current Lyddie is, she's not the person she was meant to be.'

She tried to say, 'Yes, she is loveable,' but the words turned to thorns in her throat. She'd arrived feeling negative and truculent and his empathy was cutting through her defences like a chainsaw.

He reached for her glass and filled it from the water jug that reflected the dancing candle flame and clinked with ice. 'Hey ... I didn't mean to upset you. I just wanted you to know that I'm sorry for the hurt that my family caused your family.'

She sipped the iced water. 'I appreciate that you caught some of the fallout. With your mum and dad splitting up and you ending up homeless.'

His smile was crooked. 'Oh, I had a home – the squat. It wasn't your traditional, paid-for safe harbour, but I never spent a night in a doorway. I expect I would have run back to Mum pretty sharpish if Manny hadn't been there to give me a patch of floor to doss on.'

Jed didn't miss the flash of compassion in Tamara's amber eyes. They were well-spaced eyes, upturned at the outer corners and outlined in a copper colour that picked up the red lights in her hair, with black liner over. Her lashes were big with mascara. He liked dramatic eyes. He liked drama

86

in general, if it described how Tamara Rix looked tonight, with her incredibly toned body moving under her clothes in a way that had hit him in the pit of his stomach when she'd marched into the wine bar as if for battle, hair flying like a banner. And he was trying to keep his mind off her legs for the sake of his comfort in the jeans department. The boots and skirt combination might only display nine inches of leg, but as those inches fell above the knee he could hardly keep his mind off them. It was a bastard that Tamara had come back into his life only because he'd had to admit that Dad had mown down her sister and left her in the middle of the road.

As if she read his thoughts, her eyes welled with tears. 'I was there that day, you know, when Lyddie had her accident. We were hanging out right down Main Road, where there aren't any houses. Lyddie was thrown … so far.'

His heart skipped at the pain in her eyes. 'I know. The whole village endlessly picked over every detail, trying to assimilate the reality of it.'

'Did the village say it was my fault?'

'Of course not—'

'Because it was.'

Shock sang through him. 'But—'

She made an impatient face. 'Oh, I know, your dad was driving the car. But Lyddie was chasing me because I wanted to hang out with her and her mates, including you, I suppose. She told me to clear off and, filled with childish jealousy of her teenage privileges, I shouted that I was going to tell everyone that she'd done something slutty.'

She wiped the corner of her eye with the back of her hand. A gentle grey smear of mascara marred her skin above her thumb. 'She flew at me – you remember that she was quick and athletic, then – and I took off. I did hear the car coming, but it didn't seem as great a threat at that moment as my big sister and her vengeful hands. I belted across the road.

'Then there was shrieking tyres that seemed to go on forever. A bang. And then it was so quiet.'

Tamara grabbed her champagne glass, gulping most of the dancing contents in one. 'I turned round and looked at where Lyddie ought to be. The car, a white one, was stopped up the road. And there was Lyddie, lying on the ground with her arms out, her legs crumpled and her hair fanned around her. I remember thinking: how did you get *there*?'

'Fucking hell,' Jed said, quietly. A wave of useless sympathy tightened his throat.

'I didn't move. And neither did Lyddie.' Tamara sniffed. 'I never knew who called the ambulance, but I suppose it might have been your dad. I remember the white car driving off.

'The police came. They took me home and drove Mum and Dad to Peterborough hospital. On Thorpe Road, it was, then. My grandma came to take charge of me. She ended up pretty much moving in because Mum and Dad were always at the hospital.

'The doctors thought for quite a while that Lyddie might die from the rising pressure in her skull. The brain swells up, you know? They let me see her, so I could hold her hand and talk to her but, of course,' – she managed a watery smile – 'Lyddie had gone. The old Lyddie. I stood there and pleaded with God, or someone in my head, to make her well, to take us back in time so that I could unsay what I'd said and let her go off to meet her mates, without dragging her horrible little sister along. She had operations that saved her life, but they didn't make her what she used to be. And we all had to get used to this strange girl who lay on the bed wired up like a broken robot, gradually coming back to life with jerking fits and outbursts of crying and temper, and who was never the same Lyddie again.'

Unspeaking, Jed dripped a few drops of water onto his napkin and, taking Tamara's hand, wiped the smear of mascara from the soft skin on the back of her hand. His heart lay against his ribs like a rock.

Her eyes followed his actions. 'I used to lash out at kids at school who called Lyddie "nuts" or "a loony". My heart broke watching her learning to talk again, walk again, to realise that she was never going to be the same. I used to cry every time she looked puzzled. That look of not quite understanding's all too familiar, now.

'Mum and Dad kept congratulating me on making things easier on them by behaving like a perfect little girl, when that was the last thing I wanted to do. Eventually, I broke down and told them that it was all my fault.'

Two women squealed with laughter at some wine-enhanced joke and Tamara glanced over at their table.

'And they told you it wasn't you,' Jed recaptured her attention, gently. 'I bet they were horrified that you'd been torturing yourself with those thoughts.'

A small sigh. 'Dad did. Mum hugged me and said that I couldn't have known what the consequences would be. But she cried and cried. So you can see why she's found it convenient to pin all her hatred on the driver of the white car. It was much easier to deal with than it being me.'

He still had her hand and his fingers tightened around hers. 'It wasn't you. My dad was tipsy and reckless. He was way over the speed limit. If he'd been caught he would have gone to prison.'

She looked at their hands where they lay together on the snowy tablecloth. 'I know. But if she hadn't been in the road, he couldn't have hit her, could he? Until I said what I did, we were safely wandering along on the grass verge.'

'When I passed on Dad's deathbed confession to your family, I didn't think it was possible for me to feel any worse about what happened to Lyddie. But knowing that your mother's let you share the responsibility ... I mean, what the fuck? You were *ten*. How would she feel if someone said that it was her fault because she should have taught her daughters better road sense?'

Tamara tilted her head. 'What parent doesn't wonder if they're at fault, when a child gets hurt? But if Mum's difficult, remember that Lyddie's condition affects her most. She gave up her career and will never get to that part of her life where children are adults and parents can let them live their own lives, because Lyddie's perpetually a child. Whenever Mum makes me want to explode, I try to remember that.' She glanced down at their joined hands again. But she didn't draw away, which was reason enough, he decided, to leave them as they were.

It was time to change the subject. He'd known they'd have to talk about Lyddie – it would have been too big an elephant to ignore its presence in the room – which was why he'd broached the subject so early in the evening. But now he wanted to let the elephant sidle away. He smiled. 'Your champagne glass is empty.'

'It's OK, I'm driving.' And she disengaged her hand to help herself from the water jug.

'Manny could drive you home.'

She laughed, flicking her hair back over her shoulder. It gleamed in the lights. 'I thought he was your employer's employee, not yours.'

'But I'm his boss.'

She paused in putting the water jug back on the table. 'Really?'

'In so far as I recruited him and all the household staff report to me. But he'll be OK to pick us both up – I'd do the same for him. He's on call, so he'd check Mr H didn't want him and then nip out.'

'Thanks, but it would mean me leaving my car in Bettsbrough.' And she drank from the water glass, as if that decided things.

Shame. It wasn't that he'd intended to get her drunk, but people did tend to free up with a civilised amount of alcohol bubbling inside them. And if they drove back to Middledip, the only place to eat appeared to be the village pub. The wining and dining experience wouldn't be improved by the local beer belly boys sniggering behind their hands and making 'funny' remarks, or villagers coming in with mud on their boots and tying their dogs to the tables. 'OK. Shall we eat?'

He stood back to let her go before him to the tapas bar, watching her effortless grace and the swing of her hips. At the bar, she waited to be noticed by the young guy in black who was concentrating on the appetising presentation of a platter. Jed tolerated her being kept waiting for about three seconds, before reaching over and prodding the young guy's arm. When he glanced up, Jed raised his eyebrows, nodding at Tamara.

Although he looked surprised not to be left to bestow his notice upon the clientele when he felt the time was right, the young guy picked up a plate, polished it, and turned a bright smile on Tamara. 'Madam?' As Tamara chose, he arranged her food artistically on the gleaming, white plate – cheeses, chicken, prosciutto, miniature brown breadsticks, frilly green-and-purple salad leaves, tiny tomatoes glowing red, rings of orange and yellow pepper. A vegetation rainbow. She waved away the olives, but took dressing and dips in a dish like a chrome cloverleaf, waiting while Jed selected a meal heavy on squid rings and anchovies, trusting that her cheeses would cover up any brininess in the air.

Back at the table, Jed deliberately lightened the conversation. 'Are there many people I'd remember still in the village?' He watched her mouth, her tongue tip flickering across her lips after she'd bitten into the crusty bread.

Her bright eyes gleamed at him. 'You didn't remember Tim Wysowski from your year at school. He was one of the guys in The Three Fishes.'

'Whizz? One of the beer belly boys?'

She laughed. 'I call them the blokey blokes. But yes.'

He pulled a face. 'Has he spent his entire adulthood eating pies? I recognised that other guy. Ben Bell? He was older than me, but I knew him from the school bus.'

A tiny frown nipped the skin between her eyes. 'You weren't very polite to him.'

Bell hadn't been polite to Tamara, but Jed had noticed at the time that the look she had given him had been wary, rather than admiring. He'd long ago learned to take a direct route to dealing with idiots and accepted that not everybody would appreciate his method, but it was probably best not to dwell on the episode in case that tiny frown became an actual objection. If he was to antagonise her, he might as well make it about something worthwhile. 'So about this tricky situation—'

She pointed with her fork. 'Yes, you might as well tell me. Has Emilia changed her mind?'

Wrong-footed, he hesitated. 'Why would you think that? Emilia's expecting you on Monday morning, as agreed. Manny went and picked up a yoga mat and a ton of sports wear she ordered from a shop in Peterborough.'

'Oh.' Tamara studied his face, as if trying to figure out a secret. 'I thought that you must be here to let me down gently.'

'Why?' He picked up his beer and drained the glass.

'Well ...' She shrugged. 'I couldn't think of any other reason for you to ask to see me.'

Slowly, he shook his head. 'You haven't looked in the mirror lately?'

'Oh.' Her eyes widened. 'You mean this is a date?'

'I was sort of hoping so. I asked you to lunch thinking that lunch doesn't have to be a date, it can be more about testing the water. Then you upgraded me to dinner.'

'So ... what's the tricky situation?'

He found himself smiling at the surprise in her expressive eyes. 'You seem to have a boyfriend.'

'But that didn't stop you suggesting a date?' She looked as if she didn't know whether to be affronted or intrigued.

'Evidently not. I thought I'd try and detach you. If you're not interested in that then—' He spread his hands. 'I'll have had a nice evening and lost nothing, apart from a smidgeon of pride. And I'm big enough to take that.'

Her eyes got rounder.

He gazed back, quietly enjoying himself. Women became so used to men who hid their agendas and machinated to achieve their aims, they were always astonished by a man who came out with exactly what he wanted.

As Tamara still seemed lost for words, he went on. 'I'd like to see you; I'm interested; you look great and I'm attracted to you. The following is what I anticipate you might see as obstacles.' He began to tick them off on his fingers. 'What my dad did. Your mum hates me. I was having a teenage thing with your sister when she had the accident and seeing me might make you feel disloyal. You might not feel attracted to me. You might not want to be detached from your boyfriend.'

Now a tiny smile was chasing away the shock that had made an O of her lips. 'And what are your views on those obstacles?'

He held her gaze, letting her see that she was his focus. 'I'm not my father's keeper and, however much I regret what happened, I can't change it. I'm prepared to do what I can to get Cheryl to accept that, and to see that I'm no monster.' He scooped brie onto a breadstick and dipped it in apricot chutney. 'I can see how you feel about Lyddie – not just that you suffer from survivor's guilt, but that you love her. Still, you're a rational woman who will get her head around the fact that Lyddie and I were thirteen and that, sadly, romantic relationships are unlikely for her now.'

He saw Tamara flinch and he bit into the breadstick, chewing slowly to give her time to think, while he savoured the richness of the brie and the sharpness of the chutney. His senses felt heightened by her presence and by the conversation, somehow both direct and intimate.

'Whether you feel attracted to me …? I don't think you hate me.'

She was very still, her pupils huge, eyes plainly saying, *I have no idea what to make of you. This isn't how most men act.* Well, good. He wasn't most men.

'Max – yes, I see him as the stumbling block. You looked comfortable with each other and, from the way the rest of your family were with him, he's been around for a while.' A shrug. 'If he's the love of your life, you'll tell me to get lost. Or if you have long-term plans for him, you might like it that I'm interested and flirt a bit, but, ultimately, stick with him.'

He paused to load his breadstick again. The chutney tasted a bit marmaladey, but he enjoyed fresh flavours. Tamara's eyes followed his movements. Leisurely, he bit into the breadstick. It crunched and then melted in his mouth. He'd come to this restaurant again. It was way above what he'd thought he could expect in a little market town. Another mouthful. Tamara waited. Waiting him out. Not leaping in with impetuous responses.

'But if you're not completely into Max, well ...' He let his smile flicker. An advantage to not being one of those guys who always had a smile on his face was that when he bothered with one it tended to have impact. 'My interest is significant.'

Slowly, she nodded. 'Noted.'

Then she turned her attention back to her food, emptying her plate daintily but efficiently. Drinking her water. Ordering mango juice when a server came near – he ordered another beer – touching her napkin to her lips. Then she glanced around. 'Are you up for dessert?'

Women and their desserts. 'Sure.' He went up with her and chose a dark rum-drenched pecan tart, while she went for a tall glass of green fruit-filled jelly, drizzled with cream, which she polished off with obvious relish, before ordering a cup of espresso.

Jed let her lead the conversation back to villagers he might remember – he couldn't believe Mrs Crowther still ran the shop – and those who had migrated to Bettsbrough or Peterborough. Even those who had made it out of the county, but Tamara kept up with them on Facebook. Inwardly, he was laughing. He liked it. Liked her playing her own game, not betraying herself into looking uneasy or flustered. Liked the odd considering look she sent him, which let him know that she wasn't going to pretend to ignore what he'd said.

But, oh, she was aware that the ball was in her court.

He went along with it. He'd made his play. By the Law of Conversation the response was up to her.

Vendors began threading through the tables selling charity scratch cards. 'Which charity?' Tamara asked one, a young guy wearing trainers without laces.

The young guy halted promptly. 'Homeless.'

Jed produced a ten-pound note, willing to take a punt that some of the money would find its way to a soup kitchen or something, and took two cards just before the manager zoomed in to hoof the vendor out for bothering her diners. Jed passed both cards to Tamara. 'You do the honours. You might win us a fortune.'

She studied the splurgy font on the yellow background. 'No fortunes on offer, I'm afraid. You might win a holiday or a spa day, though.' She wiped her coffee spoon on a napkin and began to scrape the silver coating from three squares on the first card. 'One holiday symbol, one question mark and one high street shopping voucher. No prize.' She took up the other card and scratched the first two squares. She looked up, eyes glowing. 'Two spa day symbols. Do you think we'll get the third?'

'Nope.'

She sighed philosophically. 'You're probably right.' She scraped the third square. 'Holiday. No luxurious spa day for us.' Discarding the neon cardboard ticket to hopes dashed, she ordered another espresso. 'What kind of interest? Are we talking platonic?'

He smiled at her abrupt return to the conversation thread that most interested him. 'No. We are not.'

She glanced down, hiding the expression in her eyes, brushing away crumbs of silver scratch card coating from the tablecloth. 'It would be against the personal code of a lot of people to hit on someone with a boyfriend.'

'I'm the pragmatic kind. It's a choice that's yours to make.'

A tiny smile tugged at one corner of her mouth before she turned away from the intriguing conversation once more. 'Is your job live-in?'

He accepted the change gracefully. 'Very much so.

Manny, Carrie and I have apartments upstairs in a separate area. I'm not permanently on call, but living in does make me kind of readily available.'

'So staff really do live in attics?'

'More like in the dormer roof, in this case. But at the back of the house, of course, as befits our lowly status.'

She nodded, gravely. 'Tiny shoebox apartments with no running water, cooking over a camp stove, that kind of thing?'

'Exactly. I sleep in a packing case and wash up in an old tin bath. Bare boards and no curtains. I could show you, if you like?' She wouldn't say yes, of course, but the rush of desire to see this clean and beautiful woman in his clean and beautiful home took him by surprise.

Although intrigue flickered, she grimaced. 'You've made it sound quite resistible, frankly.' Then she began again on the subject of the village and stayed there until she was ready to leave.

It was late when they went out into the evening. She'd parked her car in one of the spaces left when the daytime market stalls were packed away, a red hatchback with sports kit and alloy wheels. Probably the boyfriend's influence. Jed knew that Max was a motor magazine journalist. He'd made it his business to find out.

Walking her over to the car, he wished she'd let him pick her up because then he could have driven her home and she might have felt compelled to invite him in. He flirted with suggesting that she drop him home instead. Her route to Middledip would take her past the bottom of the lane after all. But it would look like a gauche play. If she wanted to be alone in the car with him, she'd offer.

She didn't.

Instead, she said, 'Goodnight,' accepting his chaste kiss on her cheek and touching his cheek fleetingly with her lips in return, discouraging any space invasion by resting her fingertips lightly against him.

Beeping her car unlocked she climbed in, swinging her legs in neatly, despite the brevity of her skirt. He watched the interior light die as she started the engine and flipped on the headlights, bright white cutting through the dusky orange the streetlights made of the dark. Then she buzzed down her window.

'Me and Max are over,' she said.

And she put the car in gear and drove away.

Jed stood very still in the dark square, voices from those leaving the surrounding pubs at the end of the evening drifting around him.

'OK, you got me,' he said to her disappearing tail lights. 'My move. Watch out.' He let himself smile. Tamara Rix. She'd knocked him off balance. He liked it. Liked the uncertainty. He'd lived an uncertain life, once, and striven hard to leave it behind, but occasionally he missed that feeling of pivoting, not knowing quite where things were headed. It kept life interesting.

Chapter Eleven

Waking early on Monday morning, Tamara was too restless to stay indoors, although she still had to reorganise to eradicate the gaps where Max's stuff used to be. That was a rainy day activity, though, rearranging the DVD collection and spreading her things into drawers allocated to him for when he'd stayed – drawers he'd largely ignored in favour of strewing his clothes over furniture and floors.

A quick shower and a muesli breakfast and then, not even pausing to be glad that there was no longer a heap of car magazines taking up one end of the sofa, she slung her purse and an exercise mat in a big holdall. She added a couple of brand new uninflated ChiBalls – as Emilia quite obviously wasn't in the way of using communal equipment – and skipped out under a china blue sky. She'd visit Lyddie at her parents' home and then walk from there to Lie Low.

But as she let herself in and dropped her bag in the hall, tension was thick in the air. By the kitchen door her mother swung away from her father, the very picture of someone trying to pretend that nothing was wrong. 'Hello, darling. Lyddie's still in the shower.'

Sean gave Tamara a forced smile. 'You look lovely.'

She glanced down at her plain black exercise pants and top. Not exactly enough to prompt 'lovely'.

'Everything OK?' she asked casually, following her parents as they moved into the kitchen. 'You look pale, Mum.'

It was rare that Cheryl would resist the opportunity to spill whatever was on her mind and, sure enough: 'We were just talking about that Jed Cassius. He called here yesterday, with more offers of cash to try to make things up to Lyddie.'

Tamara's stomach shivered. Jed had been here, while she'd been whiling away her Sunday browsing in the Queensgate Centre in Peterborough, wondering if he'd ring or text.

Sean frowned. 'He's just trying to carry out his father's last wishes. It's not an enviable task but he's trying to do the right thing.'

Cheryl snorted inelegantly and began to fill the kettle as if there were a viper in the bottom that she was trying to drown.

Tamara pulled out a white-painted kitchen chair. 'Difficult,' she said sympathetically, which could mean whatever each parent chose. She watched Cheryl bustle through the making of three mugs of instant coffee. 'So what do you think, then, Mum?'

A line dug itself between Cheryl's brows as she dispensed the mugs and took a seat. 'Think?'

'What do you think Jed should have done, when his dad confessed to having been the hit-and-run driver?' Tamara picked up her coffee mug and gazed at her mother through the steam.

Cheryl shifted. 'Well—' She stopped. Stirred her coffee. Over her shoulder, Sean, leaning against the kitchen units to drink up quickly before leaving for work, looked interested in Cheryl's reply.

Tamara reached for her mum's hand and gave it a sympathetic squeeze. 'Should he have decided to let sleeping dogs lie, do you think? Let us carry on in ignorance – even if it meant breaking his word to Don and keeping all the money left to him?' Cheryl was big on people keeping their word.

Cheryl was saved from having to come up with an answer by Lyddie's heavy footsteps down the stairs and up the hall. ''Mara! *He*llo! My hair's wet because I had a shower.' She stooped to fling her cushiony arms around her sister, making Tamara feel as if her shoulder blades were being squeezed together.

Tamara sniffed appreciatively. 'Mm, you smell lovely.' Lyddie adored 'smellies' and would happily layer on shower gel, body lotion, body spray, deodorant, talc and perfume with no regard for warring fragrances. 'Shall I dry your hair?'

'Way to go,' breathed Lyddie happily. 'Will you do it like Elrond's?'

'I'll do my best.' Tamara was practised in making her sister's hair a tribute to the Elven Lord of Rivendell from *Lord of the Rings*, although she was glad that Lyddie didn't mind if it was a bit approximate. Tamara had learned from YouTube how to make fishtail braids and weave and sculpt them artistically from the top of Lyddie's head and down her back, but that was only for when Lyddie was going somewhere special. Even Elrond had some more everyday styles that didn't take two hours to produce. 'Have you got some braid elastics?'

Cheryl got to her feet. 'In the drawer. I'll make Lyddie some hot chocolate while you fetch the hairdryer.' She, like any member of the family, automatically looked at ways of taking things to Lyddie, rather than embark on the often slow business of ushering Lyddie elsewhere. As Tamara ran up to Lyddie's room, she heard her dad shout goodbye as he left for his first meeting, and the voice of her mum overlaid with Lyddie's loud excitement. She could fit Lyddie's words to the pitch and cadence in her mind. *'Mara's going to do my hair, Mum, isn't she? Like Elrond, isn't she? My hair's wet but 'Mara's going to make it dry and do it like Elrond. Isn't she, Mum?* As so often, Tamara's heart ached.

But, as she dried her sister's lustrous brown hair, making her laugh by blowing it into her face, she did what she always did – she put aside the heartache and tried to make Lyddie happy. And if she felt at all worn down by the constant, 'You're going to make a plait at the back, aren't you, 'Mara? And long bits at the front, aren't you, 'Mara? And I'll look like Elrond, won't I, 'Mara?' she made certain never to let impatience creep into her voice.

Instead, she brushed and dried, sectioned off the top of Lyddie's hair and plaited it from root to tip – a common-or-garden plait, Lyddie wouldn't be able to see that it wasn't a fishtail braid – then sectioned off the sides at the front and, with a bit of dextrous twisting and hooking up of the braid elastics, wove a design that even Elrond would have worn without a blush. Then they went into the sitting room to admire the result in the big over-mantel mirror.

'You look like an elven queen, Lyddie. But, I have to go, now.' Tamara checked her watch, satisfied that she was leaving her sister on a high.

Immediately, Lyddie threw open her arms. 'Big hugs, 'Mara.'

Tamara let herself be squashed into Lyddie's enthusiastic embrace. 'Big hugs, Lyd.'

Walking out of the village, Tamara let herself think about Jed Cassius. Maybe he hadn't contacted her because he hadn't appreciated her imp of mischief, holding back the information that Max had awarded himself the status of ex. But she didn't think so. He'd been incredibly direct about what he wanted.

Was it the same directness that had prompted his visit to Cheryl and Sean yesterday? Was he so focused on seeing his dad's last wishes carried out? Or … having identified Cheryl's antipathy as an obstacle to getting close to Tamara, was he just attempting to clear it away?

She checked her watch and picked up her pace, enjoying the sun on her shoulders and the fresh air on her face. A few cars passed, but she didn't envy the drivers their hot little boxes. Time enough for her to be trapped this afternoon, when she drove to her two thirty class at the Bettsbrough Park Hotel.

The breeze played with her hair and rustled in her ears, and the sun made her squint. It was a beautiful walk, up Port Road and out of the village, stepping on and off the lush verges to let cars go by, then up the track and through the shade of the spinney, where the air was still and green and rang with birdsong.

At the first set of black gates she pushed the intercom button on the keypad set into the brickwork post. A moment passed, and then a tinned version of Manny's voice. 'Hello, Tamara.'

She glanced up and noticed a camera perched above her head as she answered. The gates squeaked open and she stepped through. By the time she reached them, the second set was opening, too, and she saw Manny waiting on the drive where it swept in front of the house. She tried not to wonder where Jed was. Since she'd last seen him, Manny had shaved his beard into a slim goatee and had his hair cut short. He looked different; clean cut, but kind of ordinary.

'Change of image?'

He grinned as he held open the front door and allowed her to step into the coolness of the hall. 'I like change. Emilia's waiting in the—' He broke off suddenly.

Tamara followed his gaze, which had snagged on the security monitor in a corner near the ceiling. And her mouth dried.

On-screen, Lyddie was rattling at the closed outer gates, Tamara's bag in her hand and a cross and perplexed expression on her face. Her mouth squared off as she bellowed sadly for entry. Tamara could read the dismay and frustration on her face and knew anxiety wouldn't be far away.

Somewhere a discreet alarm began to sound, *boop-boop-boop-boop*, as Lyddie shook the gate harder. 'I'll go to her,' Tamara said, breathlessly, heart beginning to thud.

She flung open the door to dash back down the drive, hearing Lyddie's forlorn wails booming on the breeze. ''Maaaaaa-ra! 'Maaaaaa-ra!' The gates began to open as Tamara ran.

As soon as Lyddie saw her, delight washed in to replace dismay, her hands flapping. 'Hello 'Mara! These stupid gates were shut tight. You forgot your bag.' Her face glowed with pleasure at being the one able to correct her sister's mistake, her Elrond hair shining in the sun as the gates parted enough to allow her to scud between them. 'You left your bag in the hall, 'Mara. I tried to catch you up, and I shouted. Didn't you hear me?'

'Afraid not.' Tamara gave her a reassuring hug, as Manny came down the drive to join them. It was uncomfortable enough that she'd performed the novel feat of turning up to meet a client with her sister trailing behind her, the last thing she needed was Lyddie bursting into tears if Tamara let her embarrassment show.

What the hell was she supposed to do now? Impossible to begin the session with Lyddie hanging around, even if she could be persuaded to sit quietly in front of a television in a room somewhere for an hour or so. But, not having a car with her, the only alternative was for Tamara to walk Lyddie home. She could ring her mother, but her dad had already taken their car to work. She couldn't send Lyddie home alone – her blood ran cold at the thought of the whizzing cars that she'd already braved by following in Tamara's wake. Lyddie didn't usually leave the village boundaries and might even turn left at the bottom of the lane instead of right.

Tamara grasped Lyddie's damp hand. 'You remember

Manny, don't you? Jed's brother, sort of.' She turned to Manny apologetically. 'I'd better explain to Emilia and walk Lyddie home. I'll just go in to see her—'

But then Lyddie burst out, with that combination of surprise and urgency with which Tamara was all too familiar, 'Ooh, need a wee!' She clutched herself emphatically and cast about, as if sizing up a likely flowerbed. 'Reeeeeeeeally need a wee, 'Mara.'

For an instant, Tamara closed her eyes. Poor Lyddie couldn't help her sudden urges, but Tamara could've done without one just now. 'Sorry,' she apologised to Manny again, trying to force her face not to heat up. 'She's not good at waiting. May we use a bathroom?'

'Of course, there's a shower room nearby that you can use.' Briskly, he led the way back into the mellow red-brick house, along the small corridor to a door near Jed's office.

'I'll go in with her in case she's freaked out by an unfamiliar high-tech flushing mechanism or cunning door lock.' Tamara whisked in behind her scuttling sister.

Inside seemed too palatial to be termed a mere 'shower room', although there was certainly a shower enclosure, one of those capacious jobs with a curved sliding glass door and shiny jets poised at interesting angles. But the room was an artwork of concealed light fittings, bulbous plumbing fixtures in gold and walls sheeted with smoky marble.

'Way to *go*,' breathed Lyddie, gazing around from her perch on the pearly white toilet. The matching bidet, alongside, had proved a handy parking space for her cardigan.

While Lyddie 'went', Tamara rang her mother.

Cheryl, judging from the snap in her voice, wasn't pleased. 'I was about to ring you. I've been worried sick. Fancy Lyddie rushing off without telling me she was going, without her phone and without taking Jabber! And now she's likely to be late for work, all because you decided to leave your bag in the hall.'

'It was a difficult situation to anticipate,' Tamara pointed out diplomatically, not sure how she was getting the blame. 'I'm going to see her home as soon as possible. And you know she turns her phone off or on silent half the time, anyway, just through playing with the buttons.' Tamara rang off, irritated.

Lyddie had finished. 'Do I have to wipe?'

'Afraid so.'

Lyddie sighed.

When they emerged, Manny was waiting, jingling car keys, with Jed beside him, his shirt black today, like his trousers. His gaze was neutral as it flicked over Tamara.

Lyddie pounded over to him. 'Jed, I had to wipe!'

'*Lyddie*,' Tamara groaned.

'And it's always me who has to do it,' Lyddie added.

'Poor you,' Jed replied, gravely. His eyes returned to Tamara. 'Manny can drive Lyddie home.'

Though grateful that Jed showed not a flicker of either amusement or dismay at Lyddie's ingenuous conversation, Tamara said, 'I'll have to go with her. Lyddie doesn't know Manny well enough to be left with him.' She could treat a slight acquaintance with huge affection, or go off on one like a child left with an unfamiliar babysitter, both equally disconcerting.

Jed didn't argue. 'Manny will bring you back. I've explained the situation to Emilia.'

'Is it a fast car?' demanded Lyddie, steering an imaginary steering wheel. She loved cars. Right now she was totally in love with Smart cars and every time she saw one she wanted to dash across and peer into its dinky interior.

'Pretty quick.' Manny smiled.

'I want to drive a car.' Lyddie's eyes widened with

excitement. 'I want to drive a big, big, fast, fast car. I'd be able to reach the pedals, I know how to turn the wheel, I want—'

'That's a wonderful solution, isn't it Lyddie? Thank you.' Tamara cut gently across Lyddie's big plans, which were never going to happen because learning to drive wasn't within Lyddie's scope. Rather than mourning that fact, it was better to refocus on the current issue, salvaging what was left of her professionalism. 'Should I see Emilia myself and explain?'

'If you want to.' Jed showed them through to the pool area and opened the door, stepping inside first. 'Tamara needs to have a word with you.'

She wondered briefly if he thought she wasn't able to open the door herself and felt like pointing out that it was well within her motor capabilities. But, well. Maybe that was how the rich did things.

Emilia put down a magazine. 'Hi! I thought …' She halted when her gaze fell on Lyddie, who'd draped her arm chummily along Tamara's shoulder and was kissing her hair. Emilia failed to hide a flash of surprised dismay.

Although her heart always sank at anything she perceived as the slightest rejection of her sister, Tamara accepted that it wasn't unreasonable for people facing an unfamiliar disability to be hesitant in their reactions. The answer was to give them a chance to see there was nothing worrying about Lyddie. So she took Lyddie's hand and moved closer, as she apologised and explained.

Emilia's smile was like plastic. 'Yes, all right. I'll see you when you've taken your sister home.'

'I had a wee in your bathroom,' Lyddie butted in, beaming. 'I nearly didn't make it, but I held on. I washed my hands. You've got gold taps. Way to go! We've got silver taps at home, haven't we, 'Mara?'

Emilia's eyes crinkled suddenly and she smiled more naturally. 'The taps are pretty aren't they? I chose them.'

Lyddie tried to pull away from Tamara, excited pink patches blooming in each cheek. 'Pretty. Very pretty. Tamara, has Emilia got poorly legs? She's got a stick. Has she got hurt?'

'I'm afraid so.' Emilia's face shadowed. Then she brightened. 'How about a drink and a cake before you go?'

Jed spoke from the doorway. 'Manny's going to drive them home.'

'Cake! Yes please,' Lyddie breathed rapturously. Cake was one of the things Lyddie loved best.

'Twenty minutes won't hurt.' Emilia didn't look at Jed as she overruled him.

By the time they'd eaten the double-choc muffins and drunk pink grapefruit juice brought in by Carrie, Lyddie had fallen in love. With Emilia.

Probably this was reinforced by the discovery that Emilia had a library of videos and DVDs tucked away on shelves behind the panelling in a TV room. Also, Emilia seemed prepared to listen, while Lyddie described the house where she lived and her room in it, her computer and her webcam, in minute detail.

By the time the twenty minutes had become forty and Emilia called Manny back, a rapturous Lyddie was clutching eight of Emily's DVDs to borrow.

When Lyddie saw the dark blue Mercedes, like a slumbering beast on the drive, her afternoon was complete. 'Way … to … *go*,' she breathed. And, once seated inside it, Tamara had to be impressed, too. She listened to the lazy grumbling engine and gazed around the immaculately luxurious interior, thinking how much Max would love a drive of this car. The gates slid open and they glided through and into the spinney, the Mercedes barely seeming to rock as it purred over the ruts.

Lyddie whiled away the short journey by talking at Manny about *Lord of the Rings*. "Mara likes Aragorn, but she helped me put a Legolas screen saver on her computer. I've got my own computer, haven't I 'Mara? But I like 'Mara's best. And I like Legolas. I *love* Legolas. Legolas can shoot two arrows at once, Legolas can slide downstairs on a shield, Legolas doesn't weigh anything so he can walk on the top of snow and jump up on galloping horses. If I was in a battle, I'd want to be on Legolas's side.'

Manny pulled up outside the square, rendered house in leafy Church Close. 'You're a bit of a scamp, aren't you, Lyddie?'

Lyddie beamed. 'My friend Mrs North's got a dog called Scamp.' And she abandoned the subject of *Lord of the Rings* in favour of launching into a list of her friends in the village.

Tamara was forced to interrupt. 'Come on, Lyddie, let's get you indoors. Mum will want to know you're safe.'

She delivered her, giggling and excited, into the hands of her mother, who had a face like a crab's claw. 'We need to talk about this, Tamara.'

'Sorry, I've got to go and Lyddie's safe. I'll call in this evening and explain what happened.' And she skipped out again quickly, sliding back in beside Manny, blowing out her cheeks. 'Please get me back to Emilia so I can get on with my job.'

He circled the car smoothly in the close and swung out onto Port Road, back to Lie Low, where Jed awaited her, his expression once again inscrutable. 'Does Lyddie wander like that very often?'

Tamara heaved a sigh. 'I think she only strayed outside her boundaries because she was following me. Normally she's very good about observing them.'

He turned to escort her back towards the pool. 'Will she remember the way back to the house?'

Tamara, dragging her hair into a ponytail on top of her head, read this as a polite suggestion that Lyddie be discouraged from paying ad hoc visits to Lie Low. She sighed. 'I aim to persuade her not to try. She might miss the turning and end up walking halfway to Bettsbrough,' she said, but her mind was on getting back to her client and re-establishing her professional persona.

Making excuses and beginning the session an hour late was not consistent with the image she liked to project. Luckily, Emilia seemed not at all bothered by the Lyddie incident and was waiting, with her new pink yoga mat and white exercise pants with vest top over a bright blue sports bra, to begin her session. 'Ready!'

Thankfully, Tamara flapped her own mat down facing Emilia's. 'I've brought some ChiBalls. They're great tools for yoga.' She began to blow the first one up. It glowed yellow in the light from the French doors as it took on its spherical form, and smelled pleasantly of lemon grass. Between puffs, she enquired how Emilia was feeling and whether she was in any more pain than usual. She then began on the basics – demonstrating how to relax down on her back on the mat in the unfortunately named corpse position.

'Is that OK for your leg? We put the ball on the knobbly bit on the back of the head, not in the neck. It won't burst, so just relax back on it. Let your eyes gently close and start to think about the breath. Think about it coming from your abdomen, making your tummy rise as you inhale and drop as you exhale. Let it be a comfortable breath. Let it deepen, oxygenating your blood and relaxing your muscles.' She took several long deep breaths of her own, concentrating on the here and now, her yoga and her yogi, rather than on her sister or her mother.

Or Jed Cassius, whose presence seemed to be reaching her through the walls of the house.

The exercise session ran to the full hour and then Emilia called Carrie to bring icy mineral water and gave Tamara enthusiastic feedback on the yoga and her leg's reaction to it. Tamara wrote down a short daily practice for Emilia to do, including heel lifts and leg raises, to help her damaged leg.

She tried not to look at her watch to check whether another thirty minutes had passed, but it seemed ages before Emilia phoned Jed.

'Tamara's ready to go, now.'

Jed came in and collected Tamara and took her through to the office to pay her, giving her his business card so that she could email the invoice to him. She wished he'd hurry. She was going to have to jog all the way home and just grab a handful of biscuits to eat as she drove to Bettsbrough for her class.

Jed caught her looking at her watch. 'Are you stuck for time, after what happened this morning?'

'A bit,' she admitted, backing towards the door.

He pulled out his car keys. 'I'll drive you.'

She didn't even bother with the socially expected 'Are you sure?' She just said, 'Oh, *thanks*,' with real gratitude, and followed him down the small corridor and out through the side of the house directly into a garage, where his BMW was parked. The garage door opened electronically as he started the engine and the car rolled smoothly onto the drive, then it shut behind them as the gates began to open. 'Very James Bond,' she observed.

'You'll need to show me where you live.' He drove down the track and turned right towards Middledip.

'It's not far.' She directed him to her end-of-terrace house in Little Dallas and he looked it over approvingly, as he drew up outside. 'Neat.'

'Kind of small compared to Lie Low.' She flipped off her seatbelt and reached for the door.

'But a palace compared to a squat.' He halted her with his hand on her arm and brushed a brief, soft kiss on her lips. 'You're welcome. Don't mention it.'

She flushed, the fresh clean smell of him shivering through her. 'Thank you.' Her lips tingled. But she thrust the feeling aside and fishing out her key, hurried to her navy-blue front door.

His car didn't move until she'd gone inside.

After a few moments, because he'd look a complete idiot if she hurried out again and caught him sitting there looking like ... well, like an idiot, Jed turned the car and drove back to Lie Low. As he drew up on the drive, he saw Manny rise from a chair beside the pond, where Emilia was sitting with one leg up on a stool in the sunshine, and waited for his stepbrother to catch him up at the house.

'Everything OK with Emilia?' Jed pushed open the door.

'She wanted to talk yoga. I guess her exercise bug is biting again. She'll probably want Tamara Rix here every day of the week.' Manny paused. 'Maybe you ought to suggest it? Or take up yoga yourself.' He winked as he left Jed at his office door.

Jed didn't respond as he went back to his desk. He knew when Manny was winding him up. It wasn't Jed's role to suggest how Emilia should spend her time. And as for him taking up yoga himself, that was ridiculous.

It would mean sharing Tamara with a whole class full of people. He was looking for ways to spend time with her alone.

Chapter Twelve

Lyddie's eyes were shadowed with fatigue by the time Tamara returned to her parents' house that evening.

'Probably from too much excitement,' said Cheryl, meaningfully, as she washed up after the evening meal. Sean's dinner sat under clingfilm on the counter, as he wasn't home from work yet. 'Lyddie, darling, you must remember about not leaving the village. It's too far for you to walk.'

'But I was with Tamara,' Lyddie protested. 'Wasn't I 'Mara?'

'I didn't know you were there, Lyd, so I couldn't check that you were OK,' Tamara had to admit.

Cheryl dried her hands and gave her eldest daughter's shoulders a squeeze. 'Tamara might've turned off without you noticing, darling, maybe if a dog came along or a nice car and you were distracted. And you didn't tell me you were leaving, or where you were going. You didn't have your phone with you, either. And you must, mustn't you? I always need to know where you are and that you're all right. Do you remember that, darling? We've talked about it often, haven't we?'

Lyddie nodded, but Cheryl still went through Lyddie's rules for the hundredth time, while Tamara looked on silently, wishing her mum didn't have to be quite so emphatic. Anyone could have seen that Lyddie had had enough. But, after a minute, Lyddie, shoulders drooping, was free to carry Jar Jar's and Chewy's cage into the sitting room to watch the Syfy Channel.

Cheryl waited for her to go, then rounded on Tamara, face tight with anger. 'That could've been a nasty episode, couldn't it?' Building up like a pressure cooker, she went through, 'all the things that could happen to darling Lyddie,' and a reprise of her many vulnerabilities, ending on, 'How am I supposed to keep her *safe*?'

It hadn't been a good day. Tamara understood that Cheryl was wound up like a toddler's toy about Don, and by association, Jed, and, because he wouldn't gang up with her against Jed, Sean, but the injustice of being made the whipping boy – girl – made words burst from her lips. 'I know you're angry, but how was I supposed to know she'd notice I didn't have my bag, and follow me? It was an unforeseen incident, which I coped with.' She didn't try to make her tone conciliatory. It wouldn't hurt her mother to realise that she couldn't just snap and snarl at Tamara on whim.

But Cheryl obviously hadn't yet arrived at that realisation. 'What on earth were you both doing in Ian Mansfield's car?'

Tamara opened her mouth and then paused. The words 'non-disclosure agreement' floated across her mind. She shut her mouth. And flushed.

Cheryl's eyes narrowed. 'What? You always make an enormous song and dance about taking responsibility for your sister, so why the sudden silence? What are you up to?'

Stung by the unwelcome note of accusation in Cheryl's voice, Tamara disregarded the NDA and flashed back, 'Jed got me some private yoga instruction work and Manny works at the same place. Manny brought us both home and he and Jed were kind and helpful. Because I'm working there twice a week, I'll see them both a lot. So suck it up,' she added, and stalked out of the following silence. Then, belatedly considering Lyddie's hatred of rows, she halted at the door to the sitting room.

The mice in their cage were in sole possession of the sofa. Lyddie and Jabber were missing. The front door was open. 'Oh, Lyddie, oh balls!' Tamara groaned aloud.

Cheryl was suddenly beside her, her Lyddie-antennae twitching. 'She's upset. She's rushed out in a mood, look, there's her phone, she hasn't taken it. Oh, why is your father always out with clients when I need him?'

'I'll find her,' Tamara snapped. 'She'll have gone to Gabe's.' She slammed out, still pulsing with anger, but sweaty with shame that they'd so far forgotten themselves as to send Lyddie flying out into the twilight like a frightened pup. Shit in shitloads. It wasn't as if they didn't know that she'd throw a wobbler at the least sniff of an argument.

The evening was still and starry. Tamara marched across The Cross and into Main Road, reaching Gabe's stony track. Her heart lifted to hear Lyddie's voice coming from the pony paddock behind the chicken run, Gabe's deep and precise tones punctuating her high-pitched distress.

She paused. It was better to give Lyddie time to wind down, to let Gabe's unflappable calm soothe her. She rang her mother. 'She's OK, she's at Gabe's.'

'Right.' Cheryl ended the call.

Tamara glared at the phone.

She had to wait until she was chilled to the bone before Lyddie's voice finally dropped to its normal gentle rhythms.

Announcing herself with a cough, Tamara approached the gate. Snobby the pony ambled over, long dark mane swinging like skeins of wool. He checked her hands and blew a polite enquiry into her pocket, but turned offish when he found both empty. No food, no affection: that was Snobby.

Lyddie and Gabe emerged from the gloom, Jabber panting on the lead and waving his feathery tail, the dressing gone from his paw now. 'I haven't seen Gabe's puppies yet,' Lyddie warned truculently. She shifted behind Gabe, as if to ward Tamara off.

Tamara reached round to her, meaning to stroke a tear track from her cheek and say, 'OK Lyd, I'll wait.'

But before the sentence was half out, Lyddie had shoved Tamara hard. '*I'm not going yet.*'

Taken by surprise, Tamara's head snapped back and she staggered. Lyddie flung down Jabber's lead and dashed through Gabe's mint-green, close-boarded door, while Jabber threaded himself between Tamara's shaking legs and laughed up at her, pretending he didn't know how to get unwound.

'I'll go with her.' Gabe strode off in Lyddie's wake.

Tamara took a couple of deep breaths, heart thumping, chest aching slightly where Lyddie had planted her hands. They knew to ignore it when she lashed out or shoved, frustrated by her powerlessness during other people's arguments. It was a while since they'd had any 'challenging behaviour' from Lyddie, but it was still unnerving.

Slowly, Tamara untangled Jabber and tied him to Snobby's fence, well away from the chicken run in case it upset any of Gabe's feathery old dames – although he was more likely to try and round them up than chase them. 'Sorry, Jabber, won't be long.'

She trod softly into the warm yellow light of Gabe's kitchen and found Lyddie sitting on the flagstones, puppies crawling all over her skirt, which was spread out around her like a fallen parachute. Her face was alight as the puppies staggered like wide-eyed little drunkards, making puppy-sized pounces on the pink laces of her trainers.

Apparently over her paddy, Lyddie giggled and cooed and stroked their backs. Her erstwhile puppynap victim, Luke, crawled into the hammock of her skirt to fall asleep.

Gabe looked at Tamara over Lyddie's head, mouthing, 'All right?'

She nodded, and shrugged, because there was no point getting upset. Lyddie wouldn't understand why.

'Well, now,' said Gabe, climbing to his feet and rubbing

his knees where they'd been in contact with the flagstones. 'I think these puppies need their sleep.'

'S'pose so.' Lyddie sighed.

'You're welcome to come again tomorrow,' he reminded her gently.

'Can I hug Princess Layer tomorrow?'

'Yes, you come around in daylight, when the chickens are out of bed.'

Tamara waited while Lyddie kissed each puppy on its domed, silky little head and tucked it back into the box and the bed of old clothes.

Then Tamara took Lyddie's arm to walk her home through the village, curtained windows glowing like squares of a multicoloured patchwork in the darkness. Jabber woofed a couple of warnings at the night breeze, but otherwise there was silence.

At home, Lyddie was abnormally co-operative about going straight to bed. She really was not good with upsets. They exhausted her.

Cheryl cornered Tamara in the hall the instant Lyddie was settled. Her hair had been 'done' that day by the mobile hairdresser and, carefully blow-dried and lacquered. It looked odd with her peach candlewick dressing gown. 'Was she dreadfully tearful? I wish you hadn't shouted, Tamara. You know how she gets if there's a row.'

Blood roared in Tamara's ears like a plane coming in to land, louder, louder, REALLY LOUD, and stupid unwanted tears prickled her eyes. Huge breath ... let it out. Control, control. Calm. Eventually she managed, 'Let's leave it, Mum,' rather than pointing out in the raucous scream she felt building up behind her eyeballs just who began the row, how unfairly, and who shouted the loudest. 'Isn't Dad home, yet?'

Untying her dressing gown belt and retying it more

tightly, as if that would control something, Cheryl pressed her lips together. 'He's gone to bed already. It's been a bad day.'

The uncharacteristic behaviour gave Tamara pause. For the first time it occurred to her to wonder whether her parents' marriage was in difficulty and a cold blade of dismay slid in between her ribs. Why did fully-grown people hurt so much when it happened? She was hardly going to qualify as a tug-of-love child, was she, passing rainy Saturday afternoons in McDonald's with her daddy and wondering if she'd have to be bridesmaid if he remarried?

And ... the cold blade twisted as she imagined Lyddie's bewilderment at a world where Sean and Cheryl lived in different houses.

As if remembering her role as a mother Cheryl patted her shoulder. 'I owe you an apology, darling. I should remember that you and Max have just parted. It's probably why you're being so difficult lately. And perhaps I was unfair earlier because Lyddie's *our* child and therefore our responsibility.'

Tamara didn't know which was more painful, her mother saying that she didn't take responsibility for Lyddie, or that she shouldn't. She'd stayed in the village because of Lyddie, hating to make her sister sad, wanting to do her bit. Maybe in assuming that that would be welcome, she'd assumed too much. Her mother seemed positively to resent her at the moment. Instead of taking the olive branch, Tamara turned for the door. 'I think I'll have an early night myself. It's been a bad day for me, too.'

Her last class on Tuesdays was at six in Middledip village hall and by seven, Tamara could hardly wait for the final spinal twists and putting her hands into prayer position to say 'namaste' to the class, before heading for home and blissful solitude. She needed space. She needed acres, football fields, whole runways of space to throw out her arms and whirl around and around, as if pushing against the walls of her life.

The day had been so hot that it was a relief to take her dinner and collapse in the dappled sun in the garden and let the long, unkempt grass cool her legs. Birds sang the evening away, leaves rustled, and Tamara ate pasta and drank wine, watching the sunspots dancing with the different shades of green.

Her village hall group had been lethargic in the hot air of the hall, sinking into their poses but not looking in the mood to stretch to their full extent. Old Harry had muttered that he would never have stayed in the village if he'd known the weather was going to be so nice. 'It would have been lovely at Wells-next-the-Sea,' he'd complained. Maybe she should make a note to ensure the weather was always bad when she was teaching yoga.

The wine was delicious. Warmed by the sun, it seeped down her throat with barely a need to swallow. Cold and white would've been a good choice, too, but this Merlot ... mmm. Just the same temperature as her blood. Wiping up the last smears of cheese sauce, she downed a second glass, feeling her brain fraying at the edges as she let herself roll down on what passed for her lawn. A most acceptable sensation.

The hush was broken only by threads of birdsong and buggy fizzing and buzzing. Young ash trees, which had seeded themselves through the hawthorn hedgerow, shivered their feathery leaves. Her garden, tucked in where the hedge turned the corner, felt pleasantly secluded. Many of the Banksiders had opted for no or low fences, which made the estate seem airy and open – or just a bit too chummy, depending upon how solitary you were. But here she could feel as if it was just her, the buzzy bugs and the singing birds.

Pulling her ponytail above her head so that the cool grass caressed her neck, Tamara crooked one arm over her eyes. She let her breath deepen and her abdomen rise, heartbeat steadying as she slowly breathed in the spicy scent of the grass and breathed out the tension from each part of her body in turn, sinking down a couple of levels towards deep relaxation.

But she became aware of a rhythmic swish intruding on her consciousness. It resolved itself in her ears to the sound of feet approaching through the uncut lawn and she lifted her arm and blinked.

A silhouette of a man was sauntering from the direction of the side of the house. 'Are you in a state of collapse?' The silhouette had Jed's voice. His hands were stuck in the pockets of his jeans and a white T-shirt was pulled tight across his chest.

She shielded her eyes to distinguish his features. One corner of his mouth quirked as he raised his eyebrows at the wine bottle.

Replacing the arm across her eyes, she sighed. 'There's still time.'

His laugh was low and the grass shifted and tickled against her leg, as he folded himself down beside her. 'I rang at your front door and your neighbour told me that you were out here.'

'Hmm. That would be Marilyn.' She might have the hedgerow instead of a neighbour on one side, but on the other the neighbour's house was close enough that its back bedroom overlooked Tamara's garden. How novel it must be to live somewhere like Lie Low, where there were no neighbours to notice that you were lying on your back in the grass, thinking of nothing on a summer's evening. At least, thinking of nothing until Jed Cassius rocked up and lay down so close that you could hear him breathe and feel his warmth across the few inches between you. Then it was difficult to think of anything but Jed Cassius.

'It's polite to offer guests hospitality,' he observed.

She pretended to consider. 'Even uninvited guests?'

'Especially uninvited guests. You might be bursting to know why the uninvited guest had the temerity to intrude on your privacy, but first you should offer him a glass of wine. It's manners. The guest is very thirsty. The guest is so thirsty he wouldn't even mind fetching his own wine glass.'

She smiled beneath her arm. 'The uninvited guest is presumptuous.'

'The guest understands his uninvited status and is anxious not to be a bother.'

'The guest has previously indicated a dislike for wine.'

'Error. The guest has previously indicated a preference for beer. Wine is OK when there's no beer.'

'Then the guest had better go in through the kitchen door and get a glass from the cupboard beside the window and another bottle of Merlot from the cubbyhole beside the fridge.'

'The guest will be delighted.'

She felt him roll away and lifted her arm a fraction so that she could watch him stride across the lawn, the late sun making a halo of his hair until he passed into shadow, opened the kitchen door and stepped inside. Then she sat up to let her eyes reaccustom themselves to the sunshine without a squint that would make Quasimodo jealous, and combed out any grass debris from her ponytail with her fingers. On Jed's return, she laid the new bottle in a patch of sun to warm and shared out the last of the glowing red liquid from the open bottle.

He settled himself on the patch of grass he'd already flattened, lounging on one elbow with his legs stretched out comfortably, and clinked his glass to hers. 'Here's to us.

Emilia wonders whether you'd like to bring Lyddie to see the alpacas? Would she like that?'

The swift change of subject made it unnecessary to react to the 'us' that had put a hitch in her breath. She'd hardly had time to change her Facebook status to *single* and it made her suspicious that already her hormones were running laps around her body whenever Jed was near. She'd never been victim to 'falling for' someone and, having watched various friends swept along by sudden passion, she was uncertain whether the experience would be all good. So much whirling excitement and inability to think straight through sweaty lust …

Jed broke into her thoughts. 'Before you ask, yes, I could have just phoned with the invitation, but I used it as an excuse to see you.'

The expression in his eyes made Tamara's brain squiggle. Damn. There you go – thoughts not going straight. She took a breath. 'That's very kind of Emilia. I'd better check with my parents—' She hesitated. 'But not tonight because I had an epic row with Mum yesterday, so I think we need a break from each other.' She frowned. 'Actually, this non-disclosure thingy is proving a bit problematic so far as Mum's concerned. Because Lyddie wandered off yesterday and Manny drove her home, I had to explain that I had a private client and that she came through you.'

His eyes gleamed with amusement. 'And was she pleased?'

'Not very.'

He sipped from his wine glass again, then let himself roll down flat on the grass, closing his eyes, balancing his glass on his chest. 'I don't think we need to take you to court over explaining that to Cheryl, especially as Emilia's invitation to Lyddie makes it impossible to keep to the letter of the NDA. Lyddie being vulnerable means that her parents will have to be involved in anything that concerns her.'

'Also, Lyddie doesn't do tact or discretion.'

A frown flitted across his face. 'Good point. That's something for Emilia and Mr H to be made aware of, but Emilia has asked me to invite you both, so ...' His wine swilled gently in the glass as he shrugged. 'Maybe you could check your schedule and let me know your availability?'

Tamara lay down on her side in the sweet-smelling grass. It seemed so much effort to sit up and Jed was preserving a distance that had let her hormones calm down to a gentle jog. The evening sky was fading to a relaxing twilight blue. 'I have my schedule in my head. Wednesdays are good —'

He held up the hand that wasn't holding the wine glass. 'Wait. You have the entire week's schedule in your head?'

The note of incredulity in his voice nettled her. 'Monday at ten, Emilia; two thirty, Bettsbrough Park Hotel; five p.m., Caradoc Gym. Caradoc Gym again at nine on Tuesday, Oasis Leisure at eleven, Middledip village hall at six. Wednesdays, just eight p.m. at the dance studio of Rowland Community College. Thursdays, two p.m. at Port Manor Hotel – which is a new venue; they've just converted some of the basement into a gym and the people from the treatment centre are administering it. Four o'clock, Bettsbrough Park Hotel; back-to-back sessions at Port-le-bain community centre at six and seven. Do I need to go on?'

'Three more days in the week,' he pointed out.

'Friday at nine, Port-le-bain community centre; ten thirty, Middledip village hall; two o'clock, Emilia. Saturday, Caradoc Gym at eleven; school studio at two. Sundays I have off. OK?'

'OK,' he agreed. 'So we're talking about Monday evening, Tuesday lunchtime, all day Wednesday, Thursday morning, Friday or Saturday evening or any time on Sunday?'

Tamara was thrown. 'You seem to have got the hang of that,' she said, eventually.

He touched his forehead. 'Memory tricks Manny taught me.'

'Oh.' She digested this. 'But we have to account for Lyddie working in the shop several days a week. They're not set days, Gwen moves her hours around.'

'Do you think your mother will stop her going because of me?'

Tamara hesitated. 'I'd like to say "no" but ...'

He groaned. 'But you can't. OK. Maybe we ought to leave it for now. The direct approach hasn't worked on Cheryl, so I'll have to try and outflank her. Leave it with me.' He propped himself up, reached for the new wine bottle and began to pick at the foil seal. 'Let's give this a chance to breathe.'

'You're obviously a connoisseur. Does it need a full yogic breath? Or will a working breath do?'

'I pick a few things up from my betters, but I don't need to be a connoisseur to spot that you're drinking wine with a twist top. Don't you know that a cork is supposed to be a mark of quality?'

She sniffed. 'Even corks aren't usually made of cork any more. And quite expensive wines can have a sensible top that I can get off without resorting to corkscrews that need mighty muscles or a degree in engineering to operate.'

He twisted off the top. 'And is this an expensive wine?' He stood his wine glass in the grass, keeping it upright with his elbow while he covered her hand to hold her glass steady as he filled it halfway. His hand was hot over hers and awareness flushed through her.

'Very. More than a fiver.'

'Wow, that much?' His hand remained on hers, while he tried to keep his own drink upright and screw the bottle top on with one hand. 'I hope you notice that I'm going to stupid lengths to have an excuse to touch you, even in the most innocent of ways?'

Her throat had dried, but she couldn't free herself to drink her wine without pulling away from his hand. And if she pulled away right when he'd drawn her attention to it, it would seem pointed. She swallowed. 'I haven't precisely asked myself why. I'm still at the stage of inwardly noting. But, as you've pointed it out …?'

His eyes glittered. 'I'm shamelessly hitting on you. My plan is to grab whatever opportunities arise, spin out whatever time I can make with you, blow on the spark that's between us and hope to fire things up. As an aside, by beginning this second glass of wine I've condemned myself to walking home as Manny's driving Mr and Mrs H to the theatre tonight, which means walking back tomorrow to retrieve my car. Pursuing a hot woman is much easier in city centres, where there's more public transport so it's easier not to fall foul of the drink-drive laws. But to return to the central topic – I want to get close to you. You know that. Even if I hadn't said so at the tapas place, the crackle between us every time we meet must tell you.'

She narrowed her eyes at him. 'Is that short for wanting to get me into bed?'

Heat glowed in his eyes. 'Obviously. But not today.'

'You're going too fast—' She made to wriggle her hand away, but then he was using it to draw her gently towards him. His lips came down soft and hot and his tongue was silk against hers, shooting flames down to the soles of her feet and igniting a couple of interesting places en route. Then he brushed the planes of her face with his lips and touched his teeth gently to her neck. It was somehow incredibly intimate, without crossing a single boundary.

'Not today,' he breathed, gently pulling at her ponytail elastic until her hair fell down around her face and he could push his fingers through it. 'It'll be all the better when it happens.'

Chapter Thirteen

On Friday morning Tamara found a 'connoisseur' lever-arm corkscrew had been left tied to her door handle with red ribbon. Carefully, she unhooked it and put it in her kitchen drawer.

She sent Jed a text. *Do I have to thank you for the corkscrew?*

His reply was prompt. *You don't have to but it would be nice. Do you want a list of ways I like to be thanked?*

Pretending to be exasperated, she returned, *I MEANT is it you who left the corkscrew? If so, thanks.*

Welcome, he replied. With *xxx* at the end. Then, seconds later, *Just let me know if you ever want the list.*

By the time her afternoon session with Emilia came around, the day had turned hazy and the sun couldn't seem to decide whether to burn through or to let the haze thicken to thunderclouds.

Jed's smile, when he let Tamara into the lofty, panelled hall, electrified the nerves in her spine. But he said no more than, 'Emilia's poolside.' And showed her through to where Emilia waited on a rattan chaise, her pink exercise mat open on the floor tiles.

'Oh good, you're here.' Her hair gleamed in its ponytail. With her looks, in low-slung exercise pants teamed with an exercise bra and strappy top, she could have stepped straight from a Nike advert.

Tamara flipped her own mat out, enjoying the steamy warmth of the room and the sunshine streaming through the many panels of glass. 'Shall we take our ChiBalls and lie down?' She paused to let Emilia settle, noticing how she favoured her right leg and was tentative about straightening it. 'You should be really comfortable. Think about your back – do you need to bring one or both of your legs in to relieve any tightness? Is the ChiBall on the knobbly bit of your head, leaving your neck free?' Tamara could see that it was, but let Emilia reach up to check. Her object was to make Emilia aware of her body, to listen to it for herself. 'Shoulders down, away from your ears … relax … chin in … palms up, let your fingers curl naturally.' Pause. 'Now let's think about your breath. You should be breathing easily and evenly through your nose. Let the breath deepen gradually, think about your abdomen rising and falling … falling, falling, expelling all that used air, allowing fresh oxygen to enter your blood stream.'

As she ran through the familiar opening routine she observed Emilia, noting the small frown that tugged between her brows, the slight fidgeting of her right foot. 'If you have to move a limb to make it more comfortable, then that's fine. Do you need to bend your right knee?'

'Slightly.' Emilia winced as she moved.

Tamara reached for a folded towel from the rung of the chaise Emilia had lately occupied and rolled it up. 'Let's try this under the knee. Any good?'

The frown vanished. 'That works.'

'OK, think about your breathing once more. Think about relaxing your face … your shoulders … let those lungs fill right up … Let's think about those facial muscles, now, getting them to release the tension they're trying to cling on to.'

Once the face and neck workout was done, Tamara moved on smoothly through a gentle stretching routine, keeping a close eye on Emilia when she was on her feet, making the session exploratory so that she could assess what could and couldn't be done and what would be most helpful to Emilia. Lunges were severely compromised, but triangles seemed a bit easier.

Then Tamara set Emilia to rolling her ChiBall slowly down the centre of her body, following it with her eyes and head until her spine rolled her down like a rag doll. 'Just hang there, letting your back stretch. Try and keep equal weight in your feet, if you can, rather than rocking back on your heels. I appreciate that that might be difficult. How uncomfortable is that for your leg? Roll up again, now, following the ball with your eyes in the same way.'

'It's not too bad. Worse when I was holding the pose.' But Emilia looked relieved when it was time to get back down on the mat for the end-of-class relaxation, the yoga for the mind, as Tamara talked her through a journey to her favourite place in her imagination, then left her there to relax.

In a class situation, she would probably spend that time doing a few poses of her own, but she didn't feel that would work so well in a one-to-one situation, so awarded herself a little relaxation of her own, sitting upright, legs crossed, as she practised deep breathing and let her muscles hang down towards the floor.

After the session, when Carrie had brought a steaming coffee pot and china mugs, Emilia stretched and sighed. 'That was wonderful. It's fantastic to be doing something again.'

'How does your leg feel?' Tamara sniffed appreciatively at the Costa Rican coffee, before taking the first delicious sip from the fine, white porcelain.

'Slightly achy. But it's just like when I'm doing my physio, so that's OK. I'll give it a go in the hot tub later.' She indicated the gently swirling water in the tub at the other end of the pool, near the French doors. Then Emilia frowned down at her leg, rubbing it ruefully. 'Look at me, getting all excited about an hour's yoga and a go in the hot tub, when I used to whizz through five hours of aerobic exercise a week. My life's unrecognisable since the accident. I'm not even a member of a gym here, because Tom seems to have to know who's with me all the time—' She stopped.

One-on-one, instructor-client relationships could deepen quite quickly, but Tamara was still surprised at Emilia volunteering this almost-criticism, even if she'd pulled herself up straight away. 'That's a shame,' she said, neutrally.

Casually, Emilia shrugged. 'He only wants to look after me. But I've gone for a private instructor because when I talked to him about taking classes, he wanted Manny or Jed to come with me.'

Tamara let her imagination toy with this information. 'So, if you took embroidery, say, Jed would have to take embroidery, too?'

Emilia's mouth curled up at the corners. 'I hadn't thought of that. Pity I'm not up to ballet. But I could do Greek,' she went on dreamily. 'Or music appreciation. Dressmaking. Bead work.'

They grinned at each other. Tamara savoured the image of Jed being obliged to take up bead work. Shame about the ballet because those lycra leggings left nothing to the imagination ...

When they'd drunk their coffee, Emilia led her through the French doors to visit the alpacas. Tamara had no objection – there were still fifteen minutes of her booked time available, apart from anything else – but it fleeted across her mind that Emilia must be lonely to want her company once the yoga was over. To pay for it, in fact.

As they rounded the corner of the house and made their way onto the paved part of the upper terrace, Jed met them. 'Are you ready to go, Tamara?'

'We're going to see the alpacas first. But I'm sure I can come and get you after that.' She only meant search him out to collect her fee, but smiled at the sudden interest in his gaze.

Emilia laughed. 'But Manny and Jed like to think they need to control anybody who enters the house. And the gates! I mean, nobody else could operate the remote control.' She didn't stop the swinging foot-foot-crutches rhythm that was carrying her across the paving towards the lawn.

'It's only to keep us safe, Emilia.' Tom Hilton's soft reproof came from behind them. Tamara jumped, turning to gaze at Mr Hilton as he stepped from the house. He threaded his way to his young wife's side, sliding an arm around her waist. 'And the best way to do that is to let Manny and Jed do their jobs, isn't it?' He squeezed her briefly.

Emilia flushed, gazing at him from under her lashes. 'But Jed's trying to hurry Tamara away and I want her to come with me to look at the alpacas.'

Tom Hilton smiled. 'Then let Jed go with you, in case you need a hand back up the slope.'

Jed stepped forward and Tom Hilton moved back, which left Emilia stumping along at the head of a train, Tamara and Jed filing behind. When Emilia paused to let Tamara draw alongside her at the foot of the steps onto the second terrace, Jed remained several paces behind. Emilia had rediscovered her smile. 'Tamara, did Jed ask you about bringing Lyddie to see the alpacas? The first baby has been born and he's so beautiful! The breeders told me that they tend to birth in batches when the weather's good, so there will probably be more any moment.' Her face was alight with pleasure as she limped along.

'It's really kind of you. Oh, isn't he gorgeous?' As they walked down the slope and neared the fence, Tamara drew in her breath to see a small, fluffy, fawn alpaca following its mother on uncertain legs, and laughed at his 'Huh?' expression.

Emilia beamed. 'He is, isn't he? I'm going to call all the babies after yoga moves, so he's going to be Warrior Two.' She giggled. 'He so doesn't look like a warrior, does he? More like a toy that's come to life. I hope I get at least one more boy because the boys have to be separated from the girls when they're a few months old and it's cruel to keep one alone. They hang out in gangs.' She turned to Jed. 'So we'll need another paddock.' She said it carelessly, in the same way she'd say they needed another sack of feed.

Tamara saw Jed's jaw tighten. 'Another paddock?'

'Definitely.'

'Can we divide this paddock into two? Or does it have to be an additional one?'

With a shrug, Emilia turned away. 'Could you ring the breeders and ask what's best?'

'And it'll mean more feeders and drinkers and another shelter?'

Emilia glanced at him again. 'I expect so.' Her tone so plainly questioned why he'd bother her with such minor details, that Tamara had to smother a grin.

Turning back to Tamara, Emilia's smile flashed. 'Jed says that his family's history with your family might mean your mum won't let Lyddie visit.'

'She does need careful handling,' Tamara acknowledged. Then, cautiously, because Emilia was employing her, after all, although she tended not to dish out her orders to Tamara in the same way that she dished them out to everyone else. 'If you're really keen on Lyddie visiting, you need to be aware that she can't sign a non-disclosure agreement. She won't understand. If it comes into her head to tell someone about the alpacas or her friend Emilia, she just will. And she works in the village shop.'

Emilia's eyes followed Warrior Two, as he tried to keep up with his mum at a drunken totter. 'Jed's already explained. I'd love it if Lyddie would call me her friend. Since my accident, I haven't made any new ones and the old ones have kind of faded, because I'm stuck here. And it seems—' She paused, biting her lip. 'Now I'm not up in London to be lavish with hospitality or invite them to share a cruise to Madeira, some of them can hardly be bothered to send an email.' She smiled crookedly. 'With Lyddie – well, I can be sure she likes me for myself, can't I?'

Tamara's heart gave a giant squeeze. 'Wow,' she said slowly. 'That caught me unawares.' She let her mind work. If Emilia was looking for a friend who would like her for herself, Tamara couldn't fault her selection. Lyddie hadn't the insight to realise that Emilia had access to oodles of money, so would never expect to be transported around the world on a yacht or invited to sumptuous parties.

'Can't you make it OK with your mum?' Emilia sounded at once coaxing and impatient.

Tamara shook herself from her thoughts. 'Um ... Let me work on her.' Cheryl was so readily perturbed these days that Tamara needed time to think what was best.

Emilia grabbed Tamara's arm uncomfortably tightly. Tears stood in her eyes. 'Thanks. Really – thanks. Jed might be one of Tom's people, but he's done good bringing you on board. I hadn't thought how fantastic it would be to have someone who worked for me, rather than for Tom. It can be—' Her eyes shone with tears. 'It can be isolating, being me. Especially since that scary stuff with the protestors that made Tom extra protective.'

She threaded her arms into her crutches. 'Let's get back up to the house. Jed can sort you out with your money.' Ignoring Jed, who was hovering as per Mr Hilton's instruction in case she needed help, she began to swing up the greensward.

'I'll visit Mum. Let me see what I can do,' Tamara promised, impulsively. Jed turned his head to regard her, but she couldn't read his expression.

At the house, Emilia illustrated that she was indeed aware of Jed's presence by standing back so that he could open the French doors for them. She then hugged Tamara and kissed her cheek, as if they were firm friends. 'I'll take that hot tub, now. My leg's a bit tired. Jed will give you my mobile number so you can let me know what your mum says about Lyddie.' Then she swung her way off around the pool.

Jed led Tamara in the other direction. 'Shall we go to my office?'

In the neat room with the glass desk, he counted out what she was owed.

Tamara took the notes he gave her and slid them into her purse. Today Jed was wearing his work persona. He was correct and courteous as he showed her to her car. 'Thanks for approaching your mum about Lyddie. You can see Emilia wants her here.'

He opened her car door for her and then pointed the remote at the gates. He was very much Jed-at-work, escorting a guest of the household with impeccable courtesy.

Quite a contrast to the Jed who had pinned her to her hall wall before he left on Tuesday evening, almost lifting her from her feet with the force of his kisses. Her toes curled just to think of it.

Trying to put him out of her mind as she whisked around the curve of the drive and could no longer see him in her mirrors, she drove directly to Church Close, wondering what Cheryl would make of Emilia's invitation. Having Emilia for a friend would be, to employ a term she usually detested, a 'normal' thing for Lyddie. A friend of her own age and gender, something most people would take for granted. Not a benevolent, retired bank manager who drove a pony; not one of the dog-walkers; not one of Gwen's customers; not even someone who knew Lyddie before she was injured and was kind to her when their paths happened to cross.

Tamara's heart ached to realise that apart from erratic overtures from fellow learning-disabled adults in Mountland Hall, Lyddie hadn't had a new friend of her own age since she ran out after Tamara in front of that car in 1993.

She hoped that Cheryl could persuade herself that it wouldn't be right to deny her the chance of one, now.

Letting herself into the house, she wondered what her mother's mood would be. It was a bit of a relief to find Cheryl relatively relaxed, indulging in a bit of 'me time' while Lyddie was at work, drinking coffee in the garden with a magazine on her lap, seemingly over her spurt of temper.

Stroking Jabber, who was only limping slightly now, Tamara seated herself on the grass and outlined her errand. 'Emilia and her husband are comfortably off and I think she's tired of freeloaders,' she ended.

Cheryl screwed up her face in thought. 'Well, darling …' They listened to each other not saying anything for several moments. 'Well, there's no reason why not, is there?' she decided, cautiously. 'If you find Emilia nice enough, then she's not going to do Lyddie any harm, is she?'

'I don't see how she could. She likes movies and animals, like Lyddie, and she's feeling isolated. I'll pop in and see Lyddie this evening and if she's keen, then I'll ring Emilia and see what we can arrange.'

Cheryl pulled a comical face. 'Do you really think that Lyddie won't be keen? Especially if there are animals involved.'

Tamara grinned, glad and relieved that her request hadn't resulted in another Mum-strop. 'She'll adore seeing the alpacas. They look like a cross between dish mops and punk-rock sheep.'

When Tamara returned that evening, the issue proved to be not whether Lyddie would want to visit Emilia and meet the alpaca herd, but whether she could be dissuaded from setting off for Lie Low instantly on foot. All the time that Tamara was on the telephone making arrangements, Lyddie bellowed excitedly in her other ear. 'We're going to visit Emilia again, aren't we, 'Mara? And she's going to show us her packers, isn't she? Isn't she, 'Mara?'

Tamara was laughing as she ended the call. 'I think Emilia gets the idea that you want to visit her, Lyd. I'm taking you tomorrow afternoon, after my second class.' At least Lyddie had Saturday off this week, so she didn't have to be contained until Sunday.

'Tomorrow?' Lyddie breathed, in bliss. 'Thank you, 'Mara.' She swept Tamara into her fiercest hug and planted four wet kisses on her cheeks. Far too excited to go to bed, even when Tamara had dragged out the old favourite, 'If you go to sleep then tomorrow will come sooner,' she giggled and chattered and clapped her hands.

So they Googled alpacas and practised saying, 'Al-pac-as, al-pac-as,' instead of 'packers' while they looked at pictures of alpacas airing their best agog expressions. Lyddie was lost in delight at the prospect of meeting the real thing. 'Are they as big as a giraffe, 'Mara? As big as an elephant?'

'No, they're not even as big as us.'

'But they've got long necks like giraffes, haven't they?'

Finally, Tamara heard her parents coming up to bed, her father's deep murmurs answering her mother's fluting and more prolific commentary, and said firmly, 'You need to get into your pyjamas, Lyddie, and we'll do a few stretches and a relaxation before you hop into bed.'

'Animal yoga?' asked Lyddie hopefully. 'Animal yoga' was one of the many ways Tamara had to keep Lyddie amused.

'OK. But pyjamas first.'

When Lyddie was arrayed in gorgeous pink seersucker with a panda face on the pocket of her pyjama jacket, teeth freshly cleaned, they got down on all fours on her bedroom carpet – also pink. Getting up or down made Lyddie wobble, but she was fine once she'd navigated her way from one to the other.

'Lion, lion,' she begged, sticking out her tongue and rolling her eyes.

Tamara was getting that end-of-a-long-day feeling and was yearning for her bed and her Kindle, so made her voice deliberately slow, focusing on soothing Lyddie down from her exuberance. 'Lion's a good pose, isn't it? It releases tension in your tongue and jaw. Have you got equal weight in your hands and knees? Look forward – that's good – and let your eyes look up to the top of your head. Stick your tongue right out—'

'Urhhhhh,' went Lyddie, enthusiastically.

'Good. Gently. Hold. Let your tongue stretch. Now a big breath out—'

'Hrruh! Hrruh! Hrruh!' Lyddie generously gave three big breaths, the 'lion's roar'.

'Lovely.' Tamara took her through it again, settling her down until she was performing the lion with less gusto and more proficiency. 'Now we'll do some lovely cat stretches. Big slow breath in as you arch your back ... tuck in your bottom and your head. Good. Big breath out, slowly, as you let your tummy and back dip and your bottom and head come up. Look forward. Other way, again, breathe in, let your back arch.' Slower and slower, until Lyddie's eyes began to look heavy.

'OK, let's lie down. Bring in your legs like a tent and we'll do some crocodiles. Breathe in as you let your knees drop towards the bed, now out. Let your head turn the other way, towards the curtains.' Tamara used objects to identify directions because left and right could be renamed 'hit and miss' so far as Lyddie was concerned. 'Good. Slow your breathing. Stretch just a little bit with your top knee. Stretch. Relax.' She let several seconds tick by. 'Now we'll do the other side. Breathe in and let your knees begin to lift ... now out as they come all the way to the top.'

In another few minutes, Lyddie was quiet and her movements were slow. Tamara was able to say, 'I'll do your relaxation when you get in bed. That's great. Comfy? Let your eyes close. Stretch your hands down towards your feet so your shoulders aren't hunched up near your ears. Relax. Let your tummy rise as you breathe in. Now let it fall as you breathe out. That's lovely. And now you're floating. Floating up, and up, and the roof's opening to let Lyddie float up to the clouds, up to the stars ... and you're warm and comfortable and leaving behind your busy day and all the things you've done ...' She remained beside the bed for several minutes after Lyddie plummeted into oblivion, watching her big sister sleep like a child. In sleep, nobody would have known that the real Lyddie had never made it to what most people experienced as adulthood. Never had a boyfriend, never driven a car, never been drunk, never had sex or had a proper career. Had missed out on so many 'normal' things.

And then, taking with her a heavy heart, Tamara let herself out of the silent house and drove off to her own little sanctuary a few minutes away at the far side of the Bankside estate.

Chapter Fourteen

I'll see you this afternoon when you bring Lyddie but we'll both have our work faces on, so hope you don't mind this by text. Come out with me on Sunday?

She didn't mind the text at all. Much better than discussing dates in front of one of the Hiltons. Breathing quickening, she replied, *It's OK. Where?*

– *Surprise. I'll pick you up at ten.*

– *Sounds good. What should I wear?*

– *No particular dress code.*

– *But do I need to be smart or comfortable?*

– *Comfortable.*

– *Comfortable but how presentable?*

– ☺ *Wtf does that mean?*

– *Like, I would hate to turn up in my hiking boots with wet weather gear and find that we're going to a jazz bistro for lunch.*

– *We're not going to a jazz bistro but I think you should upgrade from wet weather gear. You could wear your bathrobe if you want to be really comfortable.*

– *It's pink with white bunnies on.*

– *Wear it.*

She'd grinned to herself. In fact, she'd just described Lyddie's bathrobe, but he didn't have to know that. *Would look stupid with hiking boots.*

– *Lose the hiking boots. You could wear those boots with heels you wore at the tapas bar. Yeah.*

– *Let's approach this from another angle. What are you going to wear?*

– *Jeans.*

– *OK. So will I.*

– Pink with bunnies?
– Black with rips.
– I like them already.

After her class, Tamara didn't join the coffee crowd at the McDonald's half a mile up the road from the school studio, so she was at Church Close by three thirty, nearly knocked off her feet by Lyddie's excitement as she climbed from her car. "Mara, you're going to take me to 'Milia's, aren't you, 'Mara? You're going to take me to see her packers, aren't you? Can Jabber come?'

Jabber shifted paw-to-paw on Cheryl's crisp-and-cared-for lawn, ears up, as if he, too, was keen to find out about these alpacas.

Giving Lyddie a big hug, Tamara threw the expectant Jabber an apologetic look. 'I'm afraid Jabber can't come this time, Lyd. Emilia didn't invite him and you can't take dogs into people's houses when they're not invited. Bad manners.' Lyddie was familiar with the 'bad manners' reason for not doing things, as Cheryl used it to curb some of Lyddie's less welcome behaviours.

So, in a flurry of getting Jabber back into the house and Lyddie into a fleece, because the June sun had hidden behind thick cloud and allowed a chill breeze to skip around them, Tamara shouted their goodbyes to their parents, who were settled in front of Saturday afternoon sport. Lyddie climbed into the car, talking loudly about 'packers' – al-pac-as – as they set off on the short journey to Lie Low.

When they arrived at the outer gates buried in the spinney, Tamara opened the car window and announced herself via the intercom, reflecting on how familiar the action was becoming as the gates swung wide to welcome her in.

Jed stepped out of the house as they drew up. After a

fractional hesitation, it was Lyddie's door he went to open. '*Hel*lo—!' Lyddie halted.

'Jed,' Tamara supplied, suffering a pang that Lyddie recognised him as someone she'd met but couldn't download his name from her randomly functioning memory, let alone recall the Jed who'd been important to her teenaged pre-accident self.

'Jed,' Lyddie repeated, beaming as she swung her feet onto the drive, hunched over to get her balance as she thrust herself to her feet. '*Hel*lo, Jed. Me and 'Mara have come to see 'Milia and her packers. Al-pac-as.'

Jed gave her one of his rare smiles, shutting her car door. 'We'll go and find Emilia, then, shall we?' He sent Tamara a smile, too, something other than professionalism flaring briefly in his gaze as he took in her blue skinny jeans. He lifted an eyebrow. 'No rips?'

'I'm saving them.'

His gaze took in her aqua wedge-heel high tops. 'At least I've been spared the hiking boots.' Turning to Lyddie, he offered her his arm. 'Emilia's waiting for you indoors.'

Launching into the subject of Emilia at her normal volume, Lyddie ignored the proffered arm. Instead, she took his hand, directing her stream of conversation and questions right into his eyes. Jed took the development without pause, merely checking that Tamara was coming along with them before giving Lyddie his attention, letting her swing his hand without any sign of embarrassment as he led the way into the main hall, under the dogleg stairway and into a small sitting room Tamara hadn't been in before – small by Lie Low standards anyway – where Emilia was stretched out on a midnight blue chaise, idly tapping at an aluminium-case laptop. She put it aside as soon as Jed showed in the guests.

''Milia! I've come to see your packers.' Lyddie dropped Jed's hand and launched herself across the room.

Tamara was ready for her, catching her arm firmly. 'Steady, Lyddie. Remember Emilia's bad leg. We need to be careful with her, don't we?' She wasn't sure how Emilia would react to an enthusiastic Lyddie hug, possibly along with sloppy kisses.

Obediently, Lyddie halted. 'Does it hurt, 'Milia?'

Emilia scooted to the edge of the chaise and rose, shrugging into a jacket she'd had waiting on a nearby chair arm. She slipped into her crutches and came forward with a smile. 'Not most of the time. Anyway, Lyddie, I've got something really special to show you. Let's go and see.' She glanced in Jed's direction. 'I won't need you. I managed the slope perfectly well, yesterday.' She took them across the hall, across the sitting room with dark green accents where Tamara had first met Mr Hilton, and out of the door that Tamara recognised as being the one that Mr Hilton had appeared through yesterday.

Lyddie stumped along chummily beside her. One step behind, Tamara noticed that Lyddie's awkward gait was surprisingly similar to Emilia's limping one. Both had to pause at the terrace steps and shuffle to present themselves sideways to the first step. Lyddie was taking the conversational lead, mixing together an account of looking alpacas up on the internet, with one about doing animal yoga. In other circumstances, Tamara would have managed Lyddie's enthusiasm, not letting her run on uninterrupted and, perhaps, overwhelming Emilia with her undiluted attention. But if Emilia wanted Lyddie as her friend, well, this was Lyddie. Not peaceful, not restful, not necessarily coherent or fascinating.

She fell another step behind, letting her thoughts stray to where it was that Jed intended taking her tomorrow, where ripped jeans or a bathrobe might be equally acceptable.

Then, suddenly, Lyddie was shouting, 'Look, *look*!

Packers! Look, 'Mara. Packers!' And Emilia was laughing at Lyddie's delight, her hair blowing across her face as she glanced back to share the moment with Tamara.

Tamara moved closer to Lyddie, taking her arm to dissuade her from taking the rest of the slope at a run – not her steadiest gait – and perhaps precipitating an alpaca stampede. 'I think we need to be quieter. We don't want to scare the alpacas, do we? Especially the mum with the new baby.'

'We've got three babies, now,' Emilia broke in. 'There was another birth yesterday after you'd gone, and one this morning. That just leaves two to go.' She glanced at the grey sky. 'Come over to the gate, Lyddie, and you'll be able to see.'

'Al-pac-as,' Lyddie breathed, as she leaned her elbows on the top of the gate, eyes glued to the alpacas, who had paused as one, lifting their heads and gazing enquiringly as the humans arrived, ears like devil horns atop their heads. As well as little Warrior Two, there was another fawn baby and a fuzzy black one. Their legs looked hardly strong enough to carry them in deer-like steps beside their more ponderous mothers.

'Babies!' belted out Lyddie, making each alpaca draw itself up nervously and stare intently across the paddock, looking poised to turn and flee in indignation.

Gently, Tamara squeezed her arm. 'Remember we have to speak softly. If we're quiet they'll get used to us and then we can watch them all we want. Because we don't want them to run away, do we?'

Lyddie shook her head emphatically, lips squeezed firmly together.

It took only a couple of minutes for the herd members to relax into serenity, grazing, gazing, milling and murmuring.

'They keep saying "mmm",' whispered Lyddie. 'As if they like the look of us.'

Emilia laughed softly. 'It's called humming, the noise they make. People find it soothing. Do you like my alpacas?'

'I love them.' Lyddie nodded earnestly, her gaze unwaveringly on the wonderful new animals. 'I *love* them. I love their eyes and their hair and their necks.'

'I thought you might like to choose the name of one of the new babies? I'm naming them all after yoga moves. Maybe Tamara could tell you some and you could choose?'

'Lyddie does yoga, she'll be able to choose for herself,' put in Tamara, as Lyddie turned a gaze of undiluted joy on Emilia.

'Triangle,' she said, promptly. 'Can it be the little black one?'

Emilia laughed again. She looked bright and carefree. 'That's a lovely name for an alpaca baby. I'll have it put in the herd book. I think I'll call the new fawn baby Downward Dog.' She laughed again. 'You're good for me, Lyddie.'

Lyddie brushed the compliment away in favour of the interesting stuff. 'What are the mothers' names?'

Emilia pulled a face. 'They're a really boring, middle-aged collection – Duchess, Maria, Ethel, August and Twinkie. They already had their names when they arrived, of course.' She went on to tell Lyddie about what alpacas like to eat and what happened when the shearer came with his portable shearing table. On her phone she showed Lyddie pictures of the alpacas before shearing.

'Fatties,' Lyddie gurgled, joyfully. 'Big fat fluffy fatties. Like pom-poms, 'Mara.'

Finally, Emilia picked up her crutches from where she'd leaned them against the gate. 'Shall we go up and get a nice hot drink? I'm getting cold.'

'Hot chocolate?' asked Lyddie, hopefully.

'Definitely. With biscuits to dip in it.'

Lyddie sighed beatifically. 'I love biscuits. I *love* them.'

Chapter Fifteen

Jed's mini Batmobile drew up outside Tamara's house punctually the next morning and she went out without waiting for him to ring the doorbell. As he hadn't seemed to care for the idea of hiking boots and since the weather was still cool and grey, with her jeans she wore black ankle boots with studded straps that looped down to the kick-ass heel.

Jed made towards the passenger door, but she opened it for herself – men opening doors for her always made her feel vaguely fraudulent because she was quite competent with the mechanism after all – and she managed the side-and-down movement necessary to arrive elegantly in the seat of a sports car, having had opportunity to practise on some of the enormous variety of cars that Max had brought home on road tests.

Jed slid back into the driver's seat, watching as she felt for the seatbelt and then leaning over her to fish it out from behind the seat, which meant that he was in the ideal position to brush his lips across hers. He looked and smelled as if he'd just showered and shaved. 'There's something about rips,' he murmured.

Heat flared through her. 'I'm glad you're not too disappointed about the bathrobe with bunnies.'

His eyes laughed at her as he felt for the ignition and started the car. 'Another time.'

'You've got a day off?'

'I get plenty of down time. Not much at the same time as Manny, as we have to work around one another for holidays and stuff and it often means text updates while I'm away, but that's OK.'

'So, where are we going?'

Jed twisted in his seat as he manoeuvred the car around the circle that allowed those who had buried themselves this far into the estate to turn round and escape again. 'Surprise.' The car straightened up and he let it rumble along the small street and into the larger Great Hill Road, slowing for the speed bumps that had recently arrived to calm the traffic and give the village something to complain about.

'Are we going to Peterborough?'

'Around it.'

'Is this your car or Mr Hilton's?'

'Mine.'

So he could afford a pretty cool car. She didn't mind being impressed by cool cars. Especially when she didn't have anything to do except settle into the dark red leather seat, enjoy the journey and see how the day played out.

They drove past fields, past the turning to Bettsbrough, onto the parkways that encircled Peterborough, Jed weaving through the traffic that seemed to roar constantly along the parkways whatever the time of day or night, until they turned north onto the A1 and flew up the dual carriageway, past lorries trundling along like elephants holding each others' tails. Then they threaded their way through miles of lanes, before turning in under a dark green wrought iron arch on which Tamara read 'Grand Manor', picked out in gold.

'Grand Manor? Is this another of Mr Hilton's secret hideaways?'

Jed grinned. 'Kind of.'

The manor – which was pretty damned grand – was set in a pocket park with a stream burbling between manicured trees and flowering shrubs of white and pink in beds cosseted with a layer of bark.

Jed parked at the foot of a flight of semi-circular stone

steps, which climbed up to massive double doors flanked by spherical yew trees. The house itself was of uncompromising grey stone, with mullioned windows and crenellations. As they climbed from the car, a young guy in black trousers and waistcoat and a white shirt appeared at the foot of the stairs. He took Jed's keys and Jed took Tamara's hand.

Mounting the stone steps, Tamara glanced behind her as the engine started up again. 'That man seems to be taking your car.'

'They get all hurt if you don't let them park for you.'

Inside, they found a circular hall with polished wooden staircases curving up the walls to the floor above, an impressive reception desk situated in the centre, and doors opening off. It was cool, echoing, airy and perfumed.

A blonde woman in a suit rose from behind the desk. From her French plait to her French manicure, she looked as if she ought to be welcoming first-class passengers onto an airliner. A discreet black badge on her discreet black lapel read, *Imelda James, General Manager*. 'Mr Cassius, good to see you.'

Tamara flicked a glance at Jed. She'd never heard him addressed as 'Mr Cassius', but he looked comfortable with it.

'Imelda, thanks for fitting us in. This is Tamara.'

Imelda zoomed her blinding smile in on Tamara. 'Welcome to Grand Manor, Tamara. I hope you enjoy your day with us. I'm going to pass you both over to Kristi and she'll look after you.' She glanced again at Jed, as if checking for approval and waved forward a young woman with a shiny chestnut bob above the black of her tailored dress. Then Kristi wafted them through one of the doors and along a corridor and Tamara was reminded of visiting Lie Low, where she was always courteously, but firmly, escorted around.

They stepped into a bright garden room where sunshine filtered by muslin blinds fell on Lloyd Loom chairs with turquoise-striped cushions. There were other guests almost all attired in white robes and turquoise flip-flops.

Tamara exclaimed in delight. 'Oh! Are we having a spa day?'

'That's right. A visit is one of the perks of my job and I decided to take advantage of it when you failed to win one on the scratch card. I haven't done anything like this, so it's a bit of an adventure for me.' Jed pulled a mock-apprehensive face.

Kristi fetched them coffee and waterproof turquoise bags marked 'Grand Manor' discreetly in gold. 'Shall I sit down with you and we'll schedule your treatments?'

'Great.' Tamara smiled but, inwardly, she sighed. Experience told her that booking ahead was crucial to avoid the frustration of finding that everything you wanted was booked out. Still, if Jed had got a freebie through Mr Hilton, she couldn't complain.

But it only took a few happy minutes for Tamara to realise that the 'platinum package' Jed had arranged was a far cry from the spa days to which she'd occasionally treated herself. 'Platinum' seemed to signify that all she had to do was ask and a treatment was arranged – massage, facial, manicure, pedicure, wraps, mud infusion and whatever she could fit into the day. Mentally, she rubbed her hands in delight, even as she laughed at Jed making it clear that he didn't want to end up with his nails painted or his eyebrows plucked.

Kristi ran through a medical questionnaire with each of them, then smiled her bright professional smile. 'If you'd like to come with me, I'll show you to your changing facilities and then to the treatment reception, as your first treatment, the back massage, will be in twenty minutes.' She glided them along thickly carpeted corridors to individual wood-panelled cubicles about four times the size of any Tamara had encountered before. In the turquoise bag, she discovered a black tankini, flip-flops and a white towelling robe. There were even ponytail elastics and hairgrips for her to pile up her hair, and facial wipes to take off her make-up. A locker stood in the corner and the same key fitted that and the cubicle. Tamara flung off her clothes and wriggled into the neat black costume and white robe.

She stepped out to find Jed lounging on a wicker sofa in his robe, as if he expected handmaidens to appear at any moment, strong downy legs crossed comfortably at the ankles. 'I feel like an A-lister,' she said, lightly, to hide how disconcerting she found the sight of his bare chest in the V of the robe. 'I shall expect the paparazzi to be waiting outside.'

His eyes flickered as they took her in. 'We'll leave by a secret exit to confuse them.'

Kristi showed them along more carpeted corridors and put them in the hands of Steffi, who took them through to a warm room with two massage tables covered in fine fabrics. For an instant, Tamara halted. Steered smoothly into the Grand Manor experience, she hadn't given a moment's thought to what being on a spa day with Jed meant. Past spa days – spent in a less grand manner than at Grand Manor – had always been girlie affairs, when stripping off various bits of yourself felt comfortable. She hadn't considered that she'd come up close with a body she hadn't actually been personal with. Uncertainty flitted through her like butterflies finding nowhere to settle. 'We're doing this together?'

Steffi paused. 'You're on the couples platinum, aren't you?'

Jed pulled an apologetic face at Tamara. 'Sorry. I didn't

think through "couple" very well. Do you want me to go to another room?'

'That can be arranged,' said Steffi, obviously used to pandering to clients. 'But this doesn't have to be a "couply" experience.' And she pulled a white curtain between the two couches.

Tamara relaxed. 'That'll be OK.' Steffi left the area while Tamara removed her robe and top, to slide herself between the layers of filmy fabric on the couch. On the other side of the curtain she was aware of movement. Then silence. Her skin prickled to think of Jed half naked, probably thinking of her, half naked …

'What are they going to do?' he hissed.

Tamara stifled a giggle at the apprehension in his voice. 'They're going to slather us in oil and stroke us.'

'Oh.' The apprehension faded. 'That sounds … interesting.'

A knock at the door heralded the return of Steffi with another therapist, who Steffi introduced as Brodie, then sent to Jed's side of the curtain.

Steffi asked a few questions about skin sensitivity, explained what the massage would include, and then stationed herself behind Tamara's head. Tamara closed her eyes and soon lost herself in Steffi's smooth hands working almond oil scented with jasmine over her shoulders and décolleté. And, most of the time, she kept her mind on whichever part of her body was being massaged, rather than wondering which part of Jed was being worked on by Brodie.

Perhaps taking her cue from her client, Steffi worked almost silently, whereas Jed kept Brodie in low-voiced conversation. It took a few minutes for Tamara to realise that, lazy and casual as he sounded, Jed, with his capable mind, was actually talking Brodie gently through her experience of working at Grand Manor and how it compared to where she'd worked in the past.

'I like it here.' Brodie was all positivity. 'Imelda's particular about staff standards and the conditions are great.'

'What about difficult clients? Any boozy footballers or inappropriate politicians?'

Brodie was diplomatic. 'You meet all sorts but we're usually lucky with our guests. They come to relax rather than to give us trouble.'

'Do you get anybody famous?'

'We get all sorts,' she repeated vaguely. 'Would you like to turn over?'

And, in a few moments, Steffi, too, suggested, 'If you'd like to turn over …?' holding up a sarong in shades of gold and turquoise between her eyes and Tamara's body in professional discretion. Then it was Tamara's back that was subjected to the long slow sweeps of Steffi's hands, forearms and elbows. She'd asked for a hot stone massage, too, and lay comatose while preparations were made. Then, ouch, slightly hot to begin with, and firm, the hardness of the stones pushed into her muscles, chasing away any knots as they began their delicious release.

On the other side of the curtain, conversation stepped up. 'Ow! That's hot!'

'The stones will soon lose their heat,' said Brodie soothingly.

'OW!' said Jed, again. 'Are you seriously rubbing me with stones?'

Brodie sounded as if she was trying not to laugh. 'This is how hot stone therapy's usually done.'

'Not man enough?' Tamara cooed.

Pause. A sigh. 'Go on then.'

At the end of the treatment, Steffi and Brodie slipped from

the room almost noiselessly, to give them the opportunity to rouse themselves and rearrange their clothing, leaving behind them faint pan-pipes music and the sound of Tamara's and Jed's breathing.

'You were interrogating poor Brodie,' Tamara accused, without opening her eyes.

Jed sounded equally somnolent. 'I look out for Mr H's interest. That's my job.'

'Oh. So you're at work, today?'

'No. But it seems only fair to take the opportunity to check the place out while we're enjoying a freebie.'

She cracked open her eyes to peep at the thin white curtain that separated them. 'I have trouble getting a handle on what exactly your job is. One minute you seem like a modern-day butler, with a few herdsman duties thrown in, then people are calling you Mr Cassius and you're scoping out one of Mr Hilton's business interests so upscale it's almost out of the atmosphere.'

'I do whatever Mr H needs me to do, whether that concerns his household or his businesses. He pays me to look after his interests and make his life comfortable. I don't have a title or a clearly defined role.'

'The general manager of this posh venue calls you "Mr", so I think the staff see your role as defined enough.'

'Only in that they know I work closely with Mr H. Knowing that, they think it's best not to hack me off in case I have a word in the ear of the boss.'

She grinned. 'So are people going to start calling me Miss Rix because I'm working closely with Emilia? Maybe they'll start buying me flowers and chocolates and hope I'll say nice things about them?'

A heartbeat. Then Jed said, 'I don't think it's quite the same.'

'In what way?' And then, when he didn't answer, 'I

suppose you see Mr H as the one with the power because he's the one who earned the money?' The idea didn't sit comfortably and she knew that it had rung in her voice.

Jed answered with a neutral, 'No.' Then he turned the subject. 'Did you enjoy the massage? Is the stony bit always so hellishly uncomfortable?'

She stretched and sat up, swinging her legs around on the couch as she checked that the curtain was in place and reached for her tankini top. 'It was wonderful. Didn't you like it?'

'I wouldn't call it wonderful.' The rustling from his side of the curtain told her that he was up and about, too.

'Are you going to complain to Mr Hilton?' she teased. But then felt sudden compunction. She knew that discretion was a huge part of Jed's job, yet here she was interrogating him right in the heart of Mr Hilton's empire, where any old employee might be lurking. And Emilia might not have been happy to hear her relationship with her husband aired. It was her turn to change the subject. 'I'm really looking forward to the facial.'

He snorted. 'I'm going to pass on that. I'll hang out in the pool and just admire the results later.'

'I've booked manicure and pedicure, too, but I don't have to—'

'Do it. I can amuse myself. But there's a while before your next treatment, so do you want to show me what we do in a thermal spa?'

They found their way along the corridors, past other guests in sparkling white robes, drinking coffee, reading, or wandering off for their own treatments, until they reached the turquoise pool curled around rocks lavished with lush vegetation, and the thermal spa. Jed paused to read the etched glass description of the spa's delights. 'Candle pool, tropical rain room, mineral spa. What do you do with them all?'

Tamara was already pushing open the door into the heavy heated air. 'Sit, stand or float in them, depending. We'll start at the beginning and work our way around, shall we?' She felt a flutter of apprehension as they strolled past water features of pebbles and steel, anticipating the spa as a joint experience and feeling suddenly self-conscious. 'Here's the mineral spa. You just hang your robe on one of the hooks out here and go in.' She hesitated.

'Doesn't seem too difficult.' Apparently not sharing her self-consciousness, he discarded his robe. There seemed an awful lot of Jed and not a lot of black Lycra swimming shorts, which ended at mid-thigh but clung like a second skin. He waited expectantly. Trying not to feel clumsy and exposed she let her robe slip from her shoulders. As if unaware that there was now nothing much more than a couple of layers of form-hugging Lycra and a small expanse of thin air between them, she pulled open the door and entered the hot, moist, sharp-smelling steam room, her back prickling, almost able to feel his eyes on her rear view. She smiled at two women steaming gently on the other side of the small room and sank thankfully onto the hot stone bench – only to find that the walls were black and highly polished marble. She watched Jed's reflection sit down beside hers.

Slowly, he smiled. 'This is beginning to grow on me.' And then he propped his feet comfortably on the stone island in the middle of the room, tipped back his head and closed his eyes, giving Tamara the chance to get used to her lack of clothes – and check him out. His hair and skin were dampening in the cloying heat, his upper body definition impressive. She could pick out his muscles as if he were a diagram in her anatomy manual: biceps, triceps, deltoids, pectoralis major ...

When their advised ten minutes was up, Jed took her

hand to pull her to her feet. 'Come on, I want to see what happens in a tropical-storm room.'

The fluttering returned as their reflections glided across the black marble together, but she kept her voice even. 'I expect you get to stand in tropical rain. If there's hot or cold rain, I only do hot.'

By the time they'd been soaked by the tropical rain, while listening to thunder; floated in silence in the stillness of the candle room, where Tamara was seized by a fit of stifled giggles when he relaxed too much and slid suddenly off his shelf and disappeared under the water; visited a couple more detoxifying steam rooms and a lavender-scented sauna to try dry heat instead of damp heat, they felt it was time to brave the outdoor/indoor pool. Squinting, they waded into the sunshine down tiled steps, the water warm and silky, glistening off their skin. Dotted around the edges were various massage jets of water and they tried them all, laughing as the water pounded onto their shoulders or pummelled their backs, spraying the air with liquid diamonds.

Tamara was sorry when the time came to towel off and shrug into her robe and head off for her treatments. As she'd relaxed into enjoying Jed's company – and his proximity – her self-consciousness had been displaced by self-awareness, which wasn't the same thing at all. She'd been one giant buzz whenever his warm skin brushed hers. He was quite a specimen.

It was a couple of hours later when she emerged to meet him over lunch, beautifully manicured and pedicured, sporting tiger-stripe nails.

He nodded approvingly, putting down a black leather menu he'd been reading as he waited for her to show. 'I see you're into making statements.'

'Cool, aren't they?' She admired her hands with

satisfaction, her skin petal soft from being massaged and wrapped during the 'tender-care manicure'.

Lunch, a gorgeous buffet of salads, came with a tall frosted glass of champagne, which added to Tamara's sense of well-being. It was followed, after a respectable period stretched out on a lounger by the pool, by twenty minutes in the hot tub – she kept peeping at her amazing toenails to check the foils hadn't come off – where kinder jets of water tickled any lingering tension away. Beside her, Jed reclined in the whirlpool with his arms around the rim.

She let her head loll and her eyes shut. 'There's even a hair salon here.'

Jed grunted. 'Go for it, if you want.'

'But that will mean leaving you on your own again.'

His shoulder brushed hers, warm and wet, as he shrugged. 'I'll be fine.' Then he added, 'So long as you kiss me before you go.'

As there was nobody else in the hot tub right then, she let herself float briefly against his hot, wet skin while she pressed a soft kiss to the corner of his mouth and touched the spot with the tip of her tongue.

Unspeaking, Jed watched with hooded eyes as she rose from the warmth of the water. She took the steps carefully, not just in case of miss-stepping on the damp tiles but because the heat in his gaze had turned her knees to butter.

She was still thinking about him when she took her place in the hairdresser's chair as the salon chattered around her and, inspired by the power of his open admiration and the bubbly enthusiasm of her young, blonde, up-for-it stylist, Shellice, made a couple of bold choices. Amidst fragrances both perfumed and chemical, foil was soon spiking her hair as if she were a mini Statue of Liberty. When the colour had taken, Shellice stretched Tamara's hair above her head and chop-chop-chopped it, before blowing it dry with rakey fingers.

'Like it?' Shellice held a mirror up behind Tamara like an enormous silver coin, anticipation lighting her eyes.

Tamara gazed at her reflection. Colours, cut – fantastic. She looked like the product of an expensive avant-garde London salon.

'I love it. I *love* it,' she breathed. She sounded like Lyddie.

Jed, who had learned never to take a hot bath of any description for granted, remained in the whirlpool for a while after Tamara had left. He'd been incredibly aware of her, her shoulders gleaming white above the roiling water. Those tiger-stripe nails pleased him; she suited ornamentation. In another culture, he could imagine her being hung with pearls or her contours swirled with henna. Her sculpted body in a wet swimming costume almost took away his reason. He'd always thought of yoga as exercise for cissies and wusses, but having his retinas scorched by her mega-toned contours had made him revise his ideas. And made him strive to keep his gaze above her neck for fear of developing a colossal hard-on – not easily disguised in swimming trunks. A hot, heavy hard-on was a familiar sensation since the adult Tamara had marched into his life.

In one of the steamy smelly rooms – he forgot which, there were two or three, floral, spicy, mineral, indistinguishable, uncomfortable, although he'd pretended to lie back and enjoy it like everyone else, while forming the private opinion that a steam room was probably the nearest thing a man would get to a hot flush – she'd performed stretches as they'd talked, pulling her straight legs up to her nose, then uncoiling to curl her spine in the opposite direction, a look of gentle pleasure on her face. A face not one bit disappointing without make-up; milky and with the faintest trace of freckles. He'd had to look away. Had to look back. Right on the pain/pleasure threshold, he'd gripped the stone bench to prevent himself from reaching out to all that gorgeousness and running his hands over it, right there in public. There were other women aplenty wafting around the place, some in costumes much skimpier than Tamara's, but there wasn't one there to touch her.

Don't think about touching her.

The inside/outside pool had been more fun, playing in the massage jets, which were so strong that they'd made his skin itch. Not like the back massage given by Brodie. That had been good, apart from those stupid stones. He wondered how Tamara was at delivering massage. Wow. Hold that thought. No, think about it later when either properly dressed or alone …

His musings were disturbed by a young couple joining him in the hot tub. Through his lashes, he watched them settle their twenty-something bodies. They glanced at him, but when he made no acknowledgement they began a conversation about their postgraduate studies.

He listened, soaking in information. Never having been in the university system, he liked to know roughly how it worked because ignorance was seldom bliss. The girl, apparently, had almost decided on a post grad diploma, rather than a PGCE. But the boy felt that to add a PGCE to his First might keep his parents off his back, though he didn't think he'd ever actually teach – because, really, why would he want to spend all day with *children* – but he liked the look of the course.

With a surge of impatience, Jed categorised him as a lighthouse in the desert – bright, but no fucking use.

He listened as the girl dissected, with patronising sympathy, the hoops one of their friends was leaping through to work his way through his post grad studies via two jobs, a bursary, a loan and an overdraft.

Jed tried to picture her catlike self-satisfaction

disintegrating if he told her how lucky their friend was to have that life choice. How impossible it was to attend university at all if you were living outside the system. Just giving the address of the squat on an application form would have had the potential to draw the attention of 'the tax' and 'the social' on everyone existing in the squat alongside him, who, like him, were living under society's radar. Anyway, the front door had had a board screwed over the place where the letter flap and number ought to be and no handle. They'd all used the back door, through a filthy little yard, and left the locked front door to acquire a subtle empty-house, swollen-shut air of neglect.

Jed sighed and stretched, fleetingly attracting the notice of the twenty-somethings as he stood up. The girl smiled, her gaze swooping over his arms and chest, before she returned to her earnest reflection on her future as she saw it, which, he was pretty certain, wouldn't include worrying where her next mouthful of food would come from or how to survive nights so cold that she couldn't sleep for shaking. He almost sat himself down in the warm water again at the mere memory. Instead, he stepped over the side and into the comfortable life he lived now, taking a fluffy white towel from a stack, pulling on the cloud-soft robe.

He was here at Grand Manor. In luxury. Warm. Clean. Civilised.

And now he had to amuse himself until Tamara appeared again. He heaved a sigh. He was beginning to realise why he'd always left sampling the spa to Manny. A spa day might sound hedonistic, but it was boring him out of his skull.

He mooched back past the thermal spa. From the point of view of scoring points with Tamara the day seemed a screaming success, but he hadn't anticipated how much of it would be spent apart because he wouldn't have subjected himself to a manicure and a pedicure, even if it meant being in Tamara's presence. And what the hell happened during a facial? He had an image of gloops of cream or maybe crushed fruit. No. Definitely, no. So while she'd been happily closeted with beauty therapists, he'd swum thirty lengths of the indoor pool and investigated yet more massage jets and the underwater gym machines, which were quite fun. He'd admired the waterfall. Then, he'd dried off and tried a t'ai chi class, which had been OK, but he couldn't understand anybody doing it more than once in a lifetime. It was hardly kung fu.

He wouldn't be human if he hadn't noticed that he was attracting quite a few glances and even all-out eye contact from some of the women guests, but his preoccupation with Tamara made that of only passing interest. And the unnerving feeling of men being outnumbered ten to one discouraged him even from the gym room, which would normally have pulled him in for an hour's hard workout.

He turned back to assess the pool area's visual impact. Pleasing colours. Turquoise, cream, white and beige. Lots of glass looking out onto the gardens, looking up into the sky. Loungers with striped cushions, generally occupied either by a person or a proprietary robe. Palms and plants. Pebbles. Chairs of woven stuff. It was a gorgeous luxurious environment but he'd come to an important conclusion: spas were bizarre. He just didn't belong in this dressing gown club.

He needed something to do.

Imelda looked up when Jed knocked and lounged into her office. Her smile was wary, rather than welcoming. 'Everything all right?'

He dragged one of the black-leather tubular-framed chairs from beside the wall and relocated it in front of her desk. 'I thought I might as well touch base with you while I'm here – so long as you don't have appointments this afternoon?'

She looked almost regretful that she had to say no. Apprehensively she added, 'Aren't you enjoying the spa?'

He shrugged. 'Tamara's having a fantastic time, so I thought I'd leave her to it for a couple of hours. She's in the hair salon. Can you please get them to ring here when she's finished, so I can meet up with her?'

'Of course.'

Jed waited until she'd made the call. 'So. Tell me how our friend James Cochrane is doing.'

Imelda looked twitchy. 'He's still employed here.'

'Of course.' It was his job to know things like that.

'Though I wouldn't have blamed Mr Hilton for getting rid of him. I can't think what James was doing, getting mixed up with those stupid protestors. I told him how lucky he was to keep his job. Most employers would have put him in the hands of the police.'

'But we preferred not to let him drop out of sight.'

Imelda shrugged. 'Well, he's doing exactly what he was doing last time you asked. He's a personal trainer and he gives classes in Pilates, spin, cardio and fat burning. Does his job, he's punctual and respectful, the clients like him.'

'OK. Let's talk about the Grand Manor operation, then. How do you stop people from just wandering in and helping themselves to the facilities?' Jed settled back in his seat to listen to Imelda explain something that he'd already observed was impossible to prevent without aggravating the paying clientele, but would need brass balls to carry out. It was way more interesting than gloop on his face.

More than two hours passed before Imelda took the call to say that Tamara had left the salon, by which time she was looking a bit frayed and couldn't disguise the relief in her eyes when Jed jumped to his feet. His conscience twanged because it hadn't been his intention to descend on her like a messenger from the Great God Hilton. He knew that Mr H's sombre and reflective presence intimidated employees and that Jed, by extension, could be seen as a dark angel. Imelda probably thought that his visiting with Tamara hid some sinister agenda, as he usually gave any part of Hilton Kingdom due notice before he turned up. But it probably wasn't diplomatic to explain that being a client had been just too brain atrophying, once Tamara in a swimming costume had been removed from his sight.

'Everything looks great,' he said, to compensate for some of the stress. 'Your figures are good, your clients look happy and I like the staff I've met. Sorry to spoil your afternoon.'

'Not at all,' Imelda said, unconvincingly, but her shoulders relaxed for the first time since Jed had invited himself into her office.

Jed set off to find Tamara. When he saw her emerging from the changing area, he faltered mid-stride.

She giggled, her hair glowing every colour of autumn in the light from the large windows that ran down one side of the corridor. 'Is it too freaky?'

He paced slowly around her. 'It's fantastic. You just took my breath away.'

She beamed from under the shimmering, streaky, artfully tousled haircut. 'The stylist here is amazing. And the colourist.'

He lifted his hand and let her hair slither, like strands of silk, through his fingers. 'It's really cool. You look like a tiger.'

'Good. That's the idea. The colourist saw my nails and suggested we go for a theme.' She linked his arm and brushed a kiss on his cheek. 'Thanks for bringing me to the

Grand Manor. I love it. Now I've had this done I don't want to spoil it with more treatments, though.'

'There's no reason for you to have more if you don't want them.' *Result!* 'We can grab a coffee and a comfy sofa instead.' He turned her face so that he could brush her lips with his. Everything in him was telling him that this woman was going to mean something.

Even if he wasn't yet certain what.

'Dinner?' Jed suggested as they strapped themselves back into his mini Batmobile when they were ready to head home.

Tamara felt as sweet and gooey as marshmallow from being spoiled and pampered all day. In fact, marshmallow with syrup on. 'I know a place. I'll put it in your satnav.' She reached over, enjoying his intake of breath as she intruded on his space, and tapped in *PE6 9ZZ* and *39*.

'At the end of the road, turn left,' suggested the satnav woman. Jed put the car into gear and followed her directions, back along the lane, back down the A1 and around the Peterborough parkways.

An hour later, the satnav woman declared, 'You have reached your destination.' And they were outside Tamara's house.

He killed the engine, his smile slow and hot.

'Lemon chicken OK?' Tamara flicked off her seatbelt.

'Sounds great.' He followed her to her front door, waiting while she turned the key with suddenly unsteady fingers. Her pulse seemed to think that bringing Jed home was an excuse to kick off like a train, though she and yoga generally had her heart rate under control. She took a couple of deep breaths in and out of her nose, letting her abdomen inflate, settling the butterflies down to a gentle flutter instead of a Zumba boot camp.

'Come on in.' Her voice actually shook. She hadn't invited a date to this house except for Max.

But Jed seemed relaxed, settling on a stool to watch her work, apparently content in idle conversation. 'They were only just building this estate when I left.'

'And people like my parents still call it "the new village".' Tamara chopped apple, onion and celery to stuff a couple of chicken breasts, zested a lemon, made a paste of it with the lemon juice and slathered it on each piece of chicken, before sliding the tray into the oven.

She put the water on to boil, ready for the rice, and began to wash coriander leaves, which, she hoped, would take away the smell of onion on her hands. 'Today was awesome. Thank you for letting me share your freebie.'

'The pleasure was all mine.'

The memory of being in the spa together brushed its fingers across the back of her neck: his back view in swimming trunks – deltoid and trapezius muscles firm, no 'love handles' around his lats, and those glutes …

Well. Good arse, basically.

And knowing he'd had the opportunity to check her out in exactly the same way made her insides skip about. The day had been a sensuous experience and she had a sliding feeling of certainty that it wasn't over yet. It would piss her mother off big time if/when she found out, but Tamara would cross that bridge – or be hurled to the troll that lived beneath – when she came to it.

They ate at the bar in the kitchen, the nearest thing to a dining table that she owned, facing one another over the fragrant meal and a cold bottle of Pouilly Fuissé she'd been saving. She couldn't remember what she'd been saving it for, but tonight seemed to be a good time to uncork it – with the highly efficient corkscrew he'd left tied to her door, of course.

The look in Jed's eyes was giving her some idea of what Gabe had meant about a man looking at her as if he wanted to take to her to bed for a fortnight, and that was not an occasion for cheap wine.

He ate slowly, savouring the flavours. She sent a mental thank you to the 'fast but impressive' section of her favourite recipe website, that the rice had turned out perfectly pale green and fluffy and the chicken succulent, inside a toasted lemon jacket.

'That was good,' she sighed, when, finally, the chicken was no more and they'd both had second helpings of rice. 'I'll switch on the coffee machine.'

He cleared as she measured out the coffee, super aware of him, moving in and out of her space; his breathing, his heat, the shape and height of him. This man she'd had a thing about when he was the village teenage heart-throb and she was still the child's side of puberty.

And Lyddie ... Her heart flopped sadly and her movements slowed. It wasn't as if Jed was Lyddie's ex-husband or ex-lover and nor, she acknowledged with a sad frown, was he going to be Lyddie's future husband or lover. That kind of normal stuff was off Lyddie's radar and the only comfort was that Lyddie showed no signs of knowing what she'd missed.

Warm arms slid suddenly around her and she jumped.

Jed's voice was low, vibrating along her skin. 'Suddenly you look as if you're watching a weepy movie.' His cheek brushed hers and she could feel the beginnings of his stubble.

When she smiled it made the contact firmer, warmer, weakening her knees. 'A moment's weirdness about Lyddie.'

'Ah.' He kissed her ear. 'Guilt?'

She let herself rest back against him, the back of her head fitting comfortably on the scoop of his collarbone. 'I think it must be. My intellect tells me that I'm not hurting her, but my conscience isn't quite convinced.'

His arms tightened. 'Because you're used to looking out for her. You know—' He hesitated. 'She didn't even remember my name the other day, let alone the teenage snogging in the cornfield.'

She let her eyes close. 'I know.' The coffee machine began to envelope them in a coffee cloud. The warmth of his front was firm down the length of her back, his breath stirring against her skin.

'You're not going to let ancient history stop what's happening here, are you?'

Her throat dried. 'What is happening?'

He turned her to face him. 'I think we're getting close. Soon, I'm hoping we're going to get closer.' He kissed her cheekbone and then her lips, lighting a fire low in her stomach.

She fitted herself against his body, so right and tight, rising on tiptoes to brush against him with her breasts.

He groaned and stroked her tongue with his, his stubble rough and sexy against her face, his kiss an open-mouthed caress. Through one of the artfully placed rips on her thigh, he ran a fingertip across her skin. 'I've wanted to touch you all day.'

Slowly, like a question, his fingers moved upward and inside her clothes. Unhurriedly, his hands explored the planes of her back, while his lips moved down the crook of her neck, her throat, her shoulder. Slowly. Slooooowly.

Tamara let her head fall back, unable to think of anything but the heat of his mouth, the scrape of his teeth. Then she was pulling at fabric, helping him free her of her T-shirt and his fingers made short work of her bra catch, the laciness sliding off and away, as if on a breath of wind. The cooler air danced across her skin for only moments before his hands moved up and his mouth moved down. She clung to him, stroking his shoulders, as they shifted beneath her hands and he kissed and licked, nipped and teased.

The fastening of her jeans surrendered without a fight and his fingers were soon sliding inside. 'You feel fantastic.' He ran his thumbs across the soft skin of her belly, making her twitch. Smoothly, he pushed the jeans down her thighs. Then he grasped her under her arms and lifted her onto the kitchen counter and it seemed like only moments before she was completely out of her jeans – rips and all – which was pretty impressive, considering how tight she wore them. She pulled him closer, heart thundering, breath coming in bumps, wrapping her arms and legs around his hot body, rubbing against him like a pole dancer, on fire, wanting, wanting, aching and heavy for him. He was breathing like a truck, but he moved slowly, nibbling her shoulders, trailing his fingers over her.

Slowly, he explored. Her naked breasts tingled at the heat of his mouth followed by the chill of him blowing softly on her skin. Everywhere he touched became pleasure. 'Tamara,' he murmured. And his phone rang.

She gripped his shoulders. For five seconds she thought he was going to let the call go to voicemail, as his tongue shivered across her lips. Then he sighed. 'Sorry. I can't ignore that particular ring tone.'

He pulled his phone from his pocket. 'Yes, what?' He listened for several moments. Then, 'You're kidding! I only checked up on him this afternoon. Little shit.' He pulled Tamara against him, his heart pounding through the cotton of his shirt. 'OK. Yes. OK. Got it. Proceed with that.' He stabbed at his phone screen and thrust the phone back into his jeans. Then he heaved a huge frustrated sigh. 'I'm really sorry. I am *so* sorry. I can't fucking believe it. Something's happened and I have to deal with it for Mr H.'

Tamara stared up into his face. 'I thought you were off duty?' Her heart was slowing and she couldn't quite believe that, from being hot and hard and pulsing against her, he was going to leave her hanging.

He groaned, lifting her from the counter, her legs still around his waist. 'It's not that kind of job.' He buried his face in her, sucking her skin, holding her so hard that she could hardly breathe for the feel of him. He held her for a second, then, slowly, set her down on her feet, kissing his way across her neck and face. 'This sucks. But I do have to go.'

And he actually stepped away.

On a wave of embarrassed rage she snatched up her bra and top and wriggled back into them, face burning, fingers clumsy as she yanked her way back into jeans, significantly extending a couple of the rips.

'Sorry,' he repeated, helplessly. 'If it wasn't important—'

''Bye,' she said, tightly.

A big sigh, a hard kiss that she tried to thrust away, and he was picking up his car keys. And leaving.

Chapter Sixteen

Jed drove back to Lie Low, slamming the stick through the gears as if it was the car's fault that he'd had to leave Tamara half naked and wanting, while he went to attend to more problems caused by that bastard, James Cochrane. Reaching the lane up to Lie Low he stamped on the brake, slewed his car across the road and set off on foot up the grass verge at an irritated lope, peeling off into the spinney where the dusk was rendered almost dark by the canopy of leaves.

He stopped. Listened. Stepped slowly in the shadows. Paused, listened. Paused, listened. Heard a low peep, like a bird setting out on its nightly hunt. Moving towards it, he placed his feet as carefully as a cat across the carpet of leaves and pine needles. Halted. Waiting.

Then the shape of a man detached himself from a shadow and became Manny. 'Think we've missed him. I heard a car start up on the main road a couple of minutes before you turned up. Fucking nearly impossible to move silently through this terrain.'

Jed stared around, trying to pierce the gloom. 'What are we supposed to do if we get hold of him? The spinney's not Mr H's property and wandering around it on a summer's evening isn't a crime.'

'Mr H wanted us to have a word.'

Jed turned back towards where he'd left his car. 'I don't see what good that would do. Probably wind him up and make him more determined.'

'Yeah. But the boss is a frightened man, isn't he?' Manny snapped. 'I don't want Cochrane round here, either, hanging around where he's not wanted.'

By the time Jed had retrieved his car and driven up to the house, Manny and Mr H were in Manny's office checking security footage. Manny was dressed in black jeans and a long-sleeved T-shirt. Mr H's hair was slicked straight back from a forehead that wore a frown above his glasses.

Jed joined them at the PC dedicated to the CCTV. 'Have you located him on camera?'

Manny scrolled back through shots and time frames, his jaw set. 'There. That's him, isn't it?' He pointed at the screen and a shadow bearing a pale human face. 'Prowling around the fence triggered the motion sensor cameras. I gave him some room by going over the fence further along, but he took off.'

Jed zoomed in on the watchful features of James Cochrane, Mr H's nemesis. 'That's him. Wonder what he's up to? According to Imelda he's working all his shifts and keeping his nose clean at Grand Manor.' He glanced at Mr H, whose pallor illustrated that he was letting this uninvited visitor shake his composure. 'Is Emilia aware …?'

His employer shook his head. 'No. I don't know whether I should tell her or if I'd be stirring everything up for no good reason. She seems reasonably settled here.'

Neither Jed nor Manny returned an opinion. Mr H was the boss. If his wishes were that Emilia wasn't told that James Cochrane was skulking about, she wouldn't be told. With irritated little clicks of the computer mouse, Manny put a marker on the segment of digital images so that it could be easily relocated and then reset the image to real-time footage, moving from camera to camera in a programmed sweep.

Mr H sighed. 'We'll let sleeping dogs lie, for now.'

'Right,' agreed Jed and Manny. Mr H left the room, the picture of a man with something on his mind.

'Not happy,' Manny observed. He'd relaxed in his chair a little, now, as if his adrenaline rush was draining away.

'Nope.' If Jed were Mr H he would never have allowed the present situation to develop. Mr H was living on a knife-edge, just waiting for the worst to happen, trying to manage the unmanageable.

'You don't look that happy, either, little bro.' Manny cocked an eyebrow. 'You came in with a face like a slap.'

Jed tried to smooth out his scowl. 'The call came at a bad time.'

Manny let out a crack of laughter. 'It seems to be the law that when you get a red you're drinking, humping or winning a poker game.'

Jed hung his jacket over the back of a chair without commenting, running his fingers through his hair to fish out a couple of leaves and a small sludge of cobweb.

'And you don't smell of drink,' Manny continued, ruminatively. 'Win much money?'

Jed flicked the debris from his hair into the bin with distaste.

Manny grinned. 'I'm thinking of asking Tamara Rix out. She's hot, don't you think?'

Jed glared at him.

'And I already have her number …' Then Manny's eyes began to dance. 'Don't worry, I'm joking. If you hadn't made it obvious that she's on your menu, I would've already hit on her. Are you heading back to her, now?'

Jed glanced at his watch. It was only half an hour since he'd left Tamara and he was screamingly conscious that she hadn't been pleased with being pushed aside, just when she was so much on his menu that he was about to lick her all over. Would it be better to ring her to apologise, or just turn around and go back to her house? If he rang she might think he wasn't making much effort, but if he turned up she might think he was simply expecting to take up where he'd left off now there was nothing more important to do. No woman wanted to be made to feel that convenient. And he felt a deep need to shower away the residue of his trip through the undergrowth. 'I'll ring.'

But even as he pulled out his phone, Mr H trod softly back into the room, worry furrowing his forehead. 'Maybe we ought to think about relocating again.' He lowered himself into a big, green leather chair.

Jed returned his phone to his pocket and dropped into one of the other chairs, as Manny perched himself on the desk. 'It's always an option,' Jed offered, diplomatically. He didn't let his voice betray the clutch of dismay at the idea of moving out of the area. Away from Tamara Rix. 'If you think that it would prevent a repetition of this evening.'

Mr H's dark eyes swivelled to his. 'I don't suppose it would, really, would it? He could find us again. And Emilia's happy here.'

'In fact, she seems to be settling down, with her alpacas and her yoga instructor.' At a sudden smirk from Manny, Jed wished he hadn't mentioned the yoga instructor.

Mr H looked marginally cheered. 'True. If it wasn't for Cochrane turning up tonight ... well, life would be a lot simpler.' He ruminated for several moments. 'And you still think that it's better to keep employing him? I feel as if the little shit must be laughing at me.'

'I can see your point. And you might think that him turning up tonight invalidates my view that keeping him at Grand Manor is helping keep tabs on him. But, yes, I do think it's better to continue to keep him on the payroll because it goes some way towards monitoring him.'

Mr H shifted impatiently. He looked every one of his fifty-eight years tonight. 'I don't suppose we can put a tail on the man night and day, can we?'

Manny stepped into the conversation. 'If you're looking for a factual answer, yes. My skill set includes that kind of work and I have the contacts to arrange twenty-four-hour surveillance, if that's what you want. Or we can start relocating you, if you decide on that.'

'If that's what you want,' Jed agreed. He kept his voice neutral. Mr H didn't pay him to pass judgement. He paid him to be unquestioningly on Mr H's side, to provide him with information, to be his wingman, to look after his interests. It was immaterial if Jed thought putting James Cochrane under constant surveillance was the action of a desperate player and relocating, easy as Manny made that sound, was pointless. The guy with the money got to choose how the games were played.

Tom Hilton's brows drew together. 'Being the one to provide his salary does stick in my craw.'

'Then I'll find a way to get rid of him.'

The dark eyes sharpened. 'But you don't think it's a good idea?'

'If he leaves Grand Manor we'd have a harder job keeping tabs on him without setting up some form of surveillance. I'd rather have him in the tent pissing out, than outside the tent pissing in.'

Mr H gave a bark of laughter. 'I can always rely on you, Jed. Let's end the day on a few whiskies, shall we? In my study.'

As Manny nodded goodnight, Jed didn't betray his frustration as he followed his employer to the study to assume the role of barman at the drinks fridge hidden inside an oak cabinet. He and Mr H shared a love of whisky served cold, but unadulterated by ice. As they were in Mr H's sitting room, it would no doubt be something that cost hundreds of quid a bottle – not that Jed could taste the difference between that and the Glenmorangie in his own drawer.

He took out two glasses. If Mr H needed a drinking partner there was no way he'd be phoning Tamara this evening. Mr H was quite capable of drinking all night and then going to work on just a catnap in the back of the Merc, as Manny drove him to a morning meeting.

He'd have to wait and see her tomorrow. While Mr H talked he'd keep half his mind separate and uninfected by James Cochrane, holding on to the image of Tamara hot and sighing against him, her cool tiger hair hanging down her back and her sexy tiger-striped nails pricking against his skin, her expression one of horny intent.

It would be too late to phone her when Mr H had finished with him, and his blood alcohol would be too high to drive. He'd take the image of Tamara to bed with him and think of her hot body in the cool sheets. It was all he had right now.

But next time would be different.

Chapter Seventeen

Jed had not had enough sleep. He'd reached his bed so recently that he should be hunkering down for several more hours. Instead, he reached for the phone that was plugged into the charger beside him. The white figures told him it was 06.50. He rolled back against the pillows, his brain feeling unpleasantly as if it were revolving inside his skull and scraping the sides.

When would it be late enough to text? You never knew. People kept their phones on by the side of their beds and then complained bitterly when a message or call woke them up.

Give it ten minutes. The number should begin with a seven. He clamped a hand to his forehead to anchor his brain, closed his eyes and let his limbs go heavy, hoping his body clock would throw him a quick nap. About ten minutes would be good.

But instead, he thought about Tamara and the shambles of the evening before. He'd been savouring her, savouring what was to come, congratulating himself on successfully taming his instinct to wrench off the rest of her lacy underwear and plunge himself inside her … then came that bastard phone call. He opened an eye. 06.53. His head pulsed. He shut the eye again.

Trouble was, you didn't plan a mega-date like a day at Grand Manor spa and not plan for sex. It would be wrong to count on it, but you packed condoms in your wallet and let your imagination dwell on the best scenario. You told yourself that, if it happened, you'd remember your manners and *not rush it*. And even when the Tamara you'd been aching for wrapped her toned legs around your waist, you kept telling yourself that fast and hard was not the best way to go. 06.57.

And at least that bastard phone call hadn't arrived when they'd passed the delicious point of no return. Wouldn't THAT have been frustrating? To be faced with the choice of withdrawing, or making rapidly for the winning post – no doubt while she was still a mile behind. He cringed at either possibility. How to look a total freak. How to invite scorn, as well as fury. It had been bad enough having to ignore his raging hard-on and disappear. 06.59. He'd never been involved in something so frustrating, yet so pleasurable. Or so pleasurable, yet so frustrating. Shitbag, James Cochrane.

At 07.00 he reached for his phone and sent a text message to Tamara Rix. *Incredibly incredibly sorry.*

Waited. No reply.

With a sigh he gave up on sleep, rolling cautiously to the side of the bed, letting his brain keep pace with his skull. In the bathroom he squinted to protect his poor aching eyeballs from the unreasonably white tiles and shatteringly shiny chrome and decided to give his morning twenty minutes on the cross trainer a miss. While the shower warmed, he took a long draft from the cold water tap, feeling his headache fractionally loosen its talons as he stepped into the steaming shower jet, hoping it could somehow seep in through his pores and wash the alcohol from his blood.

Soaping himself, he thought about Tamara's skin, which had been as soft as … He searched for an adequate simile. He supposed a poet would say rose petals or spun silk but, hey, he was just a bloke. To him, her skin felt like woman and he liked it. And he liked her siren hair. And the tautness of her body.

He stood under the shower for a long time, but when he finally emerged naked into his bedroom there still had been no reply from Tamara.

*   *   *

Tamara had no choice but to turn up for the session at Lie Low. She was in a professional relationship with Emilia and if she'd ended up feeling totally stupid at being left on the kitchen counter like a half-dressed turkey, well, that was a problem she had with Jed, not Emilia. But it was a problem that made her unhappy.

To colour her mood blacker, last night Max had sent her a drunken text saying he was sorry he hadn't been in touch, but he was having a brilliant time out with his new colleagues. As she'd been in bed waiting for Jed to text or ring or return, her wrongful assumption that the text was going to be from him hadn't improved her mood.

But she'd decided not to let Jed see she minded, so drove through the gates and up the drive with her most professional face on and didn't even colour when Jed opened the front door as she climbed out of her car. It just bloody would be him and not Manny. 'Morning,' she said, breezing past him without making eye contact, her holdall slung over her shoulder. 'Is Emilia in the pool area? Shall I go straight through?'

His voice was soft. 'If we could just go into my office—'

Ignoring him, she chose the hallway that led to the pool, stalking past the white walls and the paintings hung in gorgeous frames.

Muttering under his breath, he caught her up. 'If we could just—'

'I know my way.' She worked at keeping her voice neutral. As if she was hardly acquainted with Jed Cassius. As if he hadn't cupped her breasts in his hands last night, kissed and licked and nibbled and— and *left*. As if she hadn't tossed and turned all night and then this morning received a single message. *Incredibly incredibly sorry.* Yes, she was sorry, too. Sorry to have been dumped like a toy stuffed in a cupboard when something better came along.

'I need to explain.' His voice was low.

'Last night would have been a good time. Not now. Emilia's waiting.' Tamara pressed on up the hall where it widened out to accommodate French doors that opened onto a paved area towards the back of the house. Into the next passage – if something eight feet wide could be termed a passage – she swung right towards the door to the pool. The back of her neck prickled with his presence, but she ploughed on. Then, as she reached for the door handle, she found herself suddenly swung away and somehow tucked between Jed and the wall.

His eyes were unnaturally bright. 'You're pissed off because I had to disappear at a delicate moment.'

'You think?'

He pressed closer, refusing to co-operate with her attempts to squirm away. 'I don't blame you, but if you won't listen now I'll just persist until you do. *Then*, if you're still pissed at me, I'll back off.'

She shrugged, as if she wasn't distracted by the pulse of his body against hers into losing the thread of her indignation.

'There was a prowler here, last night.'

Sharply, she looked up. 'In the house?'

'He didn't get that far. The cameras picked him up at the fence and he sneaked off when Manny tried to locate him. I arrived just too late to be any use.'

Tamara processed this new information, feeling her indignation melting. 'Could he have been one of the protestors?' Now that she wasn't actively trying to shove him away, her palms found a natural resting place on his biceps.

'He could have been anybody. But, in view of Mr H's history with certain people, the incident upset him. The prowler disappeared and I was about to phone you, when

Mr H asked me to join him in a nightcap.' He half smiled. His hair was sliding forward and he shook it back to maintain eye contact. 'And when he makes a request like that, my job is to say yes. His nightcaps can last most of the night – the guy has the constitution of a bull elephant. I've drunk about a gallon of coffee, but my head's rolling off my shoulders. I've showered twice and still feel as if I'm sweating whisky.'

She let herself smile. 'I wondered what it was.' In fact, all she could smell was shower gel and shampoo.

He stroked her hair back over her shoulder, his hand drifting on, down to the small of her back. 'I don't have the kind of job where I can ignore certain phone calls, or tell my boss I'm not interested when he wants to share a few drinks. I could have excused myself to the bathroom and texted you from there, but that felt tacky and wrong. I presumed you'd realise that I wouldn't get you half naked and then suddenly think of some unimportant little detail that I needed to clear up.'

'Possibly,' she acknowledged, feeling her lips curl up in a smile, her hips shifting to nestle against his.

'Believe me, it tortured me to leave. But torture occasionally finds its way into my job description. If I'm in the vicinity I'm never completely off duty, not if something significant happens. That's what Mr H pays me for and I can't promise it won't happen again. That's the first time since we came to Lie Low, but it cropped up a lot in the past.'

'When the protestors were making trouble, I presume.' It must feel horrible to have people out to get you, to be skulking around outside your home. It might make you anxious enough to stay up drinking whisky with one of the men you paid to keep you safe. But still, she added, 'You've got one hell of an inconvenient job.'

Jed's warm hands curved around her buttocks. 'Most of the time, it's a great job. You're one of the few things that has ever distracted me enough to make me wonder if it's worthwhile.' And his mouth came down on hers and she let her arms creep up around his neck as his kiss deepened, drawing her up on tiptoe to press against him.

Which was when the door to the pool area swung open. 'I saw your car draw up ages ago – *oh.*' Emilia stood in the doorway.

Tamara and Jed jumped apart. 'I—' But no pat explanation for coming into Emilia's home and kissing a member of staff sprang to Tamara's lips.

Silently, Emilia moved back.

Face burning, Tamara stepped through into the turquoise light of the pool area. The air felt hot and cloying, as if a storm was brewing.

Emilia snapped the door shut on Jed and stumped over to her pink practice mat. 'Can we get on?' Her face was shuttered.

Mortified, Tamara rolled out her own mat. She cleared her throat, searching for an appropriate apology, but Emilia clattered her crutches to the tiles and lowered herself onto her mat, rolling down on her back and closing her eyes.

It didn't seem as if she wanted to talk about it. Tamara cleared her throat again and sat cross-legged on her own mat. Deep breath. Out. Deep breath. 'Make sure you're comfortable,' she began, trying not to hear the tremor in her voice. 'Would you like the rolled up towel under your knee—'

'No, thank you.'

Tamara winced at Emilia's *froideur*. 'Then let yourself sink into your mat, think about your lower back – is it comfortable? And your shoulders, pull them down away from your ears. Let your abdomen rise and fall with the breath. A little deeper each time, until you're filling your lungs, filling them right up. Now we'll give our facial muscles a work out' — *which might get that frown off your face* — 'and relax that jaw' — *stop you grinding your teeth* — 'as tension can lead to headaches.'

The next hour crawled by. Emilia was about as responsive as she might be to an exercise class on the television, never making eye contact with Tamara or smiling or speaking. Twice, when asked a question she simply ignored it.

At the end of the session, Tamara expected to be sent straight home and/or sacked – neither of which would have been particularly unwelcome. Being so clearly on someone's shit list wasn't for her. Fourteen or fifteen hours of yoga a week usually did a pretty good job of keeping her chilled, but one hour of working with an Emilia who seemed bent on making her feel like a naughty kid, was tensing her neck like a spring.

After the final spinal twists, Emilia did manage to answer Tamara's 'Namaste' with one of her own.

Then Emilia climbed awkwardly to her feet, reached for her phone and rang Carrie, just as always. 'We'll have coffee out by the pond.' She slotted on her crutches and swung off outside, without checking to see if Tamara snatched up her things and followed.

The sunshine had returned to the summer today and the colourful garden was alive with birdsong. Between sweeps of velvet lawn, the garden was dotted with expensive-looking shrubs and dwarf trees, the kind with tortured limbs or long needles, destined to live their lives in artistic isolation so no ordinary plant should detract from their elegance.

Emilia waited to let Tamara catch up and then they made their way through rustic arches and past rockeries, over the little bridge that spanned the long, deep carp pond, the koi carp shadowing them hopefully, the movement of their oval mouths making them look as if they were muttering. Some of the koi were as big as a man's arm; palest gold to orange; white with red and black splashes; silver with brassy heads.

Near the fountain, Emilia halted. 'Could you bring a couple of those chairs up?' Tamara dragged over two heavy wooden seats that looked like thrones made from polished driftwood. They had been carved to look as if they had the feet of animals and they'd probably cost a fortune. Carrie glided up with a cafetière and tall glass coffee cups on a tray that unfolded its legs and became a table. She glanced at Emilia, received a nod of dismissal and glided off again.

Emilia propped her feet up on the bridge railing, where yolk-yellow lichen rosettes swirled across the silver oak. 'Tom's not home, nor Manny.'

'Right,' said Tamara, wondering why Emilia would share that with her.

With a perfectly manicured fingernail, Emilia began to prod at a pink-edged miniature weed that had found a home in the crack in the arm of her driftwood seat. 'But Jed being here's enough. Tom wants somebody near me all the time. He's watchful of me because of the security implications.'

'Right,' Tamara repeated, trying to find her feet in the conversation. 'Because of the protestors?'

Emilia looked up quickly. She smiled. 'Yes. But also … there's a wealth consideration.'

'Oh.' Tamara wondered just how much money a person had to have to attract a ransom deal. 'That's scary.' And rubbish so far as independence and freedom were concerned. Her heart thawed a little towards Emilia. OK, she'd been condemnatory in her silence today and maybe there was an element of poor-little-rich-girl in her manner, but a cage was a cage no matter how prettily gilded. Tamara would have hated not to be able to leave her little house and walk or drive wherever her will took her. 'The intruder last night must have worried you.'

Emilia's head jerked round. Her eyes locked on Tamara. 'What?'

Shit. Tamara halted. Jed probably shouldn't have told her about the intruder, discretion being so much a part of his job. He'd only been explaining why he'd abandoned her in a state of undress, but explaining this to Emilia, judging by her po-faced reaction to finding them in a clinch, would go down like a rat sandwich. 'I thought—' she stammered. 'Um, maybe I misunderstood.'

They stared at each other. 'Not you, too,' said Emilia softly. Tears welled in her dark eyes. 'I didn't think you'd be like them.'

'Like them?'

'Hiding things from me. Manipulating me. Keeping me stuck here.' Emilia sighed, turning away to stare blindly across the pond, past the fountain that the sunshine transformed into tinkling diamonds. She glanced behind her at the house, then swung back, eyes huge. 'I feel,' she began, fixing her gaze on Tamara with grim urgency. 'I feel ... as if I'll *die* if I don't get away from Tom Hilton.'

Chapter Eighteen

Strands of Emilia's hair escaped her ponytail and blew across her face. Her eyes were bleak. 'He won't let me go, of course.'

Tamara's stomach lurched at the despair in her voice. 'Can't you simply tell him you're not happy with your relationship?'

Emilia snorted a laugh. 'Tom doesn't react well to me wanting my own life. Being able to go where I want, with whoever I want to be with. A life like everyone else has.'

Tamara reached for the cafetière and poured the coffee. 'And have you thought of the possibilities? What you'd be facing?'

'Like how to get away, you mean? And how I'm going to live when I do? Yeah, they're the tough questions when you're dealing with a guy like Tom.'

'Why? How do you think he'll react?'

Hunching her shoulders, Emilia closed her eyes. 'Furiously,' she whispered. A tear trembled on her lower eyelid and she covered her face. 'I don't know. I don't know! I just know I can't bear it any more and sometimes I'm just so ... scared. You don't know what it's like, unless you've been controlled. I feel sick every time Tom gives me a certain look, knowing that when we're alone the shouting will start.' She wiped her eyes, sucking in air as if it were sharp and hurt her throat.

Tamara's heart expanded with sympathy. 'Everyone has the right to leave a relationship. You're an adult, free to—'

Emilia laughed, bitterly. 'You obviously don't have any idea about bullying and intimidation. About possessive men who treat you like a toy, a darling, so long as you do exactly what they say. And then, if you say the wrong thing ... they flip.

'Lots of people are scared of Tom Hilton, he's not as respectable as he seems. People don't cross him, because he always has someone who will make his wishes happen. Jed's at the top of the pyramid of his people, then Manny, then they get slightly less nasty and grubby in descending order. I feel like I'm in a prison. A black pit with Tom and Manny and Jed on patrol.'

Jed nasty and grubby? Tamara's head spun. To cover her shock, she moved into instructor mode. 'Slow down, let your breath come easily. Let it fill your lungs comfortably and without effort, don't try and tell me anything else for a minute. Slow down ... slow down. Inhale easily, now.' Her lips were moving and she could hear her own voice, calm and controlled. But it felt as if someone else was working it.

The muscles in Emilia's hands began to slacken, her breathing to ease. 'I'm sorry that I laid all that on you,' she whispered. 'But—' She stared at Tamara. Then burst out 'Look, about what I saw, earlier. You've obviously got something going with Jed. You probably think that I'm a neurotic little princess, who has nothing better to do than concoct romantic fairy tales about being locked away in a castle. But I like you, Tamara, and I can't just watch you fall for Jed's crap. I know he's hot, I know he's ripped, but he's not a very nice man. At all.'

Tamara swallowed. 'What do you mean?'

Emilia reached for the fast-cooling coffee. 'Jed and Manny – well, Tom owns them. He dragged the pair of them out of the gutter and trained them up to guard his kingdom like Dobermanns, not attacking unless they hear the word of command, but blindly obedient. Haven't you seen how Tom sets them on me? Oh, he might do it nicely – "Jed will go with you in case you need a hand" and all that shit, but he doesn't expect an argument.' She glanced around. 'And you know Manny's background? Something scary in the army? He has all the surveillance equipment. Why do you think we're sitting by this fountain? The noise will mask what we're saying.'

Tamara recoiled. 'Oh, come on. Haven't you been watching too many Tom Cruise movies?'

Miserably, Emilia slumped back in her driftwood throne. 'You obviously don't know much about parabolic directional microphones.'

Tamara stared at the other woman, thoughts scurrying like rats. Emilia's eyes were dull and disappointed, her mouth turned down and vulnerable. But she looked perfectly sane. She seemed to believe everything she was saying, but it was all so wild, so shocking, so far from Tamara's experiences. Her heart shrank at the picture Emilia had painted of Jed; she didn't want to believe in it. But Jed had left her high and dry – OK, not so dry – last night, the instant Tom Hilton had sent for him, bounding off like ... yes, like a trained dog.

Reluctantly, she took out her phone and opened her internet browser, tapping *parabolic microphone* into the search window. The screen flipped and flickered, then returned three hundred and fifty thousand results. She clicked on one. *Use for nature study, field study, law enforcement, eavesdropping and even espionage,* she read. God's balls, you could buy parabolic microphones on Amazon. They looked like hairdryers with a satellite dish on the end and earphones dangling beside. Feeling sick, Tamara stared at the screen. 'So you think Jed's listening to our conversation?'

Moodily, Emilia shook her head, pointing at the fountain. 'Parabolic microphones aren't miraculous. If you sit close to a white noise source and keep your voice low, you screw with it.' She massaged her bad leg. 'Will you tell me about the intruder? Did you find out from Jed? Tom was up drinking most of the night with him. I suppose I ought to have twigged that something was going on.'

With a huge sigh, Tamara recounted what Jed had told her, wishing it didn't fit so neatly with the bizarre scenario Emilia had just described.

Emilia paled. 'Did Jed say who it was? Have you talked to Manny about it?'

'Manny? No, how could I? You've just said he's not here.' Tamara paused for thought. 'I'm not sure if Jed said the intruder was one of the protesters who gave you grief before, or whether I suggested that and he just didn't contradict me.'

Emilia's sigh was almost a sob. 'Perfect! Someone skulking around gives them ammunition, a reason to keep me locked up.' She twisted a smile, squinting in the glare from the sun. 'They've all been unbearable since this happened.' She shifted her damaged leg.

'But that was an accident. Accidents are random and there's only a certain amount of care we can take to prevent them.'

Emilia gazed over the brilliant green of the lawn in the afternoon sun as it sloped down towards the house and an alpine bed, where a plant was just bursting into glorious cobalt-blue flower. Silver shrubs waved their frondy arms behind her throne and she leant back into them, as if seeking a spot to hide. 'Do you think Lyddie could come and visit me tomorrow?'

'You'll need to organise that with my mother. You've got the phone number, haven't you?'

'Yes, I'll ring later. I could send Manny down for her.'

Quickly, Tamara shook her head. 'Lyddie doesn't know Manny all that well and Mum will almost certainly object to putting her in a car with him alone because of the bad blood between my family and theirs. Could you ride along?'

Wearily, Emilia tipped her face back. 'I suppose so.' A beat. Then, slowly, she sat up with an expression of dawning excitement. 'Tamara, would you ask your mother to invite me to visit Lyddie? That way, she doesn't have to be in a car with Manny and Tom will probably accept it if Manny or Jed takes me there and waits outside. It would be perfectly natural for me to visit, wouldn't it, as Lyddie came here first?'

'I suppose so.' Tamara could see no real objection, but she was beginning to feel depressed by the whole situation at Lie Low. She couldn't quite find it in her heart to abandon Emilia to the half-life she described, though. 'I'll see what Mum says.'

Emilia's mood then improved enough for her to tell Tamara that her hair made her look like 'the queen of cool'. It was Tamara who found herself without much to say.

She didn't go back into the house when her time was up. Emilia picked up her phone to call Jed as usual, but Tamara said, 'Don't – I don't want to see him right now.' She left Emilia gazing at the fountain in the sunlight and made her way through an ornamental rose arch and around to the drive, fishing out her car keys. The wind had tangled her beautiful tiger hair and she felt trampled on. There was no satisfaction in having established a greater rapport with Emilia, as it had just allowed Emilia to tell her bad things about Jed.

And then he stepped out of the front door. 'You had a long chat.'

Tamara shrugged, not quite able to hold his gaze. 'It was nice to have the opportunity to get to know Emilia better.' She opened her rear car door and slid her holdall in behind the driver's seat.

'Aren't you coming in to collect your fee?'

'You can pay me double next time.'

'Mr Hilton would prefer you to be paid. Hang on and I'll get it for you.' He hesitated, as if waiting for her to reply, then ducked back inside.

Tamara got into her car, snicked on her seatbelt and started the engine. She pressed the button to roll down the window and waited. Jed had met her on the drive, which was either a big coincidence or he must have been watching her and Emilia. *Jed's at the top, then Manny, then they get slightly less nasty and grubby in descending order.*

A movement in her door mirror caught her eye and she watched Jed's approach. Self-confidence was in every stride as he grew bigger and arrived beside her, crouched at the open window and passed her the fold of notes.

'Thanks. I need to get going.'

He paused. 'Right now?'

'Right now.' She released the handbrake and he got up and stepped away, as she eased the car down the drive watching, through her mirror, him lifting his arm and pointing the remote at the gates. Let him be puzzled that she didn't share what Emilia had said about finding them together and whether she'd been angry. She felt weird and horrible. Let him feel uncomfortable, too.

She'd barely arrived home before his text arrived. *You OK?*

– *Fine thanks.*

– *Emilia didn't sack you?*

– *No*

– *Make things awkward?*

– *No*

– *You were treating me like a leper when you left so what was that? Me? The situation?*

She thought about it as she ate a salad sandwich. Then replied: *Both.*

Climbing back in her red car, she whizzed off to her class at the Bettsbrough Park Hotel, taking out her mood and her disappointment in roaring down the country lanes like a rally driver. She didn't feel much like instilling calm in others and helping them strengthen and lengthen their entire bodies, but, by the time she arrived, she was able to assume her professional persona and smile at the yogis putting down their lilac mats and lining up their trainers at the side of the studio. That's what they had every right to expect, an instructor with a smile, radiating calm and peace.

Even if, inside, she felt like the tiger her hair mimicked: jittery and growly.

Chapter Nineteen

In the early evening, Tamara was hopping out of her car outside her parents' house, intending to talk to Cheryl about Emilia, when Jed's car drew up beside her, black and low and rumbly. His expression, through the windscreen, was inscrutable.

But it wasn't his voice she heard through the open window. 'Heyyy, 'Mara! We're in Jed's car.' With a jolt, she saw Lyddie waving both hands from the other seat and Jabber's feathery tail waving from the back.

'Lyddie!' Tamara strode to the passenger door. 'How did you get there?'

'She brought Jabber to visit Emilia,' Jed reported, neutrally. 'I thought I'd better drive her straight home.'

His prompt action would explain why her phone hadn't gone into meltdown when she emerged from her afternoon class. Lyddie leaving the village on her own was an issue, and Tamara found herself beginning to smile at Jed with real gratitude. And then she remembered what Emilia had said about him and felt the smile fall from her face.

Jed frowned as he got out and let Jabber out of the back, holding on to his lead.

Lyddie fumbled with her seatbelt. 'I like Emilia. She's really cool.'

Tamara opened the door, taking her sister's arm to steady her as she heaved herself from the low car. 'You remembered the way to the house, did you? Do you remember that Mum asked you not to walk up there?'

'It's *eeeee*asy!' Lyddie boasted. 'It's up Port Road and then *this* way,' she waved her left hand, 'up that little road.' She took Jabber's lead from Jed. 'But your gates are always locked.'

'It keeps us safe.' He looked past her at Tamara.

Tamara was more than uneasy at this latest development. 'Did you have your phone, Lyddie?' Lie Low was only a little way out of the village, but definitely outside Lyddie's boundaries. Tamara was sure her mother wouldn't like it. And equally certain Tamara would get the blame.

'Here it is.' Lyddie pulled her phone out of the bum bag cinched around her ample waist. The screen was black.

Tamara pressed the button on the top and an arrow began circling in the centre. 'It's not much use if it's not switched on. Mum makes sure it's charged every night so she can ring you while you're out.'

'I was playing with it and it went off.'

'Let me show you how to turn it on again. It's this big button at the top—' But Lyddie caught the clippity-clop of an approaching pony and pushed almost through Tamara as Gabe bowled into view, perched on his little blue pony cart behind a smartly trotting Snobby. 'Gabe, Gabe! Way to go! I've been in Jed's car!'

As Gabe pulled up to chat to Lyddie and let her stroke Snobby's nose, Tamara turned back to Jed. 'Thanks for bringing her back safely. I'll try and discourage her from doing it again.'

'It would be better, wouldn't it? The gates will always be shut, although Emilia showed her how to work the intercom today. Do you think she'll remember how to do that?'

'Almost certainly she'd need showing again. Repetition, that's how she learns.' Rather than have to keep looking into Jed's eyes, hazel and watchful in the sunlight, she looked at Lyddie rubbing her face on Snobby's ears while she chattered breathlessly to Gabe, whose ponytail snaked out through the hole in his baseball cap.

Jed's fingers tapped on the car's roof. 'Obviously, it

would be safer if she didn't walk up to the house. What would happen if everyone was out?'

If everyone ever *is* out, she had to stop herself from retorting, thinking of fairy-tale princess Emilia locked in her castle. Instead she said, 'Good point,' shoving aside a mental image of Lyddie standing at the gates yelling like a calf at feeding time. He was right, of course, but she never enjoyed hearing these truths.

'Can we talk?'

'I have to go. I need to get Lyddie in to Mum.' And Tamara turned away to greet Gabe and persuade her sister to come indoors.

After Jed had driven off and Gabe and Snobby resumed their trippity-trot around the village, Tamara ushered Lyddie indoors. Her appearance was greeted by five seconds' silence – and not, as it turned out, because of Lyddie's unplanned absence. Even Jabber turned to look at her with his ears pricked.

'What do you call that hairstyle?' said Cheryl, faintly.

'Different,' Sean hedged, because he'd always try and find something neutral to say rather than admit when he hated something.

'C-o-o-o-o-l,' breathed Lyddie, who obviously hadn't noticed Tamara's hair till now. 'Way. To. Go. I want mine stripy.'

Cheryl sighed. 'Thank you, Tamara.'

Tamara shrugged. 'She ought to be able to choose her own hairstyle.' She glanced in the mirror to flick her fingers through the mocha-and-ash blonde, layered generously into her original foxy colour.

'I expect you'll be cross, but Lyddie's been visiting Emilia and Jed's just brought her home.'

'Oh, Lyddie!' Cheryl drew down her brows.

But Tamara got in a pre-emptive strike. 'It was a long

way for poor Jabber to limp. And I don't think it's ideal for Lyddie to be visiting Emilia on her own.'

'I should say not—!' started Cheryl.

'Although Jed obviously looked out for her,' interjected Sean.

Tamara put her arm around her sister. 'Do you really, really like Emilia?'

Lyddie's face shone. 'Yes! I really, really like Emilia. I *love* Emilia.'

Tamara turned to her mother with sudden resolve. 'Would you consider inviting Emilia here? I think she'd come.' She decided not to mention that the idea had originated with Emilia because how could she, without explaining that Emilia seemed to live in fear of her husband and that suddenly Tamara was wary of Jed?

All afternoon Tamara had felt sick as Emilia's confidences returned to her in ever more sinister shades. She'd thought about how flustered Imelda at Grand Manor had been around Jed and the overly respectful way she'd called him Mr Cassius – was that because she actually knew he was slightly scary? And that meeting in The Three Fishes, when Jed had suddenly dumped Bell on his arse, was it to put some manners on him, or just unthinking violence? What Jed had presented as escaping his difficult adolescent years, Emilia had described as Mr Hilton dragging Jed from the gutter. Jed spoke of never quite being off duty, but Emilia saw herself as being kept in a prison. Tamara felt as if she was living in one of those movies where the affable face of a character gradually slips to show something ugly and dark beneath.

She gave Lyddie a hard, fierce hug. 'Maybe Mum could invite Emilia here one evening and we could make cakes for when she comes.'

'Way to go,' breathed Lyddie.

Sean jingled his change in his pockets. 'I think it's a good idea. It's nice for Lyddie to have a new friend.'

And after a hesitation, Cheryl said, 'Yes. All right.'

'I'll ring her for you.' Tamara took out her phone and in minutes arrangements had been made for Emilia to visit Lyddie on Friday evening.

Emilia said simply, '*Thank* you. Really – thank you.'

And Lyddie capered around so much she made Jabber bark and caper with her, although he kept dancing out of the way to preserve his paw, Sean grinned and even Cheryl managed a smile. So Tamara was able to take Jabber to the vet's surgery in Bettsbrough to have his paw checked, feeling that she'd at least got things under control.

It wasn't until she'd returned Jabber to his mistress and driven home to find a small black BMW parked outside her house, Jed Cassius lounging against the bonnet, that she realised that he, at least, wasn't under control at all.

Chapter Twenty

'Hello,' she said, cautiously, climbing out of her car. 'Is this an official visit?'

He didn't smile. His gaze was as dark as that of a troubled spectre in a touchy mood. 'I'm here on my own time, if that's what you mean.'

Was that an answer? 'Until Mr Hilton rings you and you dash off.'

His eyes glittered. 'That could happen, but it's not likely.' He paused. 'Would you be so pissed off with me if I was a cop or a fireman? They get called out all the time.'

She nodded in acknowledgement of that fact. But she moved no closer.

He looked wary, even puzzled. 'How about we go to The Three Fishes for a drink? It seems as if the air needs clearing. It also seems as if you're not going to invite me in.'

She flushed. Last night's hot encounter made her want to take him into her house, but everything Emilia had said was whizzing around her brain and rooting her to the spot. She wasn't certain that Jed was the way that Emilia portrayed him. But she wasn't sure he wasn't.

'The pub sounds like a good idea,' she agreed. 'I'll follow you there.' She'd feel safer with her car waiting in the car park.

He sighed and rolled his eyes, but got into his car and turned it around.

Inside The Three Fishes the evening was just getting underway, with diners around the tables through the archway and the beer garden full of children whooping around the flower tubs, while parents tried the mutually exclusive feats of keeping an eye on them and relaxing.

The blokey blokes were lined up at the bar, mixing with the darts team. They said, 'Hi Tamara,' without wisecracks. Bell gave Jed a cautious look and Jed gave him a nod, as he ordered fizzy water for himself and a white-wine spritzer for Tamara.

She chose a table in the middle of the room. In movies, the guys with shady backgrounds always wanted to sit at the edge of the room so they had their backs covered and she had some hazy idea of testing Jed by selecting a table that left him exposed.

But he settled himself into the tub armchair and merely raised his eyebrows at her. 'So?'

She raised her eyebrows back. 'So, what?'

He regarded her under a darkly curled brow. 'So, are you going to tell me why you've turned into a block of ice on me and whether it's likely to be permanent? I could buy a parka and snowshoes, but I'd rather reset the thermostat.'

Drawing a pattern in the condensation on her glass, Tamara opted for creative use of the truth. 'It was really uncomfortable when Emilia found us today. It was unprofessional and she made it plain that she didn't appreciate it.'

Slowly, he nodded. 'And so you've decided to stop us before we get going?'

'It might be an idea.'

He sighed. 'A bloody crap idea.' A cheer came from the bar and his gaze flicked over to where the darts teams were exchanging friendly insults, then returned to her. 'Getting caught together was a momentary embarrassment, that's all. OK, we should have kept it "out of the office", I agree. I was tired and hung over and I got enthusiastic in wanting to make up for my disappearing trick. It won't happen again.' A ghost of a smile. 'I'm content to be your dirty secret.'

Tamara ran her fingertip around the base of her glass, trying to ignore the feeling that had skittered through her at the prospect of having a dirty secret. And it being Jed. He sounded so reasonable. Yet Emilia had made everything sound so sordid. 'What do you think of Emilia?' she asked, on impulse.

He frowned. 'Think of her?'

'Do you like her? Is she a nice woman? Are she and Tom happy—' She realised, as she watched the shutters come down over his eyes, that she'd gone about things in completely the wrong way.

'She's my employer's wife,' he said, as if that explained everything.

Whereas, actually, it explained nothing. Less than nothing. Except that discretion formed a handy screen to hide behind. For them both.

'And she's my employer,' she said, softly.

His frown got blacker. 'We're surely not taking sides?'

'Do we need to?'

He leaned forward and spoke under his breath. 'I'm still working on what you're getting at and what's on your agenda. But if you think that even to appease you I'm going to express an opinion about my employer's wife, particularly in a public place, you're mistaken.'

'Let me guess,' she whispered back. 'It's not in your job description.'

'No, it's fucking not. In fact, it's in the terms of my employment that I don't do stuff like that—'

Tamara stood up, grabbing her bag. 'We're in a pretty awkward situation, really, aren't we? I'll give that drink a miss, if you don't mind. I need to get home.'

On Friday evening, Tamara visited the house at Church Close to be there to introduce Emilia to her parents. She was greeted by a huge hug from a glitter-eyed, excited Lyddie. '*Hel*lo, 'Mara!'

Tamara hugged back. 'So what's happening, Lyd?' she teased.

Lyddie pushed her face up close. ''Milia's coming,' she breathed, hotly. 'I've been to 'Milia's house, and now 'Milia's coming to mine. That's right, isn't it, 'Mara?'

'Dead right.' Tamara returned, brushing Lyddie's hair from her face. 'Good, isn't it?'

'Way to go. 'Milia, 'Milia, 'Milia!' Lyddie began to bounce on the balls of her feet.

Tamara caught hold of both her hands. Lyddie over-excited was a Lyddie ten times more difficult to deal with. 'Before Emilia comes, tell me two things you think you might talk about together.'

The bouncing slowed, as Lyddie furrowed her brow. Her face brightened. 'Legolas.'

'Good, that's one.'

She screwed up her face. Forward planning wasn't Lyddie's thing, but she conjured up, 'DVDs?'

'Brilliant! Emilia's got lots of DVDs, hasn't she? Lots and lots all along shelves, behind wooden doors. Can you remember any you borrowed from her?'

'I'll give them back.' Lyddie looked suddenly anxious.

'Of course you will, I'm not worried about that. But can you remember what any of them were called?' And she steered her back into the sitting room, so that Cheryl and Sean could join in the game and Lyddie could be calmed by remembering *Futurama, Pitch Black* and *Skyfall*, until the doorbell rang.

''Milia!' Lyddie lurched to her feet.

'Come on, then. Let's let her in,' said Tamara.

Outside, they found Emilia beaming on the doorstep. Behind her, Manny sat at the wheel of the dark blue Mercedes Benz.

'He's waiting out there, is he?' Tamara stood back to let

Emilia edge over the doorstep on her crutches.

Emilia grinned. 'Even Tom doesn't think much can happen to me at Lyddie's house. Hey, Lyddie.'

''Milia! *Hel*lo! Hel*lo* 'Milia!'

Emilia accepted a smacking kiss, and kissed Lyddie's cheek more sedately in return. 'It's my turn to visit you, today, and meet your parents.'

'I know, I know! You're visiting me. Come on.' Hair swinging, Lyddie hauled Emilia after her by the arm. Emilia just about managed to keep up and not tangle her feet with her crutches. 'Come in the sitting room, this is Mum, and this is Dad, and this is 'Milia! Isn't it 'Mara?'

By the time Tamara had squeezed into the room, hands had been shaken and Cheryl was already vetting Emilia. But Emilia was reassuring, with her crutches and her bright smile, and soon Cheryl was smiling and glancing at Tamara to signal her approval.

Once she had drunk an obligatory cup of tea in the sitting room and eaten a slice of the date and walnut cake that Tamara had helped Lyddie make, Emilia and Lyddie disappeared upstairs to discuss films.

Watching their slow progress up the stairs, Lyddie clumping, a friendly hand at Emilia's elbow to hoist her up, Tamara had to swallow hard. She couldn't remember Lyddie having anyone else but the occasional cousin to take up to her room to hang out with since the accident. It was such an ordinary thing. But so precious to Lyddie.

Cheryl, too, was wet-eyed. 'She seems a nice woman, not hoity toity at all.' And she even smiled at Sean as well as Tamara.

Tamara decided to leave her parents alone to enjoy a couple of hours with the TV and ran upstairs, to where Lyddie was sprawling over the bed with her new friend as if they were sixteen-year-olds, eating chocolate-chip cookies that Emilia must have provided. Lyddie had chocolate around her mouth.

'See you later, Lyddie.'

Lyddie scrambled up to hug and kiss her and transfer some of the chocolate from her face to Tamara's. Then she looked anxious. 'Emilia's not leaving yet, is she? Not yet. Is she?'

'Not yet. This is so relaxing.' Emilia sighed, taking another cookie. She grinned at Tamara. 'No Manny, no Jed, no Tom.' And it looked as if Lyddie had brought her as much happiness as Emilia brought Lyddie.

Chapter Twenty-One

'Be careful of Manny. His history's chequered, apparently,' Max said.

Tamara regarded him over her lunch plate. It had been a surprise when he'd texted her on Saturday afternoon to say that he'd be back in the area on Sunday and could he see her. As she was noticing his absence from her life again, now the thing with Jed had fizzled and all she'd had planned for Sunday was to do her nails and work on a new routine to bring into her classes, she'd offered to supply lunch if he'd bring the wine. He'd actually brought something pink and *frizzante*, which wasn't his usual style. Or his old style, anyway – maybe it was part of the new Max. She looked into his dark eyes, so serious under a haircut much shorter than she was used to, and realised that he was moving on with his life.

'How, chequered?'

He fiddled with his *lollo rosso*. At least his idea of salad still looked to be more to do with pork pies and coleslaw than actual fresh leaves or tomatoes. 'I understand Manny was in the army. He was … highly effective in active situations. But there were discipline problems if he wasn't properly occupied. After the army he became a bodyguard and that's what he is now, I should think. A minder, utilising all the skills he acquired in the service. No one will get into that house if he hasn't vetted them.'

Her turn to frown. 'What house?'

He looked cagey. 'Where you're working. That weird place, all hidden in the trees.'

She cut up a leaf of rocket and pushed it onto her fork with her knife. She was getting the same hollow feeling as she'd had when Emilia had told her about Jed. 'How do you know where I'm working?'

His eyes dropped to his plate uncomfortably. 'Your mum rang me,' he admitted. 'She said it was because she hadn't had the chance to say goodbye to me and she wanted to wish me luck.'

'And instead she told you I was working in a weird place all hidden in trees?'

His eyes flicked around the room, as if the best thing to say might be lurking somewhere. 'It came up in conversation.' He sat back with a sigh. 'Tam, she's obviously worried about you hanging around with Jed Cassius and his stepbrother …' He glanced at her and then down at his abandoned salad. 'She went on about how she'd thought that you'd settled down with me and then suddenly you were hanging about with "those dreadful men" —'

Tamara let her fork clatter to her plate. 'I'll hang around with dreadful men if I want to. Not that I am. She's just niggled because she wants to hate Jed for what Uncle Don did, and me and Dad won't, and she can't bear not to be agreed with.' Realising that her fingers had tightened around her knife, she made herself lay it down on the table.

'And she said that Lyd followed you there and had to be driven home.'

Tamara nodded. 'That's true. But that's working out quite well because Lyddie—' She halted, suddenly mindful of the annoyingly ever-present non-disclosure thingy. 'What do you mean, a minder? And how on earth could Manny vet anyone?'

Max used his lettuce to scoop up the dollop of mayonnaise on his plate. 'Are you familiar with the term "background check"? If you've got the right buddies in the right part of the army – and plenty of other organisations, I expect – you can find out everything that's ever been written down about a person, without it showing up on 192.com or the Disclosure and Barring Service. If you don't mind it showing on there, you can do it from your PC. Bank accounts, property, cars, history, qualifications, criminal record, family ...'

She stared at him. Swallowed. 'What do you know about Manny? And how do you know it?'

He winked. 'A journalist protects his sources. But it wouldn't be too hard. Suppose I wanted to find out where a person had last lived, I'd search electoral records. If I wanted to know what hit the news in the period they lived there, and the local paper's archives for the period hadn't been digitised, I'd ring them. Journalists tend to do each other favours. I'd give someone a few details and they'd come back with a couple of items from their archive. There might be a feature on, say, a squaddie back from the Gulf, followed later by a lot of head-shaking over how, by now an ex-squaddie, he was cautioned by the police for putting some unfortunate bloke in hospital through overzealous close protection of a principal. There might be quotes from those who'd served with him and maybe some pop psychology about the dangers of turning men into fighting machines, or so-called close protection officers who the Security Industry Authority had never heard of.'

Tamara stared. Manny's job with the Hiltons had something to do with keeping them safe, she couldn't deny that. But she would have applied a title such as 'security manager' to the post, rather than 'minder'; a word associated in her head with the seventies television programme about dodgy deals and hooky gear and protecting a minor criminal from other criminals. Previously affable types suddenly showing their dark side if they thought the situation warranted it. Others getting hurt or frightened.

Both Jed and Manny took their roles in the Hilton household seriously, perhaps over seriously. But, even knowing that Emilia found them irksome, she'd begun to reflect on the fact that Mr Hilton was wealthy and people had caused trouble for him in the past, and had even dared to suggest to herself that maybe Jed and Manny were simply doing their jobs and weren't sinister at all.

'So you've come to warn me that Manny will have vetted me.' Max hadn't mentioned Jed's role at Lie Low and something made her not want to bring him into the discussion. 'I don't have anything to hide.'

He pulled a face. 'I just think there's something off about someone digging into your past.'

Incredulous, she laughed. 'But that's exactly what you've been doing! Using your journo connections to winkle out a couple of old newspaper reports.' And suddenly she saw exactly why non-disclosure agreements were common in the households of wealthy people. All it had taken was Cheryl to open her mouth and, even though he was more about road tests than hard news reporting, suddenly Max was poking and prying into things in a half-arsed I'm-a-journalist-so-this-is-what-I-do way, whether out of a misplaced wish to protect Tamara, or a hangover reflex to accommodate Cheryl, or maybe just plain old nosiness.

Who knew who he'd talk to next, what he'd let drop, what he'd report back to Cheryl, fuelling the image of Manny, and Jed by association, that Emilia had presented to Tamara: intimidating and sleazy?

It could be an accurate image, of course. Her stomach lurched. In which case, she'd have to maintain the current cold climate with Jed, letting her head keep in check her heart – and other bits of her that persisted in remembering how it had felt to be in Jed's hands in this very kitchen – because getting mixed up with someone who'd take a job controlling and containing a woman, even if in the lap of luxury, made her feel nauseous.

Her mind raced from one side of the problem to the other. But it wasn't as if she'd seen real evidence. If Emilia's wasn't the correct image ... her heart lurched even harder. Then she'd have to tell Jed about Cheryl interfering and Max ferreting, because both of these things had happened through her, Tamara. And she realised suddenly that what Max had called her over-developed sense of responsibility didn't only relate to her sister.

'OK, you've told me,' she said, lightly, 'and I've listened and taken it on board, and thanks for caring, although I think you're making it all sound way too cloak-and-dagger. But I hardly see Manny and he seems to have kept his nose clean lately, so I don't think you need to worry about me. And I'd be mega grateful,' she rolled her eyes, 'if you'd forget to give this information to Mum. She actually seems in quite a good mood at the moment and I wouldn't mind keeping it that way. Fancy a microwave treacle pudding?'

Max pushed the salad aside with alacrity. 'Now you're talking.'

Next day, Tamara arrived at Lie Low with her mind half made up to tell Emilia that the private yoga sessions weren't working out for her.

She'd spent what had been left of Sunday, after Max left, wondering restlessly whether she should shrug off Max's ferreting around, or whether telling Jed about it would be stupidly melodramatic.

She didn't want to tell him. A few short weeks ago, Max had been intending to buy a house that it was hazily understood she'd probably share, at some unspecified future date. And though that had fizzled out with a shockingly sudden *phht!*, he was still Max, still important to her. Also, she was reluctant to admit that it was her mother who had sparked Max's interest.

On the other hand, Tamara was employed by Emilia not Max ...

But she'd woken this morning, feeling not particularly enthusiastic about that employment. Emilia was becoming unexpectedly high maintenance, with her growing neediness and unexpected confidences. If Tamara gave up working with her, Cheryl would get off Tamara's back, Max would mind his own business and Tamara needn't worry about the shadiness, or otherwise, of Jed Cassius.

And that didn't make her feel better *at all*.

On the other hand, her conscience argued, was it right to turn her back on Emilia, who might be genuinely desperate for some tiny link with the outside world? And who had formed an unanticipated bond with Lyddie?

Tamara was still stewing, as she rolled down her car window to press the intercom button, hearing Manny's tinned voice, 'Morning, Tamara,' before the gates swung inwards. It was Manny who opened the front door, as Tamara switched off her engine and gathered up her holdall. He smiled. 'I'll show you through.'

Tamara fell in step with him, through to the back of the house. In a sleeveless T-shirt and cargo pants, Manny was solid, his shoulders thick and his arms corded. He made polite conversation about Emilia enjoying her time with Lyddie and delivered Tamara to where Emilia waited in the humid pool area, with a bottle of iced water and a magazine.

'Tamara's here, Emilia.' He stood aside for Tamara to precede him.

Emilia looked happier and more relaxed than last week. 'I'm going to have to do yoga every day if I'm going to join Lyddie in cookie feasts,' she joked, setting her magazine aside. Her pink mat was already set out and she shuffled her bottom to the edge of the chaise and pushed upright, balancing for a few moments on her good leg before allowing her right foot to the floor. 'Manny, which is better for fat burning – yoga or swimming?'

'Swimming. But I don't think you have to worry about an occasional cookie feast.' He waited for an instant, but when Emilia didn't address him again, melted quietly away.

Emilia pulled off her trainers and let herself down onto her mat. 'Your mum and dad were really sweet, Tamara. Lyddie obviously loves them to bits. And your dad took a cup of coffee out to Manny, even though your mum pulled a bit of a face and said she was sure he could have brought a flask with him because there must be a lot of waiting around when you're someone's driver.'

When she laughed she looked happy and friendly, and Tamara found herself joining in, reassured by Emilia's good mood. Her urge to disconnect herself from the strange household at Lie Low faded like the mist that had lain on the fields this morning. It wasn't an onerous job, usually, and it was certainly interesting.

So she began. 'Let's start by checking our alignment.'

By the end of the session, Emilia seemed relaxed, stretching comfortably while they drank the coffee brought by the silently smiling Carrie. 'Oh, I nearly forgot – the last two alpaca babies have arrived. When can you bring Lyddie to see them? Come on, I'll show you now. They're adorable, and both black.'

She swung up onto her crutches and led the way out into the hazy day, across the paving and the grassy terrace, down the steps and the slope. The alpacas had herded together in the middle of the field, heads up in rapt attention as Tamara and Emilia approached.

'Oh ... gorgeous!' Tamara breathed.

The new babies were distinguishable from their slightly older herd mates by their newborn totter, as if nobody had taught them how they were supposed to balance on these leg things. Their dark coats were new and fuzzy.

Once the adults had decided that the appearance of a couple of humans posed no threat, they fell to grazing again, punctuating the morning air with 'Mm. Mm. Mm.'

The cria hovered uncertainly beside their mothers, then put their ears back and tucked their heads into the mummy undercarriage to nurse. One of the mums managed to knock her baby right over with a well-meaning nudge of her nose and Tamara cried, 'Oh!' Then laughed as the baby, after a pause and a couple of flicks of its ears, gathered its legs beneath itself, gained its front knees, stuck its bottom in the air and somehow unfolded its way up again.

'Lyddie has to see these. She'll adore them,' she heard herself saying.

'Bring her this afternoon,' Emilia urged.

'She's probably working this afternoon and so am I. I could bring her on Wednesday morning.'

A dissatisfied frown wrinkled Emilia's brow. 'But I want her to see them while they're still so new and wobbly. In another couple of days they'll have found their feet.'

'I could ask Mum about this evening,' Tamara conceded, because she, too, would like to share Lyddie's joy at these gorgeous babies. 'But it's a bit of an issue with Lyddie's mealtimes because she doesn't react well to running on empty. It seems to make her much more emotional. It would be a bit of a rush for her to eat and then come out while it's still light.'

'Then you can both eat here. We'll send Manny for pizza.' Emilia shifted her weight between her good leg and her crutches. 'The three of us could toast the newborns.'

'Mum would go mad if I let Lyddie near alcohol—'

Emilia gave a snort of exasperation. 'We'll toast them in ice cream, then. Come on, Tamara!'

Tamara laughed. 'OK, hold on to yourself. I'll ring Mum and see if I can sort it.'

Emilia went back to watching the baby alpacas, the wind stirring through her ponytail, as Tamara took out her phone and rang Cheryl, who agreed immediately. 'Lyddie would absolutely love it.'

It was arranged that Tamara would pick her sister up just after six thirty, following her class at Caradoc Gym.

Then, after a few minutes, Emilia took out her own phone and spoke into it. 'Tamara's ready to leave, now,' and as Emilia began what looked like a fairly strenuous task of working her way back up the slope on her crutches, breathing harder by the time she got to the top, Tamara paced by her side and wondered whether it was Manny that Emilia had just spoken to. Or Jed.

It was Jed. By the time they'd made it back to the paving by the house, he was waiting by one of the many sets of French doors with Tamara's holdall.

Emilia popped a breathless kiss on Tamara's cheek. 'Phew. I need to sit down. Jed will look after you. See you tonight!' She turned briefly to Jed. 'Tamara's bringing Lyddie to see the new cria this evening. I'll need you or Manny to go out for pizza.' Then she turned and swung her way around the corner of the house.

Chapter Twenty-Two

Jed held the door courteously for Tamara and then led her through the quiet calm of the large hall and off to the smaller one, towards his office.

When Emilia had phoned he'd been watching the two women stand at the paddock rail, but he'd let the phone ring three times before answering and going out to watch them come up the slope. Mr H would probably have told him to get down there and help Emilia if he'd been home, but, as he wasn't, Jed had stayed where he was. Emilia wasn't always appreciative of his help.

Instead, he'd studied Tamara, the definition of her body in her dark purple and navy exercise clothes that clung to every curve. Her hair was neatly brushed up into a ball on the top of her head, accentuating her cheekbones. He was pissed off by the way he'd let things go wrong between them, but he was good at waiting games. He'd let her get over her snit.

Once in his office, he unlocked the drawer where he kept the household incidental expenses fund and counted out her fee.

'Thanks.' She tucked the money away, as if it hardly interested her. It was a decent fee for ninety minutes' work, he was aware. But Emilia had told him not to negotiate. Want something: buy it. That was her philosophy. And if Emilia was happy, Mr H was happy; if Mr H was happy, Jed's work was done.

For once, Tamara wasn't reversing towards the door in readiness to leave. A tiny frown slanted her eyebrows, as she flitted an unreadable look at him.

He leaned back in his chair. 'Everything OK?'

She blinked. Licked her lips, as if checking whether words waited on them.

Oh-kay … she was getting around to something. He crossed his ankle over his knee and let his gaze fall absently to the notes on his white pad, telling her with body language that he was relaxed, unthreatening, that his attention wasn't really fixed on her, and that it was all the same to him whether or not she vented whatever was on her mind.

'This non-disclosure thingy,' she said.

He looked up and gave her a faint questioning smile. 'What about it?'

'It's sort of bothersome.'

'Is there something I can make clearer for you?' He waved her to the seat on the other side of his desk, as if she was one of the domestic staff who'd brought him a problem.

She sank into the chair. Blue, purple and the tiger-stripe of her hair clashed gently with the green leather. She'd look much better in his flat where the neutral colours would let her vivacity glow. Even better in his bed—

'It's not that I don't understand. I just don't see how I can possibly make it work.' Once underway she began to look more confident. 'I've already explained about Lyddie's inability to practise discretion. Then there's my mum. Because of Lyddie she feels entitled to ask questions and knows I come here and that Emilia exists.' She looked down at her nails, with just a touch too much unconcern. 'And Mum hasn't signed an NDA, so it's difficult to prevent her talking to other people if the whim comes upon her.'

Ah. So it was Cheryl. 'Have you requested that she doesn't?'

She gave him a speaking glance. 'Like Canute requested the waves to just reverse a bit?' She returned to her examination of her nails. They were still in the tiger stripes.

Jed wondered how they'd feel on his naked back. With Tamara on his naked front.

'You have to remember that she knows you and Manny are at Lie Low, too, and you're a subject uppermost in her mind because of Uncle Don.'

Probably Cheryl had been talking already, then. 'Do you see a problem?'

She shrugged.

She thinks if she doesn't say it aloud, it won't be a lie. He fought a sudden urge to laugh at her amateur attempt to sound him out without him realising. He darted his agile mind over her family situation, the blameless life she led and the innocent types she associated with. He couldn't see how Tamara was going to cause the Hiltons problems. It wasn't as if she was connected in any way to those who had caused Mr H headaches in the last couple of years – particularly James bloody Cochrane.

He leaned forward and rested his elbows on the table. 'I can't really say what I want to say here,' he murmured. 'Can we meet up, later? Maybe after you and Lyddie have had your pizza with Emilia?'

Tamara looked torn. Eventually, she said, 'OK.'

He walked her out to her car, opening doors for her and taking care not to invade her space, hoping that her wariness would magically vanish if he gave her the right signals. He didn't even drop his eyes to her peachy behind as she preceded him to her sporty red hatchback, in case somehow she would know. He watched her car coast through the gates and out of sight, his mind working on what it was he'd done that had made Tamara look at him as if he might suddenly reveal himself as an alien on a mission to enslave Earth women.

When he turned away, he saw Manny and Emilia approaching one of Emilia's favourite spots, the big wooden chairs by the pond. Manny took Emilia's crutches in one hand and gave her his arm to help her over the bridge. Jed felt a surge of irrational irritation that Emilia was accepting Manny's help when she wouldn't take his.

What was it with him that was making women give him a wide berth?

It was a glorious summer evening. The sky was cloudless and the sun seemed to caress everything it touched. Tamara had linked her arm through Lyddie's because it helped keep Lyddie calm. 'Just remember to whisper, Lyddie, OK? The babies are bound to be easily frightened.'

'OK,' whispered Lyddie, stumping along between Tamara and Emilia. But then, as they negotiated the terrace steps and began to cross the grass slope to the paddock, she shouted, 'Oh, look at the BABIES!'

Ten alpaca heads flew up and swivelled in the direction of Lyddie's voice. And after a staring second, the adults turned and marched their offspring in the opposite direction.

'But they're GOING,' wailed Lyddie. 'I want to see—'

Tamara squeezed Lyddie's arm and made her voice low and soothing. 'You need to talk very quietly.'

'I want to see—' whispered Lyddie.

'Don't worry, we'll get them back up here.' Emilia whipped out her phone. 'Can you come down with some alpaca feed?' she said into it. 'I want the mums to come to this end of the paddock.'

In minutes, Jed arrived with a couple of shiny steel bowls containing a mixture of khaki pellets and beige chaff. He was wearing jeans and a navy T-shirt that clung to his chest and upper arms as he moved. 'Evening, ladies.'

'*Hel*lo, Jed,' burst out Lyddie.

'Quietly, remember.' Tamara put a finger to her lips.

'Hello, Jed,' Lyddie whispered loudly. 'I've come to see Emilia's baby packers. They're like teddies, aren't they? Are you going to get them for me?'

'Hope so.' Jed winked at her and glanced at Tamara, then swung his body over the gate and walked towards the little herd, now grazing peacefully some way off, the babies either nursing or tottering around. The two newest stuck to their mamas as if on leashes. As Jed drew closer, all ten necks extended as the huge dark eyes checked him out, ears like devil horns. 'Come on, then.' He shook the bowls enticingly. 'A little supper treat, girls.'

Two of the more matronly alpacas began trotting towards him, their cria alongside. The newest mums were the last to jostle for a turn to drop their muzzles into one of the bowls. Jed's voice came low and gentle on the breeze as he began to walk backwards, letting each adult take a turn to snack. 'Come on, bring your babies. Lyddie and Tamara have come to see you.'

Lyddie took a big breath. Instantly, Tamara gave her a warning squeeze. 'Quietly,' she whispered.

'I can see the babies,' Lyddie hissed back. 'They're like toys. They're so liddle. I can see Triangle and Warrior Two and Downward Dog.'

'The newest are the tiny black ones,' Emilia murmured, as Jed brought the herd slowly within a few yards of the fence. 'Aren't they gorgeous, Lyddie? So tottery and unsure.'

Lyddie sighed beatifically. 'The new babies walk like spiders.'

Emilia laughed and the alpacas turned their beautiful, big black eyes on her enquiringly. 'And we have to choose names. Would you like to name another one, Lyddie? What's one of your favourite yoga poses?'

Lyddie shifted excitedly, drawing the alpacas' liquid gazes. 'Corpse.'

Jed actually laughed, and Tamara covered her eyes. 'Lyddie! We can't call a beautiful baby alpaca "Corpse".'

Emilia giggled, eyes dancing. 'Can you choose something else, Lyddie? That's a bit gruesome.'

Lyddie beamed. 'Grasshopper, then.'

Emilia giggled again. 'That's better. I like that. You've just named that one over there.' She pointed at the tiniest of the cria. 'And I'll name the other one Lion,' she said, after a moment's thought.

'Lion,' agreed Lyddie, 'I can do Lion—' She made as if to get down on all fours.

Tamara hauled on her arm. 'You can do Lion pose later.'

'OK.' Lyddie launched herself suddenly at Emilia and planted a noisy kiss on her cheek. 'I'm hungry. Are we having cake? Doughnuts with cold custard in? I like cake. I love cake.'

'Manny's gone to fetch pizza, but I think Carrie's left you cakes. I don't know whether they're doughnuts, though.' Emilia smiled.

'I love pizza.' Lyddie turned and began straight away up the hill. 'I love pizza with extra cheese on. Is Jed going to eat pizza with us? I like Jed.'

Tamara cast a glance at Jed, who was putting his empty bowls together and preparing to climb back over the gate. He caught her gaze and smiled a slow smile and she felt heat flood into her face. When he looked at her like that, when he was kind to Lyddie, when he talked to alpacas in a gently soothing voice, she had a lot of trouble believing that he was as black as Emilia had him painted. And he was smiling more these days.

Once she'd seen Lyddie safely delivered to their parents, she was to meet him at The Three Fishes. The thought quickened her step as she turned and followed her sister and Emilia, both of them less than elegant on the upslope. Emilia was talking and laughing with Lyddie, blowing her hair out of her eyes as she began to run out of puff.

'Emilia, why don't you let Jed help you?' A voice from the edge of the terrace pierced the evening.

Emilia's head jerked up. Tom Hilton was standing there like an old lone wolf on his evening patrol. 'I'm fine, Tom.'

Jed overtook Tamara smoothly and quietly, making her jump more than Mr Hilton's sudden appearance had. He caught Emilia up and stationed himself at her side.

'Jed can give you his arm,' Tom Hilton persisted.

Stubbornly, Emilia kept her arms threaded through her crutches, hopping and limping along. 'I'm fine, thanks.'

'*Hel*lo,' yodelled Lyddie.

Mr Hilton's gaze moved to Tamara. 'Do you think Emilia should be doing this?' Both expression and voice were carefully neutral, yet Tamara sensed a rebuke in his question.

'I don't know of any reason that she shouldn't, if it's not increasing her pain levels or inflaming her injuries. But perhaps Emilia should check with one of her medical professionals?'

After a moment, Tom Hilton nodded. Jed fell back from Emilia's side and she and Lyddie climbed the terrace steps slowly, but surely.

'I've seen your packers,' panted Lyddie as they reached Tom Hilton, apparently unaware of any coolness from her host. 'I've seen the babies. I called one Grasshopper and 'Milia called the other Lion. He's a black lion.' She laughed.

Tom Hilton actually smiled in return. 'Let's hope he doesn't eat us.'

Lyddie burst into giggles. 'He won't. He's a packer. He's like a teddy. I like him. I love him. Are we having the pizza, soon?'

Tom Hilton caught his young wife around the waist. 'We can all eat together.'

Tamara wondered whether she imagined that Emilia

tensed at her husband's touch, whether her sudden quiet was weariness. Or anxiety. Or fear.

They went into the large sitting room. Tom Hilton was genial in a reserved way and Emilia looked as delicate as her portrait, gazing at him when he spoke and accepting his presence beside her on a small embroidered sofa.

Tamara sat with her sister on a larger velvet sofa, hoping that Lyddie wouldn't get pizza all over it if they were to eat there, noticing that Tom Hilton's suggestion that they all 'eat together' hadn't apparently meant Jed, as he'd carried on through the room and vanished through the other door.

And when Manny delivered wheel-sized pizzas a few minutes later, he, too, melted away immediately his errand was accomplished, leaving Tamara wondering why it didn't seem OK to eat with the staff, but fine to go night-long whisky drinking with them, and whether Tom Hilton was being particularly forbearing in suffering Tamara's company, as she, too, was an employee, albeit of the freelance variety.

At least it gave her the opportunity to study Emilia's interaction with her grave-faced husband, noting his brindle hair, cut expensively but conservatively. His beige polo shirt, open at the neck, was probably as casual as he got. He reminded her of her dad.

Nobody but Lyddie seemed to have a lot to say, which left the floor open for her to tell Emilia and Tom Hilton about Gabe, Luke the black puppy and Princess Layer, 'her' chicken that lived out her retirement from chicken farming in Gabe's messy garden.

Once everyone had eaten all the pizza they wanted – the leftovers were enough to feed a small nation – and chocolate brownies with coffee, tea or hot chocolate, Lyddie gave a great, uncovered yawn and announced, 'I'm tired.'

Tamara gave her sister a hug. 'I'd better get you home, then.' She took Lyddie's hand before Lyddie could say that no she wasn't tired really or that she wanted to see the cria again, and urged her to her feet. 'It's been a lovely evening, hasn't it? Grasshopper and Lion are so sweet. Let's say thank you to Emilia and Mr Hilton, shall we?'

Lyddie co-operated without demur. She was probably really tired, having expended so much energy on excitement and overeating. 'Thank you. I love your packers. I like Grasshopper best. I love him. I love Triangle, too. Bye bye, 'Milia.'

'Bye, Lyddie.' Emilia accepted Lyddie's hug and planted an affectionate kiss on her cheek. 'See you soon.'

Tom Hilton used his phone to summon Jed to see them to Tamara's car and Lyddie gave great, jaw-cracking groaning yawns all the way back to Church Close.

Chapter Twenty-Three

After dropping Lyddie off, Tamara drove home to Bankside to leave her car. A footpath between Great Hill Road and Ladies Lane took her into the back of the pub, via the beer garden.

She found Jed leaning against the bar, one foot propped on the brass rail, watching Bell and the other blokey blokes playing an inexpert game of darts. His gaze didn't waver, even when a wayward dart struck the wire and bounced off, skidding along the floor almost to his feet. Unhurriedly, he picked it up, moved up to the tatty white tape on the carpet that served as the oche, and aimed the dart at the board.

It flew straight and true into the small red segment at the top. 'Double top,' he observed.

Bell grunted.

Jed turned away and gave Tamara a half-smile, as if he'd known she was there all the time. 'What are you drinking?' When she asked for a glass of Chardonnay, he said to Janice behind the bar, 'Make that a bottle, please, with two glasses and a cooler.' Then, to Tamara, 'Let's sit outside', picking up the cooler and wine in one hand and the glasses in the other.

Bell and the rest of the blokey blokes followed their progress across the room with their eyes, until Jed turned to give them a particularly innocent smile, and then they snatched their gazes away.

Outside, dusk was falling and the air was soft. Only a few people occupied the weather-stained wooden tables, with the umbrellas stuck in the middle like giant cocktail decorations.

Jed led the way to the furthest corner, where a wild fuchsia dangled its tiny ballerina flowers right onto the table. Depositing the glasses and the wine cooler, he waited for Tamara to seat herself, then took the bench opposite, pouring wine into both glasses and lifting one in a silent toast to her.

'You can play darts,' she said, not toasting back.

'We had a dartboard in the squat. It was a major part of our entertainment – no money for computers or TVs and no electricity to power them. I got quite good.' A memory flickered across his face.

She felt a ripple of sympathy for the teenaged Jed, who had had no access to what teenagers of his era would have considered the staples of life. 'That was certainly an impressive dart.'

His eyes gleamed with amusement in the light from the pub windows. 'No it wasn't. I was aiming for the triple. But don't tell Bell.'

She laughed. The air was still and heavy, loud with the whirring of insects around the lights. Then, drinking half of her wine in one, she sighed.

'Heavy day?'

'Every day's a heavy day.' Then she wondered what on earth had made her blurt that out and retracted quickly. 'I don't mean that, not really. I'm lucky to have a career I love and that makes me feel good. There's not much in my life to complain over.'

Across the table, his eyes were fixed on her, dark in the dusk. He spoke in a voice so low that she could only just catch it.

'You don't have to hide it.'

'Hide what?'

'Hide how Lyddie's accident affected you. You talk about the guilt, the grief for the life Lyddie lost, your sympathy for how it affected your parents. But not much about what it means for you. You've built your life around your sister just as much as Cheryl and Sean have done, but without the fanfare.'

'Lyddie's not a burden.'

His hand took hers, warm and smooth. 'Any dependent person is. She can't help but be. Every time you take her out instead of hanging out with your mates, every time you unknot a situation for her, every laborious conversation or restricted walk – they're things that wouldn't have happened without Lyddie's accident. And ever since the accident, your parents have had to concentrate on Lyddie, even when you were still a kid.'

Unexpected tears scalded her eyes. No one, not even Max, had ever noticed. But she still trotted out an automatic 'I'm the lucky one. The one the car missed.'

'But nobody's too blessed to be allowed to feel pissed off with reality now and then. Who wants to be constantly thankful that they're "normal"? You're a damned saint with your sister.'

'I'm not. I just love her.' She managed a shaky laugh, hearing an echo of Lyddie's constant *I like it, I love it* declarations for anything from family to food.

'You really do. It's the genuine article – the kind of love that doesn't ask anything in return. I don't think I'd realised how rare that is. You're an extraordinary woman.'

Lost for words, she took another gulp of her wine and he topped up both glasses. She'd better slow down, or she'd be tottering about like one of the newborn alpacas.

'Was staying with Lyddie anything to do with you not leaving with Max?'

She began to say, 'Yes!' changed it to, 'Not entirely,' and, finally, 'How does it concern you?' He was still holding her hand. She wondered whether she ought to withdraw it, because holding hands with someone suggested affection and she wasn't sure whether it was safe for her to like him. But his fingers felt good around hers, his skin warm and smooth, a tiny pulse beating in his thumb as it rested in her palm.

His gaze was intent. 'Most things about you concern me, but I have to admit to a particular interest in Max. I'm looking around for reasons for you to have turned so chilly. Abandoning you at a delicate moment when Mr H needed me doesn't seem to be enough, and nor does Emilia being unimpressed with catching us in a clinch. So I thought maybe you weren't as over Max as I'd perceived. Especially as when I drove over to see you on Sunday, his car seemed to be outside your house.' He gave the faintest of smiles.

'You could have phoned first.' Her heart picked up at the thought that he'd called to see her.

'That would have given you the opportunity to brush me off. I thought my chances of a satisfactory conversation were better if I just turned up.' His thumb had moved out of her palm and was barely touching the thin skin on the inside of her wrist, somehow raising the hairs on her arm right up to the back of her neck. She actually had to suppress a shiver.

Tamara didn't want Jed to think that she still had a thing for Max. If he was the bad guy Emilia depicted, then it could lead to Jed putting Max under his microscope and somehow discovering that Max had been digging up old articles on Manny.

If he wasn't a bad guy …? Tamara didn't want Jed to think that she had a thing for anybody.

'Just because Max and I are over, doesn't mean I can't have lunch with him when he's in the area.' And then, because she didn't want Jed to ask her out again until she knew whether it was OK to let herself feel all the things she was feeling and think about him as much as she did, she tried to switch the subject, first glancing behind her to check that nobody was within hearing. 'What was it that you wanted to say about the NDA?'

'Nothing.' His thumb traced patterns over the delicate veins and sinews of her wrist, the fine bones, as silky as a snake, as light as a butterfly.

She swallowed and picked up her wine with her other hand. 'You did. You said, this afternoon, that you couldn't talk about it then, which is why we're here.'

His eyes gleamed in the lights from the pub windows. 'You had concerns about the NDA. I just said that I couldn't say what I wanted to say right then.'

'What did you want to say?' Then she read triumph in his smile and heat in his eyes and realised she'd walked right into the conversation she'd been trying to avoid. And even as her heart flipped, he pulled her nearer, leaning in to her across the warped wooden table so that all she could see was his eyes.

'I wanted to let you know that I'm still hell-bent on getting you. I want you, I'm not even close to stopping wanting you, and I'm going to carry on wanting you and trying to get close to you, unless you give me a good reason to stop.'

'Oh,' she said, weakly, a sudden flush of desire tingling down her spine.

He dropped a kiss on her palm and then one on every fingertip. Then he was leaning right over the table and his mouth was on hers, hot, hard, lightning striking, fireworks igniting, his free hand threading into her hair. 'It will happen,' he promised her, against her mouth. And he kissed her harder.

Chapter Twenty-Four

It was Tamara who broke away, her heart thundering around like an elephant on speed. She wanted to carry on kissing him, or even drag him through the darkness of the village to her bed. But the stuff Emilia had said ...

Could she just ask him? Or would that betray Emilia's confidence? If Jed passed on to Mr Hilton that Emilia's discretion was leaky, was there some chance, however small, that Emilia would suffer for it?

For several moments they stared at one another. He was breathing hard.

'Too far, too fast,' she managed.

He licked his lips. 'OK.' He didn't sound as if it was.

She picked up her glass and drained it, trying to stop her fingers from trembling on the stem. He divided the last of the bottle between their glasses before dropping it upside down in the cooler. She watched his hands.

She tore her gaze away.

Looked back. His hands were smooth, sinewy, strong. They had been on her. Hot on her skin, but not as hot as his mouth. His mouth had been ... she shivered.

Deep breath. Let it out slowly, slowly. She felt her heart steady, her pulse settle. Another: slow, deep. She couldn't want this, not yet, not till she knew what to think. She wasn't used to a man who might be dangerous, who might threaten her control. She cast around for a subject that would kill whatever it was that was crackling in the air between them.

'Tell me,' she said, 'tell me what happened on the day of Lyddie's accident.'

His eyebrows straight-lined. 'What?'

'From your point of view, I mean. It must have been weird.'

'Yes.' His gaze dropped to where he was still holding one of her hands. He traced the oval of a nail, while he made a visible effort to switch his train of thought to a new conversational track. 'There were about ten of us. We were over the fields.'

She smiled at the village kids' old expression for being outside the village, maybe walking on the edge of a cornfield or skulking about on the Carlysle Estate, out from under the eyes of adults. 'Lyddie was on her way to meet up with you.'

He nodded sombrely.

'But she had to shake me off, first.'

The flicker of a smile. 'You would have been considered way too young to hang out with us. You weren't even at senior school.' He raised pensive eyebrows. 'We heard the sirens – I don't think I'd ever heard them in the village before – so we raced back to see what was going on. Down Main Road, it seemed as if the whole world had turned to sirens and flashing blue lights. It made my eyeballs ache. The police were there and the ambulance and mums in their slippers with grave faces and men out walking their dogs. None of the adults would let us close, or tell us what had happened. I suppose they had to make sure Uncle Sean and Aunt Cheryl knew first.' He didn't seem to notice slipping back into his childhood names for Tamara's parents.

He breathed a sigh. 'It wasn't until my parents came home later that I found out. The news had whizzed around the adults. Mum and Dad were so shocked. They kept saying, "What can we do for Sean and Cheryl?" and "That poor girl." I just sat at the kitchen table. They didn't know that I'd been seeing Lyddie because teenage boys don't blab to their parents about stuff like that.' He screwed up his eyes with the effort of remembering. 'It felt unreal. I didn't know anybody who'd had a serious accident – just the occasional kid at school who broke a leg or had to have stitches. You'd hear about it, then a few days later they'd be back at school with a cast or a dressing, and then they'd get better.

'People came up to me at school and asked about Lyddie, as if I had a hotline to the hospital. In fact, if I knew anything it was only because my parents were friends with yours. Mum said Cheryl and Sean were at the hospital all the time and Lyddie had an operation, then another one.'

He sighed again, a long, far-off memory sigh. 'It began to seem real. To be obvious that Lyddie wasn't going to turn up at school any time soon. As it turned out, I never saw her again until I called at your parents' place a few weeks ago to tell them about what Dad said. And that was a different Lyddie.'

Jed lifted his gaze, squeezing her hand as if she needed comforting. And maybe she did, because an enormous aching ball of unshed tears was rising in her throat.

He went on. 'Lyddie was still in hospital when Dad applied for the new job, got it, and we moved away. I see it all in a different light now, but I saw it as a disaster at the time. I hadn't lived anywhere but Middledip and didn't fancy West London at all. But it turned out to be kind of OK. It was different to living in a village, but there were advantages because I could get on public transport into central London in a relatively short time.' He shrugged. 'The rest you know.'

'Thanks for telling me that,' she managed, huskily. 'I think I spent that time in a bubble. I either didn't know or didn't care how it affected other people.' She freed her hand and drank the last inch of her wine. 'I think I'll go home.' She didn't say 'alone' but she saw from the flicker of his eyes that he heard it.

She left him at the gate to the beer garden with a swift impersonal peck on his cheek, before she turned and strode away from him, letting the darkness hide her.

Tamara had only one class on a Wednesday, in the evening. She had housework and paperwork to do, but she never stayed indoors willingly for long, so hopped off to call on Cheryl and Lyddie.

She was beginning to feel sorry that things were chilly between her and her mother. Slightly sorry, anyway. Or perhaps regretful would be a better word. Or perhaps it was just age-old conditioning, that child thing of needing approval. And Cheryl had been OK on the occasion of Emilia's visit, so maybe she was over her stroppy patch.

The day was cold for July. She pulled up the hood of her purple fleece against a scampering breeze and as she strode out of New Street, along Ladies Lane and into Port Road, the trees tossed their heads like irritable ponies. Through their rustling, she heard steadily running footsteps behind her and glanced back.

Manny was closing on her with his easy, comfortable running stride. His white vest clung to his chest with sweat, his hair spiked damply. He grinned as he caught her up, jogging on the spot, breathing quickly but not hard. 'Visiting the family?'

She stopped. Hmm. She was heading for the family home in Church Close and he knew her family and where they'd always lived, had visited the house himself recently, but still his question triggered Max's voice in her mind. *If you've got the right buddies you can find out everything that's ever been written down about a person* ... The concept was annoying. 'You're very observant.'

His smile widened to a grin. 'I keep my eyes open.' He swivelled on his toes and glanced once up and once down the road, in an exaggerated surveillance of the terrain.

He was joking, of course, but now she thought about it, he did that a lot, checking out his surroundings; who was there, what was happening. Maybe that was what minders did? Always watchful, ready for trouble. Or maybe once a soldier, always a soldier. Or maybe her imagination was evolving Emilia's revelations into TV drama proportions.

'Enjoy your day.' And he set off, disappearing down Port Road, fast and easy on the footpath.

Tamara was still frowning over the Manny and Jed conundrum when she let herself into the house on the corner of Church Close and shouted her hello.

Lyddie bellowed in reply. 'We're upstairs, 'Mara, come and look.' And when Tamara ran up, Lyddie threw her arms around her, breathless with excitement. 'Come and see what we're doing with your room. We've been really busy, haven't we, Mum? Really busy. Look!' She beamed.

Tamara looked. It gave her an unexpectedly funny feeling to see that her old room was being taken over. She hadn't lived in it for four years, but Lyddie's dressing table and chest of drawers were *in situ* and untrafficked areas of carpet and fresh rectangles of wallpaper had been exposed by the removal of Tamara's stuff. Lyddie was going to have her room. Tamara experienced a moment's disorientation.

Cheryl snapped a metal tape measure in and out of its white case. 'We thought that Lyddie might as well have the bigger room.'

'Makes sense.' Tamara thrust away her weird feelings. They would only be reasonable if she was thinking she'd ever want to live 'at home' again, which sure as hell wasn't on her To Do list. Any occasional nights she spent here were usually Lyddie-related and when the next one arose, she could simply have Lyddie's old room.

Lyddie stumped about beaming, pausing to bear hug Tamara, a familiar but moist, hot, bone-crushing experience. 'I'm having your room! I'm going to have my computer *there*, and my bed *here*, and the wardrobe ... we got to wait for Dad to come home to move the wardrobe. And the bed.'

Tamara returned the hug. 'I could help with those.'

Cheryl hugged Tamara, too, briefly. Cheryl wasn't particularly huggy, so maybe it was her version of an olive branch. 'That would really be helpful. Dad's been working later and later, goodness knows what time he'll come home.'

The wardrobe was a bit of a monster. A very solid 1930s job inherited from grandparents, it stood on four curled legs and its doors locked with a key below a spotty mirror. Panting along the landing, Tamara struggled to keep a grip on the foot of the wardrobe, as she and Cheryl rebounded off walls and scraped their elbows on doorjambs, shuttling back and forth to achieve a suitable angle to pass into the room next door. Lyddie insisted on ushering backwards at the head of the procession, which meant Cheryl had to either bounce off her or put in a series of emergency stops, causing Tamara to bang her thighs and shins on the sharp and unforgiving boards between the curly legs. 'Ow! Have you got bricks in here, Lyddie?'

Lyddie gave her loud, kookaburra laugh. 'It's not for bricks, silly! It's for clothes. And we took them all out. Look.' She tried to reach over Cheryl to open the wardrobe door.

Cheryl put in another stop. 'Ouch, my bum! Lyddie, back up a bit, darling.'

With much panting, tutting and groaning they eventually eased the cumbersome piece of furniture into the room, heaving it around until it was finally settled with its back against the wall. Then they collapsed onto the carpet to recover.

Cheryl eased her back. 'I'd really like to make Lyddie an en suite out of her old room, but we'll have to see how much it costs.'

'It would be nice for the family to have two bathrooms,' Tamara agreed, neutrally. An en suite would mean there would be no spare room for Tamara to stay in and be supportive. Maybe they'd rather have had another bathroom all the time?

'I want a bathroom like Emilia's,' Lyddie exclaimed. 'With a toilet and that other thing to wash your bum in, and a shower without a bath under it, and gold taps.'

Tamara grinned. 'Might be a bit expensive. Better wait and see.'

'Gold taps,' she insisted, 'like Emilia's.'

They returned to the bathroom-to-be and repeated the landing struggle with Lyddie's mattress. It was more flexible than the wardrobe, but frustratingly short of things to get a grip on so they had to sort of squeeze-and-haul, seriously threatening Cheryl's hairdo.

Cheryl panted, puffing and heaving. 'How about staying for lunch? We can walk Lyddie to work after and then have a chat.'

Another olive branch? 'Lovely,' Tamara grunted, as she wrestled the mattress around the tight corner into the bedroom.

So, after Lyddie had gone to work, no doubt to bend Gwen's ear about her new bedroom and possible bathroom, and Jabber had settled with a sigh to sleep away her absence on his beanbag, Tamara stayed on to share a cup of tea, feeling pretty bloody virtuous about it because Cheryl hadn't exactly been at her most loveable recently.

Cheryl preferred tea made in a china pot and drunk from china cups and saucers, carried into the sitting room on a tray, rather than mugs at the kitchen table. She sighed as she sank into her chair and watched Tamara pour. Cheryl had inherited the cups from her mother, royal blue on the outside, but decorated with yellow roses on their white interior. It seemed a shame to cover them up with tea.

Tamara cradled her cup and sipped, feeling as if she were drinking from a big eggshell.

Cheryl picked up her cup, too. 'Has Dad said much to you?'

'What about?' Tamara asked, cautiously.

'About the situation.' Cheryl uncrossed her legs, restlessly. 'He must've taken on the evening appointments of the entire company, lately. He's making it plain he'd rather be at work than here.' She ran her fingertip around the cup. The remnants of gilt speckled the rim.

Tamara took a gulp of her tea, which was uncomfortably hot. 'It sounds as if you two need to talk.'

The mantelpiece clock ticked, the birds sang in the garden. Cheryl swung one foot. 'Was I very awful to him when Jed turned up?'

Tamara tried to be tactful. 'It was a shock for us all.'

'But was I?'

She hesitated. 'I've never been sure why you blamed Jed for what Uncle Don did, or why you should take it so personally that Dad didn't feel the same.'

Her mother turned and Tamara was shocked to see that her eyes were swimming with tears. 'I was furious and I couldn't see past that. Dad and I have had words. When I said it was a shame we didn't have the money for an en suite for Lyddie because a wet room would mean that she didn't have to clamber in and out of the bath all the time, he snapped my head off. He said that I should have thought of that before I hurled the financial compensation back in Jed's face.'

Putting down her cup, Tamara took her mother's hand. 'Talk to Dad again, Mum—'

Cheryl's eyes were pink with unshed tears. 'And then he shouted that making that room into an en suite wasn't fair to you, anyway, that you were a diamond when it came to staying here so that we can have a break now and then. He said I should get over my resentment towards you.'

Tamara recoiled. 'Resentment?' she asked, blankly, completely forgetting to say that she had a second bedroom and Lyddie could always stay there.

A tear left a trail in Cheryl's face powder. 'I gave my freedom up when Lyddie was hurt and I don't resent her, but, somehow, I feel that you've got the life I wanted. Freedom, a career that utilises your skills.'

And suddenly Tamara was on her feet. 'I've always done everything I can to help with Lyddie.'

'I know.' Cheryl scuffled around her cuffs for a tissue to blow her nose. 'I know! But that doesn't help. *I* felt so tricked and betrayed and I can't really see that *you* have anything to complain about.' Cheryl sniffed, dabbing her eyes. Then her shoulders buckled and she dropped her face in her hands. 'Isn't that h-horrible?'

Shaking, Tamara fetched a box of tissues, as her mother wept and wept, hoping the tears, the acknowledgement of the grief, would be cleansing.

Gradually Cheryl calmed, the sobs were replaced by hiccups, and she lay back as if exhausted, a fresh tissue clutched to her eyes.

Her voice emerged, muffled, from under a menthol-scented Kleenex. 'Don't suggest that Lyddie goes to Mountland Hall more often to give me a break, will you?'

'No.' Tamara had been about to suggest that very thing. 'But—'

Cheryl shook her head. 'The time will come for that. I'll get older, she'll have to be cared for more and more by others, she'll become more settled at Mountland than at home and Dad and I will know she'll be all right when we go. Because we expect her to outlive us, darling, so we have to know she'll be looked after. But I'm not ready to let her go, yet.'

Tamara opened her mouth once more, but Cheryl, removing the tissue from a red and streaky face, pre-empted her again. 'And don't suggest that you have Lyddie to give me a break, either. She's not your responsibility, darling. She's really not! You've got your life.' She touched Tamara's hand, very lightly. 'Let's limit how many lives we let Lyddie's accident compromise.'

Tamara sank down slowly. Her mind flew to the evening before and how Jed had seemed instinctively to understand and yet Max had had to be told – and now, it seemed so did her own mother, the one who should *know*.

'I don't help with Lyddie out of some over-developed sense of responsibility or duty. Or to make me look good, or you look bad, or force you to be grateful.' Her words were slow and emphatic, in time with the thumping of her heart. 'I don't do it so that I can feel smug. I love her. That's what love is – I love her in a way that makes me want to be there for her. I don't think that's going to change and, sorry, but it's not up to you to say how I should spend my time, or live my life, or love my sister. It's between me and Lyddie.'

Chapter Twenty-Five

'Wow!' Tamara halted when she saw Emilia, brilliant against the cream wall tiles of the poolside. 'You look fabulous!'

Emilia's ponytail had vanished, replaced by a sleek, ruby-streaked bob showing off catwalk cheekbones. New mulberry-coloured exercise clothes clung to her flat stomach and tight chest.

'What does Tom think of your new look?' Tamara shook out her mat beside the one Emilia had laid ready, reflecting on how coincidental it was that Emilia had had streaks and a new haircut right after Tamara had streaks and a new haircut.

Emilia flushed. 'He's ... getting used to it. He liked my hair long.'

Tamara opened her mouth to point out that it was Emilia's hair and a girl ought to be able to make up her mind about its style, but Tom Hilton walked into view outside the French doors at that moment and looked at Tamara through the glass. She nodded politely. After a few beats he moved on. 'So, Tom's home today?' She watched him move out of sight.

'They're all here today – Tom, Jed and Manny.' Emilia looked discontented. 'They might be cooking something up.'

Tamara's stomach rolled. 'Like what?'

With a shrug, Emilia pulled herself carefully off her chaise and onto her mat. 'It could be anything,' she muttered. 'Don't take any notice of me, I'm a bit jumpy. It's just that Tom looks after me a bit too well sometimes. But at least he's taking me out today. Just for some afternoon tea in aid of charity at Port Manor Hotel, but it'll be good to get away from this place.'

'Port Manor's nice. And local.' Tamara tried to be diplomatic, conscious that although she was employed by Emilia, it was very much Mr Hilton's house. And no doubt he was the one who earned the money that paid Tamara's fee. But a woman of Emilia's age and means ought to be living a never-at-home life, zooming round in a sexy, stupendous car; she was too young and gorgeous to be hidden away by an ageing husband, so that a pot of tea and plate of cakes at a local hotel was something to look forward to.

It was actually beginning to pain Tamara to see Emilia's restrictions, as if she were some exotic creature who'd been crippled by a man's cruel trap, condemned to hobble when she should dance. Tamara watched her stretch gracefully into a balance on her left leg, but not even be able to take all her weight on her right.

'OK, let's do some seated heel raises on that leg, instead,' Tamara said brightly. 'And then we'll do some forward bends and spinal twists.' In many seated poses Emilia's injury didn't show; she could easily stretch forward and grasp her feet, or hook one leg around the other and twist to look behind herself.

At the end of the session, Emilia levered to her feet and swooped up her crutches. 'Let's walk around the garden. I've told Carrie we won't be needing coffee today because I'll be awash with the stuff at the charity do.'

Though Tamara would have preferred to remain in the warmth of the pool area and, actually, didn't see why she should do without coffee because Emilia chose to, she accepted her role as hired help and let Emilia lead the way over the bridge to the driftwood thrones and the fountain.

Emilia seated herself and sighed. 'I was hoping to visit

Lyddie tonight. Do you think it'll be OK?' Although she smiled, there seemed an underlying despondency, even desperation, in her manner.

'You'll have to ask my mother.' Tamara watched her tap-tap-tapping her crutch on the floor, shifting her leg, pulling her fleece around her.

'I rang your parents last night to invite Lyddie at the weekend, but Cheryl said Lyddie would be away.'

'Yes, at Mountland Hall. She goes into respite care one weekend in four.'

Emilia's eyes were clear in the sunshine. 'Does she have treatment?'

'Some occupational therapy, simple cooking tasks, that sort of thing. Lyddie's full of you being her new friend.'

Emilia smiled the smile that made her beautiful, the one that eclipsed the anxiety in her face. 'She's fantastic. I haven't had a friend like her since I was a teenager.'

'It's certainly ... uncomplicated.' Lyddie was happy if she could please those she loved, watch TV, play on her computer and adore her animals. She made few demands, harboured no grudges, asked no favours. Tamara wondered how long it would be before Emilia wanted more conventional friendships with people able to live independent lives.

Then the thought brought a surge of traitorousness that made her feel quite cold. To make up for it, she took out her phone and offered, 'I'll ring Mum for you, now, if you like.'

Emilia's brilliant smile flashed again. 'Thank you! It would be great to be with someone who's so easy to be with.' She threw a nervous glance at the house. 'You've no idea what it's like to feel you're always under someone's watchful eyes.'

Tamara made the call, heart in her boots at how trapped Emilia seemed to feel. And if Jed was instrumental in that ...

'Mum says it's fine,' she was happy to report, two minutes later. And Emilia beamed like a child who had been given exactly what she'd wanted for Christmas.

Because Emilia needed to change her clothes, Jed came early to escort Tamara to his office to collect her fee. Lost in conjecture about whether Jed was jailer or protector, she was monosyllabic as he took his time over his obligations and asked how the session had gone, how Lyddie was. Eventually, he walked her to her car.

Instead of opening the door for her, he rested his hand against it. 'Not even lukewarm today. You OK?'

Behind him, the garage door opened with a mechanical grumble and the dark blue Mercedes rolled out, Manny at the wheel. He flashed a grin and drove the car up to the front door. Almost immediately, Mr Hilton and Emilia came out of the house, Emilia changed out of her exercise gear and into a pale green silk dress. Before climbing into the back of the car, she looked at Tamara and then at Jed. Immediately, Tamara made to open her own car door, obliging Jed to remove his hand so that she could throw in her bag and mat as she answered, briefly, 'Fine.'

The gates opened, the Mercedes swept out, and, slowly, the gates closed behind it.

'Why is it that when a woman says "fine" she really means "fuck off and die"?'

Surprised into looking up and meeting his eyes, she saw no hint of the menace that Emilia seemed to associate with this difficult-to-read man. There was interest, wariness, amusement. And uncertainty? Concern? 'I don't mean that. I mean I'm fine. Not fabulous, but not under threat of death.'

'"Fine" covers quite a window, then.'

Reluctantly, she smiled. 'Suppose it does.'

'Would a nice cup of strong coffee take you a step closer

to "fabulous"? Seems to me that you're owed a cup and, as most of the household has just left the building, I'm about to have one myself.'

So he'd noticed that Emilia hadn't seen the necessity to provide refreshment today. She glanced at her watch. Coffee sounded tempting. She refused to acknowledge that spending time with Jed, even time clouded by suspicion, was tempting too.

'Suppose I could.'

'Good.' Closing her car door, he led her around the garage to an entrance to Lie Low that she'd never noticed.

'Where are we going?'

'My shoebox apartment. I have running water now.'

She felt a little jolt. For some reason she'd assumed he'd take her to his office and call Carrie for coffee, just like Emilia did.

She halted at the foot of the stairs.

Jed looked around impatiently. 'What's up?'

He knew what was up. She was a woman and he was a man. A man who, for some reason, she couldn't decide whether to like or not. The prospect of entering his lair had set off her inner rape alarm and she was poised to fly. He didn't understand why, but he had to go through the whole gaining her trust thing all over again.

Raising his hands in the age-old gesture of surrender, he injected a judicious iota of boredom into his voice. 'I'll leave the doors open and you can run at the first sign of my turning into a slavering beast.' Then, fishing for his key, he resumed his climb up the stairs.

When he'd unlocked his front door, he looked back. Tamara was following, warily. Passing through the door ahead of her, he kicked off his shoes and headed for the kitchen, letting her follow or not. Her footsteps halted on the threshold. He glanced back to see her start after him. She'd been wearing those things that couldn't make up their mind whether to be trainers or sandals, but now her feet were bare but for purple nail varnish sinking delicately, into the carpet pile.

He turned away to prevent himself from swinging back and sweeping her up against the white wall. Or flat on her back under him on the floor, her hair a bright splash against the cream carpet, her skin pale satin as he got her naked. He could deal with those stretchy clothes in seconds. She'd probably be wearing a sports bra and those things could be a bloody nuisance but—

Get hold of yourself!

He kept his back to her as he took down mugs, white porcelain with *'le café noir'* fired onto them in fine black cursive script. The coffee machine, part of a stainless steel bank of appliances, was on. He filled the little drawer with beans and selected 'strong cup', adding a tot of cream to his cup while hers was filling. 'Biscuit?'

'No, thanks.'

He had full command of himself now and let himself face the kitchen doorway, where she stood eyeing him, tiger hair glowing in the afternoon light, falling back as he approached with a mug in each hand, then following him into the sitting room. Even her wariness of him seemed to enhance his image of her as clean and nice. He didn't know what it was she had against him, but it seemed as if it must spring from rightness and morality.

He deposited the mugs on the glass coffee table and dropped onto the chaise end of the massive black and white sofa, swinging his feet up, making himself comfortable as if there was truly nothing more in his mind than taking a quick coffee break in his favourite spot, a bank of remote controls and his e-reader beside him. He didn't betray, by so much as a fleeting glance at her breasts, how aware he was of her. The top she was wearing fastened with eleven small hooks down the front. He'd tested his peripheral vision by counting them. He could have a lot of fun with eleven hooks. He wondered how fast he could flip them open. Then how slowly ...

She settled herself further along the massive sofa combination. 'Thanks.'

He lifted his mug. 'Costa Rican.'

She sipped. 'It's good.' Her gaze left him and travelled slowly around the room, over the framed monochrome photos on the wall, the floor-length black curtains, glass lampshades, the huge TV and speakers. 'You lied about your apartment.'

He shrugged. 'I do have carpets and curtains, and more than a gas ring for coffee.'

'It's fantastic.' Her gaze took in the sitting room door as if checking that, good to his word, he'd left her exit clear. 'Is it— Is it important to you to live somewhere this sumptuous?'

Taken aback at the speed with which she'd seen straight to his centre, he sipped his coffee before he replied. 'Sumptuous? No. I'm just lucky that my job carries a spacious apartment and that I earn enough to fit it out indulgently. I only have myself to please, so why not?' And then, because revealing himself to her felt kind of right 'If I ever had to go back to living in a squat to survive, I could, but I prefer to live somewhere as unlike the squat as I can make it. I like nice smells and being clean.' It flashed across his mind to tell her that, on the other hand, he could be very dirty, if he wanted. But inappropriate remarks weren't going to improve his image in her eyes.

She looked uncertain. 'You won't ever have to go back to that, will you?'

'I've made provision against it.' There was a bank account with quite a lot of money in it, and enough would remain to keep him for a couple of years, even if he succeeded in getting Sean and Cheryl to accept his half of his dad's house proceeds.

When she'd finished her drink, he glanced at his watch. 'Better get back to work,' he said, gathering up the coffee mugs.

In the hall he trod back into his shoes and opened the door for her – because it was good manners, not just an opportunity to watch her bottom swinging – and saw her back to her car. Behaving in an absolutely non-threatening manner, he'd demonstrated that she could trust him even with his bed in proximity, a huge sofa for him to coax her down onto, the carpet, the kitchen counter, the shower, just about any hard surface ... yet he hadn't so much as kissed her cheek or taken her hand.

But as she was getting into her car, he spoke into her ear. 'The temperature rose a degree or two, in there. I'll keep working towards something hotter.' And winked when she blushed.

It had been a long day. Tamara had detected a sense of undercurrents at Lie Low; something that Emilia wasn't revealing, but was feeling deeply. In the depths of her eyes, Tamara could read secrets. She hated, absolutely hated, to think of Emilia being hemmed in and controlled. It made her irritable and disappointed with the world.

Or ... she kept letting the thought in as she conducted her afternoon classes. Was whatever was happening to Emilia making Tamara feel uncomfortable simply because Jed was implicated? Every time she saw Jed, she felt as if he was pulling on a rubber band with her on the other end. But then, every time she saw Emilia, she felt as though she had to resist Jed, because Jed was a potentially painful landing place.

Tamara yearned to give in and hurtle in his direction even when, like today, he behaved as if he was her Sunday school teacher.

Her restlessness was increased by there not being much in her social life right now. The trouble with having a boyfriend who was your best friend, was that when he moved on you had nobody to bitch to about it. Lyddie, however large a slice of Tamara's heart she owned, wasn't the confidante a healthy sister might be. And though Tamara knew loads of her yogis well enough to meet for coffee before or after a class, she'd never hooked up with any of them at other times.

So she prepared to spend Friday evening at home with QI on the television and her laptop on her knee. She opened Rowland Community College's social networking page. Maybe a 'How are *you*?' conversation with an old school buddy would soon become, 'We must meet up!'

She was giggling over a post from someone who had shared Tamara's hatred of chemistry lessons, when her Skype icon burst into life and Lyddie's avatar flashed. Tamara answered, and Lyddie loomed, her big smile stretched by the fish-eye effect of the webcam. 'Shall we Skype, 'Mara?'

'Hiya, Lyddie! Have you logged on by yourself? Well done. Has Emilia gone home already?' She checked her watch. It was only eight thirty.

In answer, Lyddie's image slid around and off the screen and Tamara was treated to a moving jigsaw of disjointed images before the screen greyed over with just a sunburst of light at one side. Frowning, Tamara listened to muffled voices.

Then an image slid back onto the screen and settled down.

It was Emilia.

'This is a huge cheek.' Her silvery voice floated from the speakers in sync with her slightly jerky lip movements. 'But I need to speak to you. I'm really sorry to do it like this ...' Her image shrugged. 'But you know how things are at home.'

Lyddie appeared behind Emilia, the webcam's fisheyed view showed Lyddie with a pouch fastened untidily about her waist and lightweight earphones looping over her head. 'Hello 'Mara! I'm letting 'Milia use my computer and I'm using her little stereo.' Her voice was unnecessarily loud to combat the music feeding directly into her ears, like an old lady shouting over her deafness. Emilia had evidently made an expedient exchange of personal possessions – she got to use Lyddie's computer as a hotline to Tamara, and at the same time prevented Lyddie from listening in while she used it.

So as not to infect Lyddie with her disquiet over this arrangement, Tamara grinned and waved reassuringly. Lyddie waved back and turned her attention to the iPod, poking and pressing at the buttons. Probably Emilia had already set the equipment on 'hold' so that no amount of exploring of the buttons would stop the music.

Tamara felt a sliding sensation of dismay that Emilia was going to the lengths of getting herself into Tamara's parents' home and finding Tamara in cyber-space. 'What's up?'

Emilia blinked. 'Confidential, right?'

Tamara frowned. 'I suppose so. As long as it's nothing dicey. Or anything that affects Lyddie.'

'Even if you decide not to help?'

'I suppose so. What's with all the secrecy?' Her voice was sharp. She wasn't sure she liked Lyddie being manipulated like this. It made her feel as if she wasn't looking after her sister properly. Although she couldn't actually detect danger in anything Emilia was doing, there was something disquieting about her being with Lyddie in the room Tamara had grown up in, while Tamara could only look into the scene through her computer. 'Maybe I ought to just join you at Mum and Dad's house—'

'Um ...' Emilia screwed up her forehead in alarm. 'I really wish you wouldn't. It would make your mum and dad wonder if something's going on.'

It was on the tip of Tamara's tongue to point out that setting up this elaborate line of communication was actually what most people would consider 'something going on'.

Emilia squinted at Tamara's expression. 'I'm making travel plans. I'm going to visit my mother in Canada. She's had cancer and, although she's got the all clear, I want to spend more time with her. She's had a hysterectomy and a mastectomy and I want to see her.'

A click from Tamara's mental tumblers. She nodded slowly. 'On your own?'

'Yes.' Emilia nodded back. Then her eyes skidded guiltily away. 'You know why it's going to be difficult to get away, after what I told you about Tom.' She sighed heavily.

Tamara felt anxiety settling like a gremlin on her shoulder. 'And he wouldn't even be OK about you visiting your mother?'

Behind Emilia, Lyddie was doing a seated bum-shuffle on the end of the bed, hands waggling.

Silence. Then Emilia said quietly. 'I'm not coming back. So I need to get away without Tom knowing.'

Chapter Twenty-Six

Worry wormed through Tamara's belly. 'Are you certain you're going about things in the best way? There are people you can talk to. People who can coach you on how to assert yourself with your husband, non-confrontational methods—'

Emilia heaved a sigh huge enough to make the speakers crackle, clutching the sides of her head in the universal indication of frustration, ruffling her sleek new bob. 'Truth is, I've had enough of being Tom's wife! It can be a fucking hazardous occupation.'

Behind her, Lyddie stood up and began to dance, bum out.

'I know that domination from your partner can seem an insurmountable problem—'

Emilia snorted. 'If it were only him!' She glanced around to check that Lyddie was still occupied. 'The thing is, my accident – well, it wasn't an accident. It was an "on purpose".'

Tamara felt the blood drain from her face. A distant buzz began and she thought it must be coming from her ears. Surely Emilia couldn't mean what she thought she meant? 'On purpose?'

Emilia rubbed the heels of her hands into her eyes, as if suddenly terribly, terribly tired. 'Tom has enemies. You know that, right?'

Tamara swallowed. 'The protestors?'

She could see Emilia's hands balling into fists. 'I haven't got time to go into every little detail, but yes. And they might have a point, frankly. Tom's involved in a wide spectrum of stuff, everything from legitimate through shady to downright immoral, if not actually illegal. How do you think he got so rich? Anyway, Manny and Jed weren't around the night it happened. Tom went apeshit at them and so they got scared for their cushy jobs, I suppose, which is why they're both trailing around after me like annoying kids.' She stopped, gulping a couple of breaths.

'When what happened?' Tamara shook her head.

'Two men got into my hotel suite when I was asleep and Tom was out on business with Jed; Manny was driving them. The men tipped me off the balcony. I suppose I was lucky not to land on my head and spend the rest of my life as a veg—' She broke off abruptly and cast a mortified look behind her at Lyddie.

Tamara was too dumbstruck to take offence at any clumsy allusions to head injury. 'Shit,' she breathed. 'This is like something from a nine o'clock drama.'

Emilia licked her lips nervously, fingers drumming on the chair arm. 'So that's why we're hiding away up in the country; why Manny and Jed are minding me like a princess.' She laughed shortly. 'And the real reason that Tom has turned from possessive to obsessive. But I want to see my mum.'

She scrabbled for a tissue and dabbed at her eyes. 'Mum and Tom don't get on, so Tom would never go with me to Canada.' Her voice broke. 'I know it's one of the first places he'd look for me, but once I've seen Mum I can disappear and Mum can come with me, if she wants. But I must get away from Tom Hilton, from the prison he's gradually created. And from the kind of attention he attracts from violent bastards who don't mind who suffers as long as they get their point across.'

Tamara was assailed with a horrible image of poor Emilia being dragged bodily from her bed, hoiked over a balcony and tossed into the black night. But she also had to think about Lyddie, who had stopped dancing and was fiddling with her earphones. It only needed her to decide to yank them off and she'd hear Emilia's tear-filled voice and fly immediately into 'a state', as Cheryl would call it, tossing her arms around and squealing and maybe shoving Emilia. Emilia wouldn't know how to calm her, she'd be knocked off her limping feet, Cheryl would run upstairs and get angry. It would all be uncomfortable to witness through a bloody webcam. 'I wish you hadn't involved my sister in this—'

But then Emilia's face was twisting, words swarming in the air like angry bees. 'Aren't you listening to me, Tamara? I've told you what my life's like. I need to leave Tom Hilton! And Manny's so bloody clever with his high-risk close-surveillance training. Tom doesn't employ him for nothing. Manny can listen to anything going on in any room in the house. Why do you think Tom's humouring me, letting me have my little yoga classes – so long as they take place in Lie Low?'

'Calm down!' Tamara hissed uncomfortably. 'You'll upset Lyddie.' She paused for thought, as Emilia cast an apologetic look over her shoulder to where Lyddie was frowning again at the iPod. Emilia's story seemed unbelievable. Incredible. But, made enough sense that it couldn't be ignored. 'Is this for real? You're seriously using my sister and me as a blind for leaving your husband?'

'Very real.' Emilia sniffed. 'I'm sorry. I suppose I am kind of using you, but I'm desperate. I look for opportunities to make contacts with the outside world all the time – I tried to form a friendship with the alpaca breeders, but it didn't work out. Even though Manny's outside in the car, he thinks I'm safely penned in here and can't get up to anything. He's not worried about my mobile because he can intercept cell-phone signals and I've never found a way to

247

get myself a satellite phone. That's why I thought of using Skype. I've already used it to talk to Mum tonight because I really needed to.' Distractedly, she glanced at her watch. 'Tamara, please will you do something for me?'

One eye on Lyddie, Tamara was cautious. 'What?'

'Next time you come to the house ... will you give me a lift when you leave, and say you're bringing me to see Lyddie?'

'But surely Manny will simply pick up his keys and take you himself?'

'Not if we do it when Manny's out driving Tom. Then it's just Jed and he likes you, he trusts you and he's got a thing for you. I've heard you talk to him and you don't take any of his shit. You can be impatient with him, brush his protests aside and he'll probably just think it's funny, in his weird way.'

Emilia might be right. But Tamara wasn't liking it. She felt cornered. 'I'm not comfortable in getting involved.'

Emilia thrust her face closer to the camera, so it looked as if she was looking through a fish bowl. 'How comfortable are you with me being controlled like this until the day Tom dies? How comfortable will you be with horrible men coming after me and crippling my other leg? You were the one who told me that there was an intruder at the fence recently. The others kept it from me. And that's why – because I might be a target again and it's easier for them to control me if I think I'm safe.' The urgency in her face transcended the slight disjointedness of webcam images.

'I've been lying awake at nights, turning it over and over. I could only come up with one way of getting away from this situation – and this is it. It's down to you. Please say you can rescue me. All you have to do is drop me at Church Close and Mum will arrange the rest.'

Tamara's stomach clenched and she wished, desperately,

that she'd turned Emilia down as a client in the first place. That Emilia hadn't become friendly with Lyddie, involving her in her sad, controlled, life.

But, at least, Emilia bunking off to Canada would mean an end to Tamara's involvement, and she could easily push Jed to a proper distance. With Emilia gone, Mr Hilton and his retinue might leave the area, anyway.

Poor Lyddie would lose her lovely new friend, though. Tamara swore to herself. Never again would she get involved with a weird private client who lived a freaky hermit life, no matter how hurt she was and no matter how much she paid.

'And what happens when Jed or Manny come banging at my parents' door?'

Emilia bit her lip. 'If they weren't home ...?'

'Yes, we'll all arrange our lives around you, shall we?' Tamara let out on a spurt of temper. Then, seeing Emilia's woebegone face, felt a stab of grudging compunction. 'Leave it with me. Now get off my sister's computer, give her a big hug and tell her it's time for you to go. And go home while I think about this.'

Emilia's lip quivered. 'Monday, Tamara, please? Manny's driving Tom down to London on Monday, so it can be then. Please, Tamara! Please! I'm so scared.'

Fresh outrage swelled in Tamara's chest. 'You're putting me on the spot—'

Lyddie pulled off the earphones and dropped the iPod on the bed disconsolately. ''Mara, I don't like all of 'Milia's music. 'Milia, the music's changed to rap and I don't like it. There's no tune.'

'I'll try,' Tamara whispered to Emilia. Then she raised her voice to Lyddie. 'Never mind, Lyd. How about you come over to the computer and talk to me for a minute? Emilia has to get ready to go home, now.'

'When I've sent one more email,' Emilia corrected her, brightly. 'Do you mind if I use your computer while you talk to Tamara, Lyddie?'

Lyddie beamed her big, trusting smile. "Course not. We don't mind, do we, 'Mara?'

Chapter Twenty-Seven

Tamara changed her mind eight times before Monday.

Should she help Emilia?

Of course she should; Emilia was a woman in jeopardy.

But if Tom Hilton – and Jed and Manny – were half what Emilia said, would that put Tamara and her family at risk?

Her only loyalty to Emilia was as a fairly recent client. OK, they'd been friendly, but she wasn't so short of buddies that she'd actually call Emilia a friend.

But what was wrong with giving a client a lift into the village, if it helped that client escape from an intolerable situation? Tom Hilton had no right to appoint jailers; her client was an independent person with every right to quit her marital home.

Tom Hilton paid the fees …

More fool him. Emilia was her client.

When she rolled through the gates and pulled up on the drive, Tamara felt hollow and damp-palmed, as if waiting for an exam to begin. Jed was waiting for her. He opened her car door, the muscles of his tanned forearm moving under his skin.

'What's the temperature today?' One corner of his mouth lifted.

She shrugged, dragging her holdall from the back seat, searching his eyes for whether he was the kind of man who would act as an unwanted guardian. 'I haven't decided yet.' It was the truth, but it sounded as if she was some silly capricious female only on nodding terms with the word 'rational'.

Instantly, Jed frowned, gaze sharpening. 'That's an odd reaction.'

She shrugged again, trying to look vague. Hell, she was as jumpy as … as an Emilia. Maybe she was getting a glimmer of understanding of how it made you feel to have Jed's stare boring into you when you didn't want it. 'It's you who's been saying I'm changeable,' she invented. 'I'm just proving your point.' No, that was wrong, too, his frown became more ferocious and she could almost see his brain working.

'I never said you were changeable. I said you'd changed towards me. There's a difference. My whole point is that you're *not* changeable, so the change must have happened for a reason. And I don't think that it's unreasonable for me to be curious about what that is.' He stayed her with a hand on her arm. 'So why don't you tell me? I'm a big boy and I can take it. Halitosis? BO? Have I said something that offends some principle you hold dear?'

His tone might be bantering, but Tamara could see real puzzlement behind it. And maybe hurt? Or was that her imagination? She'd hardly slept since Friday. Perhaps sleep deprivation was making her imagination loop the loop. Perhaps that was why she was experiencing an overwhelming urge to simply tell him what Emilia had said and hope he'd refute it with an explanation that would put him in a good light, like Emilia suffering from a delusional condition or persecution complex, which meant she would spin wild and whirly stories about perfectly innocent people.

But that didn't seem very likely because if Emilia had a mental health or emotional issue Tamara would naturally have been informed.

As she followed Jed – too miserable even to appreciate his amazing glutes – through the house to where Emilia waited by the pool like an outcast mermaid, she sadly acknowledged that Emilia's explanation of the way things were at Lie Low was, unfortunately, all too plausible.

Emilia pulled herself to her feet as soon as Jed showed

Tamara into the poolside area. She was pale, but composed. 'Great to see you.'

Feeling as if she was in a bad dream, Tamara summoned up a smile. 'Ready to relax? I thought we'd work on weight-bearing, today. Your injured leg won't be able to take so much as the other, but it will benefit you, I think. We'll roll down to relax first, though.'

'Fantastic,' said Emilia, brightly, faux-happy. But Tamara could see her tension and that when she bit her lip, it was to prevent the fall of tears that stood in her eyes.

The hour dragged by. Instead of the floating feeling of contentment that yoga usually brought, Tamara felt heavy with dread as she rolled up her mat and followed Emilia out to the driftwood thrones by the fountain, which was tinkling incongruously in the sunshine.

Emilia limped restlessly around the pond, gazing down at the fish gaping up at her with their bulging eyes and cartoon mouths as she gabbled meaninglessly about yoga, the sessions that had obviously all been part of the design to keep Tamara coming to the house so that, eventually, Emilia could use her.

And Lyddie.

Finally, Emilia took the throne beside Tamara's, dropping her voice until it could be lost in the plink-plinky-plink of the dancing water. 'I was scared to death you wouldn't come today.'

'You want to go through with—?'

'Of course. Just get me through those gates and into the village. You're not going to let me down, are you?' Emilia's eyes were feverish, pleading.

In contrast, Tamara could hear her own voice was all doubt. 'You're a hundred per cent certain are you? Because the consequences aren't necessarily all yours. I've given Mum tickets to take Lyddie to the pictures this afternoon, pretending somebody gave them to me to make it worthwhile rearranging Lyddie's hours at the shop. I'm going to deflect as much attention as I can from them, but you must see that Jed or Manny, or even Mr Hilton, will ask questions.'

Emilia clenched her hands. 'Don't back out, Tamara! *Please.* I'm sorry to involve your family when you've all been so good to me, but I've got to get away. I just want to have my own life. And I don't want to end up hurt again—'

Tamara cast around for more obstacles. 'I presume you've thought about finance?'

Emilia reached into her yoga pants. 'I've got your money here, because you obviously can't get involved with going into Jed's office today.'

'I didn't mean my fee,' Tamara said, stiffly. 'I'm asking if you're going to starve in Canada.'

For a moment, Emilia's eyes softened. 'I can get at money. And Mum'll make sure I'm OK.' Her eyes flickered around the garden, darting from the pale pink anemones to the dustier pink hydrangeas clustered on their bushes like old-fashioned bathing hats.

Tamara sighed and waved away the fold of money. 'What do you think Jed is – stupid? You wouldn't normally sully your hands with paying the hired help, so he's bound to smell a stinky great rat if you suddenly get all helpful now. I'll have to go into his office. You wander around to the front of the house and lurk somewhere near the car.'

'I've got a bag hidden in the bushes,' whispered Emilia. 'I took it out early this morning, through the garage, after the alarm was off and nobody was about.'

'This is beginning to seem ridiculously cops and robbers,' snapped Tamara. 'You'd better put it in the boot while I talk to Jed. I haven't locked the car. This place is like Fort Knox, anyway.'

Slowly, they sipped their drinks. The time seemed to crawl. Tamara looked down at the animal-like feet on the big driftwood seats and wished they'd carry her off. She couldn't think of anything she wanted to say. She felt as if she was paying a personal cost for Emilia's freedom and that the cost would be her relationship with Jed. A chill weight wrapped itself around her heart as she tried to make herself realise that Jed was a baddie. His boss was dodgy. His stepbrother had been in trouble with the law. His dad had knocked Lyddie cartwheeling through the air and run away ... She stopped. None of those were things that Jed had done; she was as bad as her mother, damning him for his associations.

She began a new mental list. Conspiring against Emilia was unacceptable and helping exert that kind of control showed that he was unscrupulous. He was hot, he had a great behind, his eyes creased at the corners in place of a proper smile, when he'd touched her, her skin had burned—

She halted. Her list had gone off track somewhere.

Setting her cup down with a clatter, she jumped to her feet. 'Ring Jed as usual, then give me two minutes before you start moving. I'll meet you at the car.'

She swung her bag over her shoulder, while Emilia made the usual 'Tamara's leaving now' call, then she strolled towards the house.

Jed met her as she stepped through the French doors. 'Leaving early?'

'I've something I need to do.' Tamara glanced back, giving him the opportunity to see that Emilia had gone to stand on the bridge, gazing down through still water at the carp as if lost in thought, her crutches hooked loosely around her elbows.

His eyebrows rose a fraction. 'Come through, then.'

She didn't take a seat while he opened his stupid cash

box and counted out her money. Sadly, she watched his deft movement, the strength in his hands. Silently, she said goodbye.

His eyes sparked up at her. 'You OK?'

She gave a tiny shrug. 'Fine.'

'So "fine" means Arctic temperatures, today?'

She repeated the shrug, keeping her eyes on the thick green carpet. Emilia would have had time to get halfway to the car by now.

He studied her. 'Why don't we have a glass of wine later? Or dinner? Tamara, your attitude's beginning to burn me. I don't know what it is in your expression when you look at me – but I don't like it.'

Tamara offered a regretful smile and swept up the money he'd laid on the desk. It would be her last fee from Emilia, but she wasn't sorry. She couldn't wait to get out of this oppressive house, with its weird inhabitants and their dysfunctional lives. She couldn't wait never to see Jed Cassius again. Her treacherous eyes burned at the thought. 'I'm sorry. But I just can't.'

She checked her watch. Emilia should be ready. 'I'm afraid I need to go.'

He rose, not stepping aside as she moved towards the door, but he didn't stop her when she brushed past and walked on soft legs from the house. As usual, he fell in behind her, watching her to her car, just as every visitor to this bloody house seemed to be controlled and escorted.

Out in the sunshine, Emilia emerged casually from around the corner. Tamara called, 'If you want to see Lyddie, hop in and I'll give you a lift. Lyddie'll be thrilled.'

'Fantastic.' Emilia opened the passenger door.

Immediately, Jed stepped forward. 'You didn't say you were going visiting, Emilia. I'll take you.'

Tamara gave him her best impatient frown, as Emilia

reversed herself into the front seat. 'I'm perfectly capable of driving her to see my sister. She can ring you when she's ready to come home in an hour or two.'

'Mr H would prefer me to be with her.'

Tamara dropped herself into the driving seat. 'Follow behind if you so want to spend the afternoon sitting in the car in Church Close, but I'm not hanging around because I've got things to do before my next class.' Then she was starting her car, putting it in gear and swinging it around to make for the gates ... which remained closed.

She pressed the horn, a quick, light reminder.

'He's not going to open it,' breathed Emilia. Her good foot tapped nervously.

Tamara watched in the rear-view mirror. 'He's thinking about it.' She pipped the horn twice more, then opened the window and twisted around to stick her arms out and tap on her watch.

Finally, Jed's hand rose, the one holding the remote control ... and the gates began to open. The moment the aperture was wide enough, Tamara drove sedately out.

'Quickly!' hissed Emilia, swinging round to look behind her.

As soon as she was out of Jed's sight, Tamara put her foot down, nipping through the spinney, whipping down the track, swinging right onto Port Road, whizzing along the half-mile to the village.

At the entrance to Church Close a taxi was waiting, engine running. Not having to be told the next step, Tamara pulled in behind it.

'*Thank* you. Open the boot for me to get my bag.'

Tamara pressed the boot-release button and Emilia bundled herself out of the door, round the back of the car to the boot, then came back into sight limping swiftly over to the taxi, hauling a big cylindrical black holdall-on-wheels that looked heavy enough to be filled with rocks.

Obviously, even running away from an abusive husband necessitated an impressive cache of personal possessions. She threw her crutch inside the cab and fell in after it. The taxi was already leaving as the door shut, speeding down the road and swinging left at The Cross.

Tamara stared at the empty road it left behind.

Then, shaky with anticlimax, she drove off slowly, turning left into Main Road and home to Bankside.

Indoors, she made herself a stiffening cup of coffee, mulling over what she'd say to Jed when he arrived. Her heart was dancing a rumba and her breath fluttering in her throat as she wiped her palms on her yoga pants. She told herself she'd nothing to worry about. Had done nothing wrong.

It took about ten minutes, just long enough for him to try fruitlessly for an answer at her parents' house, she supposed, then he was banging on her door.

Obviously, she had to respond. Her car was outside. She took her phone with her, pretending to be part-way through a call. When she saw Jed, she let her eyebrows lift. 'This isn't a good time.' And then, inspiration striking, 'I'm speaking to Max.' That might help keep him at a distance.

His eyes went dark and still. 'Is Emilia here?'

'Emilia?' She shook her head, shrugging for good measure, saying into the phone in a clipped and irritated manner, 'Sorry about this, I'll be with you in half a minute.' Then to Jed, using her you're-being-a-bit-of-a-fool voice, 'I dropped Emilia off to visit Lyddie, didn't I?'

He swore comprehensively, snatching out his mobile. 'There's no one answering the door at your parents' house. I've tried the house phone, too, and just get the answering machine.'

She let her eyes widen and her mouth drop open. 'You're kidding?'

His eyes were flinty. 'Any chance you could phone your parents' mobiles for me? You'll appreciate that I can't just let Emilia evaporate.'

She sighed like the most put-upon woman in England. 'No, I suppose it's "not part of your job". Hang on, then.' And, into the phone, 'I'm sorry, Max, but could I call you back in five minutes? It's unavoidable.' Pretending to ring off, she clicked on her mother's name in her phone contacts in the certain knowledge that, in the darkness of the Odeon, it would be switched off. Cheryl had fixed ideas on the appropriate use of mobile phones and wouldn't even put hers on silent while she was in a cinema or a restaurant. She listened briefly, then ended the call. 'Sorry. Went straight to voicemail.'

Jed's eyes glinted with fury. 'Do you know where Emilia is?'

Tamara sighed and looked at her watch. 'Haven't we just covered this? I just dropped her off. I didn't hang around to check she walked up a garden path safely. Can we end this now, please? I want to speak to Max.' Then she closed the door on Jed's baffled face.

She stood still in her hallway, wishing she felt pleased with herself, wishing for some sense of satisfaction at having helped Emilia outwit him. Wishing she didn't somehow feel as if she'd just hung Jed out to dry.

Chapter Twenty-Eight

During her classes at Bettsbrough Park Hotel and then at the Caradoc Gym, Tamara tried hard to put Jed and Emilia out of her mind. She spent the slack time between her classes drinking lattes with some of the yogis from the hotel in the comfortable coffee bar, laughing at anecdotes, treating everyone to chocolate brownies. And fighting down feelings of guilt.

If Jed was a good guy, she felt guilty at conniving at something that would get him into trouble with his boss – maybe even lose him his job. If he wasn't ... that she might have involved her parents and her sister was unsettling. Belatedly, she wished she'd told Emilia she couldn't help her fly the nest.

After her last class she drove home gloomily, showered and changed, and then her mother rang. 'What's all this fuss about Emilia, do you know?'

Fresh guilt washed in. 'Emilia?'

'Jed Cassius has been on the phone asking if she was here. I said that she wasn't, but what did it have to do with him? He went all gruff on me and hung up.'

The guilt washed out a bit. Jed obviously didn't think that Cheryl knew anything, which was reasonable, as she didn't.

'Weird,' she breezed. 'How was the movie?'

'Lyddie loved it. She's so full of popcorn she hasn't even asked for biscuits.'

Tamara's guilt receded still further. Evidently, she'd managed the situation – Emilia was free and Lyddie and Cheryl had enjoyed a nice afternoon at the cinema. She set out for an evening at The Three Fishes to distract herself.

And really, Bell, less than beautiful in a black cross-back vest that allowed hams of swinging flesh to escape, jelly belly and thighs shaking along with his roars of laughter, ought to have been sufficient to distract anyone from anything. But even through his beeriest obnoxiousness about Tamara and Max not being an item any more and Bell being perfectly willing to 'take her on', Tamara couldn't shake off her gloom.

The expression in Jed's eyes as he'd tried to locate Emilia was proving hard to forget. He'd been worried. Whether that worry was for his job or for Emilia revolved uneasily in Tamara's mind. A sinking sensation was telling her that she might have allowed Jed to become collateral damage without being certain that he'd earned it.

By nine, she'd eaten an omelette, chatted to Janice behind the bar, turned down a marriage proposal from Bell with a sweet 'Not in this lifetime', chatted with two girls she'd been to school with who had left their husbands to the babysitting, and had had enough.

The evening outside was clammy after a humid day. She glanced up Main Road where the speed camera stood, charred now since someone tied a firework to it, but still, sadly, functioning. Then she turned away, heading across the playing fields, past the village hall and into Port Road. She needed to make sure Jed and Manny hadn't turned up at Church Close to make life difficult, and there would be something comforting about seeing Lyddie, feeling her sister's big soft arms around her and receiving a shower of damp kisses.

But Lyddie wasn't in front of the TV with Chewy and Jar Jar, as Tamara had hoped. She must have gone early to bed because when Tamara let herself in the front door with her key, only Jabber lolloped up the hall to welcome her and her parents were evidently too caught up in a furious under-voiced row-in-progress, to notice that their youngest daughter had just walked in.

Tamara was just in time to hear Cheryl explode. 'But why should we worry about what I told Jed when he phoned? I'm more worried about Emilia, if she's disappeared.'

Tamara halted uncertainly, a sinking feeling under her knicker elastic, wishing that her conscience had let her go home so she didn't have to listen to this.

Frustration rang in Sean's every word. 'I think Jed's in a mess and I'm sorry if he is, that's all. There was no need to be obstructive. You could have just said that you hadn't seen her and weren't expecting her. He's obviously worried to have rung back. He hasn't done anything to us. It was his father.' A silence. Then Sean's voice dropped dangerously low. 'You don't know anything about Emilia's disappearance, do you?'

'No. But I rather wish I did, so that I could refuse to tell him about it,' spat Cheryl unreasonably.

Turning, giving Jabber a last pat, Tamara made a quick exit, not sure she could maintain an air of innocence if her dad sliced questions at her as he had at her mum. And if Jed came looking again for Emilia, it was probably best if they genuinely knew nothing. Blank looks would be a sturdy defence.

She searched for her conviction that she'd done the right thing in helping Emilia. It had seemed reasonably clear cut, at one time, but Jed's face kept swimming before her eyes. Would he be in big trouble with Mr Hilton for letting his beloved Emilia slip away? Would Jed lose his job and that detergent-ad apartment that was obviously so important to him?

She wished she could be certain that he deserved that fate. But then she realised she'd much rather know that he didn't. For then she could just get on with feeling like slime for having let him take the fall.

On Tuesday, Tamara's doorbell sounded as she was eating porridge. Having decided to dismiss yesterday's escapade as nothing to do with her, and to try to forget that Jed's dismay, when he'd realised Emilia had slipped away, sat oddly with his habitual gritty reserve, she opened the door.

In a moment Manny's boot prevented it shutting again. The navy-blue Merc squatted at the roadside behind him. He didn't smile.

Belatedly, Tamara realised it might've been expedient to ignore the bell while she was alone in the house. 'What's up?' she demanded, as if mystified.

He looked as if he'd slept in his black trousers and shirt. After a moment, he managed to paste on an expression that passed as pleasant, if preoccupied. 'Tamara, I need to find Emilia. I must make sure she's all right. We're worried.'

Tamara looked down at the foot jammed in the door. 'What are you doing?' She went for bewilderment rather than irritation. If Manny was the Manny that Emilia depicted, then it was probably wise not to antagonise him.

He didn't move. 'I have to find Emilia. Mr Hilton's doing his crust.'

She tested the door gently as she gazed at him wide-eyed. 'Do you mean Emilia's *still missing*?' The door wouldn't budge. She paused for effect, hoping she looked suitably shocked and amazed. 'Then Mr Hilton must report it to the police! As you obviously already know, I gave Emilia a lift into the village yesterday. I don't know what happened to her after that – it could be anything!'

He ignored the suggestion about the police. 'Jed says that Sean was at work and your mother took Lyddie to the cinema yesterday afternoon, so why would Emilia think it was a good time to visit?'

Tamara shrugged, as if she were as baffled as he. 'Yes, why *would* she ask me to drop her at the Close? It doesn't make sense. Are you saying she just vanished? Has someone kidnapped her or something? I know the Hiltons have had threats in the past and she once told me that the wealthy could be targeted.' She almost clasped her hand to her mouth, but dismissed it as too theatrical.

Manny's eyes narrowed. He glanced behind him. One dark glass car window began to slide down and Tamara realised that Tom Hilton was waiting in the back of the Mercedes. Manny's voice dropped. 'Emilia left in your car and we need to know where she is. Come on, Tamara. What the fuck's going on?'

The inference that he had a good idea, and was giving her a chance to come clean, made sweat break out between her shoulders. 'I'm afraid I don't know.'

'You picked up someone else, didn't you?'

'No, who would I pick up?' she snapped, happy that she could answer that one with a clear conscience.

'Was someone else waiting for her?'

There she was on shakier ground, as the taxi driver had been waiting. But she had no trouble sounding puzzled because he seemed surprisingly wound up by the disappearance of his boss's wife. 'I just dropped her at my parents' house. It's not my job to count people on pavements or cars on roads.'

'What did she have with her? A bag?' Manny persisted.

'Yes, I think so. A black one. Women often do have bags with them.' He couldn't argue with her stating the bleeding obvious.

'How big?'

'Not big enough to have anybody in it,' she retorted,

deliberately misunderstanding. 'Big for a handbag, small for a suitcase. Just a bag.' Tamara glanced at Tom Hilton, who stared inscrutably back. She gave another tug at the door, wondering whether Manny was tired of standing on one leg yet. No, he looked as if he had impressive core muscles. 'Has Mr Hilton asked the police for help?'

Manny's expression became set.

Tamara let understanding wash over her face, as if the penny had just dropped. 'Then I presume that he knows that the situation is that his wife has chosen not to tell him her plans. But that's her choice, isn't it? She lies outside our control.'

Manny thrust out his chin. 'Has she run off with her boyfriend again? It didn't end well last time, did it?'

Tamara paused. 'Who?' Boyfriend? Not mother? Run off *again*? Last time?

Manny pressed as she hesitated. 'Didn't she tell you? Emilia and Mr Hilton have had their difficulties. It was when Emilia tried to disappear in the middle of the night with her boyfriend that she fell from the balcony. Of course, the slimeball vanished when people ran to see what she was screaming about.'

'That's how she fell?' Not violent protestors tipping her out onto a cruel and unforgiving patio?

'Yes, and if she's gone, she's gone. But there are reasons why we need to find her.'

'What are they?' Tamara asked, curiously. She felt as if she was in some kind of game where everyone knew the answers but had to guess the right questions.

He shook his head, his eyes guarded. 'I can't tell you.'

'The same reasons Mr Hilton's had her living behind electric gates with monitors everywhere? I'm not that surprised if she's had enough of it, to be honest.'

He sighed. 'There are reasons that Mr H is as he is, and

I'm not saying that I think he always does the right thing. But I do see why he does it.'

She tried again to close the door against his boot. 'Well, anyway, it's not really my business, is it? I'm obviously just incidental to whatever's been going on between you all at Lie Low. And I'd really appreciate it if you'd move your foot.'

Manny let out a tiny sigh of frustration, half-closing his eyes. 'Tamara, if you know something, it would be for the best if you shared it with me.'

Her heart dipped. It wasn't that his tone was threatening. It was just … firm. 'Are you getting the sack because you've let her slip away?'

Instantly, he lifted his lids, fastening onto this speck of sympathy. 'No. I wasn't with her when she slipped off. Jed was. Would you care if Jed lost his job over it?'

She shrugged. *Yes. A bit.* 'I don't see why he should lose his job. You guys were given a pretty impossible task, to shut a grown woman away from the world.'

Manny abandoned that line of attack and returned to trying to winkle out information. 'Emilia might not be Mrs Truth and Honesty, but Mr H is desperate to find her.' He watched her face. 'Look, I'll share some background info, because it might make you … remember something. The bloke, James Cochrane, is a weak self-centred shit who likes the high life. He's worked in Mr H's businesses as a personal trainer for quite some time and Mr H hasn't sacked him, despite Cochrane having a thing with Emilia, because Jed thought it was better to have some idea where Cochrane is, at least some of the time. Emilia is just the latest on his list of rich women. He's like a tick. He climbs on board and sucks out all the blood, then drops off and waits for the next rich bitch to get the hots for him, at whichever gym or spa he's working at.'

Oh. Tamara felt that dropping sensation that comes with an unsuspected revelation.

'Cochrane will soon get sick of a crippled female partner. He'll find a way of parting Emilia from her money – I can judge her future by his past. And Emilia hasn't had to work for a living for years, so she'll find herself in Queer Street. She's a bloody nuisance sometimes but I – we – need to know she's OK. I need to track her down. I really do.'

Tamara gazed into his eyes, trying to read them, feeling hollow and uncertain. Either Emilia hadn't trusted her with the truth or Manny was spinning lies as fast as the words would fall from his mouth. 'This James Cochrane guy isn't one of these mythical protestors, then?'

Manny snorted scornfully. 'Not really – and they're not mythical. He joined them briefly to distract us all from who he really is and what he was doing, that's all. He's not a man with strong moral convictions. He's some pretty boy that fancies himself as a personal trainer and Emilia let herself be taken in by him for a while.'

Then the rear door of the Mercedes opened and Tom Hilton unfolded himself out of the back seat, adjusted his jacket and traversed the short path. He stared at Tamara for a second and she tried to look back neutrally, though her heart was banging in her ears.

'Do you know where my wife is, Ms Rix?' He looked sad.

A question she could answer. 'No.'

He nodded, even more colourless than usual. 'I'm sorry that Emilia has used and manipulated you. Jed rather allowed himself to be distracted by you, and Emilia was on that like a weasel scenting eggs.' He sighed. 'Ms Rix, I suppose you know that before she met me, Emilia used to be an actress? When she wants to, she can make most of us believe anything she wants us to. It's not your fault.

You're gullible, and as soon as she met your sister, Emilia saw exactly how to use you both for her own ends. I could see it happening but, even so, the way she executed her exit strategy took me by surprise.' With a final look, he turned back towards his car. 'You're wasting your time, Manny.'

But Manny seemed unwilling to accept defeat. 'I need to find her.' His eyes burned. Then, with lightning speed, his hand was on Tamara's wrist, his fingers digging in painfully. 'Where is she? Who's she with?'

Tamara yelped as she was yanked forward, toppling into thin air until ending up with a *whoof* against him. Once she was off balance, he shifted his grip to a bear hug and lifted her easily back over the step and inside the house. Trapped between him and the wall, she felt his breath hot on her cheek. 'What do you know, Tamara?'

Struggling to free an arm, wedge her feet against the door, the door jamb, anything, she became aware of another car door slamming, someone shouting her name.

A someone who was mighty pissed off. 'Manny! Stop it *now*.'

Over Manny's shoulder, she caught a glimpse of Jed, his face as sour as early plums as he stormed across the pavement and the path, ignoring the Merc and Mr Hilton standing by its open door, looking back.

'Make him stop!' she tried to yell, but her lips were numb and her lungs too constricted by his weight to fuel any volume of noise.

Jed snapped at his stepbrother as he stalked into the fray. 'Put her down, you goat. Let me handle this. *Get off her!*'

'She knows something,' Manny growled.

Then, suddenly, she was free and Manny was searching for his footing on the path outside, glaring at Jed as if uncertain how he got out there, but not liking it. Deprived of support, Tamara flailed sideways through the kitchen door, tripping over the threshold, bumping hard onto her bum on the quarry tiles. Then Manny was striding back to the Mercedes and Jed was hauling Tamara to her feet, slamming the front door shut.

'Bad idea to piss Manny off,' Jed said, breathing hard.

Tamara yanked her hands out of his. 'I didn't piss him off,' she retorted. 'He got pissed off all on his own. He spun in here like a Tasmanian devil.'

'Oh, stop.' Jed was all muscle and anger, snapping sentences into her face. 'You very obviously know more than you're telling, so cut the injured dignity. Are you going to tell us what you know?'

'No,' Tamara snapped back, smoothing her hair and pulling up the strap of her top. 'I have to leave to take a class. Piss off.'

'Gladly.'

And then Tamara's ears were ringing to the slamming of the door, with Jed on the outside of it.

She coaxed her trembling legs to a kitchen stool, using her breathing to calm her heart rate. Hopefully, that was the worst of it. Manny had had his tantrum, Tom Hilton had been coldly contemptuous, Jed had lost his temper. Tamara had survived. She tried to stop the muscle around her knees going all cowardy custard on her.

It would be best if she focused on her own worries, such as how Lyddie would react to the knowledge that her best friend Emilia was gone.

Chapter Twenty-Nine

A week of silence. At least, from the Lie Low camp.

The rest of the world kept turning. Tamara crossed Emilia's sessions from her schedule, went with Lyddie to visit Gabe, and shut the blokey blokes up for once by walking into The Three Fishes and buying them all a drink, just for the hell of seeing their stupefied faces. She knew Jed wouldn't be there, but she glanced around, anyway.

She knew he wouldn't call her, but she kept checking her phone.

There was no way he'd turn up at her house, but she occasionally glanced outside for cars.

She didn't want to be pursued by the sort of man Jed Cassius was – probably … possibly – so she shouldn't miss him at all. But, somehow, she lived in a constant state of expecting him. Fruitlessly.

To occupy herself, Tamara invited Lyddie to stay at the weekend. 'Why don't you two go away?' she suggested to Cheryl, with some hazy idea that her parents might then stop snapping at one another. 'I don't have Emilia's session on Friday now, so I can have Lyddie from lunchtime. Is she due at the shop?'

'Only on Sunday.' A pause. 'I suppose it wouldn't do any harm for me and your father to get away.'

'Do it, then. She can come to my Saturday classes and we'll have lunch at the bakery in Bettsbrough. She'll love it.'

To make an occasion of the weekend, Tamara bought Lyddie's favourite biscuits and various other treats, along with new bedclothes for the spare room featuring plenty of Lyddie's favourite pink: cherry blossoms on a sage-green background.

''Mara, way to go-o!' Lyddie hallooed the moment she arrived in Sean's car on Friday, clutching a huge backpack and Jabber's beanbag, Jabber panting and wagging on his lead beside her. 'I'm on holiday to your house, aren't I? Your house, your house!' She did a little stiff-legged skip. 'I'm going to sleep here for two nights. And Jabber, eh? And Jabber. We've brought his bed.'

'I've been looking forward to it for days.' Tamara joined in an enthusiastic hug, almost swamped by the love emanating from her sister.

After examining the spare room with its new bed covers, Lyddie demolished a plate of lasagne, 'I love lasagne!' and they watched the Syfy Channel together, eating popcorn, 'I love popcorn!' Then, they put on their shoes to go out into a perfect lavender-and-navy summer evening to walk Jabber.

Lyddie beamed. 'Can we visit Gabe?'

'Of course. You can go and see how the puppies are getting on and feed the chickens.'

'And stroke Snobby.' Lyddie gave a huge sigh of contentment. 'I love Snobby. I love his nose.' She stroked Tamara's nose – none too gently.

Tamara laughed. 'I think Snobby's nose is better designed for stroking than mine.'

'And can I take carrots? Then he'll let me stroke him. Otherwise, he does this.' Lyddie demonstrated how Snobby tossed his head about to avoid the hand of a would-be stroker who didn't have the forethought to bring a bribe.

'I bought some specially.' Tamara giggled at Lyddie being a pony, hair flying in all directions, as she shook her head and blew out her lips. Whatever the state of her own heart, at least she could share Lyddie's moments of happiness.

Tears burned her eyes as she fetched the carrots and linked arms with her sister to be towed behind Jabber along the footpath to Ladies Lane, the ford, and along the track behind the cottages of Main Road, a shortcut to Gabe's.

And soon Lyddie was stroking Snobby's nose as she fed him the carrots. Then Gabe good-naturedly let her get 'her' chicken, Princess Layer, out of the run before he shut the hen house up for the night. And Princess Layer was such a fat and comfortable hen that she allowed herself to sit in Lyddie's lap and be stroked, her bronze feathers sleek and shiny.

'Princess Layer likes me, Princess Layer loves me,' crooned, Lyddie contentedly, seated cross-legged on the ground, her hair a cloak around her shoulders.

Tamara looked on and decided not to tell Lyddie that Emilia had gone away until it was unavoidable. Why spoil this happy weekend?

Chapter Thirty

Jed fed the alpacas. Emilia was a fair-weather herd owner and he'd taken enough of the rainy days, and the Emilia-can't-be-bothered days, to be familiar with the measures of alpaca pellets and alfalfa. He frowned as he went into the paddock and set out the feed bowls, watching the girls hurry over, jostling gently, swapping bowls and letting the crias dance out of their way.

Something was going on at the house.

He could taste it.

He'd come down to the paddock so that he could think and watch, while all the time looking as if he had nothing more on his mind than chatting to these fleeces on legs, which they answered with contented humming. He supposed that if Emilia didn't come back, Tom would sell the herd. Jed would miss the alpacas. They'd grown on him, with their mad haircuts and oversized eyes.

There was no sign of Emilia coming home. Jed had always known that she'd leave again, sooner or later.

And Mr H was gutted. Jed had known that he would be. If the time bomb hadn't been James Cochrane, it would have been someone else. A thirty-year age gap might work in some marriages, but not one that Emilia was any part of. If Mr H hadn't been able to see that, or had kidded himself, well, it hadn't been Jed's responsibility to tell him things he didn't want to hear. Mr H wasn't the first rich guy to find a fit young woman putting him on her wedding list.

Now Mr H was hurt, angry and upset.

Jed's frown grew.

But Mr H was much more angry and upset than Jed would have anticipated. Or angry and upset in the wrong way. For one thing, he wasn't drinking things over with Jed – he was spending his time with Manny, or shut away on long phone calls.

The alpacas had slowed in their crunching, now. A couple of the babies were playing: Triangle and Downward Dog. Stupid names. Typical Emilia. Pandering to Tamara, not by the obvious flattery route of asking her to name the babies, but by calling them after yoga positions and giving Lyddie input. Changing her hair when Tamara changed her hair. Indirect, but deadly effective. Tamara probably hadn't even realised that she was being courted.

He swore. He hadn't done much more than vaguely suspect it himself. Mr H had been in such a panic at James Cochrane nosing around their perimeter, like a grizzly at a campsite, that they'd all been looking outwards while Emilia's ticket to ride had been invited in among them.

Well … he half smiled. He'd been looking at Tamara all right, but not in case she somehow got mixed up in Emilia leaving Mr H. For himself, if Mr H hadn't been so upset, Jed would have been grateful that Tamara had got Emilia off his back so effectively.

The bowls empty, Jed stacked them, pausing to gaze at his own reflection in the stainless steel, his hair tossing in the breeze. Was Mr H unsubtly punishing him for losing Emilia by taking his late-night whiskies with Manny?

Jed wasn't fragile about stuff like that. It was just one of several things that weren't adding up. Mr H hadn't sacked him or even bollocked him for Emilia's loss, but he wasn't confiding in him either. He shrugged. Maybe Mr H had got Manny to get together a tracking team to find Emilia and he knew that Jed would point out all the disadvantages of that, so he'd chosen simply to freeze Jed out. But Manny, too, seemed abstracted and bothered.

In fact, the atmosphere in the house was bloody tense.

He turned and strode back up the slope, dropping the feed bowls off in the little shed. He felt underemployed. Mr H was indoors, nursing his grievances instead of working. If he wasn't asking for anything and if Emilia wasn't around to need nursemaiding, then there was only the household to oversee. Without Emilia's interference, the household ticked along with little arbitration from Jed. Carrie shopped, made meals and provided coffee, the gardeners gardened, the cleaners cleaned.

It was Friday afternoon, but there was no visit from Tamara to look forward to.

That thought nestled uncomfortably heavily in Jed's gut, along with the memory of her chilly evasiveness. Her gaze, when she looked at him, had been shuttered. Wary. It was the wariness that bothered him. What the fuck had he done? He could have understood it if she'd never looked at him with desire in her amber eyes. He'd told past women about his time as what certain newspapers referred to as 'the dregs of society' and sensed their distaste. They liked a man with a degree or two and a nice tidy background. They showed their support for those down on their luck with a purchase of *The Big Issue*. They were turned off by someone who'd fought his way to respectability the hard way – well, that was OK.

But Tamara had seemed to have more integrity.

Not long ago, he'd looked into her eyes and been sure it was only a matter of time before he'd be making the kind of love to her that would cause supernovas in far off galaxies. He'd gone so far as to toy with hows and wheres – although the hot interlude in her kitchen had almost decided both.

His mouth quirked as he remembered his urgency blanking out his half-evolved next-date plan of taking her on the Eurostar to Paris, migrating to a nearby hotel, hopefully. And he knew just the hotel, where they could lounge in the rooftop pool and drink champagne, looking out over the city towards the Eiffel Tower. That would have been some date. He'd imagined kissing her all the way down to their room and unwrapping her like a gift, her hair damp from the pool, as she tipped back her head and …

And then, on the edge of her kitchen counter, he'd almost ended up firing himself into her like a missile because she was just so firm and hot and silky and his wanting her had been such a blind ambition that he'd have willingly sacrificed Paris rooftops and sunset sex to be inside her.

He wished he had. He wished he hadn't been so focused on savouring that kitchen-counter encounter and drawing it out to be something incredible. Because since he'd lost control sufficiently to put Tamara's fine body between his and the wall and go deaf to Emilia opening the door at the wrong moment, Tamara had gradually pushed him out in the cold.

Then, damned if Mr H, of all people, wasn't pushing him out in the cold, too. Courteous but withdrawn, apparently putting Jed on some half-arsed form of gardening leave simply by asking nothing of him and allotting him no tasks.

Jed turned and stalked up the slope to the house, taking out the remote on his key fob to open the garage door. He'd go somewhere. He was sufficiently his father's son to enjoy a fast drive for the pure hell of it and maybe that would settle his fidgets.

From the corner of his eye, as he waited for the big silver shutter to roll itself up and out of the way, he saw Manny watching him through the window of the small sitting room Mr H used, before turning to talk to someone in the room, gesticulating in Jed's direction.

It increased his sense of something being 'off'.

Without letting on that he'd noticed anything, Jed entered the garage, opened the car and started it without closing either car or garage door. Then he slid from the driver's seat and let himself quietly into the house, soft stepping along the small hall and into the big one, until he was outside the door to Mr H's sitting room.

'I don't know how you expect me to solve this one. It's a mess,' Manny was saying, obviously irritated.

Then Mr H, sad and strained: 'Find her. I thought you could find anyone.'

Manny laughed. 'Yes, I probably can, given time, but I can't do the impossible. If she's left the country on a perfectly valid passport in a perfectly lawful way, she's gone. She's made fucking fools of us.'

'There's nothing lawful about that holdall full of cash!'

'Exactly! That's the issue—'

Jed found himself suddenly in the room, glaring into Manny's and Mr H's boggling eyes. 'What fucking holdall full of cash?'

Chapter Thirty-One

Tamara hadn't cleared up after lunch because it had seemed much more fun to walk Lyddie to work the long way round so that they could see the puppies again. Gabe was finding them homes and so puppy time was at a premium and they were huge fun, pouncing on each other, attacking shoelaces with deadly intent and tiny teeth.

After a chat with Gwen at Crowthers' shop, and having left Lyddie proudly behind the counter, Tamara deposited Jabber in his own back garden with a couple of Bonios and a bowl of water. The garden at Church Close was Jabber-proof, which hers wasn't, and she planned to walk Lyddie home to her parents' house after work, when Cheryl and Sean would be back. Lyddie could make her own way home, but Tamara didn't have anything better to do and she'd feel happier if she knew her parents were home when Lyddie returned.

When Tamara reached her own house she could hardly believe her eyes. A black BMW Z4 was parked outside, a man in its driver's seat. Approaching cautiously, she watched him gazing through the windscreen, apparently staring at the hedge. He didn't look around. Heart skipping, she walked past the car and up her garden path, letting herself into the house without glancing over her shoulder.

In the kitchen, she occupied herself by washing up and wiping surfaces. After a few minutes, she checked through her sitting room window. It was the kind that took up a lot of the wall, three sizeable plain glass panes above a bottom segment of obscure glass, so she had a good view. He hadn't driven away.

She tried to ignore his brooding presence, but she was on

edge for the sound of her doorbell as she ran upstairs and packed Lyddie's backpack to take along when she called for her at the shop after work. She cleaned her teeth, took down her hair from its plastic hair clamp and brushed it out about her shoulders, straight and glossy.

Then she ran downstairs to glare out of the sitting room window. The car was still there. Jed still stared at the hedge. Shoving her bare feet into silver flip-flops, she threw open her front door and strode across the garden, around the car, to bang on the driver's window with the side of her fist. 'What's the idea?'

Slowly, Jed turned to look at her. His eyes were flat. After a few seconds, he pressed a button and the window hummed down. 'I'm trying to decide whether there's any point.' Unsmiling, fatigue and sadness lay in grooves around his eyes. In the sunshine they were more green than hazel, like stream water.

'In what?'

'In speaking to you.'

'None if you're going to carry on talking in riddles.'

He shrugged with his eyebrows and turned back to his contemplation of the hedge.

Weird. All the quiet energy that usually characterised him was missing. At least, the energy was. The quiet had hung around.

Exasperated, Tamara swung away.

Intrigued, she turned back. 'OK, I'll buy it. Come in and we'll find out if there is any point.'

After a few seconds, when he looked as if he wasn't sure whether to bother, he opened the car door and uncoiled himself from the driver's seat, padding behind her into the house like a stalking leopard.

Unable to shake off her mother's training sufficiently not to offer hospitality, but equally unequal to facing him across the kitchen with the spectre of their earlier selves making out on the worktop, she put him in the sitting room, while she made a pot of coffee – extra strong, because he looked as if he needed the caffeine hit. And it would probably pay her to be alert, too.

Vaguely troubled by his uncharacteristic inertia, she gave him the largest mug, then curled up in an armchair. 'What's up?'

He eased his neck, as if trying to get the tension out. 'I've had a bad day.'

She waited.

He said nothing.

'Want to tell me about it?'

'Don't know.' He sighed and fixed his eyes blankly on the white woman-in-tree-pose figurine that stood on Tamara's carpet near the television.

They drank their coffee. Tamara was mystified. She watched Jed frown. Sigh. And not tell her something that he so plainly thought he *might* tell her, that she buzzed with curiosity. What could have happened to turn him into a zombie?

Draining her coffee mug, Tamara slapped it down on the table. Jed didn't even blink. So she moved from the chair to the sofa, landing beside him with a deliberate bounce. Slowly, he turned and looked at her. If she'd had any intention of getting waspish, it died at the trouble she saw in his eyes.

Her stomach dipped. 'Is it something bad?' she said, gently.

With a sigh, he let his head rock back against the sofa. 'Pretty bad. Potentially fucking bad.' His eyes were still unfocused, as if at least part of him was off on some journey in his mind.

'And you can't tell me?' She realised that her hand had

settled on his forearm when the muscle shivered beneath her fingertips.

'On one level I want to. You can probably fill in some blanks that will provide me with personal satisfaction, even if it doesn't change anything. But there's some stuff it might be better if you don't know. Because if you don't know, you can't be implicated.'

Alarmed, she let her fingers tighten on his arm. 'Implicated in what?'

His gaze drifted down to her mouth. 'On the other hand, if you know the whole truth you might be better able to defend yourself.'

She recoiled. 'Defend myself? From who?' A nasty thought ricocheted into her brain. 'Mr Hilton? And Manny? And ... well, you? Or the protestors? They wouldn't come after me like they did Emilia, would they?'

His gaze fastened back on hers like a trap and suddenly he had snapped back to life. 'What the fuck are you talking about? Why should you have to defend yourself from us? Particularly *me*? And what the fuck have the protestors got to do with anything?'

Although his gaze bored into her, Tamara couldn't look away and she wished fervently that she'd kept her mouth shut. Now he was going to dig for what she knew and she wasn't at all sure it was a good idea to share Emilia's accusations. If they contained any truth ...

His frown grew blacker as silent seconds ticked by.

Uncomfortably, she slid her hand from his arm.

His stare didn't waver. Slowly, he said, 'I have absolutely no idea what you're talking about, but it's beginning to feel as if not telling you what's happened is doing more harm than good – even if you don't believe me about my part in things. I suppose that one of the reasons I've been reluctant to spill is in case it makes me look bad.' He smiled a crooked smile. 'But then you're so icy towards me, anyway ...' Some of the tension faded from the clean lines of his face, as if released by him coming to a decision.

'It's the police you need to worry about. Not Mr H or Manny. And definitely not me.'

Chapter Thirty-Two

Tamara felt as if he'd jumped on her belly with both boots. 'The *police*?'

He half turned, one knee crooking up as a place to rest his elbow. 'OK, here's the whole story.' He paused. 'I've discovered that Mr H's been stupid enough to involve himself in something criminal.' He swallowed, hard. 'And Manny, too.'

Tamara's heart began a slow downward spiral. Exactly as Emilia said. Shady. Dodgy. And Manny. So … she blinked, her eyes burning. So, Jed must be, too. She drew herself away. 'It might be better for you not to say any more.' Her voice was thin as she forced it from her aching throat. 'Emilia told me Mr Hilton's dodgy.'

Surprise flickered in his eyes. 'So Emilia knew, did she? That explains a lot.' He rubbed his chin. He didn't look worried or angry at Tamara already being in possession of the truth, just mildly disconcerted.

Rage at his lack of concern or conscience blossomed in her chest. She forgot to be cautious, letting scorn invade her voice just so he knew exactly what she thought of petty crooks and self-appointed jailers. 'Manny's his minder and you and him were meant to keep Emilia under lock and key. But she was too clever, wasn't she? And,' she added, defiantly, 'yes, I helped her. And I'm glad I did.'

Jed froze. One segment of his brain was noting how hot Tamara looked when she was angry, her lips thinning, eyes glittering – he hadn't thought that she had a temper and had assumed that serenity was what you attained from spending half the week in a headstand. But the rest of his mind was circling what she'd just said, trying to get a handhold.

'Lock and key?'

'Don't bother denying it.' She blinked, as if she might cry. 'Emilia told me how Mr Hilton controlled her, via you and Manny, pretending it was all for her own good. How she wasn't allowed to leave Lie Low without you. She couldn't even go to classes, could she? That's why she had to hire me to come to her house.' Contempt rang in every word. Contempt for him. And it stung like a nest full of wasps.

'For someone who believes that I'm such a scumbag,' he growled, 'you're being a bit fucking incautious in what you're saying and the way you're saying it. Aren't you scared I'll "put you under lock and key", too?'

She halted, confusion clouding her eyes.

'Emilia had you come to the house because Emilia's a fucking princess.' His breath was threatening to choke him. 'You really think—?' With an effort, he uncurled his fists and shook out his shoulders. Then spoiled the effect by gritting his teeth. 'You've obviously let that bitch do a number on you. So let me tell you a few truths about Emilia. She was nobody. She called herself an actress, and she certainly had been to some minor league drama school, but she didn't get through the course. When Mr H met her she was in promotions, wearing a sexy dress and a sultry smile in the foyer of a theatre, trying to get suckers to patronise some arts company.'

Tamara had fallen silent. She was looking like she had a stick in the wrong place, but she seemed to be listening.

Jed rubbed his eyes. He'd hardly slept last night, lying in bed, his fears swooping around him like bats in the darkness. 'Mr H fell for her like a ton of bricks. It was completely out of character. He'd never been married. He hadn't even lived with a woman, although there had been women in his life. We could see that Emilia wasn't in love with him, but she had no trouble loving his bank account and his yacht and his apartment in Gibraltar. So she played him like a fool and he acted exactly like one, and married her.'

The distrust in Tamara's eyes shifted slightly.

'Manny and me, we hated her.' He paused to try and loosen his throat with a swig of coffee. 'She was a giant pain in the arse. She ordered us around, never said please and thank you and deliberately caused us aggro. And anything she wanted, Tom fell over himself to give her or instruct us to get for her. I suppose he knew, at the bottom of himself, that she was only with him for the lifestyle and the dosh, and so he gave it to her in spades.'

'So why did you stick it out?'

He grimaced. 'You may remember the little matter of me not having qualifications? And my only employment record being with Mr H? But, mainly, it was because, Emilia aside, I love my job. Mr H is a good businessman and a good employer and he gave me respect. He put me in a position where I got respect from the rest of the world, too. Why should I give that up? Manny had to put up with more from her because he knows about fitness and she'd use him as a personal trainer at home, sometimes, breaking into his evenings to waffle on about her diet and her fitness regime.

'But I was pretty sure that Emilia wouldn't be an issue forever. She'd stick around for a few years, enjoy what Mr H could give her, then use his money to hire a shithot lawyer to divorce him and take him for every penny she could. But then it seemed as if I had overestimated her.' He shook his head. 'She couldn't even wait out the few years it would take for the courts to see her as a good spouse, rather than an opportunistic gold-digger. She began an affair.'

'Was it true what Manny told me about that guy

called James Cochrane, then?' Shock had taken the place of distrust in Tamara's face. The stiffness of outrage had seeped from her body.

'You've got it. He worked at a spa Mr H has in west London. Emilia frittered away a good part of every week lying around letting people pamper her, or taking fucking silly exercise classes.'

'Exercise classes aren't fucking silly.'

Recalling who he was talking to, he backtracked. 'No, OK. But aerobics was the nearest thing to work she did. And she had to have a personal trainer at the spa, of course – Cochrane. She was sneaking out to him when she fell and smashed her leg up. Until then she'd had the intelligence and grace to conduct her affair discreetly, so at least Mr H didn't get his nose rubbed in it. But she'd had a row with lover boy and he came creeping into the garden to try for the big make-up scene. I was working in Mr H's study, which happened to be at the foot of the stairs, so she thought she'd climb down to Cochrane – but she fell.'

Tamara's lips parted indignantly. 'She told me the protestors threw her over the balcony!'

He shook his head, feeling weak with relief that she actually seemed to be coming around to believing him. 'They didn't. I was outside to her in seconds. Cochrane was with her – until he saw me.'

Her mouth shut, the lips pressing together over any more words. Her eyes waited for him to go on.

'Mr H should have divorced her then, but I suppose she spun him a story and they made up and stayed married.' He closed his eyes for a moment. 'I was so elated thinking we were going to get rid of her. Then so disappointed when she managed to cling to her throne. Mr H did have trouble with protestors at around the same time; it was in all the papers and James Cochrane geed up the more extreme elements, using information he got through Emilia, so they'd know Mr H's movements and be lying in wait to pelt the car with eggs or scream abusive slogans as he went to business meetings. With that going on, sometimes right outside the house, Emilia had had all the excuse she needed to say she felt safe at the spa and spend half her life there – until she made her balcony mistake.

'So then, in his turn, Mr H used the protestors – as a reason to move out of London and put a bit of distance between him and the world. He said he was protecting himself and his wife, but in my opinion he was giving in to his obsession with her, keeping tabs on her. And I suppose it suited her to co-operate while she healed. It really was a pretty terrible injury.'

Tamara's eyes were wide. 'If everything you say is true, why did she feel the need to enact the elaborate scenario that she did to get away from Mr Hilton? She doesn't sound short of bottle. If she just left him, the courts would award her plenty of his money.'

His guts rolled. 'I only found out yesterday.' His voice emerged as a croak and he had to swallow hard before he could tell her the rest. 'Emilia may have told you Mr H is shady, but it might surprise you to know that I actually wouldn't work for a crook.'

He felt a shaft of satisfaction at a flicker of guilt and dismay in her eyes. But then his conscience made him add, 'At least, I didn't know he was involved in anything. But like a lot of successful businessmen, he resents paying tax at every turn. Accountants look for tax efficiencies, but it's difficult to avoid paying over huge portions of profits to the government.'

He paused. This was the part that he'd been reluctant to share. If it all came out the police would probably want to talk to her, which would be uncomfortable for her and possibly raise eyebrows in the village but, ultimately, would sooner or later be over. They'd be a lot less likely to believe that Jed was squeaky clean though. Tom Hilton's aide-de-camp. The young lad that had come out of a squat to live in a great apartment in the Hilton's own home. Yeah, right, he thought, bitterly.

But Tamara was waiting, a thousand questions in her eyes. He swallowed, and forced himself to admit the truth. 'I've just found out that he, and a few guys like him, have been a bit creative in finding ways to keep money unrecorded – cash transactions "off the books". Gradually, they legitimised it via property bought abroad. Money laundering.'

Shame curled him up inside at her horrified expression and he had to take another breath before completing his confession. 'The latest "project" involved five people putting in a whole lot of money. The cash was all at Lie Low, for some operational reason, around half a million in used notes – a reason involving Manny being the muscle, driving whichever of them was moving cash from one place to another, apparently. Which meant nice cash-in-pocket bonuses for him. My cool older brother conniving at money laundering.' He laughed without humour. 'Anyway. Emilia's taken the cash. And the other four people are not happy.' He paused to wipe sweat from his forehead with his wrist. 'Cloning software has suddenly appeared on the PC linked to CCTV. They suspect that Emilia has made a copy of the hard drive, although everyone's surprised she'd know how. So now they're frightened.'

'Why would she do that?' Tamara had turned quite pale.

He snorted. 'One of the guys in on the deal, Gil Burton, is a scrap-metal merchant and the scrap business can be made pretty opaque. The police have shown interest in his dealings in the past and he's very anxious to avoid a repetition. Frankly, he's frightened that from the safety of another country, Emilia will tell the police – or the taxman, who's probably scarier than any number of policemen so far as Gil's concerned – about the little money-laundering caper and produce security footage of Gil and the others visiting Lie Low. If you own a lot, you have a lot to lose. Being found guilty of tax evasion can land you in prison and lose you a lot of your assets.'

Tamara's eyebrows shot up. 'Half a million's a fortune to me but not to Emilia. Why would she exchange it for the half of everything she'd get in a divorce?'

'She won't,' he said, simply. 'She'll keep the cash and get loads more than half of everything now that she has the information as leverage. Mr H can't inform on her stealing the cash without admitting that he's committed a criminal act, ruining himself and implicating others. So he's going to be easy meat in the divorce settlement.'

'Wow, half a million in cash,' she said. 'No wonder her bag seemed heavy.'

Absently, he lifted a hand and touched her hair, slipping its softness through his fingers. 'I hope you'll agree that if I was supposed to be keeping Emilia "under lock and key", I've made a pretty shitty job of it. I'm reluctantly impressed that her acting talents are good enough to convince you that I'm that kind of monster. Though I seem to have been played for a fool by everyone while I did my best to earn my generous salary by being the perfect employee, including putting up with Mr H's obsession for his nightmare of a wife. It seems that I was essential to the respectable side of Mr H and carefully excluded from the rest. I had no idea of his creative tax evasion. Mr H and Manny knew I'd never condone it. And though I was responsible for bringing you to Lie Low, I'd never knowingly have let anyone involve you – however scummy you may think I am.'

Chapter Thirty-Three

Tamara's heart flipped in shock. 'Involved? I'm not involved. How am I involved?'

'Who helped Emilia abscond with a big bag of cash?'

'I didn't!' she began, indignantly.

His eyebrows lifted.

'I didn't mean to,' she amended, shock and panic clawing at her throat. 'Wow. That bitch. She seriously set me up?'

'Deadly seriously.' He sighed. '"Serious" is a word that's been in my head a lot, since yesterday. Mr H and Manny may be in serious shit. I may even be myself, by association. I've told Mr H I'm leaving, but the shit could certainly still fly in my direction, if I can't get behind the fan.'

He let his hand drop from her hair. 'In the event of an investigation, I think the police will soon recognise you as a dupe. It may take them a little longer with me. Life would certainly have been easier if I hadn't found out because if it comes out and I haven't reported it, they may want to know why. I think that if they ask me direct questions and I deny any knowledge of the answers, that's an offence in itself.'

'Are you going to report it?'

Wordlessly, he shook his head.

'What about if there's an investigation?'

He looked stricken. 'I'm desperately hoping there won't be because I can't bear to think of Manny behind bars, not even if he's been an idiot. And' – his Adam's apple bobbed – 'Mr H did a lot for me. He gave me the means to rejoin society. I've lived in comfort, afforded a nice car and holidays abroad. I'd absolutely hate to repay that by being instrumental in putting him away. But if it's him or me ...?' The eyes he fixed on Tamara shone with emotion. 'I like being squeaky clean. And I don't like my head being served up to the cops on a plate.'

Heart trembling for him, she took his hand. 'I'm sorry I badgered you into telling me.'

His fingers closed around hers. 'None of this is your fault.'

Although she still felt as if she was in a nightmare, Tamara was conscious of a rising sense of peace. Jed wasn't a baddie. But that meant that … Heat rose to her cheeks. 'I owe you a huge apology. When Emilia told me that you and Manny were employed to control her, I had trouble believing it. But I never totally disbelieved it. She was so plausible. Told just enough of the truth to fill my mind with doubts. I've never been so glad to be proved wrong.'

'It certainly showed me that you can take the man out of the gutter, but he'll always stink,' Jed said heavily. 'You didn't give me a chance to explain. You just got more remote.'

Her face was in flames of shame. 'I didn't want to believe it. Maybe I never truly did. But you're not the only one capable of feeling loyalty to an employer's confidence – and she presented herself as a woman in jeopardy. If I broke her trust, what might I have been responsible for? Mr Hilton, Manny and you, you can present a pretty intimidating group. I had no experience of the scenario she created. Mr Hilton called me gullible and I suppose I was. But—' She swallowed a sudden ball in her throat. 'I was also miserable that we ended up on opposite sides of the fence. And you wouldn't believe how glad I am to find out I've been lied to and manipulated. Even if I've spoiled everything,' she finished miserably.

Jed looked away, out of the window behind her, his expression shuttered. Slowly, he freed his hands from hers, leaving her feeling suddenly cold as he withdrew. The silence seemed to go on and on.

Then his narrow gaze flicked to her. 'Do you care if it's spoiled?'

'Yes.' And then, as his gaze remained locked with hers, more indignantly, 'Yes, of course I care. But haven't I been made a fool of just as much as you? Maybe more! Arch bitch Emilia's used me and Lyddie as cats' paws. She fooled me like Mr Hilton fooled you and so I don't see that you've got any particular claim to the moral high ground—'

Suddenly she was being scooped onto his lap, his arms like bands around her, his breath hot on her neck. He nuzzled her hair, making her scalp tingle.

'When I first moved into the squat, one of the guys there went for me. He gave me such a kick in the guts, I thought I'd never breathe again. When you froze me out, I felt like that again.'

Her head tilted, giving his mouth access to her throat, letting his tongue trace patterns from the lobe of her ear to the deliciously ticklish crook of her neck. Delicately, he slipped down her straps, so that he could nip and kiss her collarbone. Slowly, slowly, pulling, as the fabric seemed reluctant to surmount her breasts, until it gave up and her dress shot down to her waist. She gasped, first at the rush of air on her naked skin and then at the rush of heat, as he moved in with his mouth.

He groaned deep in his throat, digging in his pocket for his phone. 'I'm turning this off. The only person that's going to stop me this time is you.' He dropped the phone on the carpet and then his hand skimmed deliciously up her bare legs and under her dress.

She arched and twisted sideways, pulling him with her, on top of her on the softness of the sofa. 'I'm not stopping you,' she gasped, in case he hadn't got that. Her blood sang in her veins as he grasped her underwear and slid it down her legs, lifting himself, them both, to allow it clear passage, his mouth still travelling her breasts in hot trails that cooled deliciously.

Then 'Sofa's too small.' He pulled her against the firmness of his body and rolled them both onto the floor, landing her on top of him with a grunt. They rolled again as he pulled up the fabric of her skirt, hot hands touching, stroking, hot mouth sucking, kissing. Tamara pulled at his T-shirt, desperate to get his naked flesh against hers. His back, lean and strong under her palms, his firm buttocks downy, his chest hot against her, making her breasts ache with desire.

Levering himself up, he went for the fastening of his jeans. 'This isn't going to wait.' He swore as he wrestled with the zipper. 'I've waited too long. I don't care if the ceiling caves in or the house catches fire. I am going to get inside you.'

'Ohhh, yeahhh!' She tried to help, getting in his way, making him laugh as he wriggled out of his clothes.

Then 'Fuck. Condom.' He grabbed for the jeans he'd just kicked off, while she arched up to taste the hollow of his throat as he dug in his pocket, braced on one hand, ripping the foil with his teeth, sorting himself out deftly with the other hand.

Then his tip was against her and he paused. 'Later,' he said, 'I'm going to make love to you inch by inch. I'm going to be the most considerate, generous lover in the world. But right this minute, we're going to—'

'Fuck,' she said. And lifted her hips as he drove forward. And again and again, her arms and legs wound around him as she threw back her head and—

The doorbell rang. 'No!' he protested.

'Ignore it,' she gasped, juddering against him, breathing in the scent of arousal on his skin. 'I'm not expecting anyone.'

He ignored it.

The doorbell rang again. For longer.

'Ig ... nore ... it!' She gritted her teeth, moving faster, wanting, nearly getting, refusing to let anything interfere. 'Just ignore it.'

He ignored it. And fucked and bucked, and sent her right over the edge.

Tamara cried out at the relief, the release, the waves of pleasure.

And then she heard a voice right by the window. 'Perhaps she walked to meet Lyddie and we've missed them somewhere along the way. But her car's here— Oh! *Ta-MARA!*'

Tamara froze.

Above her, Jed froze, too. 'Tell me that's not Auntie Cheryl,' he managed, between heaving breaths.

Chapter Thirty-Four

His heart thundered and his skin prickled. Adrenaline flooded through him, but whether it was the exultation of finally coming inside Tamara, or horror that Tamara's mother's scandalised voice had just come from a window immediately behind his naked backside, he wasn't certain.

Beneath him, the Tamara who had been a crescendo of movement only moments earlier, let her limbs flop. 'I'm afraid it is.'

Gently, she pushed against his chest, but he was reluctant to withdraw from her heat, to unpeel his skin from the satin and softness he was pressed into. He brushed kisses on her eyes, her cheeks, her mouth, his heart still pounding against the wonderfully mobile flesh of her breast.

Cheryl's voice had distanced itself from the immediate vicinity of the window, but was still close enough to be heard, rising and falling, rapid with exasperation. Then Sean's voice, soothing.

'I think I'd rather face the police,' Jed muttered.

Tamara gave a sudden – and, in his view, inappropriate – snort of laughter, making her muscles do interesting things around him. 'I'll go out and ... I don't know what I'll say, actually. But you could lurk in here—'

'Like a creep? Yeah, right.' Bowing to the inevitable, he withdrew, careful of the condom, and rolled aside so that she could pull up or down the parts of her dress as necessary and sit up to repossess and replace her underwear. It didn't take long for him to rearrange his own clothing. He couldn't see an obvious repository for the condom, so tied it off and tucked it in his shirt pocket.

Tamara climbed reluctantly to her feet. 'This is going to be fun.'

'Not,' he agreed gloomily.

But when Tamara let her parents into the house, apart from a rapier glare in his direction and an icy 'Quite finished?', he found his behaviour wasn't Cheryl's major focus.

'Where's Lyddie?' she demanded.

Tamara glanced at her watch. 'Oh …! I wasn't watching the clock—'

'Evidently.' Cheryl's acidity could have stripped paint. 'The shop's closed. Did you ask her to come back here or go home?'

'I said I'd meet her at the shop,' Tamara admitted guiltily. Her cheeks were scarlet with mortification. 'Have you tried her phone?'

Cheryl's mouth opened again but Sean, balancing his wife's less-endearing qualities with level-headedness as he so frequently did, cut her off. 'Yes, but it just goes to voicemail.' He gave his wife a meaningful look. 'I think we need to focus on finding out where she is and leave any recriminations till later. We'll walk from here to the shop and if we don't find her, we'll walk on to our house. Tamara, you walk from here to Gabe's and from there to our house. That way, we stand a good chance of intercepting her.'

'I'll drive to Lie Low, in case she's on her way there,' volunteered Jed, glad to have something positive to contribute.

Cheryl frowned. 'But Emilia's not there, now, is she? Although I suppose Lyddie could have forgotten.'

Tamara looked stricken. 'I haven't told her about Emilia. I didn't want to spoil her weekend.'

Sean sighed. 'In that case, that's a good offer, Jed, thank you.'

As it didn't seem he could piss Cheryl off any more than he already had, Jed pulled Tamara into his arms and kissed her. 'Don't worry. We'll find her.'

'No,' Gabe said, brow furrowing, strands of silver hair wafting from his ponytail in the late afternoon breeze. 'I haven't seen her today. But let's just check around the place, shall we?'

They looked around the outhouses and in the hen run, where Princess Layer pecked the ground with the other old dames, and in Snobby's paddock, but there was no Lyddie. 'She'll turn up,' he said, squeezing Tamara's shoulders. 'I'll stay in case she wanders here and ring you if she does.'

'And I'll ring you if we find her elsewhere.' Tamara tried to sound equally as reassuring, though her heart was bounding in her chest like a scared rabbit. For the fiftieth time she tried Lyddie's mobile, but it was still going to voicemail. She left a message, even knowing that Lyddie would never remember how to retrieve it.

Jogging home, she paused at the homes of some of Lyddie's dog-walking friends, breathless, her legs like chewed string. She even ran into The Three Fishes. 'Has anybody seen Lyddie? Has anybody seen my sister?' Her voice was hoarse from fear and running.

There were few people in apart from the ever-present blokey blokes watching Sky Sports and drinking pints of bitter.

'I saw her this afternoon.' Bell, for once, forwent the opportunity to act like a prat in Tamara's presence. 'I stopped at the shop for some batteries. She was chatting away, as usual. Here. Have a swig.' He offered her his beer.

Tamara gulped most of it, too grateful to soothe her rasping throat to worry about Bell germs. 'Thanks,' she gasped. Her chest felt bound by iron bands of anxiety.

This was her fault. Lyddie was vulnerable. She knew, she'd always known that Lyddie could be preyed upon by the wrong kind of man or could get lost or do something dangerous that left her helpless and hurt. That was why she had firm boundaries. That was why everyone got uptight when she slipped outside them.

She rang her parents as she ran on in the direction of her home, but they had no news, of course, or they would have rung her. It was just that Tamara couldn't quite believe that Lyddie wasn't there. Wasn't at Tamara's house. Wasn't anywhere.

By the time she got back to Church Close, she was wiping away tears of frustration and fear. And anger at herself for failing Lyddie, again.

Cheryl was white and strained. 'Where can she be? Is it time to call the police?'

Sean put his arms around her. 'I think it's a bit early for that. Perhaps Jed will find her.'

'He's taking his time about letting us know what's happening,' said Cheryl, waspishly.

But then Jabber let out a volley of barks and galloped to the front door and Lyddie was somehow in the hall, fussing Jabber as he flung himself at her in a paroxysm of delight. 'Mum, I'm ever so hungry, can I have biscuits? Can I have lots of biscuits? Lots?'

Weak with relief, Tamara realised, dimly, that Jed was behind Lyddie, but she could think of nothing but hauling her sister into her arms. '*Lyddie*! Where have you been?'

'Can I have some biscuits?' demanded Lyddie, brushing Tamara off and stumping towards the kitchen. 'I'm hungry.'

Cheryl and Sean took their turns to hug Lyddie every bit as hard as Tamara had. Jed stepped indoors and, giddy with relief, Tamara slumped against him. His body was reassuringly solid and his arms felt like a haven.

Cheryl's voice was tight with unshed tears. 'Where have you *been*, darling? You know you should have either stayed at the shop to wait for Tamara or walked straight home.'

'Can I have some biscuits?' Lyddie persisted.

Even choked with relief, Sean managed to be the voice of reason. 'Probably won't get anything out of her if she's famished.'

They all trailed Lyddie to the kitchen, where a custard cream and a garibaldi were devoured in two mouthfuls. As nobody had thought about preparing a meal and they were so glad to see Lyddie home anyway, Cheryl filled the plate with a random selection and Lyddie stuffed another two biscuits in her mouth at once. Then everyone turned to Jed expectantly.

His arm was still around Tamara. 'She's fine. She's just had a small adventure.'

Cheryl clucked in distress, stroking Lyddie's hair.

'Apparently only Mr H was at the house. Lyddie had been at the gate—'

'Look, Bourbons! And choc-chip cookies and pink wafers. I love pink wafers. I *love* pink wafers. Pink wafers are my favourite. I don't like Mr Hilton.'

Jed lifted his voice. 'Because Mr H didn't have any of your phone numbers, he'd put Lyddie in his car ready to bring her straight back.'

Lyddie nodded. 'It's got leather seats. It's a blue one, with black windows. It's the car Manny drives, but Mr Hilton says it's his.' Lyddie put down her biscuits in order to saw at an imaginary steering wheel. ''Milia wasn't at home. 'Milia likes pink wafers. I like 'Milia. Mr Hilton said he doesn't know where she is. He asked me, he kept asking me, if I had seen 'Milia. But I haven't, have I? Can I ring 'Milia and go and see her?'

As Tamara thought it highly unlikely that she'd ever see

Emilia again, she temporised. 'Not if she's not there, Lyd. She's probably gone away for a while. I think Emilia can afford lots and lots of holidays, don't you?'

Lyddie's smile fled. 'Mr Hilton's not on holiday. He's horrible.'

Tamara's stomach lurched. 'How?'

Jed's hand settled reassuringly on Tamara's back. When she looked up into his eyes, she was confused to see laughter dancing there. 'Lyddie, you don't have to take any notice of Mr H being angry. It doesn't matter.'

She beamed at him. 'I should've just got out of the car sooner, shouldn't I? But I needed a wee. A big one.'

'Suddenly?' said Tamara, light dawning.

She nodded. 'I did a bit – quite a bit – in Mr Hilton's car. On the seat. I shouted, "I'm weeing!" and Mr Hilton shouted, "Get out quick!" and I got out and went away, behind a bush, like I'm supposed to, Tamara.'

'Did you get wet socks?'

Lyddie nodded philosophically. 'Trainers, too.'

Gravely, Jed said, 'That's when I turned up. Mr H didn't know whether to demand to know whether I'd found anything out about Emilia, talk about ... another situation, or insist that I ring Lyddie's family.' He winked at Tamara. 'But I think my phone must still be at your house, so I said I'd see Lyddie home and he settled for that. I put her in the car and came straight here.' He smiled slowly at Lyddie. 'You know, I'd quite like to have a wee in Mr Hilton's car, too.'

Lyddie roared with delight, eyes shining. 'Jed wants to wee in Mr Hilton's car! I like Jed, he's naughty.'

Even Cheryl managed to send Jed a smile, as she held out her hand to her daughter. 'If you've weed on your clothes we'd better get you upstairs to shower and change, hadn't we? And maybe someone should clean Jed's seat.'

'I sat on a carrier bag,' Lyddie said, indignantly. 'A green one.'

When, twenty minutes later, Cheryl trod back downstairs with a fresh and fragrant Lyddie, she crossed without hesitation to Jed. 'You were great, today.' She gave a faint smile. 'Although I'm not very keen on finding you, um ...' She searched for a phrase. 'In full swing—'

'*Mum!*' yelped Tamara, appalled.

'—I'm sorry I blamed you for what Don did.'

Jed gave one of his rare smiles. 'That's good. Because it's going to be really difficult for Tamara if we're not speaking. And I'm not going away any time soon.' He paused. 'I'd still like you to have the money for Lyddie. Take her on holiday or something.'

Cheryl looked uncertain.

Swiftly, he provided a ladder for her climb down. 'Maybe you could at least have a family conference with Sean and Tamara before you make up your mind to definitely turn it down anyway. Or maybe Tamara and I could take her to Disneyland once in a while. Will you think about it?'

Graciously, Cheryl nodded. 'OK, I will.' And, with a visible effort 'Thank you.'

Much later, when Lyddie had gone to bed and Tamara had shared a wordless hug with her parents, who seemed much happier together – perhaps because they'd just spent a weekend away or perhaps because they'd been brought closer by adversity, or even perhaps because Cheryl had forgiven Jed for his father's sins – Tamara let Jed drive her home. She felt as if her heart would take weeks to recover from the emotional roller coaster of the day.

Indoors, he pulled her into his arms. 'I need to make it up to you.'

'What?' She let herself relax against him.

'The, um … lack of finesse, this afternoon.'

She giggled. 'When you were "in full swing", you mean?'

He groaned against her neck, his hands sliding down to cup her buttocks. 'Don't. I may be scarred for life by that conversation. Let's go upstairs where nobody can look in through windows.' His tongue flicked her ear and her heart danced into a rhythm that indicated that it wasn't going to take weeks to recover after all. 'If this afternoon was a sprint, I owe you a marathon.'

'I'm not even in training,' she teased. Then she stopped talking to let him run his tongue along her lips, as her hands wandered down the breadth of his back so that she could pull his shirt out of his jeans, trace his spine and enjoy how well he was put together.

'Another reason to take things slowly.' He caught her hands as he steered her towards the stairs, treading backwards before her, smiling a bedroom smile as he slid her straps down her arms. 'You have amazing shoulders.'

'How can shoulders be amazing?' She let him draw her along, floating on a cloud of lustful anticipation.

'All of you is. You're toned and taut and edible.' They reached the landing. 'Is this one your room? You've driven me nuts for weeks and now it's my turn.' He crossed to the window to close her blinds.

'How would anyone be able to see in?' she protested.

He made a mock-cautious face. 'They can get around the side of your house with a ladder.' Then he turned on the lamps and piled her pillows in the middle of the bed, eyes glittering. 'I hope you don't have plans for this evening.'

'I'm all yours.' Her breathing was uneven. And, damn, she was meant to be in charge of her breathing. She was a yoga instructor. Breathing was one of her things. She couldn't even smooth it down into a rhythmic working breath as he inched down the fabric of her dress, making her skin prickle, sending her temperature soaring with the heat of his mouth, his tongue, his fingertips. Infinitely slowly, he eased the fabric over the tips of her breasts.

Sinking down onto the bed he settled her astride his lap. Tamara let her head fall back, her hair hanging down.

She'd never realised being in a marathon would feel so good.

Chapter Thirty-Five

It was late. Very late in the evening when Tamara's phone rang.

Although she was bone weary, she hadn't been able to sleep. She was lying along her pillows watching television, enjoying the sensation of Jed having passed out with his head on her belly, his emerging stubble tickling the soft sensitive skin with every breath. At the ring tone he stirred, blinked, resettled himself contentedly and sank back into sleep.

The phone screen told Tamara that the call was coming from an unknown number.

But the voice turned out not to be unknown. In fact, it was cooingly familiar. 'I just thought you might like to know I've arrived safely.'

Tamara pressed the mute button on the TV remote. 'In Canada? How's your "mum"?'

Jed roused, hauling himself up onto one elbow so that he could press his ear close to the phone, as if he hadn't been deeply asleep only moments earlier. Tamara shifted it away from her head a little so he could hear.

Emilia hesitated, obviously alerted by the coldness of Tamara's tone. 'Ah.' And she laughed.

'Are you with James?'

Emilia gave up any pretence. 'You don't want to know.'

'Manny thinks you're with him. He came here, shouting the odds, shoving me around, convinced I knew.'

A giggle echoed over the airwaves. 'Poor Manny, I expect he's furious at being outwitted. But he should have seen it coming, really. Sorry if he got a bit lively with you.' Emilia didn't sound sorry. She sounded lazily amused and deeply self-satisfied.

Tamara felt like hissing and spitting. Through gritted teeth she asked, 'Are you calling for any reason other than to gloat about your cleverness?'

'Not now,' chimed Emilia, with exaggerated and irritating cheer. 'I thought it was worth a call to lay some more misinformation for you to pass on, in the hopes of confusing Manny. Information is such power, don't you think? And therefore open to abuse.' She laughed. And rang off.

Tamara snatched the phone from her ear, fury burning in her heart. 'Bitch. She didn't even ask after Lyddie or whether her smartarsed scheming caused trouble for my family.'

'There wasn't much about that call to like,' Jed said slowly, frowning. 'What was the thing about information being power?'

'No idea.' Staring at the phone in thought, Tamara clicked onto her activity log.

Jed, his frown cutting ever-deeper furrows between his brows, watched her fingers on the screen. 'Hasn't she blocked the number she called from? That's a bit cocky,' he said, slowly.

'So it's not only in movies that people can be traced by their mobile phones?'

'No. It's easy with the right equipment. Even if she bins the phone, the prefix should tell us which country she's in, which is a start.'

Tamara stared at the number on her screen, mulling over the wrongs and rights of the situation. Or, rather, the wrongs and wrongs. 'I could go to the police with this, couldn't I? She's stolen a lot of dodgy money.'

He tensed. 'You could. A lot of people would think you should. We'd all have to be interviewed and investigated, of course. Mr H and his buddies would go to prison.' He turned to search her eyes. 'Is that what you're going to do?'

She tried to think it through. 'If I go to the police with the information, it's not just Mr Hilton, is it? Manny would probably be in very deep, very hot water.'

He nodded tensely. 'No "probably" about that.' His eyes held a plea.

She sighed. 'I don't care much about Mr Hilton, but you care a lot about Manny.' The older stepbrother had looked after him, in his own haphazard way, when Jed was a disenfranchised teen. Manny had been stupid, but Tamara knew that a little bit of Jed would wither to know Manny was in prison.

'And the police might never believe that you know nothing about money hidden from the tax man,' she said.

'They'd probably question you pretty closely too, as you did drive the getaway car when Emilia left Lie Low with a bag full of cash belonging to other people.' Then he added fairly 'But I'm almost certain they don't prosecute anyone unless they have what they call guilty knowledge.'

Alarm inched up Tamara's spine. 'I don't think I want to put it to the test.' She felt suddenly cold. 'I've got the Lie Low landline number.' She opened her contacts screen.

He jerked back, his eyes blazing with incredulity. 'You don't seriously think you're going to talk to him about this on a *mobile phone*?'

She began to tremble. 'I don't know! Shouldn't I?'

'No,' he said, with quiet emphasis. 'It really isn't secure or wise. Or good for my heart.'

She flung the phone down as if it was a scorpion and covered her eyes. 'I can't believe this is happening. It feels as if I'm in a really tacky film. This is going to rumble on and on, isn't it? Emilia can yank my chain whenever she feels like it. And Mr Hilton and Manny obviously don't believe that I know nothing. What am I going to do?'

Roughly, he pulled her into his arms, stroking her back in

silence for several minutes. Finally, he sighed. 'We'd better go and see Mr H. And Manny. Not because I think the number is going to prove as useful as you might think, but because keeping it from them is probably going to prove to be the wrong thing to do.' His voice was grim.

Jed drove Tamara the few minutes to Lie Low with a feeling of unreality, tension filling every nook and cranny of the car. Tamara was staring straight ahead, as if she might see something lurking in the darkness if she took her eyes away from the reassuring pool of brightness cast by the headlights.

Jed opened the gates with the remote and took her hand reassuringly after they climbed from the car. 'Don't worry. We'll get through this. Just leave everything to me.' He wished he felt as sure as he tried to sound. Emilia's phone call had seriously spooked him and he wasn't even sure why.

He led her into the house, lifting his voice. 'It's me.'

'Yeah, we saw,' answered Manny's voice drily.

Jed headed for Mr Hilton's small sitting room, where Mr Hilton and Manny waited in green leather armchairs, a bottle and two glasses on a table between them. The bottle cap was off and the spicy smell of whisky lay heavy on the air. Tom Hilton looked exhausted. Manny looked wary. His eyes flicked to Tamara, and back to Jed.

'Tamara needs to talk to you.' Jed steered Tamara to a chair and then pulled up one for himself, close enough that she'd be able to feel his arm brushing hers. She was shaking again. He laced his fingers with hers, trying to read his erstwhile employer's expression. Mr H wasn't giving anything away. Mentally, Jed crossed his fingers that this was going to work out OK.

'I did help her,' Tamara blurted out before Jed could open the conversation, control things, keep the mood even, as he'd intended. What part of 'Just leave everything to me' had she misheard? But she was ignoring Jed and looking Tom Hilton dead in the eye. 'She had a taxi waiting in Church Close. She told me she had to get away because she was scared of you and she was going to Canada, to her mother's.'

Mr Hilton's gaze turned to ice. 'She doesn't speak to her mother and her mother doesn't live in Canada. She lives in Kent.'

Audibly, Tamara swallowed. 'That's not much of a shock. She's such a good liar that it's impossible to tell where the truth ends and her crap begins. But I helped her because she convinced me that you were pretty much keeping her prisoner here. And that the protestors had hurt her before and she was scared of it happening again. I know now that she was just spinning me a story.'

Inclining his head in silent acknowledgement, Mr Hilton waited for her to go on.

She took a big breath. 'She rang me tonight.'

Mr Hilton stiffened. 'Why would she do that?'

'*What?*' snapped Manny simultaneously. His gaze was as intent as any hawk's.

Jed turned and looked at him, trying to catch his eye, to remind him that Tamara was with Jed. With *Jed*. She wasn't there to be snapped at. But Manny just leaned forward in his chair, eyes boring into Tamara.

Tamara's gaze darted between Manny and Mr H. 'She said she meant to give me new misinformation to send you off on the wrong trail. And Manny. When I made it obvious that I knew the truth, she just rang off. I want to give you the number. In case … you can use it.'

Tom Hilton stared. 'If I can use it,' he asked coldly, 'why give it to me?'

'Because I don't want you on my back trying to get

information out of me that I don't have. I don't want you taking some half-arsed revenge or pestering my family. But I also don't want you to go after her and take the money back, because then she'd probably inform on you, wouldn't she? And I understand she has stuff that might make the police take her seriously. Then they would want to talk to all of us.'

Again, Mr H inclined his head. 'Undoubtedly.' His eyes flickered to Jed. 'I take it that discretion is no longer part of your job description?'

Stonily, Jed met his eyes. 'I'm being selective. And that's the best you can hope for – in the circumstances.' Jed shifted in his chair. He wasn't happy about the way that things were going, but he wasn't quite sure why. Silently, he cursed Emilia Hilton for phoning Tamara when she did. A stressful, nervy meeting was not the perfect end to a perfect evening in bed.

Tamara took a deep breath. 'I thought maybe ... the phone number gives you the country prefix, at least. If you could find her, you could share the money with her. Then you couldn't inform on her and she couldn't inform on you. That would put the rest of us in the clear.'

Jed didn't betray his inner sigh. There was something reassuring about thinking there were such idealists in the world. And that one of them was Tamara. But ... like that was going to work.

Tom Hilton stared. 'The money is the lesser part of the problem. The information Emilia holds could be used against me and your solution won't stop her using it to leverage a very favourable divorce settlement. I could lose a lot.'

'Let's try it,' contradicted Manny roughly. 'I should be able to get a fix on her if we've got her mobile number. If she's not inclined to be co-operative, she'll find I can make things uncomfortable for her. And Cochrane.'

Slowly, Tom Hilton turned to look at him. 'And just what would that achieve? If she hasn't blocked her number, there's probably a reason. How hard would it be to buy a disposable phone and let the number register just before she changes countries? Not all information is good information.'

Not all information is good information. Jed recognised one of Manny's own mantras. Just like – his heart tripped over – *Information is power.* And he realised what it was about Emilia's phone conversation that was bothering him. *Information is power.*

Information.

He looked at Manny just as his stepbrother jumped to his feet and began to pace along the absurdly expensive carpet that lent its rich green presence to the room. Horrible knowledge whirled around his brain. He could see a train wreck coming and he couldn't think how to prevent it. Furiously, his mind worked on what he could say, how he could say it, to get both Tamara and Manny out of that room before the train began to plough through them all.

And like a bad dream he saw something pass across the face of Mr H. A thought, a suspicion … A realisation.

Then Mr H was staring at Manny, as if he'd grown horns and a forked tail. 'How did Emilia get the information?' he asked hoarsely.

Manny stopped mid-stride.

'How did she get the information she's holding over my head, Manny? The copy of the hard drive from the PC linked to the surveillance system?'

Dimly, Jed was aware of Tamara glancing at him. Gazing around the room, puzzled by an atmosphere suddenly as sharp as razor blades.

Slowly, Mr H rose to his feet. He and Manny were about the same height, although, unlike him, the younger man was built of sinew and stone.

'It's always bothered me how Emilia would know how to clone a hard disc,' Mr H said softly.

Manny looked like a cornered fox. 'Software. You can download it. I told you all about it.'

'But not how Emilia got the password to the surveillance computer. The only three people who should know that password are in this room.'

Tamara made a near-soundless '*Ohhhhh* …'

Jed felt anger and disappointment war in his chest. *Manny*. For fuck's sake. What a stupid mistake to make. What a whole bunch of stupid, stupid mistakes. But the thought scampered across his mind that at least Mr H had no reason to bother Tamara now. Information was emerging – but it wasn't via the Rix family.

Manny took several steps back, eyes flicking warily between Jed and Mr H, making sure nobody could get between him and the door.

Tom Hilton's voice snapped out like a whip. 'So what is there between you and my wife?'

Silence.

Manny's gaze tangled with Jed's. Jed read regret there. An apology.

Manny cleared his throat. 'It's probably better that I don't say too much. Except she has duped me as much as she's duped you.'

In slow motion, Tom Hilton's knees buckled and his backside hit his chair with a thud. He stared at Manny like a dog will stare at a snake. 'Not you, Manny. Tell me you weren't so stupid.'

Manny said, '"Sorry" isn't really enough, is it?' His chin jutted. 'I don't have a defence. I'd better pack my stuff.' But he was looking at Jed, not Tom Hilton. Slowly, silently, he stepped backwards towards the door. Then he was gone.

Mr H stared after him. And then at Jed. 'He conspired against me – with my *wife*? Tell me it's not true.'

Jed pulled himself to his feet. His legs felt as if they had flu. Aching. Weak. Beside him, Tamara, too, rose silently. 'I can't tell you that.' He sighed. 'But I can tell you that I didn't know.'

A laugh that was almost a sob. 'As if I didn't know that, Jed. Mr Clean. You don't have to tell me. And now I've lost my woman, just as you've got yours.' He held his forehead in his hand, as if his head was suddenly painful and heavy.

'Yeah. I'm sorry. I know now how love feels.' Jed, towing Tamara, made to follow Manny.

Tom Hilton lurched suddenly to his feet. 'Whisky?'

Jed slowed, but didn't stop. 'I don't think so.'

'You're not really leaving?'

'I am. You let me get up to my arse in crap, even though you had the number for the plumber.'

Pain flashed across Tom Hilton's face. 'What will you do?'

Jed shrugged. 'I'll think of something. Something local, because of Tamara. I'll come back to move my stuff in the next few days.' He hesitated at the desolation in Tom Hilton's face. He thought about his stepbrother. 'You know, you might do worse than to ask Manny to stay. He might be able to find Mrs H for you. A man with a grudge can be implacable.'

Like a beaten man, Tom Hilton sank back into his chair. 'Will you ask him?'

'I'll talk to him now.'

He was aware of Tamara's small, trusting hand in his as he strode along the passageways. At the door to the outside, he paused. He turned to face her. Her eyes were enormous, her wild hair still tossed from their time in bed. 'Would you be frightened if I asked you to wait in the car?'

After a moment, she reached up and pressed her lips to his. 'No.' Then she took the car keys he handed to her and stepped out onto the drive. He watched her until she was safely settled in the passenger seat. When she looked back to where he stood he raised his hand and mimed her locking the doors. A moment later, the lights of his car flashed and went dark, showing that she'd complied.

Heart tied like a weight around his ankles, he turned and took the few strides to the door to the staff quarters, treading heavily up the stairs until he stood outside his stepbrother's door. He rattled the handle. 'Manny?'

Silence.

'I'm on my own.'

Several seconds, then the door opened. He stepped inside. Manny was already walking across the hall to his bedroom and Jed followed. On the bed was a large khaki rucksack, already half full. Manny began to move swiftly between drawers and the wardrobe, compiling a basic-needs kit. Jed could almost see him ticking items off in his head.

He spoke in a low voice, knowing the chances were that the housekeeper, Carrie, would be in her apartment, and he didn't want to be overheard. 'What happened? Idiot.' He sat down on a stool, watching six pairs of socks and six pairs of boxers disappear into the pack.

Manny laughed humourlessly. 'I was tempted. Bitch. She took me for a ride. I thought we were in it together, we were going to leave together. I came up with the whole plan, explained why the taxman can be scarier to these rich business dudes than the grim reaper, did the cloning software stuff, set the whole fucking thing up.' He began rolling T-shirts into tight compact rolls. 'And she fucked off without me. Probably with Cochrane. Or maybe not.' He looked up suddenly. 'Did Tamara give you the details?'

'No,' said Jed uncompromisingly. 'She doesn't know where Emilia went or with who.'

Manny smiled, faintly, grabbed his passport out of a drawer, stuffed it in a sidepocket of the pack and dragged the chord tight with a snap, then hefted the pack, hesitating. 'Sorry to fuck up so royally on your watch.'

Jed shrugged. 'I'm voluntarily unemployed. But you could stay. Mr H is willing to talk about you going after Emilia.' His heart was beating oddly at the idea of Manny going away. Memories of the day he'd packed his own bag and left home, a sad and angry teenager, and run straight to Manny, rose up to shut off his breath.

Manny laughed, a hard, unhappy sound. 'Give that sharp little bastard something to hold over my head? Don't think so.'

Then he turned and gave Jed a hard hug. 'Watch yourself.'

Jed hugged him back. 'And you.'

He followed his stepbrother down the stairs and out into the darkness. In a few steps Manny had melted away, taking only the bag on his back.

Jed raised a reassuring hand to Tamara, knowing she'd be able to see him in the light from the doorway. Then he went back into the house, down the familiar hallway, past the office he'd called his own.

Tom Hilton was waiting exactly where Jed had left him.

'I was too late. He'd already gone,' Jed lied.

Chapter Thirty-Six

Tamara could hardly keep her eyes open as they drove back to her house. The village was dark, apart from street lamps and Jed was silent. It was about two, she calculated, and she felt as if she'd been awake forever, with all the furore around Lyddie going missing … and making love with Jed. Both the sprint and the marathon. Then the unreality of being involved in Mr H's dodgy dealings, the kind that didn't happen every day in Middledip. Her head felt enormous and over-sensitive with fatigue. She yawned a jaw-cracking yawn. 'So, what happened?'

Jed took the turning into Great Hill Road. 'Manny's out of there.'

She studied his profile. Set. Withdrawn. 'Where will he go?'

He shrugged.

Alarm uncoiled in her belly. 'That won't just be it, though, will it? How will you stay in touch? Your phones—'

He brought the car to a halt outside her house. Killed the engine. Sighed and turned to face her. Even in the light from a street lamp, his expression was bleak. 'Our phones go with our jobs. There's going to be a lot of confusion with Manny taking off and me not being there. The household phone contract was one of the things I administered for Mr H, but it's inevitable that, before much longer, both of those phones will cease to work. I suppose I should have left mine behind already.' He fished it out of his pocket and turned it over in his hand.

'Call him now,' she urged, her heart aching for the emptiness in his face. 'Make sure he copies his phone book, because he has my number so he can get in touch.'

He gave the faint smile that came more from his eyes than his mouth. 'He'll have switched the phone off. Probably left it behind. Phones are traceable, you know. He won't want to risk Mr H deciding that he's been too easy on him, or any of Mr H's slightly shady buddies deciding that he owes them for what he made it possible for Emilia to take.' A sigh shook through him. 'I hope you're right that he'll contact me through you. He will have his phone book backed up somewhere he can access remotely. He'd say it was standard operating procedure.'

Tamara leaned forward and touched her lips to his. 'He won't just forget you. He never has before. He's your family.'

He sighed again. 'Speaking of family, what are you going to tell your mother about this?'

'Nothing,' said Tamara promptly. 'I've signed a non-disclosure agreement.'

He laughed softly, pulling her closer, holding her close. 'Wc both have. Useful.'

Upstairs, indoors, they undressed one another slowly, rolled beneath the covers and switched off the lamps. There was no light from streetlights at the rear of the house and the darkness that settled around them was complete. Tamara sank into the crook of Jed's arm with a contented hum, her nakedness against his nakedness, her cheek against the dusting of hairs on his chest.

She yawned so hard, her eyes watered. Tomorrow, or sometime, they'd have to talk about what they were and where they were going. They'd talk about heavy stuff at a later date. Not tonight. Tonight she was sooooo tired ... sooooo tired she needed to just drift away ...

'I meant it,' he said.

'Tomorrow,' she mumbled. 'I need to sleep.'

He kissed the top of her head. 'OK. So long as you know.'

'OK.' She snuggled closer, sliding one of her bare legs over his, settling more comfortably. And she began to drift away …

'What?' she said, blinking awake. 'What did you mean? What do I know?'

'Tomorrow,' he murmured. 'You need to sleep.'

She elbowed him. 'No. I need to know.'

He laughed. 'Yeah. You do need to know.'

'*What?* What do I need to know?'

He turned her in his arms and kissed her, cradling her head, making love to her mouth with his. Finally, he said, 'I know now how love feels. You need to know that I understand about Lyddie. I love you too much to try and take you away from her.' Evidently, he hadn't got the memo about discussing heavy stuff at a later date.

'*Is* this love?' Her heart surged hotly, beating hard at the thought.

He sounded impatient. 'What else could it be? And what you have for Lyddie is love. I won't suggest you have to prove your love for me is strongest. I don't know what I'm going to do for a job yet – but it will be here, near you. I haven't been able to shake you from my mind since that first day I visited your parents and you walked in. It took ten seconds before I had a coherent thought.'

'Oh,' she said, snuggling again into his hot firm body, feeling his fine hairs move over her skin in a kind of erotic massage. 'I had loads of coherent thoughts. Like "Wow, it's Jed Cassius … who I used to have such a giant crush on".'

'You had a crush on me?' One of his hands had begun to trace lazy circles from her waist and over her buttocks.

'I was a really sad case. A pathetic lovesick little kid.' Her heart gave a great kick at the way those words from the past had found their way into her mouth just when everything she wanted was within her grasp – in fact, in her bed. Her hand slid over his ribs, following the curve up to his chest, feeling his heart beating against her palm. Hers was suddenly beating harder. She took a deep breath.

'That's what Lyddie called me, that day – a pathetic lovesick little kid. I'd told her that I liked you, too, and she laughed and I was so hurt and … that's why I was angry enough to yell that I was going to spread lies about her.' She took in a long wavering breath. 'She was so angry. That's why I ran. That's why she followed me into the road—'

And then he was hushing her and stroking her back and she realised that her voice had risen and she was on the brink of tears.

'Tamara,' he whispered. 'It was my old man who careered round the bend too fast and was too tipsy to hit the brakes in time. It wasn't your fault, whatever you and Lyddie were arguing about.'

She let his words seep over her, like balm. 'I just wanted you to know.'

He held her closer, harder, so that he pressed against every inch of her body. 'Why? In case it stopped me loving you? It's never stopped Lyddie loving you. Love's a pretty robust thing. You can trust in it. You can trust in me.'

He dropped a kiss on the end of her nose. 'Now tell me more about this crush.'

About the Author

Sue Moorcroft is a working writer. *Is This Love?* is her ninth novel and sixth novel with Choc Lit – *Starting Over, All That Mullarkey, Want to Know a Secret?, Love & Freedom* and *Dream a Little Dream. Love & Freedom* won the 2011 Best Romantic Novel of the Year Award from the Festival of Romance and *Dream a Little Dream* was shortlisted for a 2013 Romantic Novel Award.

Sue has published over a hundred short stories, articles and several serials in magazines. She was a runner-up in the Ford Fiesta Short Story Competition and a winner of the Katie Fforde Bursary Award. She's a creative writing tutor for distance learning and residential courses in the UK and abroad. She has written courses for the London School of Journalism and, with her tutor's hat on: *LOVE WRITING – How to Make Money Writing Romantic or Erotic Fiction* (published Jan 2010). She is Vice Chairman of the Romantic Novelists' Association.

www.suemoorcroft.com
www.suemoorcroft.wordpress.com
www.twitter.com/suemoorcroft
www.facebook.com/sue.moorcroft.3

More Choc Lit

From Sue Moorcroft

Starting Over

New home, new friends, new love. Can starting over be that simple?

Tess Riddell reckons her beloved Freelander is more reliable than any man – especially her ex-fiancé, Olly Gray. She's moving on from her old life and into the perfect cottage in the country.

Miles Rattenbury's passions? Old cars and new women! Romance? He's into fun rather than commitment. When Tess crashes the Freelander into his breakdown truck, they find that they're nearly neighbours – yet worlds apart. Despite her overprotective parents and a suddenly attentive Olly, she discovers the joys of village life and even forms an unlikely friendship with Miles. Then, just as their relationship develops into something deeper, an old flame comes looking for him ...

Is their love strong enough to overcome the past? Or will it take more than either of them is prepared to give?

Visit www.choc-lit.com for more details including the first two chapters and reviews, or simply scan barcode using your mobile phone QR reader.

All That Mullarkey

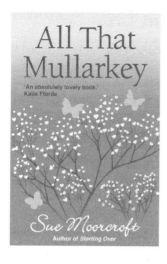

**Revenge and love:
it's a thin line ...**

The writing's on the wall for
Cleo and Gav. The bedroom
wall, to be precise. And it says
'This marriage is over.'

Wounded and furious, Cleo
embarks on a night out with
the girls, which turns into
a glorious one-night stand
with ...

Justin, centrefold material and irrepressibly irresponsible.
He loves a little wildness in a woman – and he's in the right
place at the right time to enjoy Cleo's.

But it's Cleo who has to pick up the pieces – of a marriage
based on a lie and the lasting repercussions of that night.
Torn between laid-back Justin and control-freak Gav, she's a
free spirit that life is trying to tie down. But the rewards are
worth it!

Visit www.choc-lit.com for more details
including the first two chapters and
reviews, or simply scan barcode using
your mobile phone QR reader.

Want to Know a Secret?

Money, love and family. Which matters most?

When Diane Jenner's husband is hurt in a helicopter crash, she discovers a secret that changes her life. And it's all about money, the kind of money the Jenners have never had.

James North has money, and he knows it doesn't buy happiness. He's been a rock for his wayward wife and troubled daughter – but that doesn't stop him wanting Diane.

James and Diane have something in common: they always put family first. Which means that what happens in the back of James's Mercedes is a really, really bad idea.

Or is it?

Visit www.choc-lit.com for more details including the first two chapters and reviews, or simply scan barcode using your mobile phone QR reader.

Love & Freedom

*Winner of the Festival of Romance
Best Romantic Read Award 2011*

New start, new love.

That's what Honor Sontag
needs after her life falls apart,
leaving her reputation in
tatters and her head all over
the place. So she flees her
native America and heads for
Brighton, England.

Honor's hoping for a much-
deserved break and the chance to find the mother who
abandoned her as a baby. What she gets is an entanglement
with a mysterious male whose family seems to have a finger
in every pot in town.

Martyn Mayfair has sworn off women with strings attached,
but is irresistibly drawn to Honor, the American who keeps
popping up in his life. All he wants is an uncomplicated
relationship built on honesty, but Honor's past threatens to
undermine everything. Then secrets about her mother start
to spill out ...

Honor has to make an agonising choice. Will she live
up to her dutiful name and please others? Or will she
choose freedom?

Visit www.choc-lit.com for more details
including the first two chapters and
reviews, or simply scan barcode using
your mobile phone QR reader.

Dream a Little Dream

What would you give to make your dreams come true?

Liza Reece has a dream. Working as a reflexologist for a troubled holistic centre isn't enough. When the opportunity arises to take over the Centre she jumps at it. Problem is, she needs funds, and fast, as she's not the only one interested.

Dominic Christy has dreams of his own. Diagnosed as suffering from a rare sleep disorder, dumped by his live-in girlfriend and discharged from the job he adored as an Air Traffic Controller, he's single-minded in his aims. He has money, and plans for the Centre that don't include Liza and her team.

But dreams have a way of shifting and changing and Dominic's growing fascination with Liza threatens to reshape his. And then it's time to wake up to the truth ...

Visit www.choc-lit.com for more details including the first two chapters and reviews, or simply scan barcode using your mobile phone QR reader.

More from Choc Lit

If you enjoyed Sue's story, you'll enjoy the
rest of our selection. Here's a sample:

Please don't stop the music

Jane Lovering

  *Winner of the 2012 Best
Romantic Comedy Novel
of the Year*

*Winner of the 2012 Romantic
Novel of the Year*

How much can you hide?

Jemima Hutton is determined
to build a successful new
life and keep her past a dark
secret. Trouble is, her jewellery business looks set to fail –
until enigmatic Ben Davies offers to stock her handmade belt
buckles in his guitar shop and things start looking up, on all
fronts.

But Ben has secrets too. When Jemima finds out he used
to be the front man of hugely successful Indie rock band
Willow Down, she wants to know more. Why did he desert
the band on their US tour? Why is he now a semi-recluse?

And the curiosity is mutual – which means that her own
secret is no longer safe …

Visit www.choc-lit.com for more details
including the first two chapters and
reviews, or simply scan barcode using
your mobile phone QR reader.

The Silent Touch of Shadows

Christina Courtenay

Festival of Romance

Winner of the 2012 Best Historical Read from the Festival of Romance

What will it take to put the past to rest?

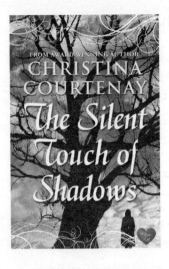

Professional genealogist Melissa Grantham receives an invitation to visit her family's ancestral home, Ashleigh Manor. From the moment she arrives, life-like dreams and visions haunt her. The spiritual connection to a medieval young woman and her forbidden lover have her questioning her sanity, but Melissa is determined to solve the mystery.

Jake Precy, owner of a nearby cottage, has disturbing dreams too, but it's not until he meets Melissa that they begin to make sense. He hires her to research his family's history, unaware their lives are already entwined. Is the mutual attraction real or the result of ghostly interference?

A haunting love story set partly in the present and partly in fifteenth century Kent.

Visit www.choc-lit.com for more details including the first two chapters and reviews, or simply scan barcode using your mobile phone QR reader.

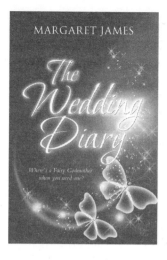

The Wedding Diary
Margaret James

Where's a Fairy Godmother when you need one?

If you won a fairy-tale wedding in a luxury hotel, you'd be delighted – right? But what if you didn't have anyone to marry? Cat Aston did have a fiancé, but now it looks like her Prince Charming has done a runner.

Adam Lawley was left devastated when his girlfriend turned down his heartfelt proposal. He's made a vow never to fall in love again.

So – when Cat and Adam meet, they shouldn't even consider falling in love. After all, they're both broken hearted. But for some reason they can't stop thinking about each other. Is this their second chance for happiness, or are some things just too good to be true?

Visit www.choc-lit.com for more details including the first two chapters and reviews, or simply scan barcode using your mobile phone QR reader.

A Stitch in Time
Amanda James

A stitch in time saves nine ... or does it?

Sarah Yates is a thirty-something history teacher, divorced, disillusioned and desperate to have more excitement in her life. Making all her dreams come true seems about as likely as climbing Everest in stilettos.

Then one evening the doorbell rings and the handsome and mysterious John Needler brings more excitement than Sarah could ever have imagined. John wants Sarah to go back in time ...

Sarah is whisked from the Sheffield Blitz to the suffragette movement in London to the Old American West, trying to make sure people find their happy endings. The only question is, will she ever be able to find hers?

Visit www.choc-lit.com for more details including the first two chapters and reviews, or simply scan barcode using your mobile phone QR reader.

CLAIM YOUR FREE EBOOK

of

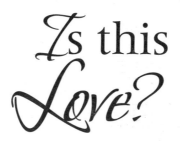

You may wish to have a choice of how you read *Is this Love?*. Perhaps you'd like a digital version for when you're out and about, so that you can read it on your ereader, iPad or even a Smartphone. For a limited period, we're including a **FREE** ebook version along with this paperback.

To claim, simply visit ebooks.choc-lit.com or scan the QR Code.

You'll need to enter the following code:

Q121308

Introducing Choc Lit

We're an independent publisher creating
a delicious selection of fiction.
Where heroes are like chocolate – irresistible!
Quality stories with a romance at the heart.

Choc Lit novels are selected by genuine readers like yourself.
We only publish stories our Choc Lit Tasting Panel want to
see in print. Our reviews and awards speak for themselves.

We'd love to hear how you enjoyed *Is this Love?*.
Just visit www.choc-lit.com and give your feedback.
Describe Jed in terms of chocolate
and you could win a Choc Lit novel in our
Flavour of the Month competition.

Available in paperback and as ebooks from most stores.

Visit: www.choc-lit.com for more details.

Keep in touch:
Sign up for our monthly newsletter Choc Lit Spread for
all the latest news and offers: www.spread.choc-lit.com.
Follow us on Twitter: @ChocLituk and Facebook: Choc Lit.

Or simply scan barcode using your mobile phone QR reader:

*Choc Lit
Spread*

Twitter

Facebook